JOB:
A Comedy of Justice

Books by Robert A. Heinlein

Assignment in Eternity
The Best of Robert
  Heinlein
* Between Planets
Beyond This Horizon
* Citizen of the Galaxy
The Door into Summer
Double Star
Expanded Universe: More
  Worlds of Robert A.
  Heinlein
* Farmer in the Sky
Farnham's Freehold
* Friday
Glory Road
The Green Hills of Earth
* Have Space Suit—Will
  Travel
I Will Fear No Evil
* JOB: A Comedy of Justice
The Man Who Sold the
  Moon
The Menace from Earth
Methuselah's Children
The Moon Is a Harsh
  Mistress
The Notebooks of Lazarus
  Long

The Number of the Beast
Orphans of the Sky
The Past Through Tomor-
  row: "Future History"
  Stories
Podkayne of Mars
The Puppet Masters
* Red Planet
Revolt in 2100
* Rocket Ship Galileo
* The Rolling Stones
Sixth Column
* Space Cadet
* The Star Beast
* Starman Jones
Starship Troopers
Stranger in a Strange
  Land
Three by Heinlein
Time Enough for Love
* Time for the Stars
Tomorrow the Stars (Ed.)
* Tunnel in the Sky
The Unpleasant Profes-
  sion of Jonathan Hoag
Waldo & Magic, Inc.
The Worlds of Robert A.
  Heinlein

* Available from Del Rey Books

JOB:
A Comedy of Justice
Robert A. Heinlein

A Del Rey Book

BALLANTINE BOOKS • NEW YORK

A Del Rey Book
Published by Ballantine Books

Copyright © 1984 by Robert A. Heinlein

Library of Congress Cataloging in Publication Data

Heinlein, Robert A. (Robert Anson), 1907–
  Job, a comedy of justice.

  "A Del Rey book."
  I. Title.
PS3515.E288J6 1984   813'.54   84-3091
ISBN 0-345-31357-7
ISBN 0-345-32060-3 (lim. ed.)

Manufactured in the United States of America

First Edition: September 1984

9 8 7 6 5 4 3 2 1

To Clifford D. Simak

*Behold, happy is the man whom God correcteth:
therefore despise not thou the chastening of
the Almighty.*
Job 5:17

I

*When thou walkest through the fire,
thou shalt not be burned.*
Isaiah 43:2

The fire pit was about twenty-five feet long by ten feet wide, and perhaps two feet deep. The fire had been burning for hours. The bed of coals gave off a blast of heat almost unbearable even back where I was seated, fifteen feet from the side of the pit, in the second row of tourists.

I had given up my front-row seat to one of the ladies from the ship, delighted to accept the shielding offered by her well-fed carcass. I was tempted to move still farther back . . . but I *did* want to see the fire walkers close up. How often does one get to view a miracle?

"It's a hoax," the Well-Traveled Man said. "You'll see."

"Not really a hoax, Gerald," the Authority-on-Everything denied. "Just somewhat less than we were led to expect. It won't be the whole village—probably none of the hula dancers and certainly not those children. One or two of the young men, with calluses on their feet as thick as cowhide, and hopped up on opium or some native drug, will go down the pit at a dead run. The villagers will cheer and our kanaka friend there who is translating for us will strongly suggest that we should tip each of the fire walkers, over and above what we've paid for the luau and the dancing and this show.

"Not a complete hoax," he went on. "The shore excursion brochure listed a 'demonstration of fire walking.'

1

That's what we'll get. Never mind the talk about a whole village of fire walkers. Not in the contract." The Authority looked smug.

"Mass hypnosis," the Professional Bore announced.

I was tempted to ask for an explanation of "mass hypnosis"—but nobody wanted to hear from me; I was junior—not necessarily in years but in the cruise ship *Konge Knut*. That's how it is in cruise ships: Anyone who has been in the vessel since port of departure is senior to anyone who joins the ship later. The Medes and the Persians laid down this law and nothing can change it. I had flown down in the *Count von Zeppelin*, at Papeete I would fly home in the *Admiral Moffett*, so I was forever junior and should keep quiet while my betters pontificated.

Cruise ships have the best food and, all too often, the worst conversation in the world. Despite this I was enjoying the islands; even the Mystic and the Amateur Astrologer and the Parlor Freudian and the Numerologist did not trouble me, as I did not listen.

"They do it through the fourth dimension," the Mystic announced. "Isn't that true, Gwendolyn?"

"Quite true, dear," the Numerologist agreed. "Oh, here they come now! It will be an odd number, you'll see."

"You're so learned, dear."

"Humph," said the Skeptic.

The native who was assisting our ship's excursion host raised his arms and spread his palms for silence. "Please, will you all listen! *Mauruuru roa*. Thank you very much. The high priest and priestess will now pray the Gods to make the fire safe for the villagers. I ask you to remember that this is a religious ceremony, very ancient; please behave as you would in your own church. Because—"

An extremely old kanaka interrupted; he and the translator exchanged words in a language not known to me—Polynesian, I assumed; it had the right liquid flow to it. The younger kanaka turned back to us.

"The high priest tells me that some of the children are making their first walk through fire today, including that baby over there in her mother's arms. He asks all of you to keep perfectly silent during the prayers, to insure the safety of the children. Let me add that I am a Catholic. At this point I always ask our Holy Mother Mary to watch over our children—and I ask all of you to pray for them in your own way. Or at least keep silent and think good thoughts for them. If the high priest is not satisfied that there is a reverent attitude, he won't let the children enter the fire—I've even known him to cancel the entire ceremony."

"There you have it, Gerald," said the Authority-on-Everything in a third-balcony whisper. "The build-up. Now the switch, and they'll blame it on us." He snorted.

The Authority—his name was Cheevers—had been annoying me ever since I had joined the ship. I leaned forward and said quietly into his ear, "If those children walk through the fire, do you have the guts to do likewise?"

Let this be a lesson to you. Learn by my bad example. Never let an oaf cause you to lose your judgment. Some seconds later I found that my challenge had been turned against me and—somehow!—all three, the Authority, the Skeptic, and the Well-Traveled Man, had each bet me a hundred that *I* would not dare walk the fire pit, stipulating that the children walked first.

Then the translator was shushing us again and the priest and priestess stepped down into the fire pit and everybody kept very quiet and I suppose some of us prayed. I know I did. I found myself reciting what popped into my mind:

"Now I lay me down to sleep.

"I pray the Lord my soul to keep—"

Somehow it seemed appropriate.

The priest and the priestess did not walk through the fire; they did something quietly more spectacular and (it seemed to me) far more dangerous. They simply stood in the fire pit, barefooted, and prayed for several minutes. I could see their lips move. Every so often the old priest sprinkled something into the pit. Whatever it was, as it struck the coals it burst into sparkles.

I tried to see what they were standing on, coals or rocks, but I could not tell . . . and could not guess which would be worse. Yet this old woman, skinny as gnawed bones, stood there quietly, face placid, and with no precautions other than having tucked up her lava-lava so that it was almost a diaper. Apparently she fretted about burning her clothes but not about burning her legs.

Three men with poles had been straightening out the burning logs, making sure that the bed of the pit was a firm and fairly even footing for the fire walkers. I took a deep interest in this, as I expected to be walking in that pit in a few minutes—if I didn't cave in and forfeit the bet. It seemed to me that they were making it possible to walk the length of the fire pit on rocks rather than burning coals. I hoped so!

Then I wondered what difference it would make—recalling sun-scorched sidewalks that had blistered my bare feet when I was a boy in Kansas. That fire had to be at least seven hundred degrees; those rocks had been soaking in that fire for several hours. At such temperatures was there any real choice between frying pan and fire?

Meanwhile the voice of reason was whispering in my ear that forfeiting three hundred was not much of a price to pay to get out of this bind . . . or would I rather walk the rest of my life on two barbecued stumps?

Would it help if I took an aspirin?

The three men finished fiddling with the burning logs and went to the end of the pit at our left; the rest of the villagers gathered behind them—including those darned kids! What were their parents thinking about, letting them risk something like this? Why weren't they in school where they belonged?

The three fire tenders led off, walking single file down the center of the fire, not hurrying, not dallying. The rest of the men of the village followed them, a slow, steady procession. Then came the women, including the young mother with a baby on her hip.

When the blast of heat struck the infant, it started to cry. Without varying her steady pace, its mother swung it up and gave it suck; the baby shut up.

The children followed, from pubescent girls and adolescent boys down to the kindergarten level. Last was a little girl (nine? eight?) who was leading her round-eyed little brother by the hand. He seemed to be about four and was dressed only in his skin.

I looked at this kid and knew with mournful certainty that I was about to be served up rare; I could no longer back out. Once the baby boy stumbled; his sister kept him from falling. He went on then, short sturdy steps. At the far end someone reached down and lifted him out.

And it was *my* turn.

The translator said to me, "You understand that the Polynesia Tourist Bureau takes no responsibility for your safety? That fire can burn you, it can kill you. These people can walk it safely because they have faith."

I assured him that I had faith, while wondering how I could be such a barefaced liar. I signed a release he presented.

All too soon I was standing at one end of the pit, with my trousers rolled up to my knees. My shoes and socks and hat and wallet were at the far end, waiting on a stool. That was my goal, my prize—if I didn't make it, would they cast lots for them? Or would they ship them to my next of kin?

He was saying: "Go right down the middle. Don't hurry but don't stand still." The high priest spoke up; my mentor listened, then said, "He says not to run, even if your feet burn. Because you might stumble and fall down. Then you might never get up. He means you might die. I must add that you probably would not die—unless you breathed flame. But you would certainly be terribly burned. So don't hurry and don't fall down. Now see that flat rock under you? That's your first step. *Que le bon Dieu vous garde.* Good luck."

"Thanks." I glanced over at the Authority-on-Everything, who was smiling ghoulishly, if ghouls smile. I gave him a mendaciously jaunty wave and stepped down.

I had taken three steps before I realized that I didn't feel anything at all. Then I did feel something: scared. Scared silly and wishing I were in Peoria. Or even Philadelphia. Instead of alone in this vast smoldering waste. The far end of the pit was a city block away. Maybe farther. But I kept plodding toward it while hoping that this numb paralysis would not cause me to collapse before reaching it.

I felt smothered and discovered that I had been holding my breath. So I gasped—and regretted it. Over a fire pit that vast there is blistering gas and smoke and carbon dioxide and carbon monoxide and something that may be Satan's halitosis, but not enough oxygen to matter. I chopped off that gasp with my eyes watering and my throat raw and tried to estimate whether or not I could reach the end without breathing.

Heaven help me, I could not *see* the far end! The smoke had billowed up and my eyes would barely open and would not focus. So I pushed on, while trying to remember the formula by which one made a deathbed confession and then slid into Heaven on a technicality.

Maybe there wasn't any such formula. My feet felt odd and my knees were coming unglued . . .

"Feeling better, Mr. Graham?"

I was lying on grass and looking up into a friendly, brown face. "I guess so," I answered. "What happened? Did I walk it?"

"Certainly you walked it. Beautifully. But you fainted right at the end. We were standing by and grabbed you, hauled you out. But you tell me what happened. Did you get your lungs full of smoke?"

"Maybe. Am I burned?"

"No. Oh, you may form one blister on your right foot. But you held the thought perfectly. All but that faint, which must have been caused by smoke."

"I guess so." I sat up with his help. "Can you hand me my shoes and socks? Where is everybody?"

"The bus left. The high priest took your pulse and checked your breathing but he wouldn't let anyone disturb you. If you force a man to wake up when his spirit is still walking about, the spirit may not come back in. So he believes and no one dares argue with him."

"I won't argue with him; I feel fine. Rested. But how do I get back to the ship?" Five miles of tropical paradise would get tedious after the first mile. On foot. Especially as my feet seemed to have swelled a bit. For which they had ample excuse.

"The bus will come back to take the villagers to the boat that takes them back to the island they live on. It then could take you to your ship. But we can do better. My cousin has an automobile. He will take you."

"Good. How much will he charge me?" Taxis in Polynesia are always outrageous, especially when the drivers have you at their mercy, of which they have none. But it occurred to me that I could afford to be robbed as I was bound to show a profit on this jape. Three hundred minus one taxi fare. I picked up my hat. "Where's my wallet?"

"Your wallet?"

"My billfold. I left it in my hat. Where is it? This isn't funny; my money was in it. And my cards."

"Your money? *Oh! Votre portefeuille.* I am sorry; my English is not perfect. The officer from your ship, your excursion guide, took care of it."

"That was kind of him. But how am I to pay your cousin? I don't have a franc on me."

We got that straightened out. The ship's excursion escort, realizing that he would be leaving me strapped in rescuing my billfold, had prepaid my ride back to the ship. My kanaka friend took me to his cousin's car and introduced me to his cousin—not too effectively, as the cousin's English was limited to "Okay, Chief!" and I never did get his name straight.

His automobile was a triumph of baling wire and faith. We went roaring back to the dock at full throttle, frightening chickens and easily outrunning baby goats. I did not pay much attention as I was bemused by something that had happened just before we left. The villagers were waiting for their bus to return; we walked right through them. Or started to. I got kissed. I got kissed by all of them. I had already seen the Polynesian habit of kissing where we would just shake hands, but this was the first time it had happened to me.

My friend explained it to me: "You walked through their fire, so you are an honorary member of their village. They want to kill a pig for you. Hold a feast in your honor."

I tried to answer in kind while explaining that I had to return home across the great water but I would return someday, God willing. Eventually we got away.

But that was not what had me most bemused. Any unbiased judge would have to admit that I am reasonably sophisticated. I am aware that some places do not have America's high moral standards and are careless about indecent exposure. I know that Polynesian women used to run around naked from the waist up until civilization came along—shucks, I read the *National Geographic*.

But I never expected to *see* it.

Before I made my fire walk the villagers were dressed just as you would expect: grass skirts but with the women's bosoms covered.

But when they kissed me hello-goodbye they were not. Not covered, I mean. Just like the *National Geographic*.

Now I appreciate feminine beauty. Those delightful differences, seen under proper circumstances with the shades decently drawn, can be dazzling. But forty-odd (no, even) of them are intimidating. I saw more human, feminine busts than I had ever seen before, total and cumulative, in my entire life. The Methodist Episcopal Society for Temperance and Morals would have been shocked right out of their wits.

With adequate warning I am sure that I could have enjoyed the experience. As it was, it was too new, too much, too fast. I could appreciate it only in retrospect.

Our tropical Rolls-Royce crunched to a stop with the aid of hand brake, foot brake, and first-gear compression; I looked up from bemused euphoria. My driver announced, "Okay, Chief!"

I said, "That's not my ship."

"Okay, Chief?"

"You've taken me to the wrong dock. Uh, it looks like the right dock but it's the wrong ship." Of that I was certain. M.V. *Konge Knut* has white sides and superstructure and a rakish false funnel. This ship was mostly red with four tall black stacks. Steam, it had to be—not a motor vessel. As well as years out of date. "No. No!"

"Okay, Chief. *Votre vapeur! Voilà!*"

"*Non!*"

"Okay, Chief." He got out, came around and opened the door on the passenger side, grabbed my arm, and pulled.

I'm in fairly good shape, but his arm had been toughened by swimming, climbing for coconuts, hauling in fishnets, and pulling tourists who don't want to go out of cars. I got out.

He jumped back in, called out, "Okay, Chief! *Merci bien! Au 'voir!*" and was gone.

I went, Hobson's choice, up the gangway of the strange vessel to learn, if possible, what had become of the *Konge Knut*. As I stepped aboard, the petty officer on gangway watch saluted and said, "Afternoon, sir. Mr. Graham, Mr. Nielsen left a package for you. One moment—" He lifted the lid of his watch desk, took out a large manila envelope. "Here you are, sir."

The package had written on it: *A. L. Graham, cabin C109.* I opened it, found a well-worn wallet.

"Is everything in order, Mr. Graham?"

"Yes, thank you. Will you tell Mr. Nielsen that I received it? And give him my thanks."

"Certainly, sir."

I noted that this was D deck, went up one flight to find cabin C109.

All was not quite in order. My name is not "Graham."

II

*The thing that hath been, it is that which
shall be, and that which is done is that
which shall be done, and there is
no new thing under the sun.*
Ecclesiastes 1:9

Thank heaven ships use a consistent numbering system. Stateroom C109 was where it should be: on C deck, starboard side forward, between C107 and C111; I reached it without having to speak to anyone. I tried the door; it was locked—Mr. Graham apparently believed the warnings pursers give about locking doors, especially in port.

The key, I thought glumly, is in Mr. Graham's pants pocket. But where is Mr. Graham? About to catch me snooping at his door? Or is he trying my door while I am trying his door?

There is a small but not zero chance that a given key will fit a strange lock. I had in my own pocket my room key from the *Konge Knut*. I tried it.

Well, it was worth trying. I stood there, wondering whether to sneeze or drop dead, when I heard a sweet voice behind me:

"Oh, Mr. Graham!"

A young and pretty woman in a maid's costume— Correction: stewardess' uniform. She came bustling toward me, took a pass key that was chained to her belt, opened C109, while saying, "Margrethe asked me to watch for

11

you. She told me that you had left your cabin key on your desk. She let it stay but told me to watch for you and let you in."

"That's most kind of you, Miss, uh—"

"I'm Astrid. I have the matching rooms on the port side, so Marga and I cover for each other. She's gone ashore this afternoon." She held the door for me. "Will that be all, sir?"

I thanked her, she left. I latched and bolted the door, collapsed in a chair and gave way to the shakes.

Ten minutes later I stood up, went into the bathroom, put cold water on my face and eyes. I had not solved anything and had not wholly calmed down, but my nerves were no longer snapping like a flag in a high wind. I had been holding myself in ever since I had begun to suspect that something was seriously wrong, which was—when? When nothing seemed quite right at the fire pit? Later? Well, with utter certainty when I saw one 20,000-ton ship substituted for another.

My father used to tell me, "Alex, there is nothing wrong with being scared . . . as long as you don't let it affect you until the danger is over. Being hysterical is okay, too . . . afterwards and in private. Tears are not unmanly . . . in the bathroom with the door locked. The difference between a coward and a brave man is mostly a matter of timing."

I'm not the man my father was but I try to follow his advice. If you can learn not to jump when the firecracker goes off—or whatever the surprise is—you stand a good chance of being able to hang tight until the emergency is over.

This emergency was not over but I had benefited by the catharsis of a good case of shakes. Now I could take stock.

Hypotheses:

a) Something preposterous has happened to the world around me, or

b) Something preposterous has happened to Alex

Hergensheimer's mind; he should be locked up and sedated.

I could not think of a third hypothesis; those two seemed to cover all bases. The second hypothesis I need not waste time on. If I were raising snakes in my hat, eventually other people would notice and come around with a straitjacket and put me in a nice padded room.

So let's assume that I am sane (or nearly so; being a little bit crazy is helpful). If I am okay, then the world is out of joint. Let's take stock.

That wallet. Not mine. Most wallets are generally similar each to other and this one was much like mine. But carry a wallet for a few years and it fits you; it is distinctly yours. I had known at once that this one was not mine. But I did not want to say so to a ship's petty officer who insisted on "recognizing" me as "Mr. Graham."

I took out Graham's wallet and opened it.

Several hundred francs—count it later.

Eighty-five dollars in paper—legal tender of "The United States of North America."

A driver's license issued to A. L. Graham.

There were more items but I came across a window occupied by a typed notice, one that stopped me cold:

Anyone finding this wallet may keep any money in it as a reward if he will be so kind as to return the wallet to A. L. Graham, cabin C109, S.S. KONGE KNUT, Danish American Line, or to any purser or agent of the line. Thank you. A.L.G.

So now I knew what had happened to the *Konge Knut;* she had undergone a sea change.

Or had *I?* Was there truly a changed world and therefore a changed ship? Or were there two worlds and had I somehow walked through fire into the second one? Were there indeed two men and had they swapped destinies? Or had Alex Hergensheimer metamorphized into Alec

Graham while M.V. *Konge Knut* changed into S.S. *Konge Knut?* (While the North American Union melted into the United States of North America?)

Good questions. I'm glad you brought them up. Now, class, are there any more questions—

When I was in middle school there was a spate of magazines publishing fantastic stories, not alone ghost stories but weird yarns of every sort. Magic ships plying the ether to other stars. Strange inventions. Trips to the center of the earth. Other "dimensions." Flying machines. Power from burning atoms. Monsters created in secret laboratories.

I used to buy them and hide them inside copies of *Youth's Companion* and of *Young Crusaders*, knowing instinctively that my parents would disapprove and confiscate. I loved them and so did my outlaw chum Bert.

It couldn't last. First there was an editorial in *Youth's Companion:* "Poison to the Soul—Stamp it Out!" Then our pastor, Brother Draper, preached a sermon against such mind-corrupting trash, with comparisons to the evil effects of cigarettes and booze. Then our state outlawed such publications under the "standards of the community" doctrine even before passage of the national law and the parallel executive order.

And a cache I had hidden "perfectly" in our attic disappeared. Worse, the works of Mr. H. G. Wells and M. Jules Verne and some others were taken out of our public library.

You have to admire the motives of our spiritual leaders and elected officials in seeking to protect the minds of the young. As Brother Draper pointed out, there are enough exciting and adventurous stories in the Good Book to satisfy the needs of every boy and girl in the world; there was simply no need for profane literature. He was not urging censorship of books for adults, just for the impressionable young. If persons of mature years wanted to read such fantastic trash, suffer them to do so—although he, for one, could not see why any grown man would *want* to.

I guess I was one of the "impressionable young"—I still miss them.

I remember particularly one by Mr. Wells: *Men Like Gods*. These people were driving along in an automobile when an explosion happens and they find themselves in another world, much like their own but better. They meet the people who live there and there is explanation about parallel universes and the fourth dimension and such.

That was the first installment. The Protect-Our-Youth state law was passed right after that, so I never saw the later installments.

One of my English professors who was bluntly opposed to censorship once said that Mr. Wells had invented every one of the basic fantastic themes, and he cited this story as the origin of the multiple-universes concept. I was intending to ask this prof if he knew where I could find a copy, but I put it off to the end of the term when I would be legally "of mature years"—and waited too long; the academic senate committee on faith and morals voted against tenure for that professor, and he left abruptly without finishing the term.

Did something happen to me like that which Mr. Wells described in *Men Like Gods?* Did Mr. Wells have the holy gift of prophecy? For example, would men someday actually fly to the moon? Preposterous!

But was it more preposterous than what had happened to me?

As may be, here I was in *Konge Knut* (even though she was not *my Konge Knut)* and the sailing board at the gangway showed her getting underway at 6 p.m. It was already late afternoon and high time for me to decide.

What to do? I seemed to have mislaid my own ship, the Motor Vessel *Konge Knut*. But the crew (some of the crew) of the Steamship *Konge Knut* seemed ready to accept me as "Mr. Graham," passenger.

Stay aboard and try to brazen it out? What if Graham comes aboard (any minute now!) and demands to know what I am doing in his room?

Or go ashore (as I should) and go to the authorities with my problem?

Alex, the French colonial authorities will love you. No baggage, only the clothes on your back, no money, not a sou—no passport! Oh, they will love you so much they'll give you room and board for the rest of your life . . . in an oubliette with a grill over the top.

There's money in that wallet.

So? Ever heard of the Eighth Commandment? That's *his* money.

But it stands to reason that *he* walked through the fire at the same time you did but on this side, this world or whatever—or his wallet would not have been waiting for you. Now *he* has *your* wallet. That's logical.

Listen, my retarded friend, do you think logic has anything to do with the predicament we are in?

Well—

Speak up!

No, not really. Then how about this? Sit tight in this room. If Graham shows up before the ship sails, you get kicked off the ship, that's sure. But you would be no worse off than you will be if you leave now. If he does *not* show up, then you take his place at least as far as Papeete. That's a big city; your chances of coping with the situation are far better there. Consuls and such.

You talked me into it.

Passenger ships usually publish a daily newspaper for the passengers—just a single or double sheet filled with thrilling items such as "There will be a boat drill at ten o'clock this morning. All passengers are requested—" and "Yesterday's mileage pool was won by Mrs. Ephraim Glutz of Bethany, Iowa" and, usually, a few news items picked up by the wireless operator. I looked around for the ship's paper and for the "Welcome Aboard!" This latter is a booklet (perhaps with another name) intended to make the passenger newly aboard sophisticated in the little world of the ship: names of the officers, times of meals, location of barber shop, laundry, dining room, gift shop (notions, magazines, toothpaste), and how to place a morning call, plan of the ship by decks, location of life preserver, how to find your lifeboat station, where to get your table assignment—

"Table assignment"! Ouch! A passenger who has been aboard even one day does not have to ask how to find his table in the dining room. It's the little things that trip you. Well, I'd have to bull it through.

The welcome-aboard booklet was tucked into Graham's desk. I thumbed through it, with a mental note to memorize all key facts before I left this room—if I was still aboard when the ship sailed—then put it aside, as I had found the ship's newspaper:

The King's Skald it was headed and Graham, bless him, had saved all of them from the day he had boarded the ship . . . at Portland, Oregon, as I deduced from the place and date line of the earliest issue. That suggested that Graham was ticketed for the entire cruise, which could be important to me. I had expected to go back as I had arrived, by airship—but, even if the dirigible liner *Admiral Moffett* existed in this world or dimension or whatever, I no longer had a ticket for it and no money with which to buy one. What do these French colonials do to a tourist who has no money? Burn him at the stake? Or merely draw and quarter him? I did not want to find out. Graham's roundtrip ticket (if he had one) might keep me from having to find out.

(If he didn't show up in the next hour and have me kicked off the ship.)

I did not consider remaining in Polynesia. Being a penniless beachcomber on Bora-Bora or Moorea may have been practical a hundred years ago but today the only thing free in these islands is contagious disease.

It seemed likely that I would be just as broke and just

as much a stranger in America but nevertheless I felt that I would be better off in my native land. Well, Graham's native land.

I read some of the wireless news items but could not make sense of them, so I put them aside for later study. What little I had learned from them was not comforting. I had cherished deep down an illogical hope that this would turn out to be just a silly mixup that would soon be straightened out (don't ask me how). But those news items ended all hoping.

I mean to say, what sort of world is it in which the "President" of Germany visits London? In my world Kaiser Wilhelm IV rules the German Empire. A "president" for Germany sounds as silly as a "king" for America.

This might be a pleasant world . . . but it was *not* the world I was born into. Not by those weird news items.

As I put away Graham's file of *The King's Skald* I noted on the top sheet today's prescribed dress for dinner: "Formal."

I was not surprised; the *Konge Knut* in her other incarnation as a motor vessel was quite formal. If the ship was underway, black tie was expected. If you didn't wear it, you were made to feel that you really ought to eat in your stateroom.

I don't own a tuxedo; our church does not encourage vanities. I had compromised by wearing a blue serge suit at dinners underway, with a white shirt and a snap-on black bow tie. Nobody said anything. It did not matter, as I was below the salt anyhow, having come aboard at Papeete.

I decided to see if Mr. Graham owned a dark suit. And a black tie.

Mr. Graham owned lots of clothes, far more than I did. I tried on a sports jacket; it fit me well enough. Trousers? Length seemed okay; I was not sure about the waistband—and too shy to try on a pair and thereby risk being caught by Graham with one leg in his trousers. What does one say? Hi, there! I was just waiting for you and thought I would pass the time by trying on your pants. Not convincing.

He had not one but two tuxedos, one in conventional black and the other in dark red—I had never heard of such frippery.

But I did not find a snap-on bow tie.

He had black bow ties, several. But I have never learned how to tie a bow tie.

I took a deep breath and thought about it.

There came a knock at the door. I didn't jump out of my skin, just almost. "Who's there!" (Honest, Mr. Graham, I was just waiting for you!)

"Stewardess, sir."

"Oh. Come in, come in!"

I heard her try her key, then I jumped to turn back the bolt. "Sorry, I had forgotten that I had used the dead bolt. Do come in."

Margrethe turned out to be about the age of Astrid, youngish, and even prettier, with flaxen hair and freckles across her nose. She spoke textbook-correct English with a charming lilt to it. She was carrying a short white jacket on a coat hanger. "Your mess jacket, sir. Karl says the other one will be ready tomorrow."

"Why, thank you, Margrethe! I had forgotten all about it."

"I thought you might. So I came back aboard a little early—the laundry was just closing. I'm glad I did; it's much too hot for you to wear black."

"You shouldn't have come back early; you're spoiling me."

"I like to take good care of my guests. As you know." She hung the jacket in the wardrobe, turned to leave. "I'll be back to tie your tie. Six-thirty as usual, sir?"

"Six-thirty is fine. What time is it now?" (Tarnation, my watch was gone wherever Motor Vessel *Konge Knut* had vanished; I had not worn it ashore.)

"Almost six o'clock." She hesitated. "I'll lay out your clothes before I go; you don't have much time."

"My dear girl! That's no part of your duties."

"No, it's my pleasure." She opened a drawer, took out a dress shirt, placed it on my/Graham's bunk. "And you know why." With the quick efficiency of a person who knows exactly where everything is, she opened a small desk drawer that I had not touched, took out a leather case, from it laid out by the shirt a watch, a ring, and shirt studs, then inserted studs into the shirt, placed fresh underwear and black silk socks on the pillow, placed evening pumps by the chair with shoe horn tucked inside, took from the wardrobe that mess jacket, hung it and black dress trousers (braces attached) and dark red cummerbund on the front of the wardrobe. She glanced over the layout, added a wing collar, a black tie, and a fresh handkerchief to the stack on the pillow—cast her eye over it again, placed the room key and the wallet by the ring and the watch—glanced again, nodded. "I must run or I'll miss dinner. I'll be back for the tie." And she was gone, not running but moving very fast.

Margrethe was so right. If she had not laid out everything, I would still be struggling to put myself together. That shirt alone would have stopped me; it was one of the dive-in-and-button-up-the-back sort. I had never worn one.

Thank heaven Graham used an ordinary brand of safety razor. By six-fifteen I had touched up my morning shave, showered (necessary!), and washed the smoke out of my hair.

His shoes fit me as if I had broken them in myself. His trousers were a bit tight in the waist—a Danish ship is no place to lose weight and I had been in the Motor Vessel *Konge Knut* for a fortnight. I was still struggling with that consarned backwards shirt when Margrethe let herself in with her pass key.

She came straight to me, said, "Hold still," and quickly

buttoned the buttons I could not reach. Then she fitted that fiendish collar over its collar buttons, laid the tie around my neck. "Turn around, please."

Tying a bow tie properly involves magic. She knew the spell.

She helped me with the cummerbund, held my jacket for me, looked me over and announced, "You'll do. And I'm proud of you; at dinner the girls were talking about you. I wish I had seen it. You are very brave."

"Not brave. Foolish. I talked when I should have kept still."

"Brave. I must go—I left Kristina guarding a cherry tart for me. But if I stay away too long someone will steal it."

"You run along. And thank you loads! Hurry and save that tart."

"Aren't you going to pay me?"

"Oh. What payment would you like?"

"Don't tease me!" She moved a few inches closer, turned her face up. I don't know much about girls (who does?) but some signals are large print. I took her by her shoulders, kissed both her cheeks, hesitated just long enough to be certain that she was neither displeased nor surprised, then placed one right in the middle. Her lips were full and warm.

"Was that the payment you had in mind?"

"Yes, of course. But you can kiss better than that. You know you can." She pouted her lower lip, then dropped her eyes.

"Brace yourself."

Yes, I can kiss lots better than that. Or could by the time we had used up that kiss. By letting Margrethe lead it and heartily cooperating in whatever way she seemed to think a better kiss should go I learned more about kissing in the next two minutes than I had learned in my entire life up to then.

My ears roared.

For a moment after we broke she held still in my arms

and looked up at me most soberly. "Alec," she said softly, "that's the best you've ever kissed me. Goodness. Now I'm going to run before I make you late for dinner." She slipped out of my arms and left as she did everything, quickly.

I inspected myself in the mirror. No marks. A kiss that emphatic ought to leave marks.

What sort of person was this Graham? I could wear his clothes . . . but could I cope with his woman? Or was she his? Who knows?—I did not. Was he a lecher, a womanizer? Or was I butting in on a perfectly nice if somewhat indiscreet romance?

How do you walk back through a fire pit?

And did I want to?

Go aft to the main companionway, then down two decks and go aft again—that's what the ship's plans in the booklet showed.

No problem. A man at the door of the dining saloon, dressed much as I was but with a menu under his arm, had to be the head waiter, the chief dining-room steward. He confirmed it with a big professional smile. "Good evening, Mr. Graham."

I paused. "Good evening. What's this about a change in seating arrangements? Where am I to sit tonight?" (If you grab the bull by the horns, you at least confuse him.)

"It's not a permanent change, sir. Tomorrow you will be back at table fourteen. But tonight the Captain has asked that you sit at his table. If you will follow me, sir."

He led me to an oversize table amidships, started to seat me on the Captain's right—and the Captain stood up and started to clap, the others at his table followed suit, and shortly everyone in the dining room (it seemed) was standing and clapping and some were cheering.

I learned two things at that dinner. First, it was clear that Graham had pulled the same silly stunt I had (but it still was not clear whether there was one of us or two of us—I tabled that question).

Second, but of major importance: Do not drink ice-cold Aalborg akvavit on an empty stomach, especially if you were brought up White Ribbon as I was.

III

Wine is a mocker, strong drink is raging—
Proverbs 20:1

I am not blaming Captain Hansen. I have heard that Scandinavians put ethanol into their blood as antifreeze, against their long hard winters, and consequently cannot understand people who cannot take strong drink. Besides that, nobody held my arms, nobody held my nose, nobody forced spirits down my throat. I did it myself.

Our church doesn't hold with the doctrine that the flesh is weak and therefore sin is humanly understandable and readily forgiven. Sin can be forgiven but just barely and you are surely going to catch it first. Sin should suffer.

I found out about some of that suffering. I'm told it is called a hangover.

That is what my drinking uncle called it. Uncle Ed maintained that no man can cope with temperance who has not had a full course of intemperance . . . otherwise when temptation came his way, he would not know how to handle it.

Maybe I proved Uncle Ed's point. He was considered a bad influence around our house and, if he had not been Mother's brother, Dad would not have allowed him in the house. As it was, he was never pressed to stay longer and was not urged to hurry back.

Before I even sat down at the table, the Captain offered me a glass of akvavit. The glasses used for this are not large; they are quite small—and that is the deceptive part of the danger.

The Captain had a glass like it in his hand. He looked me in the eye and said, "To our hero! *Skaal!*"—threw his head back and tossed it down.

There were echoes of *"Skaal!"* all around the table and everyone seemed to gulp it down just like the Captain.

So I did. I could say that being guest of honor laid certain obligations on me—"When in Rome" and all that. But the truth is I did not have the requisite strength of character to refuse. I told myself, "One tiny glass can't hurt," and gulped it down.

No trouble. It went down smoothly. One pleasant ice-cold swallow, then a spicy aftertaste with a hint of licorice. I did not know what I was drinking but I was not sure that it was alcoholic. It seemed not to be.

We sat down and somebody put food in front of me and the Captain's steward poured another glass of schnapps for me. I was about to start nibbling the food, Danish hors d'oeuvres and delicious—smorgasbord tidbits—when someone put a hand on my shoulder.

I looked up. The Well-Traveled Man—

With him were the Authority and the Skeptic.

Not the same names. Whoever (Whatever?) was playing games with my life had not gone that far. "Gerald Fortescue" was now "Jeremy Forsyth," for example. But despite slight differences I had no trouble recognizing each of them and their new names were close enough to show that someone, or something, was continuing the joke.

(Then why wasn't my new name something like "Hergensheimer"? "Hergensheimer" has dignity about it, a rolling grandeur. Graham is a so-so name.)

"Alec," Mr. Forsyth said, "we misjudged you. Duncan and I and Pete are happy to admit it. Here's the three thousand we owe you, and—" He hauled his right hand out from behind his back, held up a large bottle. "—the best champagne in the ship as a mark of our esteem."

"Steward!" said the Captain.

Shortly the wine steward was going around, filling glasses at our table. But before that, I found myself again standing up, making *Skaal!* in akvavit three times, once to each of the losers, while clutching three thousand dollars (United States of North America dollars). I did not have time then to wonder why three hundred had changed to three thousand—besides, it was not as odd as what had happened to the *Konge Knut*. Both of her. And my wonder circuits were overloaded anyhow.

Captain Hansen told his waitress to place chairs at the table for Forsyth and company, but all three insisted that their wives and table mates expected them to return. Nor was there room. Not that it would have mattered to Captain Hansen. He is a Viking, half again as big as a house; hand him a hammer and he would be mistaken for Thor—he has muscles where other men don't even have places. It is very hard to argue with him.

But he jovially agreed to compromise. They could go back to their tables and finish their dinners but first they must join him and me in pledging Shadrach, Meshach, and Abed-nego, guardian angels of our shipmate Alec. In fact the whole table must join in. "Steward!"

So we said *"Skaal!"* three more times, while bouncing Danish antifreeze off our tonsils.

Have you kept count? That's seven, I think. You can stop counting, as that is where I lost track. I was beginning to feel a return of the numbness I had felt halfway through the fire pit.

The wine steward had completed pouring champagne, having renewed his supply at a gesture from the Captain. Then it was time to toast me again, and I returned the compliment to the three losers, then we all toasted Captain Hansen, and then we toasted the good ship *Konge Knut*.

The Captain toasted the United States and the whole room stood and drank with him, so I felt it incumbent to answer by toasting the Danish Queen, and that got me toasted again and the Captain demanded a speech from me. "Tell us how it feels to be in the fiery furnace!"

I tried to refuse and there were shouts of "Speech! Speech!" from all around me.

I stood up with some difficulty, tried to remember the speech I had made at the last foreign missions fund-raising dinner. It evaded me. Finally I said, "Aw, shucks, it wasn't anything. Just put your ear to the ground and your shoulder to the wheel and your eyes on the stars and you can do it too. Thank you, thank you all and next time you must come to my house."

They cheered and we skaaled again, I forget why, and the lady on the Captain's left got up and came around and kissed me, whereupon all the ladies at the Captain's table clustered around and kissed me. That seemed to inspire the other ladies in the room, for there was a steady procession coming up to claim a buss from me, and usually kissing the Captain while they were about it, or perhaps the other way around.

During this parade someone removed a steak from in front of me, one I had had plans for. I didn't miss it too much, because that endless orgy of osculation had me bewildered, plus bemusement much like that caused by the female villagers of the fire walk.

Much of this bemusement started when I first walked into the dining room. Let me put it this way: My fellow passengers, female, really should have been in the *National Geographic*.

Yes. Like that. Well, maybe not quite, but what they did wear made them look nakeder than those friendly villagers. I'm not going to describe those "formal evening dresses" because I'm not sure I could—and I *am* sure I shouldn't. But none of them covered more than twenty percent of what ladies usually keep covered at fancy evening affairs in the world I grew up in. Above the waist I mean. Their skirts, long, some clear to the floor, were nevertheless cut or slit in most startling ways.

Some of the ladies had tops to their dresses that covered everything . . . but the material was transparent as glass. Or almost.

And some of the youngest ladies, girls really, actually did belong in the *National Geographic*, just like my villagers. Somehow, these younger ladies did not seem quite as immodest as their elders.

I had noticed this display almost the instant I walked in. But I tried not to stare and the Captain and others kept me so busy at first that I really did not have time to sneak glances at the incredible exposure. But, look— when a lady comes up and puts her arms around you and insists on kissing you, it is difficult *not* to notice that she isn't wearing enough to ward off pneumonia. Or other chest complaints.

But I kept a tight rein on myself despite increasing dizziness and numbness.

Even bare skin did not startle me as much as bare words—language I had never heard in public in my life and extremely seldom even in private among men only. "Men," I said, as gentlemen don't talk that way even with no ladies present—in the world I knew.

The most shocking thing that ever happened to me in my boyhood was one day crossing the town square, noticing a crowd on the penance side of the courthouse, joining it to see who was catching it and why . . . and finding my Scoutmaster in the stocks. I almost fainted.

His offense was profane language, so the sign on his chest told us. The accuser was his own wife; he did not dispute it and had thrown himself on the mercy of the court—the judge was Deacon Brumby, who didn't know the word.

Mr. Kirk, my Scoutmaster, left town two weeks later and nobody ever saw him again—being exposed in the stocks was likely to have that effect on a man. I don't know what the bad language was that Mr. Kirk had used, but it couldn't have been too bad, as all Deacon Brumby could give him was one dawn-to-dusk.

That night at the Captain's table in the *Konge Knut* I

heard a sweet lady of the favorite-grandmother sort address her husband in a pattern of forbidden words involving blasphemy and certain criminal sensual acts. Had she spoken that way in public in my home town she would have received maximum exposure in stocks followed by being ridden out of town. (Our town did not use tar and feathers; that was regarded as brutal.)

Yet this dear lady in the ship was not even chided. Her husband simply smiled and told her that she worried too much.

Between shocking speech, incredible immodest exposure, and effects of two sorts of strange and deceptive potions lavishly administered, I was utterly confused. A stranger in a strange land, I was overcome by customs new and shocking. But through it all I clung to the conviction that I must appear to be sophisticated, at home, unsurprised. I must not let anyone suspect that I was not Alec Graham, shipmate, but instead Alexander Hergensheimer, total stranger . . . or something terrible might happen.

Of course I was wrong; something terrible had already happened. I was indeed a total stranger in an utterly strange and confusing land . . . but I do not think, in retrospect, that I would have made my condition worse had I simply blurted out my predicament.

I would not have been believed.

How else? I had trouble believing it myself.

Captain Hansen, a hearty no-nonsense man, would have bellowed with laughter at my "joke" and insisted on another toast. Had I persisted in my "delusion" he would have had the ship's doctor talk to me.

Still, I got through that amazing evening easier by holding tight to the notion that I must concentrate on acting the part of Alec Graham while never letting anyone suspect that I was a changeling, a cuckoo's egg.

There had just been placed in front of me a slice of princess cake, a beautiful multilayered confection I recalled from the other *Konge Knut*, and a small cup of coffee, when the Captain stood up. "Come, Alec! We go to the lounge now; the show is ready to start—but they can't start till I get there. So come on! You don't want all that sweet stuff; it's not good for you. You can have coffee in the lounge. But before that we have some man's drinks, henh? Not these joke drinks. You like Russian vodka?"

He linked his arm in mine. I discovered that I was going to the lounge. Volition did not enter into it.

That lounge show was much the mixture I had found earlier in M.V. *Konge Knut*—a magician who did improbable things but not as improbable as what I had done (or been done to?), a standup comedian who should have sat down, a pretty girl who sang, and dancers. The major differences were two I had already been exposed to: bare skin and bare words, and by then I was so numb from earlier shock and akvavit that these additional proofs of a different world had minimal effect.

The girl who sang just barely had clothes on and the lyrics of her songs would have caused her trouble even in the underworld of Newark, New Jersey. Or so I think; I have no direct experience with that notorious sink of iniquity. I paid more attention to her appearance, since here I need not avert my eyes; one is *expected* to stare at performers.

If one admits for the sake of argument that customs in dress can be wildly different without destroying the fabric of society (a possibility I do not concede but will stipulate), then it helps, I think, if the person exhibiting this difference is young and healthy and comely.

The singer was young and healthy and comely. I felt a twinge of regret when she left the spotlight.

The major event was a troupe of Tahitian dancers, and I was truly not surprised that they were costumed bare to the waist save for flowers or shell beads—by then I would have been surprised had they been otherwise. What was still surprising (although I suppose it should not have

been) was the subsequent behavior of my fellow passengers.

First the troupe, eight girls, two men, danced for us,
much the same dancing that had preceded the fire walk
today, much the same as I had seen when a troupe had
come aboard M.V. *Konge Knut* in Papeete. Perhaps you
know that the hula of Tahiti differs from the slow and
graceful hula of the Kingdom of Hawaii by being at a
much faster beat and is much more energetic. I'm no expert on the arts of the dance but at least I have seen both
styles of hula in the lands where each was native.

I prefer the Hawaiian hula, which I had seen when the
Count von Zeppelin had stopped at Hilo for a day on her
way to Papeete. The Tahitian hula strikes me as an ath-
letic accomplishment rather than an art form. But its
very energy and speed make it still more startling in the
dress or undress these native girls wore.

There was more to come. After a long dance sequence
which included paired dancing between girls and each of
the two young men—in which they did things that would
have been astonishing even among barnyard fowl (I kept
expecting Captain Hansen to put a stop to it), the ship's
master of ceremonies or cruise director stepped forward.

"Ladeez and gentlemen," he announced, "and the rest
of you intoxicated persons of irregular birth—" (I am
forced to amend his language.) "Most of you setters and
even a few pointers have made good use of the four days
our dancers have been with us to add the Tahitian hula
to your repertoire. Shortly you'll be given a chance to
demonstrate what you've learned and to receive diplomas as authentic Papeete papayas. But what you don't
know is that others in the good ole knutty *Knut* have been
practicing, too. Maestro, strike up the band!"

Out from behind the lounge stage danced a dozen more
hula dancers. But these girls were not Polynesian; these
girls were Caucasian. They were dressed authentically,
grass skirts and necklaces, a flower in the hair, nothing

else. But instead of warm brown, their skins were white; most of them were blondes, two were redheads.

It makes a difference. By then I was ready to concede that Polynesian women were correctly and even modestly dressed in their native costume—other places, other customs. Was not Mother Eve modest in her simplicity before the Fall?

But white women are grossly out of place in South Seas garb.

However, this did not keep me from watching the dancing. I was amazed to see that these girls danced that fast and complex dance as well (to my untutored eye) as did the island girls. I remarked on it to the Captain. "They learned to dance that precisely in only four days?"

He snorted. "They practice every cruise, those who ship with us before. All have practiced at least since San Diego."

At that point I recognized one of the dancers—Astrid, the sweet young woman who had let me into "my" stateroom—and I then understood why they had had time and incentive to practice together: These girls were ship's crew. I looked at her—stared, in fact—with more interest. She caught my eye and smiled. Like a dolt, a bumpkin, instead of smiling back I looked away and blushed, and tried to cover my embarrassment by taking a big sip of the drink I found in my hand.

One of the kanaka dancers whirled out in front of the white girls and called one of them out for a pair dance. Heaven save me, it was Margrethe!

I choked up and could not breathe. She was the most blindingly beautiful sight I had ever seen in all my life.

"Behold, thou art fair, my love; behold, thou art fair; thou hast doves' eyes within thy locks: thy hair is as a flock of goats, that appear from Mount Gilead.

"Thy navel is like a round goblet, which wanteth not liquor: thy belly is like a heap of wheat set about with lilies.

"Thy two breasts are like two young roes that are twins.

"Thou art all fair, my love; there is no spot in thee." ·

IV

Although affliction cometh not forth of the dust,
neither doth trouble spring out of the ground;
yet man is born unto trouble,
as the sparks fly upward.
Job 5:6–7

I slowly became aware of myself and wished I had not; a most terrible nightmare was chasing me. I jammed my eyes shut against the light and tried to go back to sleep.

Native drums were beating in my head; I tried to shut them out by covering my ears.

They got louder.

I gave up, opened my eyes and lifted my head. A mistake—my stomach flipflopped and my ears shook. My eyes would not track and those infernal drums were tearing my skull apart.

I finally got my eyes to track, although the focus was fuzzy. I looked around, found that I was in a strange room, lying on top of a bed and only half dressed.

That began to bring it back to me. A party aboard ship. Spirits. Lots of spirits. Noise. Nakedness. The Captain in a grass skirt, dancing heartily, and the orchestra keeping step with him. Some of the lady passengers wearing grass skirts and some wearing even less. Rattle of bamboo, boom of drums.

Drums—

Those weren't drums in my head; that was the boom-

ing of the worst headache of my life. Why in Ned did I let
them—

Never mind "them." You did it yourself, chum.

Yes, but—

"Yes, but." Always "Yes, but." All your life it's been
"Yes, but." When are you going to straighten up and take
full responsibility for your life and all that happens to
you?

Yes, but *this* isn't my fault. I'm not A. L. Graham. That
isn't my name. This isn't my ship.

It isn't? You're not?

Of course not—

I sat up to shake off this bad dream. Sitting up was a
mistake; my head did not fall off but a stabbing pain at
the base of my neck added itself to the throbbing inside
my skull. I was wearing black dress trousers and apparently nothing else and I was in a strange room that was
rolling slowly.

Graham's trousers. Graham's room. And that long,
slow roll was that of a ship with no stabilizers.

Not a dream. Or if it is, I can't shake myself out of it.
My teeth itched, my feet didn't fit. Dried sweat all over
me except where I was clammy. My armpits— Don't even
think about armpits!

My mouth needed to have lye dumped into it.

I remembered everything now. Or almost. The fire pit.
Villagers. Chickens scurrying out of the way. The ship
that wasn't my ship—but was. Margrethe—

Margrethe!

*"Thy two breasts are like two roes—thou art all fair, my
love!"*

Margrethe among the dancers, her bosom as bare as
her feet. Margrethe dancing with that villainous kanaka,
and shaking her—

No wonder I got drunk!

Stow it, chum! You were drunk before that. All you've
got against that native lad is that it was he instead of

you. You wanted to dance with her yourself. Only *you* can't dance.

Dancing is a snare of Satan.

And don't you wish you knew how!

"*—like two roes*"! Yes. I do!

I heard a light tap at the door, then a rattle of keys. Margrethe stuck her head in. "Awake? Good." She came in, carrying a tray, closed the door, came to me. "Drink this."

"What is it?"

"Tomato juice, mostly. Don't argue—drink it!"

"I don't think I can."

"Yes, you can. You must. Do it."

I sniffed it, then I took a small sip. To my amazement it did not nauseate me. So I drank some more. After one minor quiver it went down smoothly and lay quietly inside me. Margrethe produced two pills. "Take these. Wash them down with the rest of the tomato juice."

"I never take medicine."

She sighed, and said something I did not understand. Not English. Not quite. "What did you say?"

"Just something my grandmother used to say when grandfather argued with her. Mr. Graham, take those pills. They are just aspirin and you need them. If you won't cooperate, I'll stop trying to help you. I'll— I'll swap you to Astrid, that's what I'll do."

"Don't do that."

"I will if you keep objecting. Astrid would swap, I know she would. She likes you—she told me you were watching her dance last night."

I accepted the pills, washed them down with the rest of the tomato juice—ice-cold and very comforting. "I did until I spotted you. Then I watched you."

She smiled for the first time. "Yes? Did you like it?"

"You were beautiful." (And your dance was obscene. Your immodest dress and your behavior shocked me out of a year's growth. I hated it—and I wish I could see it all over again this very instant!) "You are very graceful."

The smile grew dimples. "I had hoped that you would like it, sir."

"I did. Now stop threatening me with Astrid."

"All right. As long as you behave. Now get up and into the shower. First very hot, then very cold. Like a sauna." She waited. "'Up,' I said. I'm not leaving until that shower is running and steam is pouring out."

"I'll shower. After you leave."

"And you'll run it lukewarm, I know. Get up, get those trousers off, get into that shower. While you're showering, I'll fetch your breakfast tray. There is just enough time before they shut down the galley to set up for lunch . . . so quit wasting time. Please!"

"Oh, I can't eat breakfast! Not today. No." Food—what a disgusting thought.

"You *must* eat. You drank too much last night, you know you did. If you don't eat, you will feel bad all day. Mr. Graham, I've finished making up for all my other guests, so I'm off watch now. I'm fetching your tray, then I'm going to stay and see that you eat it." She looked at me. "I should have taken your trousers off when I put you to bed. But you were too heavy."

"You put me to bed?"

"Ori helped me. The boy I danced with." My face must have given me away, for she added hastily, "Oh, I didn't let him come into your room, sir. I undressed you myself. But I did have to have help to get you up the stairs."

"I wasn't criticizing." (Did you go back to the party then? Was he there? Did you dance with him again? "—*jealousy is cruel as the grave; the coals thereof are coals of fire*—" I have no right.) "I thank you both. I must have been a beastly nuisance."

"Well . . . brave men often drink too much, after danger is over. But it's not good for you."

"No, it's not." I got up off the bed, went into the

bathroom, said, "I'll turn it up hot. Promise." I closed the door and bolted it, finished undressing. (So I got so stinking, rubber-limp drunk that a native boy had to help get me to bed. Alex, you're a disgusting mess! And you haven't any right to be jealous over a nice girl. You don't own her, her behavior is not wrong by the standards of this place—wherever this place is—and all she's done is mother you and take care of you. That does not give you a claim on her.)

I did turn it up hot, though it durn near kilt poor old Alex. But I left it hot until the nerve ends seemed cauterized—then suddenly switched it to cold, and screamed.

I let it stay cold until it no longer felt cold, then shut it off and dried down, having opened the door to let out the moisture-charged air. I stepped out into the room . . . and suddenly realized that I felt wonderful. No headache. No feeling that the world is ending at noon. No stomach queasies. Just hunger. Alex, you must never get drunk again . . . but if you do, you must do exactly what Margrethe tells you to. You've got a smart head on her shoulders, boy—appreciate it.

I started to whistle and opened Graham's wardrobe.

I heard a key in the door, hastily grabbed his bathrobe, managed to cover up before she got the door open. She was slow about it, being hampered by a heavy tray. When I realized this I held the door for her. She put down the tray, then arranged dishes and food on my desk.

"You were right about the sauna-type shower," I told her. "It was just what the doctor ordered. Or the nurse, I should say."

"I know, it's what my grandmother used to do for my grandfather."

"A smart woman. My, this smells good!" (Scrambled eggs, bacon, lavish amounts of Danish pastry, milk, coffee—a side dish of cheeses, *fladbrød*, and thin curls of ham, some tropic fruit I can't name.) "What was that your grandmother used to say when your grandfather argued?"

"Oh, she was sometimes impatient."

"And you never are. Tell me."

"Well— She used to say that God created men to test the souls of women."

"She may have a point. Do you agree with her?"

Her smile produced dimples. "I think they have other uses as well."

Margrethe tidied my room and cleaned my bath (okay, okay, *Graham's* room, *Graham's* bath—satisfied?) while I ate. She laid out a pair of slacks, a sport shirt in an island print, and sandals for me, then removed the tray and dishes while leaving coffee and the remaining fruit. I thanked her as she left, wondered if I should offer "payment" and wondered, too, if she performed such valet services for other passengers. It seemed unlikely. I found I could not ask.

I bolted the door after her and proceeded to search Graham's room.

I was wearing his clothes, sleeping in his bed, answering to his name—and now I must decide whether or not I would go whole hawg and *be* "A. L. Graham" . . . or should I go to some authority (American consul? If not, whom?), admit the impersonation, and ask for help?

Events were crowding me. Today's *King Skald* showed that S.S. *Konge Knut* was scheduled to dock at Papeete at 3 p.m. and sail for Mazatlán, Mexico, at 6 p.m. The purser notified all passengers wishing to change francs into dollars that a representative of the Bank of Papeete would be in the ship's square facing the purser's office from docking until fifteen minutes before sailing. The purser again wished to notify passengers that shipboard indebtedness such as bar and shop bills could be settled only in dollars, Danish crowns, or by means of validated letters of credit.

All very reasonable. And troubling. I had expected the ship to stop at Papeete for twenty-four hours at the very least. Docking for only three hours seemed preposterous—why, they would hardly finish tying up before it would be time to start singling up for sailing! Didn't they have to pay rent for twenty-four hours if they docked at all?

Then I reminded myself that managing the ship was not my business. Perhaps the Captain was taking advantage of a few hours between departure of one ship and arrival of another. Or there might be six other reasons. The only thing I should worry about was what I could accomplish between three and six, and what I *must* accomplish between now and three.

Forty minutes of intense searching turned up the following:

Clothes, all sorts—no problem other than about five pounds at my waistline.

Money—the francs in his billfold (must change them) and the eighty-five dollars there; three thousand dollars loose in the desk drawer that held the little case for Graham's watch, ring, shirt studs, etc. Since the watch and jewelry had been returned to this case, I assumed conclusively that Margrethe had conserved for me the proceeds of that bet that I (or Graham) had won from Forsyth and Jeeves and Henshaw. It is said that the Lord looks out for fools and drunkards; if so, in my case He operated through Margrethe.

Various impedimenta of no significance to my immediate problem—books, souvenirs, toothpaste, etc.

No passport.

When a first search failed to turn up Graham's passport, I went back and searched again, this time checking the pockets of all clothes hanging in his wardrobe as well as rechecking with care all the usual places and some unusual places that might hide a booklet the size of a passport.

No passport.

Some tourists are meticulous about keeping their passports on their persons whenever leaving a ship. I prefer not to carry my passport when I can avoid it because losing a passport is a sticky mess. I had not carried mine the day before . . . so now mine was gone where the woodbine twineth, gone to Fiddler's Green, gone where Motor Vessel *Konge Knut* had gone. And where was that? I had not had time to think about that yet; I was too busy coping with a strange new world.

If Graham had carried his passport yesterday, then it too was gone to Fiddler's Green through a crack in the fourth dimension. It was beginning to look that way.

While I fumed, someone slipped an envelope under the stateroom door.

I picked it up and opened it. Inside was the purser's billing for "my" (Graham's) bills aboard ship. Was Graham scheduled to leave the ship at Papeete? Oh, no! If he was, I might be marooned in the islands indefinitely.

No, maybe not. This appeared to be a routine end-of-a-month billing.

The size of Graham's bar bill shocked me . . . until I noticed some individual items. Then I was still more shocked but for another reason. When a Coca-Cola costs two dollars it does not mean that a Coke is bigger; it means that the dollar is smaller.

I now knew why a three-hundred-dollar bet on, uh, the *other* side turned out to be three thousand dollars on this side.

If I was going to have to live in this world, I was going to have to readjust my thinking about all prices. Treat dollars as I would a foreign currency and convert all prices in my head until I got used to them. For example, if these shipboard prices were representative, then a first-class dinner, steak or prime rib, in a first-class restaurant, let's say the main dining room of a hotel such as the Brown Palace or the Mark Hopkins—such a dinner could easily cost ten dollars. Whew!

With cocktails before dinner and wine with it, the tab

might reach fifteen dollars! A week's wages. Thank heaven I don't drink!

You don't what?

Look—last night was a very special occasion.

So? So it was, because you lose your virginity only once. Once gone, it's gone forever. What was that you were drinking just before the lights went out? A Danish zombie? Wouldn't you like one of those about now? Just to readjust your stability?

I'll never touch one again!

See you later, chum.

Just one more chance but a good one—I hoped. The small case that Graham used for jewelry and such had in it a key, plain save for the number eighty-two stamped on its side. If fate was smiling, that was a key to a lockbox in the purser's office.

(And if fate was sneering at me today, it was a key to a lockbox in a bank somewhere in the forty-six states, a bank I would never see. But let's not borrow trouble; I have all I need.)

I went down one deck and aft. "Good morning, Purser."

"Ah, Mr. Graham! A fine party, was it not?"

"It certainly was. One more like that and I'm a corpse."

"Oh, come now. That from a man who walks through fire. You seemed to enjoy it—and I know I did. What can we do for you, sir?"

I brought out the key I had found. "Do I have the right key? Or does this one belong to my bank? I can never remember."

The purser took it. "That's one of ours. Poul! Take this and get Mr. Graham's box. Mr. Graham, do you want to come around behind and sit at a table?"

"Yes, thank you. Uh, do you have a sack or something that would hold the contents of a box that size? I would take it back to my desk for paper work."

"'A sack'— Mmm . . . I could get one from the gift

shop. But— How long do you think this desk work will take you? Can you finish it by noon?"

"Oh, certainly."

"Then take the box itself back to your stateroom. There is a rule against it but I made the rule so we can risk breaking it. But try to be back by noon. We close from noon to thirteen—union rules—and if I have to sit here by myself with all my clerks gone to lunch, you'll have to buy me a drink."

"I'll buy you one anyhow."

"We'll roll for it. Here you are. Don't take it through any fires."

Right on top was Graham's passport. A tight lump in my chest eased. I know of no more lost feeling than being outside the Union without a passport . . . even though it's not truly the Union. I opened it, looked at the picture embossed inside. Do I look like that? I went into the bathroom, compared the face in the mirror with the face in the passport.

Near enough, I guess. No one expects much of a passport picture. I tried holding the photograph up to the mirror. Suddenly it was a good resemblance. Chum, your face is lopsided . . . and so is yours, Mr. Graham.

Brother, if I'm going to have to assume your identity permanently—and it looks more and more as if I had no choice—it's a relief to know that we look so much alike. Fingerprints? We'll cope with that when we have to. Seems the U.S. of N.A. doesn't use fingerprints on passports; that's some help. Occupation: Executive. Executive of *what?* A funeral parlor? Or a worldwide chain of hotels? Maybe this is not going to be difficult but merely impossible.

Address: Care of O'Hara, Rigsbee, Crumpacker, and Rigsbee, Attys at Law, Suite 7000, Smith Building, Dallas. Oh, just dandy. Merely a mail drop. No business address, no home address, no business. Why, you phony, I'd love to poke you in the snoot!

(He can't be too repulsive; Margrethe thinks well of him. Well, yes—but he should keep his hands off Margrethe; he's taking advantage of her. Unfair. *Who* is taking advantage of her? Watch it, boy, you'll get a split personality.)

An envelope under the passport contained the passenger's file copy of his ticket—and it was indeed round trip, Portland to Portland. Twin, unless you show up before 6 p.m., I've got a trip home. Maybe you can use my ticket in the *Admiral Moffett*. I wish you luck.

There were some minor items but the bulk of the metal box was occupied by ten sealed fat envelopes, business size. I opened one.

It contained thousand-dollar bills, one hundred of them.

I made a fast check with the other nine. All alike. One million dollars in cash.

V

The wicked flee when no man pursueth:
but the righteous are bold as a lion.
Proverbs 28:1

Barely breathing, I used gummed tape I found in Graham's desk to seal the envelopes. I put everything back but the passport, placed it with that three thousand that I thought of as "mine" in the little drawer of the desk, then took the box back to the purser's office, carrying it carefully.

Someone else was at the front desk but the purser was in sight in his inner office; I caught his eye.

"Hi," he called out. "Back so soon?" He came out.

"Yes," I agreed. "For once, everything tallied." I passed the box to him.

"I'd like to hire you for this office. Here, nothing ever tallies. At least not earlier than midnight. Let's go find that drink. I need one."

"So do I! Let's."

The purser led me aft to an outdoor bar I had not noticed on the ship's plan. The deck above us ended and the deck we were on, D deck, continued on out as a weather deck, bright teak planks pleasant to walk on. The break on C deck formed an overhang; under it was this outdoor spread canvas. At right angles to the bar were long tables offering a lavish buffet lunch; passengers were queued up for it. Farther aft was the ship's swimming pool; I could hear splashing, squeals, and yells.

43

He led me on aft to a small table occupied by two junior officers. We stopped there. "You two. Jump overboard."

"Right away, Purser." They stood up, picked up their beer glasses, and moved farther aft. One of them grinned at me and nodded, as if we knew each other, so I nodded and said, "Hi."

This table was partly shaded by awning. The purser said to me, "Do you want to sit in the sun and watch the girls, or sit in the shade and relax?"

"Either way. Sit where you wish; I'll take the other chair."

"Um. Let's move this table a little and both sit in the shade. There, that does it." He sat down facing forward; perforce I sat facing the swimming pool—and confirmed something I thought I had seen at first glance: This swimming pool did not require anything as redundant as swim suits.

I should have inferred it by logic had I thought about it—but I had not. The last time I had seen it—swimming without suits—I had been about twelve and it had been strictly a male privilege for boys that age or younger.

"I said, 'What will you drink, Mr. Graham?'"

"Oh! Sorry, I wasn't listening."

"I know. You were looking. What will it be?"

"Uh . . . a Danish zombie."

He blinked at me. "You don't want that at this time of day; that's a skull splitter. Mmm—" He waggled his fingers at someone behind me. "Sweetheart, come here."

I looked up as the summoned waitress approached. I looked and then looked twice. I had seen her last through an alcoholic haze the night before, one of two redheads in the hula chorus line.

"Tell Hans I want two silver fizzes. What's your name, dear?"

"Mr. Henderson, you pretend just one more time that you don't know my name and I'll pour your drink right on your bald spot."

"Yes, dear. Now hurry up. Get those fat legs moving."

She snorted and glided away on limbs that were slender and graceful. The purser added, "A fine girl, that. Her parents live just across from me in Odense; I've known her since she was a baby. A smart girl, too. Bodel is studying to be a veterinary surgeon, one more year to go."

"Really? How does she do this and go to school, too?"

"Most of our girls are at university. Some take a summer off, some take a term off—go to sea, have some fun, save up money for next term. In hiring I give preference to girls who are working their way through university; they are more dependable—and they know more languages. Take your room stewardess. Astrid?"

"No. Margrethe."

"Oh, yes, you are in one-oh-nine; Astrid has portside forward on your deck, Margrethe is on your side. Margrethe Svensdatter Gunderson. Schoolteacher. English language and history. But knows four more languages—not counting Scandinavian languages—and has certificates for two of them. On one-year leave from H. C. Andersen Middle School. I'm betting she won't go back."

"Eh? Why?"

"She'll marry a rich American. Are you rich?"

"*Me?* Do I look rich?" (Could he possibly know what is in that lockbox? Dear God, what does one do with a million dollars that isn't yours? I can't just throw it overboard. Why would Graham be traveling with that much in cash? I could think of several reasons, all bad. Any one of them could get me in more trouble than I had ever seen.)

"Rich Americans never look it; they practice not looking rich. North Americans, I mean; South Americans are another fish entirely. Gertrude, thank you. You are a good girl."

"You want this drink on your bald spot?"

"You want me to throw you into the pool with your

clothes on? Behave yourself, dear, or I'll tell your mother. Put them down and give me the chit."

"No chit; Hans wanted to buy a drink for Mr. Graham. So he decided to include you, this once."

"You tell him that's the way the bar loses money. Tell him I take it out of his wages."

That's how I happened to drink two silver fizzes instead of one . . . and was well on my way toward a disaster such as the night before, when Mr. Henderson decided that we must eat. I wanted a third fizz. The first two had enabled me to quit worrying over that crazy box full of money while enhancing my appreciation of the poolside floor show. I was discovering that a lifetime of conditioning could wash away in only twenty-four hours. There was nothing sinful about looking at feminine loveliness unadorned. It was as sweetly innocent as looking at flowers or kittens—but far more fun.

In the meantime I wanted another drink.

Mr. Henderson vetoed it, called Bodel over, spoke to her rapidly in Danish. She left, returned a few minutes later carrying a loaded tray—smorgasbord, hot meat balls, sweet pastry shells stuffed with ice cream, strong coffee, all in large quantities.

Twenty-five minutes later I still appreciated the teenagers at the pool, but I was no longer on my way to another alcoholic catastrophe. I had sobered up so much that I now realized that I not only could not solve my problems through spirits but must shun alcohol until I did solve them—as I did not know how to handle strong drink. Uncle Ed was right; vice required training and long practice—otherwise for pragmatic reasons virtue should rule even when moral instruction has ceased to bind.

My morals certainly had ceased to bind—or I could not have sat there with a glass of Devil's brew in my hand while I stared at naked female flesh.

I found that I had not even a twinge of conscience over

anything. My only regret involved the sad knowledge that I could not handle the amount of alcohol I would have enjoyed. *"Easy is the descent into Hell."*

Mr. Henderson stood up. "We tie up in less than two hours and I have some figures to fudge before the agent comes aboard. Thanks for a nice time."

"Thank *you*, sir! *Tusind tak!* Is that how you say it?"

He smiled and left. I sat there for a bit and thought. Two hours till we docked, three hours in port—what could I do with the opportunities?

Go to the American consul? Tell him *what?* Dear Mr. Consul, I am not he whom I am presumed to be and I just happened to find this million dollars—

Ridiculous!

Say nothing to anyone, grab that million, go ashore and catch the next airship for Patagonia?

Impossible. My morals had slipped—apparently they were never very strong. But I still had this prejudice against stealing. It's not only wrong; it's undignified.

Bad enough that I'm wearing his clothes.

Take the three thousand that is "rightfully" yours, go ashore, wait for the ship to sail, then get back to America as best you can?

Stupid idea! You would wind up in a tropical jail and your silly gesture would not do Graham any good. It's Hobson's choice again, you knothead; you must stay aboard and wait for Graham to show up. He won't, but there might be a wireless message or something. Bite your nails until the ship sails. When it does, thank God for a trip home to God's country. While Graham does the same for his ticket home in the *Admiral Moffett*. I wonder how he likes being named Hergensheimer? Better than I like "Graham" I'll bet. A proud name, Hergensheimer.

I got up, ducked around to the far side, and went up two decks to the library, found it unoccupied save for a woman working on a crossword puzzle. Neither of us wanted to be disturbed, which made us good company. Most of the bookcases were locked, the librarian not being present, but there was a battered encyclopedia— just what I needed as a start.

Two hours later I was startled by a blast indicating that we had a line to the dock; we had arrived. I was loaded with strange history and stranger ideas and none of it digested. To start with, in this world William Jennings Bryan was never president; in 1896 McKinley had been elected in his place, had served two terms and had been followed by someone named Roosevelt.

I recognized none of the twentieth-century presidents.

Instead of more than a century of peace under our traditional neutrality, the United States had repeatedly been involved in foreign wars: 1899, 1912–17, 1932 (with *Japan!*), 1950–52, 1980–84, and so on right up to the current year—or current when this encyclopedia was published; *King's Skald* did not report a war now going on.

Behind the glass of one of the locked cases I spotted several history books. If I was still in the ship three hours from now, I must plan on reading every history book in the ship's library during the long passage to America.

But names of presidents and dates of wars were not my most urgent need; these are not daily concerns. What I urgently needed to know, lest ignorance cause me anything from needless embarrassment to catastrophe, was the differences between my world and this world in how people lived, talked, behaved, ate, drank, played, prayed, and loved. While I was learning, I must be careful to talk as little as possible and to listen as much as possible.

I once had a neighbor whose knowledge of history seemed limited to two dates, 1492 and 1776, and even with those two he was mixed up as to what events each marked. His ignorance in other fields was just as profound; nevertheless he earned an excellent living as a paving contractor.

It does not require a broad education to function as a social and economic animal . . . as long as you know when to rub blue mud into your bellybutton. But a mistake in local customs can get you lynched.

I wondered how Graham was doing? It occurred to me that his situation was far more dangerous than mine . . . if I assumed (as apparently I must) that he and I had simply swapped places. It seemed that my background could make me appear eccentric here—but *his* background could get Graham into serious trouble in my world. A casual remark, an innocent act, could land him in the stocks. Or worse.

But he might find his worst trouble through attempting to fit himself fully into my role—if indeed he tried. Let me put it this way: On her birthday after we had been married a year I gave Abigail a fancy edition of *The Taming of the Shrew*. She never suspected that I had been making a statement; her conviction of her own righteousness did not embrace the possibility that in my heart I equated her to Kate. If Graham assumed my role as her husband, the relationship was bound to be interesting for each of them.

I would not knowingly wish Abigail on anyone. Since I had not been consulted, I did not cry crocodile tears.

(What would it be to bed with a woman who did not always refer to marital relations as "family duties"?)

Here I have in front of me a twenty-volume encyclopedia, millions of words packed with all the major facts of this world—facts I urgently need. What can I squeeze out of it quickly? Where to start? I don't want Greek art, or Egyptian history, or geology—but what *do* I want?

Well, what did you first notice about this world? This ship itself. Its old-fashioned appearance compared with the sleek lines of the M.V. *Konge Knut*. Then, once you were aboard, the lack of a telephone in your-Graham's stateroom. The lack of passenger elevators. Little things that gave it an air of the luxury of grandfather's day.

So let's see the article on "Ships"—volume eighteen.

Yes, sir! Three pages of pictures . . . and they all have

that Mauve-Decade look. S.S. *Britannia*, biggest and fastest North Atlantic liner, 2000 passengers, only sixteen knots! And looks it.

Let's try the general article on "Transportation"—

Well, well! We aren't too surprised, are we? No mention of airships. But let's check the index volume— Airship, nothing; dirigible, zero; aeronautics—see "Balloon."

Ah, yes, a good article on free ballooning, with the Montgolfiers and the other daring pioneers—even Salomon Andrée's brave and tragic attack on the North Pole. But either Count von Zeppelin never lived, or he never turned his attention to aeronautics.

Possibly, after his service in the Civil War, he returned to Germany and there never found the atmosphere receptive to the idea of air travel that he enjoyed in Ohio in my world. As may be, this world does not have air travel. Alex, if you have to live here, how would you like to "invent" the airship? Be a pioneer and tycoon, and get rich and famous?

What makes you think you could?

Why, I made my first airship flight when I was only twelve years old! I know all about them; I could draw plans for one right now—

You could? Draw me production drawings for a lightweight diesel, not over one pound per horsepower. Specify the alloys used, give the heat treatments, show work diagrams for the actual operating cycles, specify fuels, state procurement sources, specify lubricants—

All those things can be worked out!

Yes, but can *you* do it? Even knowing that it can be done? Remember why you dropped out of engineering school and decided you had a call for the ministry? Comparative religion, homiletics, higher criticism, apologetics, Hebrew, Latin, Greek, all require scholarship . . . but the slipstick subjects require brains.

So I'm stupid, am I?

Would you have walked through that fire pit if you had brains enough to come in out of the rain?

Why didn't you stop me?

Stop you? When did you ever listen to *me?* Quit evading—what was your final mark in thermodynamics?

All right! Assume that I can't do it myself—

Big of you.

Lay off, will you? Knowing that something *can* be done is two thirds of the battle. I could be director of research and guide the efforts of some really sharp young engineers. They supply the brains; I supply the unique memory of what a dirigible balloon looks like and how it works. Okay?

That's the proper division of labor: You supply memory, they supply brains. Yes, that could work. But not quickly, not cheaply. How are you going to finance it?

Uh, sell shares?

Remember the summer you sold vacuum cleaners?

Well . . . there's that million dollars.

Naughty, naughty!

"Mr. Graham?"

I looked up from my great plans to find a yeoman from the purser's office looking at me. "Yes?"

She handed me an envelope. "From Mr. Henderson, sir. He said you would probably have an answer."

"Thank you." The note read: "Dear Mr. Graham: There are three men down here in the square who claim to have an appointment with you. I don't like their looks or the way they talk—and this port has some very strange customers. If you are not expecting them or don't wish to see them, tell my messenger that she could not find you. Then I'll tell them that you've gone ashore. A.P.H."

I remained balanced between curiosity and caution for some long, uncomfortable moments. They did not want to see me; they wanted to see Graham . . . and whatever it was they wanted of Graham, I could not satisfy their want.

You *know* what they want!

So I suspect. But, even if they have a chit signed by Saint Peter, I can't turn over to them—or to anyone— that silly million dollars. You know that.

Certainly I know that. I wanted to be sure that you knew it. All right, since there are no circumstances under which you will turn over to a trio of strangers the contents of Graham's lockbox, then why see them?

Because I've got to *know!* Now shut up. I said to the yeoman, "Please tell Mr. Henderson that I will be right down. And thank you for your trouble."

"My pleasure, sir. Uh, Mr. Graham . . . I saw you walk the fire. You were wonderful!"

"I was out of my silly mind. Thanks anyhow."

I stopped at the top of the companionway and sized up the three men waiting for me. They looked as if they had been type-cast for menace: one oversize job about six feet eight with the hands, feet, jaw, and ears of glandular giantism; one sissy type about one quarter the size of the big man; one nothing type with dead eyes. Muscles, brain, and gun—or was it my jumpy imagination?

A smart person would go quietly back up and hide.

I'm not smart.

VI

Let us eat and drink, for tomorrow we shall die.
Isaiah 22:13

I walked down the stairs, not looking at the three, and went directly to the desk of the purser's office. Mr. Henderson was there, spoke quietly as I reached the counter. "Those three over there. Do you know them?"

"No, I don't know them. I'll see what they want. But keep an eye on us, will you, please?"

"Right!"

I turned and started to walk past that lovable trio. The smart boy said sharply, "Graham! Stop there! Where you going?"

I kept moving and snapped, "Shut up, you idiot! Are you trying to blow it?" Muscles stepped into my path and hung over me like a tall building. The gun stepped in behind me. In a fake prison-yard style, from the side of my mouth, I said, "Quit making a scene and get these apes off the ship! You and I must talk."

"Certainly we talk. *Ici!* Now. Here."

"You utter fool," I answered softly and glanced nervously up, to left and right. "Not here. Cows. Bugs. Come with me. But have Mutt and Jeff wait on the dock."

"*Non!*"

"God save us! Listen carefully." I whispered, "You are going to tell these animals to leave the ship and wait at the foot of the gangway. Then you and I are going to walk out on the weather deck where we can talk without being

53

overheard. Otherwise we do *nothing!*—and I report to Number-One that you blew the deal. Understand? Right *now!* Or go back and tell them the deal is off."

He hesitated, then spoke rapidly in French that I could not follow, my French being mostly of the *La plume de ma tante* sort. The gorilla seemed to hesitate but the gun type shrugged and started toward the gangway door. I said to the little wart, "Come on! Don't waste time; the ship is about to sail!" I headed aft without looking to see whether or not he was following. I set a brisk pace that forced him to follow or lose me. I was as much taller than he as that ape was taller than I; he had to trot to stay at my heels.

I kept right on going aft and outside, onto the weather deck, past the open bar and the tables, clear to the swimming pool.

It was, as I expected, unoccupied, the ship being in port. There was the usual sign up, CLOSED WHILE SHIP IS IN PORT, and a nominal barrier around it of a single strand of rope, but the pool was still filled. I stepped over the rope and stood with my back to the pool. He followed me; I held up a hand. "Stop right there." He stopped.

"Now we can talk," I said. "Explain yourself, and you'd better make it good! What do you mean, calling attention to yourself by bringing that muscle aboard? And a Danish ship at that! Mr. B. is going to be very, very angry with you. What's your name?"

"Never mind my name. Where's the package?"

"What package?"

He started to sputter; I interrupted. "Cut the nonsense; I'm not impressed. This ship is getting ready to sail; you have only minutes to tell me exactly what you want and to convince me that you should get it. Keep throwing your weight around and you'll find yourself going back to your boss and telling him you failed. So speak up! What do you want?"

"The package!"

I sighed. "My old and stupid, you are stuck in a rut.

We've been over that. What sort of a package? What's in it?"

He hesitated. "Money."

"Interesting. How much money?"

This time he hesitated twice as long, so again I interrupted. "If you don't know how much money, I'll give you a couple of francs for beer and send you on your way. Is that what you want? Two francs?"

A man that skinny shouldn't have such high blood pressure. He managed to say, "American dollars. One million."

I laughed in his face. "What makes you think I've got that much? And if I had, why should I give it to *you*? How do I know you are supposed to get it?"

"You crazy, man? You know who am I."

"Prove it. Your eyes are funny and your voice sounds different. I think you're a ringer."

"'Ringer'?"

"A fake, a phony! An impostor."

He answered angrily—French, I suppose. I am sure it was not complimentary. I dug into my memory, repeated carefully and with feeling the remark that a lady had made last night which had caused her husband to say that she worried too much. It was not appropriate but I intended simply to anger him.

Apparently I succeeded. He raised a hand, I grabbed his wrist, tripped myself, fell backwards into the pool, pulling him with me. As we fell I shouted, "Help!"

We splashed. I got a firm grip on him, pulled myself up as I shoved him under again. "Help! He's drowning me!"

Down we went again, struggling with each other. I yelled for help each time my head was above water. Just as help came I went limp and let go.

I stayed limp until they started to give me mouth-to-mouth resuscitation. At that point I snorted and opened my eyes. "Where am I?"

Someone said, "He's coming around. He's okay."

I looked around. I was flat on my back alongside the pool. Someone had done a professional job of pulling me out with a dip-and-jerk; my left arm felt almost dislocated. Aside from that I was okay. "Where is he? The man who pushed me in."

"He got away."

I recognized the voice, turned my head. My friend Mr. Henderson, the purser.

"He did?"

That ended it. My rat-faced caller had scrambled out as I was being fished out and had streaked off the ship. By the time they had finished reviving me, Nasty and his bodyguards were long gone.

Mr. Henderson had me lie still until the ship's doctor arrived. He put a stethoscope on me and announced that I was okay. I told a couple of small fibs, some near truths, and an evasion. By then the gangway had been removed and shortly a loud blast announced that we had left the dock.

I did not find it necessary to tell anyone that I had played water polo in school.

The next many days were very sweet, in the fashion that grapes grow sweetest on the slopes of a live volcano.

I managed to get acquainted (reacquainted?) with my table mates without, apparently, anyone noticing that I was a stranger. I picked up names just by waiting until someone else spoke to someone by name—remembered the name and used it later. Everyone was pleasant to me—I not only was not "below the salt," since the record showed that I had been aboard the full trip, but also I was at least a celebrity if not a hero for having walked through the fire.

I did not use the swimming pool. I was not sure what swimming Graham had done, if any, and, having been "rescued," I did not want to exhibit a degree of skill inconsistent with that "rescue." Besides, while I grew accustomed to (and even appreciative of) a degree of nudity shocking in my former life, I did not feel that I could manage with aplomb being naked in company.

Since there was nothing I could do about it, I put the mystery of Nastyface and his bodyguard out of my mind.

The same was true of the all-embracing mystery of who I am and how I got here—nothing I could do about it, so don't worry about it. On reflection I realized that I was in exactly the same predicament as every other human being alive: We don't know who we are, or where we came from, or why we are here. My dilemma was merely fresher, not different.

One thing (possibly the only thing) I learned in seminary was to face calmly the ancient mystery of life, untroubled by my inability to solve it. Honest priests and preachers are denied the comforts of religion; instead they must live with the austere rewards of philosophy. I never became much of a metaphysician but I did learn not to worry about that which I could not solve.

I spent much time in the library or reading in deck chairs, and each day I learned more about and felt more at home in this world. Happy, golden days slipped past like a dream of childhood.

And every day there was Margrethe.

I felt like a boy undergoing his first attack of puppy love.

It was a strange romance. We could not speak of love. Or I could not, and she did not. Every day she was my servant (shared with her other passenger guests) . . . and my "mother" (shared with others? I did not think so . . . but I did not know). The relationship was close but not intimate. Then each day, for a few moments while I "paid" her for tying my bow tie, she was my wonderfully sweet and utterly passionate darling.

But only then.

At other times I was "Mr. Graham" to her and she called me "sir"—warmly friendly but not intimate. She was willing to chat, standing up and with the door open; she often had ship's gossip to share with me. But her manner was always that of the perfect servant. Correction: the perfect crew member assigned to personal service. Each day I learned a little more about her. I found no fault in her.

For me the day started with my first sight of her—usually on my way to breakfast when I would meet her in the passageway or spot her through an open door of a room she was making up . . . just "Good morning, Margrethe" and "Good morning, Mr. Graham," but the sun did not rise until that moment.

I would see her from time to time during the day, peaking each day with that golden ritual after she tied my tie.

Then I would see her briefly after dinner. Immediately after dinner each evening I would return to my room for a few minutes to refresh myself before the evening's activities—lounge show, concert, games, or perhaps just a return to the library. At that hour Margrethe would be somewhere in the starboard forward passageway of C deck, opening beds, tidying baths, and so forth—making her guests' staterooms inviting for the night. Again I would say hello, then wait in my room (whether she had yet reached it or not) because she would come in shortly, either to open my bed or simply to inquire, "Will you need anything more this evening, sir?"

And I would always smile and answer, "I don't need a thing, Margrethe. Thank you." Whereupon she would bid me good night and wish me sound sleep. That ended my day no matter what else I did before retiring.

Of course I was tempted—daily!—to answer, "You know what I need!" I could not. *Imprimis:* I was a married man. True, my wife was lost somewhere in another world (or I was). But from holy matrimony there is no release this side of the grave. Item: Her love affair (if such it was) was with Graham, whom I was impersonating. I could not refuse that evening kiss (I'm not that angelically perfect!) but in fairness to my beloved I could not go beyond it. Item: An honorable man must not offer less than matrimony to the object of his love . . . and that I was both legally and morally unable to offer.

So those golden days were bittersweet. Each day brought one day nearer the inescapable time when I must leave Margrethe, almost certainly never to see her again.

I was not free even to tell her what that loss would mean to me.

Nor was my love for her so selfless that I hoped the separation would not grieve her. Meanly, self-centered as an adolescent, I hoped that she would miss me as dreadfully as I was going to miss her. Childish puppy love— certainly! I offer in extenuation the fact that I had known only the "love" of a woman who loved Jesus so much that she had no real affection for any flesh-and-blood creature.

Never marry a woman who prays too much.

We were ten days out from Papeete with Mexico almost over the skyline when this precarious idyll ended. For several days Margrethe had seemed more withdrawn each day. I could not tax her with it as there was nothing I could put my finger on and certainly nothing of which I could complain. But it reached crisis that evening when she tied my tie.

As usual I smiled and thanked her and kissed her.

Then I stopped with her still in my arms and said, "What's wrong? I know you can kiss better than that. Is my breath bad?"

She answered levelly, "Mr. Graham, I think we had better stop this."

"So it's 'Mr. Graham,' is it? Margrethe, what have I done?"

"You've done nothing!"

"Then— My dear, you're crying!"

"I'm sorry. I didn't intend to."

I took my handkerchief, blotted her tears, and said gently, "I have never intended to hurt you. You must tell me what's wrong so that I can change it."

"If you don't know, sir, I don't see how I can explain it."

"Won't you try? Please!" (Could it be one of those cyclic emotional disturbances women are heir to?)

"Uh . . . Mr. Graham, I knew it could not last beyond the end of the voyage—and, believe me, I did not count on any more. I suppose it means more to me than it did to you. But I never thought that you would simply end it, with no explanation, sooner than we must."

"Margrethe . . . I do not understand."

"But you *do* know!"

"But I don't know."

"You *must* know. It's been eleven days. Each night I've asked you and each night you've turned me down. Mr. Graham, aren't you ever again going to ask me to come back later?"

"Oh. So *that's* what you meant! Margrethe—"

"Yes, sir?"

"I'm not 'Mr. Graham.'"

"Sir?"

"My name is 'Hergensheimer.' It has been exactly eleven days since I saw you for the first time in my life. I'm sorry. I'm terribly sorry. But that is the truth."

VII

Now therefore be content, look upon me;
for it is evident unto you if I lie.
Job 6:28

Margrethe is both a warm comfort and a civilized adult. Never once did she gasp, or expostulate, or say, "Oh, no!" or "I can't believe it!" At my first statement she held very still, waited, then said quietly, "I do not understand."

"I don't understand it either," I told her. "Something happened when I walked through that fire pit. The world changed. This ship—" I pounded the bulkhead beside us. "—is not the ship I was in before. And people call me 'Graham' . . . when I *know* that my name is Alexander Hergensheimer. But it's not just me and this ship; it's the whole world. Different history. Different countries. No airships here."

"Alec, what is an airship?"

"Uh, up in the air, like a balloon. It *is* a balloon, in a way. But it goes very fast, over a hundred knots."

She considered it soberly. "I think that I would find that frightening."

"Not at all; it's the best way to travel. I flew down here in one, the *Count von Zeppelin* of North American Airlines. But this world doesn't have airships. That was the point that finally convinced me that this really is a different world—and not just some complicated hoax that someone had played on me. Air travel is so major a part

of the economy of the world I knew that it changes everything else not to have it. Take— Look, do you believe
me?"

She answered slowly and carefully, "I believe that you
are telling the truth as you see it. But the truth I see is
very different."

"I know and that's what makes it so hard. I— See here,
if you don't hurry, you're going to miss dinner, right?"

"It does not matter."

"Yes, it does; you must not miss meals just because I
made a stupid mistake and hurt your feelings. And if I
don't show up, Inga will send somebody up to find out
whether I'm ill or asleep or whatever; I've seen her do it
with others at my table. Margrethe—my very dear!—I've
wanted to tell you. I've waited to tell you. I've needed to
tell you. And now I can and I must. But I can't do it in
five minutes standing up. After you turn down beds
tonight can you take time to listen to me?"

"Alec, I will always take all the time for you that you
need."

"All right. You go down and eat, and I'll go down and
touch base at least—get Inga off my neck—and I'll meet
you here after you turn down beds. All right?"

She looked thoughtful. "All right. Alec— Will you kiss
me again?"

That's how I knew she believed me. Or wanted to believe me. I quit worrying. I even ate a good dinner, although I hurried.

She was waiting for me when I returned, and stood up
as I came in. I took her in my arms, pecked her on the
nose, picked her up by her elbows and sat her on my
bunk; then I sat down in the only chair. "Dear one, do
you think I'm crazy?"

"Alec, I don't know what to tink." (Yes, she said "tink."
Once in a long while, under stress of emotion, Margrethe
would lose the use of the theta sound. Otherwise her En-

glish accent was far better than my tall-corn accent, harsh as a rusty saw.)

"I know," I agreed. "I had the same problem. Only two ways to look at it. Either something incredible did happen when I walked through the fire, something that changed my whole world. Or I'm as crazy as a pet 'coon. I've spent days checking the facts . . . and the world *has* changed. Not just airships. Kaiser Wilhelm the Fourth is missing and some silly president named 'Schmidt' is in his place. Things like that."

"I would not call Herr Schmidt 'silly.' He is quite a good president as German presidents go."

"That's my point, dear. To me, any German president looks silly, as Germany is—in *my* world—one of the last western monarchies effectively unlimited. Even the Tsar is not as powerful."

"And that has to be my point, too, Alec. There is no Kaiser and there is no Tsar. The Grand Duke of Muscovy is a constitutional monarch and no longer claims to be suzerain over other Slavic states."

"Margrethe, we're both saying the same thing. The world I grew up in is gone. I'm having to learn about a different world. Not a totally different world. Geography does not seem to have changed, and not all of history. The two worlds seem to be the same almost up to the beginning of the twentieth century. Call it eighteen-ninety. About a hundred years back something strange happened and the two worlds split apart . . . and about twelve days ago something equally strange happened to me and I got bounced into this world." I smiled at her. "But I'm not sorry. Do you know why? Because *you* are in this world."

"Thank you. It is important to me that you are in it, too."

"Then you do believe me. Just as I have been forced to believe it. So much so that I've quit worrying about it.

Just one thing really bothers me— What became of Alec Graham? Is he filling my place in my world? Or what?"

She did not answer at once, and when she did, her answer did not seem responsive. "Alec, will you please take down your trousers?"

"What did you say, Margrethe?"

"Please. I am not making a joke and I am not trying to entice you. I must see something. Please lower your trousers."

"I don't see— All right." I shut up and did as she asked—not easy in evening dress. I had to take off my mess jacket, then my cummerbund, before I was peeled enough to let me slide the braces off my shoulders.

Then, reluctantly, I started unbuttoning my fly. (Another shortcoming of this retarded world—no zippers. I did not appreciate zippers until I no longer had them.)

I took a deep breath, then lowered my trousers a few inches. "Is that enough?"

"A little more, please—and will you please turn your back to me?"

I did as she asked. Then I felt her hands, gentle and not invasive, at my right rear. She lifted a shirttail and pulled down the top of my underwear pants on the right.

A moment later she restored both garments. "That's enough. Thank you."

I tucked in my shirttails and buttoned up my fly, reshouldered the braces and reached for the cummerbund. She said, "Just a moment, Alec."

"Eh? I thought you were through."

"I am. But there is no need to get back into those formal clothes; let me get out casual trousers for you. And shirt. Unless you are going back to the lounge?"

"No. Not if you will stay."

"I will stay; we must talk." Quickly she took out casual trousers and a sports shirt for me, laid them on the bed. "Excuse me, please." She went into the bath.

I don't know whether she needed to use it or not, but

she knew that I could change more comfortably in the stateroom than in that cramped shipboard bathroom.

I changed and felt better. A cummerbund and a boiled shirt are better than a straitjacket but not much. She came out, at once hung up the clothes I had taken off, all but the shirt and collar. She removed studs and collar buttons from these, put them away, and put shirt and collar into my laundry bag. I wondered what Abigail would think if she could see these wifely attentions. Abigail did not believe in spoiling me—and did not.

"What was that all about, Margrethe?"

"I had to see something. Alec, you were wondering what had become of Alec Graham. I now know the answer."

"Yes?"

"He's right here. You are he."

At last I said, "That, just from looking at a few square inches on my behind? What did you find, Margrethe? The strawberry mark that identifies the missing heir?"

"No, Alec. Your 'Southern Cross.'"

"My what?"

"Please, Alec. I had hoped that it would restore your memory. I saw it the first night we—" She hesitated, then looked me square in the eye. "—made love. You turned on the light, then turned over on your belly to see what time it was. That was when I noticed the moles on your right buttock cheek. I commented on the pattern they made, and we joked about it. You said that it was your Southern Cross and it let you know which end was up."

Margrethe turned slightly pink but continued to look me firmly in the eye. "And I showed you some moles on my body. Alec, I am sorry that you do not remember it but please believe me: By then we were well enough acquainted that we could be playful about such things without my being forward or rude."

"Margrethe, I don't think you could ever be forward or

rude. But you're putting too much importance on a chance arrangement of moles. I've got moles all over me; it doesn't surprise me that some of them, back where I can't see easily, are arranged in a cross shape. Or that Graham had some that were somewhat similar."

"Not 'similar.' Exactly the same."

"Well— There is a much better way to check. In the desk there in my wallet. Graham's wallet, actually. Driver's license. His. His thumbprint on it. I haven't checked it because I have never had the slightest doubt that he was Graham and that I am Hergensheimer and that we are not the same man. But we *can* check. Get it out, dear. Check it yourself. I'll put a thumbprint on the mirror in the bath. Compare them. Then you will know."

"Alec, I do know. You are the one who doesn't believe it; you check it."

"Well—" Margrethe's counterproposal was reasonable; I agreed to it.

I got out Graham's driver's license, then placed a print on the bath mirror by first rubbing my thumb over my nose for the nose's natural oil, so much greater than that of the pad of the thumb. I found that I could not see the pattern on the glass too well, so I shook a little talcum onto my palm, blew it toward the mirror.

Worse. The powder that detectives use must be much finer than shaving talcum. Or perhaps I don't know how to use it. I placed another print without powder, looked at both prints, at my right thumb, at the print on the driver's license, then checked to see that the license did indeed designate print of right thumb. It did. "Margrethe! Will you come look, please?"

She joined me in the bath. "Look at this," I said. "Look at all four—my thumb and three prints. The pattern in all four is basically an arch—but that simply trims it down to half the thumbprints in the world. I'll bet you even money that your own thumbprints have an arch pattern. Honest, can you tell whether or not the thumbprint on that card was made by *this* thumb? Or by my left thumb; they might have made a mistake."

"I cannot tell, Alec. I have no skill in this."

"Well— I don't think even an expert could tell in this light. We'll have to put it off till morning; we need bright sunlight out on deck. We also need glossy white paper, stamp-pad ink, and a magnifying glass . . . and I'll bet Mr. Henderson will have all three. Will tomorrow do?"

"Certainly. This test is not for me, Alec; I already know in my heart. And by seeing your 'Southern Cross.' Something has happened to your memory but you are still you . . . and someday we will find your memory again."

"It's not that easy, dear. I *know* that I am not Graham. Margrethe, do you have any idea what business he was in? Or why he was on this trip?"

"Must I say 'him'? I did not ask your business, Alec. And you never offered to tell me."

"Yes, I think you must say 'him,' at least until we check that thumbprint. Was he married?"

"Again, he did not say and I did not ask."

"But you implied— No, you flatly stated that you had 'made love' with this man whom you believe to be me, and that you have been in bed with him."

"Alec, are you reproaching me?"

"Oh, no, no, no!" (But I was, and she knew it.) "Whom you go to bed with is your business. But I must tell you that *I* am married."

She shut her face against me. "Alec, I did not try to seduce you into marriage."

"Graham, you mean. I was not there."

"Very well. Graham. I did not entrap Alec Graham. For our mutual happiness we made love. Matrimony was not mentioned by either of us."

"Look, I'm sorry I mentioned the matter! It seemed to have some bearing on the mystery; that's all. Margrethe, will you believe that I would rather strike off my arm—

or pluck out my eye and cast it from me—than hurt you, ever, in any way?"

"Thank you, Alec. I believe you."

"All that Jesus ever said was: 'Go, and sin no more.' Surely you do not think I would ever set myself up as more severely judgmental than was Jesus? But I was not judging you; I was seeking information about Graham. His business, in particular. Uh, did you ever suspect that he might be engaged in something illegal?"

She gave a ghost of a smile. "Had I ever suspected anything of the sort, my loyalty to him is such that I would never express such suspicion. Since you insist that you are not he, then there it must stand."

"Touché!" I grinned sheepishly. Could I tell her about the lockbox? Yes, I must. I had to be frank with her and had to persuade her that she was not being disloyal to Graham/me were she to be equally frank. "Margrethe, I was not asking idly and I was not prying where I had no business to pry. I have still more trouble and I need your advice."

Her turn to be startled. "Alec . . . I do not often give advice. I do not like to."

"May I tell you my trouble? You need not advise me . . . but perhaps you may be able to analyze it for me." I told her quickly about that truly damning million dollars. "Margrethe, can you think of any legitimate reason why an honest man would be carrying a million dollars in cash? Travelers checks, letters of credit, drafts for transferring monies, even bearer bonds— But *cash?* In that amount? I say that it is psychologically as unbelievable as what happened to me in the fire pit is physically unbelievable. Can you see any other way to look at it? For what *honest* reason would a man carry that much cash on a trip like this?"

"I will not pass judgment."

"I do not ask you to judge; I ask you to stretch your imagination and tell me why a man would carry with him a million dollars in cash. Can you think of a reason? One as farfetched as you like . . . but a reason."

"There could be many reasons."

"Can you think of one?"

I waited; she remained silent. I sighed and said, "I can't think of one, either. Plenty of criminal reasons, of course, as so-called 'hot money' almost always moves as cash. This is so common that most governments—all governments, I believe—assume that any large amount of cash being moved other than by a bank or by a government is indeed crime money until proved otherwise. Or counterfeit money, a still more depressing idea. The advice I need is this: Margrethe, what should I do with it? It's not mine; I can't take it off the ship. For the same reason I can't abandon it. I can't even throw it overboard. What *can* I do with it?"

My question was not rhetorical; I had to find an answer that would not cause me to wind up in jail for something Graham had done. So far, the only answer I could think of was to go to the only authority in the ship, the Captain, tell him all my troubles and ask him to take custody of that awkward million dollars.

Ridiculous. That would just give me a fresh set of bad answers, depending on whether or not the Captain believed me and on whether or not the Captain himself was honest—and possibly on other variables. But I could not see any outcome from telling the Captain that would not end in my being locked up, either in jail or in a mental hospital.

The simplest way to resolve the situation would be to throw the pesky stuff overboard!

I had moral objections to that. I've broken some of the Commandments and bent some others, but being financially honest has never been a problem to me. Granted, lately my moral fiber did not seem to be as strong as I had thought, but nevertheless I was not tempted to steal that million even to jettison it.

But there was a stronger objection: Do you know any-one who, having a million dollars in his hands, could bring himself to destroy it?

Maybe you do. I don't. In a pinch I might turn it over to the Captain but I would not destroy it.

Smuggle it ashore? Alex, if you ever take it out of that lockbox, you have stolen it. Will you destroy your self-respect for a million dollars? For ten million? For five dollars?

"Well, Margrethe?"

"Alec, it seems to me that the solution is evident."

"Eh?"

"But you have been trying to solve your problems in the wrong order. First you must regain your memory. Then you will know why you are carrying that money. It will turn out to be for some innocent and logical pur-pose." She smiled. "I know you better than you know yourself. You are a good man, Alec; you are not a crimi-nal."

I felt a mixture of exasperation at her and of pride in what she thought of me—but more exasperation than pride. "Confound it, dear, I have *not* lost my memory. I am not Alec Graham; I am Alexander Hergensheimer, and that's been my name all my life and my memory is sharp. Want to know the name of my second-grade teacher? Miss Andrews. Or how I happened to have my first airship ride when I was twelve? For I do indeed come from a world in which airships ply every ocean and even over the North Pole, and Germany is a monarchy and the North American Union has enjoyed a century of peace and prosperity and this ship we are in tonight would be considered so out of date and so miserably equipped and slow that no one would sail in it. I asked for help; I did not ask for a psychiatric opinion. If you think I'm crazy, say so . . . and we'll drop the subject."

"I did not mean to anger you."

"My dear! You did not anger me; I simply unloaded on

you some of my worry and frustration—and I should not have done so. I'm sorry. But I do have real problems and they are not solved by telling me that my memory is at fault. If it were my memory, saying so would solve nothing; my problems would still be there. But I should not have snapped at you. Margrethe, you are all I have . . . in a strange and sometimes frightening world. I'm sorry."

She slid down off my bunk. "Nothing to be sorry about, dear Alec. But there is no point in further discussion tonight. Tomorrow— Tomorrow we will test that thumbprint carefully, in bright sunlight. Then you will see, and it could have an immediate effect on your memory."

"Or it could have an immediate effect on your stubbornness, best of girls."

She smiled. "We will see. Tomorrow. Now I think I must go to bed. We have reached the point where we are each repeating the same arguments . . . and upsetting each other. I don't want that, Alec. That is not good."

She turned and headed for the door, not even offering herself for a goodnight kiss.

"Margrethe!"

"Yes, Alec?"

"Come back and kiss me."

"Should I, Alec? You, a married man."

"Uh— Well, for heaven's sake, a kiss isn't the same as adultery."

She shook her head sadly. "There are kisses and kisses, Alec. I would not kiss the way we have kissed unless I was happily willing to go on from there and make love. To me that would be a happy and innocent thing . . . but to you it would be adultery. You pointed out what the Christ said to the woman taken in adultery. I have not sinned . . . and I will not cause you to sin." Again she turned to leave.

"Margrethe!"

"Yes, Alec?"

"You asked me if I intended ever again to ask you to

come back later. I ask you now. Tonight. Will you come back later?"

"Sin, Alec. For you it would be sin . . . and that would make it sin for me, knowing how you feel about it."

"'Sin.' I'm not sure what sin is. I do know I need you . . . and I think you need me."

"Goodnight, Alec." She left quickly.

After a long while I brushed my teeth and washed my face, then decided that another shower might help. I took it lukewarm and it seemed to calm me a little. But when I went to bed, I lay awake, doing something I call thinking but probably is not.

I reviewed in my mind all the many major mistakes I have made in my life, one after another, dusting them off and bringing them up sharp in my head, right to the silly, awkward, inept, self-righteous, asinine fool I had made of myself tonight, and, in so doing, how I had wounded and humiliated the best and sweetest woman I have ever known.

I can keep myself uselessly occupied with self-flagellation for an entire night when my latest attack of foot-in-mouth disease is severe. This current one bid fair to keep me staring at the ceiling for days.

Some long time later, after midnight and more, I was awakened by the sound of a key in the door. I fumbled for the bunk light switch, found it just as she dropped her robe and got into bed with me. I switched off the light.

She was warm and smooth and trembling and crying. I held her gently and tried to soothe her. She did not speak and neither did I. There had been too many words earlier and most of them had been mine. Now was a time simply to cuddle and hold and speak without words.

At last her trembling slowed, then stopped. Her breathing became even. Then she sighed and said very softly, "I could not stay away."

"Margrethe. I love you."

"Oh! I love you so much it hurts in my heart."

• • •

I think we were both asleep when the collision happened. I had not intended to sleep but for the first time since the fire walk I was relaxed and untroubled; I dropped off.

First came this incredible jar that almost knocked us out of my bunk, then a grinding, crunching noise at ear-splitting level. I got the bunk light on—and the skin of the ship at the foot of the bunk was bending inward.

The general alarm sounded, adding to the already deafening noise. The steel side of the ship buckled, then ruptured as something dirty white and cold pushed into the hole. As the light went out.

I got out of that bunk any which way, dragging Margrethe with me. The ship rolled heavily to port, causing us to slide down into the angle of the deck and the inboard bulkhead. I slammed against the door handle, grabbed at it, and hung on with my right hand while I held Margrethe to me with my left arm. The ship rolled back to starboard, and wind and water poured in through the hole—we heard it and felt it, could not see it. The ship recovered, then rolled again to starboard—and I lost my grip on the door handle.

I have to reconstruct what happened next—pitch dark, mind you, and a bedlam of sound. We were falling—I never let go of her—and then we were in water.

Apparently when the ship rolled back to starboard, we were tossed out through the hole. But that is just reconstruction; all I actually know is that we fell, together, into water, went down rather deep.

We came up and I had Margrethe under my left arm, almost in a proper lifesaver carry. I grabbed a look as I gulped air, then we went under again. The ship was right alongside us and moving. There was cold wind and rumbling noise; something high and dark was on the side away from the ship. But it was the ship that scared me— or rather its propeller, its screw. Stateroom C109 was far forward—but if I didn't get us well away from the ship almost at once, Margrethe and I were going to be chewed into hamburger by the screw. I hung onto her and stroked hard away from the ship, kicking strongly—and exulted as I felt us getting away from the hazard of the ship . . . and banged my head something brutal against blackness.

VIII

So they took up Jonah, and cast him forth into the sea: and the sea ceased from her raging.
Jonah 1:15

I was comfortable and did not want to wake up. But a slight throb in my head was annoying me and, willy-nilly, I did wake. I shook my head to get rid of that throb and got a snootful of water. I snorted it out.

"Alec?" Her voice was nearby.

I was on my back in blood-warm water, salt water by the taste, with blackness all around me—about as near to a return to the womb as can be accomplished this side of death. Or was this death? "Margrethe?"

"Oh! Oh, Alec, I am so relieved! You have been asleep a long time. How do you feel?"

I checked around, counted this and that, twitched that and this, found that I was floating on my back between Margrethe's limbs, she being also on her back with my head in her hands, in one of the standard Red-Cross life-saving positions. She was using slow frog kicks, not so much moving us as keeping us afloat. "I'm all right. I think. How about you?"

"I'm just fine, dearest!—now that you're awake."

"What happened?"

"You bumped your head against the berg."

"Berg?"

"The ice mountain. Iceberg."

(Iceberg? I tried to remember what had happened.) "What iceberg?"

"The one that wrecked the ship."

Some of it came tumbling back, but it still did not make an understandable picture. A giant crash as if the ship had hit a reef, then we were dumped into water. A struggle to get clear—I did bump my head. "Margrethe, we're in the tropics, as far south as Hawaii. How can there be icebergs?"

"I don't know, Alec."

"But—" I started to say "impossible," then decided that, from me, that word was silly. "This water is too warm for icebergs. Look, you can quit working so hard; in salt water I float as easily as Ivory soap."

"All right. But do let me hold you. I almost lost you once in this darkness; I'm frightened that it might happen again. When we fell in, the water was cold. Now it's warm; so we must not be near the berg."

"Hang onto me, sure; I don't want to lose you, either." Yes, the water had been cold when we fell into it; I remembered. Or cold compared with a nice warm cuddle in bed. And a cold wind. "What happened to the iceberg?"

"Alec, I don't know. We fell into the water together. You grabbed me and got us away from the ship; I'm sure that saved us. But it was dark as December night and blowing hard and in the blackness you ran your head into the ice.

"That is when I almost lost you. It knocked you out, dear, and you let go of me. I went under and gulped water and came up and spat it out and couldn't find you.

"Alec, I have never been so frightened in all my life. You weren't anywhere. I couldn't see you; I reached out, all sides, and could not touch you; I called out, you did not answer."

"I'm sorry."

"I should not have panicked. But I thought you had drowned. Or were drowning and I was not stopping it.

But in paddling around my hand struck you, and then I grabbed you and everything was all right—until you didn't answer. But I checked and found that your heart was steady and strong, so everything was all right after all, and I took you in the back carry so that I could hold your face out of water. After a long time you woke up— and now everything is truly all right."

"You didn't panic; I'd be dead if you had. Not many people could do what you did."

"Oh, it's not so uncommon; I was a guard at a beach north of København two summers—on Fridays I gave lessons. Lots of boys and girls learned."

"Keeping your head in a crunch and doing it in pitch darkness isn't learned from lessons; don't be so modest. What about the ship? And the iceberg?"

"Alec, again I don't know. By the time I found you and made sure that you were all right and then got you into towing position—by the time I had time to look around, it was like this. Nothing. Just blackness."

"I wonder if she sank? That was one big wallop she took! No explosion? You didn't hear anything?"

"I didn't hear an explosion. Just wind and the collision sounds you must have heard, then some shouts after we were in the water. If she sank, I did not see it, but— Alec, for the past half hour, about, I've been swimming with my head pushed against a pillow or a pad or a mattress. Does that mean the ship sank? Flotsam in the water?"

"Not necessarily but it's not encouraging. Why have you been keeping your head against it?"

"Because we may need it. If it is one of the deck cushions or sunbathing mats from the pool, then it's stuffed with kapok and is an emergency lifesaver."

"That's what I meant. If it's a flotation cushion, why are you just keeping your head against it? Why aren't you on it, up out of the water?"

"Because I could not do that without letting go of you."

"Oh. Margrethe, when we get out of this, will you

kindly give me a swift kick? Well, I'm awake now; let's find out what you've found. By Braille."

"All right. But I don't want to let go of you when I can't see you."

"Honey, I'm at least as anxious not to lose track of you. Okay, like this: You hang onto me with one hand; reach behind you with the other. Get a good grip on this cushion or whatever it is. I turn over and hang onto you and track you up to the hand you are using to grip the pillow thing. Then we'll see—we'll both feel what we have and decide how we can use it."

It was not just a pillow, or even a bench cushion; it was (by the feel of it) a large sunbathing pad, at least six feet wide and somewhat longer than that—big enough for two people, or three if they were well acquainted. Almost as good as finding a lifeboat! Better—this flotation pad included Margrethe. I was minded of a profane poem passed around privately at seminary: "A jug of wine, a loaf of bread, and thou—"

Getting up onto a mat that is limp as an angleworm on a night as black as the inside of a pile of coal is not merely difficult; it is impossible. We accomplished the impossible by my hanging on to it with both hands while Margrethe slowly slithered up over me. Then she gave me a hand while I inched up and onto it.

Then I leaned on one elbow and fell off and got lost. I followed Margrethe's voice and bumped into the pad, and again got slowly and cautiously aboard.

We found that the most practical way to make best use of the space and buoyancy offered by the mat was to lie on our backs, side by side, starfished like that Leonardo da Vinci drawing, in order to spread ourselves as widely as possible over the support.

I said, "You all right, hon?"

"Just fine!"

"Need anything?"

"Not anything we have here. I'm comfortable, and re-laxed—and you are here."

"Me, too. But what would you have if you could have anything you want?"

"Well . . . a hot fudge sundae."

I considered it. "No. A chocolate sundae with marsh-mallow syrup, and a cherry on top. And a cup of coffee."

"A cup of chocolate. But make mine hot fudge. It's a taste I acquired in America. We Danes do lots of good things with ice cream, but putting a hot sauce on an ice-cold dish never occurred to us. A hot fudge sundae. Better make that a double."

"All right. I'll pay for a double if that's what you want. I'm a dead game sport, I am—and you saved my life."

Her inboard hand patted mine. "Alec, you're fun—and I'm happy. Do you think we're going to get out of this alive?"

"I don't know, hon. The supreme irony of life is that hardly anyone gets out of it alive. But I promise you this: I'm going to do my best to get you that hot fudge sun-dae."

We both woke up when it got light. Yes, I slept and I know Margrethe did, too, as I woke a little before she did, listened to her soft snores, and kept quiet until I saw her eyes open. I had not expected to be able to sleep but I am not surprised (now) that we did—perfect bed, perfect si-lence, perfect temperature, both of us very tired . . . and absolutely nothing to worry about that was worth worry-ing about because there was nothing, nothing whatever, to do about our problems earlier than daylight. I think I fell asleep thinking: Yes, Margrethe was right; a hot fudge sundae was a better choice than a chocolate marsh-mallow sundae. I know I dreamt about such a sundae—a quasi-nightmare in which I would dip into it, a big bite . . . lift the spoon to my mouth, and find it empty. I think that woke me.

She turned her head toward me, smiled and looked about sixteen and utterly heavenly. ("—*like two young roes that are twins. Thou art all fair, my love; there is no spot in thee.*") "Good morning, beautiful."

She giggled. "Good morning, Prince Charming. Did you sleep well?"

"Matter of fact, Margrethe, I haven't slept so well in a month. Odd. All I want now is breakfast in bed."

"Right away, sir. I'll hurry!"

"Go along with you. I should not have mentioned food. I'll settle for a kiss. Think we can manage a kiss without falling into the water?"

"Yes. But let's be careful. Just turn your face this way; don't roll over."

It was a kiss mostly symbolic rather than one of Margrethe's all-out specials. We were both quite careful not to disturb the precarious stability of our make-do life raft. We were worried about something more important than being dumped into the ocean—at least I was.

I decided to broach it, take it out where we could worry about it together. "Margrethe, by the map just outside the dining room we should have the coast of Mexico near Mazatlán just east of us. What time did the ship sink? If it sank. I mean, what time was the collision?"

"I don't know."

"Nor do I. After midnight, I'm sure of that. The *Konge Knut* was scheduled to arrive at eight a.m. So that coast line could be over a hundred miles east of us. Or it could be almost on top of us. Mountains over there, we may be able to see them when this overcast clears away. As it did yesterday, so it probably will today. Sweetheart, how are you on long-distance swimming? If we can see mountains, do you want to try for it?"

She was slow in answering. "Alec, if you wish, we will try it."

"That wasn't quite what I asked."

"That is true. In warm sea water I think I can swim as long as necessary. I did once swim the Great Belt, in water colder than this. But, Alec, in the Belt are no sharks. Here there are sharks. I have seen."

I let out a sigh. "I'm glad you said it; I didn't want to have to say it. Hon, I think we must stay right here and hold still. Not call attention to ourselves. I can skip breakfast—especially a shark's breakfast."

"One does not starve quickly."

"We won't starve. If you had your druthers, which would you pick? Starvation? Or death by sunburn? Sharks? Or dying of thirst? In all the lifeboat and Robinson Crusoe stories I've ever read our hero had something to work with. I don't have even a toothpick. Correction: I have you; that changes the odds. Margrethe, what do you think we ought to do?"

"I think we will be picked up."

I thought so, too, but for a reason I did not want to discuss with Margrethe. "I'm glad to hear you say that. But why do you think so?"

"Alec, have you been to Mazatlán before?"

"No."

"It is an important fishing port, both commercial fishing and sport fishing. Since dawn hundreds of boats have put out to sea. The largest and fastest go many kilometers out. If we wait, they will find us."

"May find us, you mean. There is a lot of ocean out here. But you're right; swimming for it is suicide; our best bet is to stay here and hold tight."

"They will be looking for us, Alec."

"They will? Why?"

"If *Konge Knut* did not sink, then the Captain knows when and where we were lost overboard; when he reaches port—about now—he will ask for a daylight search. But if she did sink, then they will be scouring the whole area for survivors."

"Sounds logical." (I had another idea, not at all logical.)

"Our problem is to stay alive till they find us, avoiding sharks and thirst and sunburn as best we can—and all of that means holding still. Quite still and all the time. Except that I think we should turn over now and then, after the sun is out, to spread the burn."

"And pray for cloudy weather. Yes, all of that. And maybe we should not talk. Not get quite so thirsty—eh?"

She kept silent so long that I thought she had started the discipline I had suggested. Then she said, "Beloved, we may not live."

"I know."

"If we are to die, I would choose to hear your voice, and I would not wish to be deprived of telling you that I love you—now that I may!—in a futile attempt to live a few minutes longer."

"Yes, my sweetheart. Yes."

Despite that decision we talked very little. For me it was enough to touch her hand; it appeared to be enough for her, too.

A long time later—three hours at a guess—I heard Margrethe gasp.

"Trouble?"

"Alec! Look there!" She pointed. I looked.

It should have been my turn to gasp, but I was somewhat braced for it: high up, a cruciform shape, somewhat like a bird gliding, but much larger and clearly artificial. A flying machine—

I knew that flying machines were impossible; in engineering school I had studied Professor Simon Newcomb's well-known mathematical proof that the efforts of Professor Langley and others to build an aerodyne capable of carrying a man were doomed, useless, because scale theory proved that no such contraption large enough to carry a man could carry a heat-energy plant large enough to lift it off the ground—much less a passenger.

That was science's final word on a folly and it put a stop to wasting public monies on a will-o'-the-wisp. Research and development money went into airships, where it belonged, with enormous success.

However, in the past few days I had gained a new angle on the idea of "impossible." When a veritable flying machine showed up in our sky, I was not greatly surprised.

I think Margrethe held her breath until it passed over us and was far toward the horizon. I started to, then forced myself to breathe calmly—it was such a beautiful thing, silvery and sleek and fast. I could not judge its size, but, if those dark spots in its side were windows, then it was enormous.

I could not see what pushed it along.

"Alec . . . is that an airship?"

"No. At least it is not what I meant when I told you about airships. This I would call a 'flying machine.' That's all I can say; I've never seen one before. But I can tell you one thing, now—something very important."

"Yes?"

"We are not going to die . . . and I now know why the ship was sunk."

"Why, Alec?"

"To keep me from checking a thumbprint."

IX

For I was an hungred, and ye gave me meat:
I was thirsty, and ye gave me drink:
I was a stranger, and ye took me in.
Matthew 25:35

"Or, to put it more nearly exactly, the iceberg was there and the collision took place to keep me from checking my thumbprint against the thumbprint on Graham's driver's license. The ship may not have sunk; that may not have been necessary to the scheme."

Margrethe did not say anything.

So I added gently, "Go ahead, dear; say it. Get it off your chest; I won't mind. I'm crazy. Paranoid."

"Alec, I did not say that. I did not think it. I would not."

"No, you did not say it. But this time my aberration cannot be explained away as 'loss of memory.' That is, if we saw the same thing. What did you see?"

"I saw something strange in the sky. I heard it, too. You told me that it was a flying machine."

"Well, I think that is what it should be called—but you can call it a, uh, a 'gumpersaggle' for all of me. Something new and strange. What is this gumpersaggle? Describe it."

"It was something moving in the sky. It came from back that way, then passed almost over us, and disappeared there." (She pointed, a direction I had decided was north.) "It was shaped something like a cross, a crucifix. The crosspiece had bumps on it, four I think. The front end had eyes like a whale and the back end had flukes like a whale. A whale with wings—that's what it looked like, Alec; a whale flying through the sky!"

"You thought it was alive?"

"Uh, I don't know. I don't think so. I don't know what to think."

"I don't think it was alive; I think it was a machine. A flying machine. A boat with wings on it. But, either way—a machine or a flying whale—have you ever in your life seen anything like it?"

"Alec, it was so strange that I have trouble believing that I saw it."

"I know. But you saw it first and pointed it out to me—so I didn't trick you into thinking that you saw it."

"You wouldn't do that."

"No, I would not. But I'm glad you saw it first, dearest girl; that means it's real—not something dreamed up in my fevered brain. That thing did not come from the world you are used to . . . and I can promise you that it is not one of the airships I talked about; it is not from the world I grew up in. So we're now in still a third world." I sighed. "The first time it took a twenty-thousand-ton ocean liner to prove to me that I had changed worlds. This time just one sight of something that simply could not exist in my world is all I need to know that they are at it again. They shifted worlds when I was knocked out—I think that's when they did it. As may be, I think they did it to keep me from checking that thumbprint. Paranoia. The delusion that the whole world is a conspiracy. Only it's not a delusion."

I watched her eyes. "Well?"

"Alec . . . could it possibly be that both of us imagined it? Delirious, perhaps? We've both had a rough experience—you hit your head; I may have hit mine when the iceberg struck."

"Margrethe, we would not each have the same delirium dream. If you wake up and find that I'm gone, that could be your answer. But I'm not gone; I'm right here. Besides, you would still have to account for an iceberg as far south as we are. Paranoia is a simpler explanation. But the conspiracy is aimed at me; you just had the misfortune to be caught in it. I'm sorry." (I wasn't really sorry. A raft in the middle of the ocean is no place to be alone. But with Margrethe it was "paradise enow.")

"I still think that sharing the same dream is—*Alec, there it comes again!*" She pointed.

I didn't see anything at first, then I did: A dot that grew into a cruciform shape, a shape that I now identified as "flying machine." I watched it grow.

"Margrethe, it must have turned around. Maybe it saw us. Or they saw us. Or he saw us. Whatever."

"Perhaps."

As it came closer I saw that it was going to pass to our right rather than overhead. Margrethe said suddenly, "It's not the same one."

"And it's not a flying whale—unless flying whales hereabouts have wide red stripes down their sides."

"It's not a whale. I mean 'it's not alive.' You are right, Alec; it is a machine. Dear, do you really think it has people inside it? That scares me."

"I think I would be more scared if it did not have people inside it." (I remembered a fantastic story translated from the German about a world peopled by nothing but automatic machines—not a pleasant story.) "Actually, it's good news. We both know now that our seeing the first one was not a dream, not an illusion. That nails down the fact that we are in another world. Therefore we are going to be rescued."

She said hesitantly, "I don't quite follow that."

"That's because you are still trying to avoid calling me paranoid—and thank you, dear, but my being paranoid is the simplest hypothesis. If the joker pulling the strings had intended to kill me, the easy time to do it would have been with the iceberg. Or earlier, with the fire pit. But he's not out to kill me, at least not now. He's playing with

me, cat and mouse. So I'll be rescued. So will you, because we're together. You were with me when the iceberg
hit—your bad luck. You're still with me now, so you'll be
rescued—your good luck. Don't fight it, dear. I've had
some days to get used to it, and I find that it is all right
once you relax. Paranoia is the only rational approach to
a conspiracy world."

"But, Alec, the world ought not to be that way."

"There is no 'ought' to it, my love. The essence of philosophy is to accept the universe as it is, rather than try
to force it into some preconceived shape." I added,
"Wups! Don't roll off. You don't want to be a snack for a
shark just after we've had proof that we are going to be
picked up!"

For the next hour or so nothing happened—unless you
count sighting two regal sailfish. The overcast burned
away and I began to be anxious for an early rescue; I
figured they owed me that much! Not let me get a third-
degree sunburn. Margrethe might be able to take a bit
more sun than I; she was blonde but she was tanned a
warm toast color all over—lovely! But I was raw frog-
belly white except for my face and hands—a full day of
tropic sun could put me into hospital. Or worse.

The eastern horizon now seemed to show a gray un-
evenness that could be mountains—or so I kept telling
myself, although there isn't much you can see when your
viewpoint is about seven inches above water line. If those
were indeed mountains or hills, then land was not many
miles away. Boats from Mazatlán should be in sight any
time now . . . if Mazatlán was still there in this world.
If—

Then another flying machine showed up.

It was only vaguely like the other two. They had been
flying parallel to the coast, the first from the south, the
second from the north. This machine came out from the
direction of the coast, flying mostly west, although it
zigzagged.

It passed north of us, then turned back and circled around us. It came low enough that I could see that it did indeed have men in it, two I thought.

Its shape is hard to explain. Imagine first a giant box kite, about forty feet long, four feet wide, and about three feet between two kite surfaces.

Imagine this box kite placed at right angles to a boat shape, somewhat like an Esquimau's kayak but larger, much larger—about as large as the box kite.

Underneath all this are two more kayak shapes, smaller, parallel to the main shape.

At one end of this shape is an engine (as I saw later) and at the front end of that is an air propeller, like a ship's water propeller—and this I saw later, also. When I first saw this unbelievable structure, the air screw was turning so extremely fast that one simply could not see it. But one could hear it! The noise made by this contraption was deafening and never stopped.

The machine turned toward us and tilted down so that it headed straight toward us—like nothing so much as a pelican gliding down to scoop up fish.

With us the fish. It was frightening. To me, at least; Margrethe never let out a peep. But she did squeeze my fingers very hard. The mere fact that we were not fish and that a machine could not eat us and would not want to did not make this dive at us less terrifying.

Despite my fright (or because of it) I now saw that this construction was at least twice as big as I had estimated when I saw it high in the sky. It had two teamsters operating it, seated side by side behind a window in the front end. The driving engine turned out to be two, mounted between the box-kite wings, one on the right of the teamsters' position, one on the left.

At the very last instant the machine lifted like a horse taking a hurdle, and barely missed us. The blast of wind it created almost knocked us off our raft and the blast of sound caused my ears to ring.

It went a little higher, curved back toward us, glided

again but not quite toward us. The lower twin kayak shapes touched the water, creating a brave comet's tail of spume—and the thing slowed and stopped and stayed there, on the water, and did not sink!

Now the air screws moved very slowly and I saw them for the first time . . . and admired the engineering ingenuity that had gone into them. Not as efficient, I suspected, as the ducted air screws used in our dirigible airships, but an elegant solution to a problem in a place where ducting would be difficult or perhaps impossible.

But those infernally noisy driving engines! How any engineer could accept that, I could not see. As one of my professors said (back before thermodynamics convinced me that I had a call for the ministry), noise is always a byproduct of inefficiency. A correctly designed engine is as silent as the grave.

The machine turned and came at us again, moving very slowly. Its teamsters handled it so that it missed us by a few feet and almost stopped. One of the two inside it crawled out of the carriage space behind the window and was clinging by his left hand to one of the stanchions that held the two box-kite wings apart. His other hand held a coiled line.

As the flying machine passed us, he cast the line toward us. I snatched at it, got a hand on it, and did not myself go into the water because Margrethe snatched at me.

I handed the line to Margrethe. "Let him pull you in. I'll slide into the water and be right behind you."

"No!"

"What do you mean, 'No'? This is no time to argue. Do it!"

"Alec, be quiet! He's trying to tell us something."

I shut up, more than a little offended. Margrethe listened. (No point in my listening; my Spanish is limited to *"Gracias"* and *"Por favor."* Instead I read the lettering on the side of the machine: *EL GUARDACOSTAS REAL DE MÉXICO.*

"Alec, he is warning us to be very careful. Sharks."

"Ouch."

"Yes. We are to stay where we are. He will pull gently on this rope. I think he means to get us into his machine without us going into the water."

"A man after my own heart!"

We tried it; it did not work. A breeze had sprung up; it had much more effect on the flying machine than it had on us—that water-soaked sunbathing pad was practically nailed down, no sail area at all. Instead of being able to pull us to the flying machine, the man on the other end of the line was forced to let out more line to keep from pulling us off into the water.

He called out something; Margrethe answered. They shouted back and forth. She turned to me. "He says to let loose the rope. They will go out and come back, this time directly at us, but slowly. As they come closest, we are to try to scramble up into the *aeroplano*. The machine."

"All right."

The machine left us, went out on the water and curved back. While waiting, we were not bored; we had the dorsal fin of a huge shark to entertain us. It did not attack; apparently it had not made up its mind (what mind?) that we were good to eat. I suppose it saw only the underside of the kapok pad.

The flying machine headed directly toward us on the water, looking like some monstrous dragonfly skimming the surface. I said, "Darling, as it gets closest, you dive for the stanchion closest to you and I'll push you up. Then I'll come up behind you."

"No, Alec."

"What do you mean, 'No'?" I was vexed. Margrethe was such a good comrade—then suddenly so stubborn. At the wrong time.

"You can't push me; you have no foundation to push from. And you can't stand up; you can't even sit up. Uh, you scramble to the right; I'll scramble to the left. If either of us misses, then back onto the pad—fast! The *aeroplano* will come around again."

"But—"

"That's how he said to do it."

There was no time left; the machine was almost on top of us. The "legs" or stanchions joining the lower twin shapes to the body of the machine bridged the pad, one just missing me and the other just missing Margrethe. "Now!" she cried. I lunged toward my side, got a hand on a stanchion.

And almost jerked my right arm out by the roots but I kept on moving, monkey fashion—got both hands on that undercarriage, got a foot up on a horizontal kayak shape, turned my head.

Saw a hand reaching down to Margrethe—she climbed and was lifted onto the kite wing above, and disappeared. I turned to climb up my side—and suddenly levitated up and onto the wing. I do not ordinarily levitate but this time I had incentive: a dirty white fin too big for any decent fish, cutting the water right toward my foot.

I found myself alongside the little carriage house from which the teamsters directed their strange craft. The second man (not the one who had climbed out to help) stuck his head out a window, grinned at me, reached back and opened a little door. I crawled inside, head first. Margrethe was already there.

The space had four seats, two in front where the teamsters sat, and two behind where we were.

The teamster on my side looked around and said something, and continued—I noticed!—to look at Margrethe. Certainly she was naked, but that was not her fault, and a gentleman would not stare.

"He says," Margrethe explained, "that we must fasten our belts. I think he means this." She held up a buckle on the end of a belt, the other end being secured to the frame of the carriage.

I discovered that I was sitting on a similar buckle, which was digging a hole into my sunburned backside. I hadn't noticed it up to then, too many other things demanding attention. (Why didn't he keep his eyes to himself! I felt myself ready to shout at him. That he had, at great peril to himself, just saved her life and mine did not that moment occur to me; I was simply growing furious that he would take such advantage of a helpless lady.)

I turned my attention to that pesky belt and tried to ignore it. He spoke to the other man beside him, who responded enthusiastically. Margrethe interrupted the discussion. "What are they saying?" I demanded.

"The poor man is about to give me the shirt off his back. I am protesting . . . but I'm not protesting so hard as to put a stop to it. It's very gallant of them, dear, and, while I'm not foolish about it, I do feel more at ease among strangers with some sort of clothing." She listened, and added, "They're arguing as to which one has the privilege."

I shut up. In my mind I apologized to them. I'll bet even the Pope in Rome has sneaked a quick look a time or two in his life.

The one on the right apparently won the argument. He squirmed around in his seat—he could not stand up—and got his shirt off, turned and passed it back to Margrethe. "*Señorita. Por favor.*" He added other remarks but they were beyond my knowledge.

Margrethe replied with dignity and grace, and chatted with them as she wiggled into his shirt. It covered her mostly. She turned to me. "Dear, the commander is *Teniente* Anibal Sanz Garcia and his assistant is *Sargento* Roberto Dominguez Jones, both of the Royal Mexican Coast Guard. Both the Lieutenant and the Sergeant wanted to give me a shirt, but the Sergeant won a finger-guessing game, so I have his shirt."

"It's mighty generous of him. Ask them if there is anything at all in the machine that I can wear."

"I'll try." She spoke several phrases; I heard my name. Then she shifted back to English. "Gentlemen, I have the honor to present my husband, *Señor* Alexandro Graham Hergensheimer." She shifted back to Spanish.

Shortly she was answered. "The Lieutenant is devastated to admit that they have nothing to offer you. But he promises on his mother's honor that something will be found for you just as quickly as we reach Mazatlán and the Coast Guard headquarters there. Now he urges both of us to fasten our belts tightly as we are about to fly. Alec, I'm scared!"

"Don't be. I'll hold your hand."

Sergeant Dominguez turned around again, held up a canteen. *"Agua?"*

"Goodness, yes!" agreed Margrethe. *"Sí sí sí!"*

Water has never tasted so good.

The Lieutenant looked around when we returned the canteen, gave a big smile and a thumbs-up sign old as the Colosseum, and did something that speeded up his driving engines. They had been turning over very slowly; now they speeded up to a horrible racket. The machine turned as he headed it straight into the wind. The wind had been freshening all morning; now it showed little curls of white on the tops of the wavelets. He speeded his engines still more, to an unbelievable violence, and we went bouncing over the water, shaking everything.

Then we started hitting about every tenth wave with incredible force. I don't know why we weren't wrecked.

Suddenly we were twenty feet off the water; the bumping stopped. The vibration and the noise continued. We climbed at a sharp angle—and turned and started down again, and I almost-not-quite threw up that welcome drink of water.

The ocean was right in front of us, a solid wall. The Lieutenant turned his head and shouted something.

I wanted to tell him to keep his eyes on the road!—but I did not. "What does he say?"

"He says to look where he points. He'll point us right at it. *El tiburón blanco grande*—the great white shark that almost got us."

(I could have done without it.) Sure enough, right in the middle of this wall of water was a gray ghost with a fin cutting the water. Just when I knew that we were going to splash right down on top of it, the wall tilted away from us, my buttocks were forced down hard against the seat, my ears roared, and I again missed throwing up on our host only by iron will.

The machine leveled off and suddenly the ride was almost comfortable, aside from the racket and the vibration.

Airships are ever so much nicer.

The rugged hills behind the shoreline, so hard to see from our raft, were clearly in sight once we were in the air, and so was the shore—a series of beautiful beaches and a town where we were headed. The Sergeant looked around, pointed down at the town, and spoke. "What did he say?"

"Sergeant Roberto says that we are home just in time for lunch. *Almuerzo*, he said, but notes that it's breakfast—*desayuno*—for us."

My stomach suddenly decided to stay awhile. "I don't care what he calls it. Tell him not to bother to cook the horse; I'll eat it raw."

Margrethe translated; both our hosts laughed, then the Lieutenant proceeded to swoop down and place his machine on the water while looking back over his shoulder to talk to Margrethe—who continued to smile while she drove her nails through the palm of my right hand.

We got down. No one was killed. But airships are much better.

Lunch! Everything was coming up roses.

X

In the sweat of thy face shalt thou eat bread,
till thou return unto the ground—
Genesis 3:19

A half hour after the flying machine splashed down in
the harbor of Mazatlán Margrethe and I were seated with
Sergeant Dominguez in the enlisted men's mess of the
Coast Guard. We were late for the midday meal but we
were served. And I was clothed. Some at least—a pair of
dungaree trousers. But the difference between bare naked
and a pair of pants is far greater than the difference between cheap work trousers and the finest ermine. Try it
and you'll see.

A small boat had come out to the flying machine's
mooring; then I had to walk across the dock where we
had landed and into the headquarters building, there to
wait until these pants could be found for me—with
strangers staring at me the whole time, some of them
women. I know now how it feels to be exposed in stocks.
Dreadful! I haven't been so embarrassed since an unfor-
tunate accident in Sunday school when I was five.

But now it was done with and there was food and drink
in front of us and, for the time being, I was abundantly
happy. The food was not what I was used to. Who said
that hunger was the best sauce? Whoever he was, he was
right; our lunch was delicious. Thin cornmeal pancakes
soaked with gravy, fried beans, a scorching hot stew, a
bowl of little yellow tomatoes, and coffee strong, black,

95

and bitter—what more could a man want? No gourmet ever savored a meal as much as I enjoyed that one.

(At first I had been a bit miffed that we ate in the enlisted men's mess rather than going with Lieutenant Sanz to wherever the officers ate. Much later I had it pointed out to me that I suffered from a very common civilian syndrome, i.e., a civilian with no military experience unconsciously equates his social position to that of officers, never to that of enlisted men. On examination this notion is obviously ridiculous—but it is almost universal. Oh, perhaps not universal but it obtains throughout America . . . where every man is "as good as anyone else and better than most.")

Sergeant Dominguez now had his shirt back. While pants were being found for me, a woman—a charwoman, I believe; the Mexican Coast Guard did not seem to have female ratings—a woman at headquarters had been sent to fetch something for Margrethe, and that something turned out to be a blouse and a full skirt, each of cotton and in bright colors. A simple and obviously cheap costume but Margrethe looked beautiful in it.

As yet, neither of us had shoes. No matter—the weather was warm and dry; shoes could wait. We were fed, we were dressed, we were safe—and all with a warm hospitality that caused me to feel that Mexicans were the finest people on earth.

After my second cup of coffee I said, "Sweetheart, how do we excuse ourselves and leave without being rude? I think we should find the American consul as early as possible."

"We have to go back to the headquarters building."

"More red tape?"

"I suppose you could call it that. I think they want to question us in more detail as to how we came to be where we were found. One must admit that our story is odd."

"I suppose so." Our initial interview with the Commandant had been less than satisfactory. Had I been alone I think he simply would have called me a liar . . . but it is difficult for a male man bursting with masculine ego to talk that way to Margrethe.

The trouble was the good ship *Konge Knut.*

She had not sunk, she had not come into port—she had never existed.

I was only moderately surprised. Had she turned into a full-rigged ship or a quinquereme, I would not have been surprised. But I had expected some sort of vessel of that same name—I thought the rules required it. But now it was becoming clear that I did not understand the rules. If there were any.

Margrethe had pointed out to me a confirming factor: This Mazatlán was not the town she had visited before. This one was much smaller and was not a tourist town— indeed the long dock where the *Konge Knut* should have tied up did not exist in this world. I think that this convinced her quite as much as the flying machines in proving to her that my "paranoia" was in fact the least hypothesis. She had been here before; that dock was big and solid; it was gone. It shook her.

The Commandant had not been impressed. He spent more time questioning Lieutenant Sanz than he spent questioning us. He did not seem pleased with Sanz.

There was another factor that I did not understand at the time and have never fully understood. Sanz's boss was "Captain" (or *"Capitán"*); the Commandant also was "Captain." But they were not the same rank.

The Coast Guard used navy ranks. However, that small part of it that operated flying machines used army ranks. I think this trivial difference had an historical origin. As may be, there was friction at the interface; the four-stripes or seagoing Captain was not disposed to accept as gospel anything reported by a flying-machine officer.

Lieutenant Sanz had fetched in two naked survivors with a preposterous story; the four-striper seemed inclined to blame Sanz himself for the unbelievable aspects of our story.

Sanz was not intimidated. I think he had no real respect for an officer who had never been higher off the water than a crow's nest. (Having ridden in his death trap, I understood why he was not inclined to genuflect to a sea-level type. Even among dirigible balloon pilots I have encountered this tendency to divide the world into those who fly and those who do not.)

After a bit, finding himself unable to shake Sanz, unable to shake Margrethe, and unable to communicate with me except through Margrethe, the Commandant shrugged and gave instructions that resulted in us all going to lunch. I thought that ended it. But now we were going back for more, whatever it was.

Our second session with the Commandant was short. He told us that we would see the immigration judge at four that afternoon—the court with that jurisdiction; there was no separate immigration court. In the meantime here was a list of what we owed—arrange payment with the judge.

Margrethe looked startled as she accepted a piece of paper from him; I demanded to know what he had said.

She translated; I looked at that billing.

More than eight thousand pesos!

It did not take a deep knowledge of Spanish to read that bill; almost all the words were cognates. *"Tres horas"* is three hours, and we were charged for three hours' use of *"aeroplano"*—a word I had heard earlier from Margrethe; it meant their flying machine. We were charged also for the time of Lieutenant Sanz and Sergeant Dominguez. Plus a multiplying factor that I decided must mean applied overhead, or near enough.

And there was fuel for the *aeroplano,* and service for it.

"Trousers" are *"pantalones"*—and here was a bill for the pair I was wearing.

A *"falda"* was a skirt and a *"camisa"* was a blouse—and Margrethe's outfit was decidedly not cheap.

One item surprised me not by its price but by being included; I had thought we were guests: two lunches, each at twelve pesos.

There was even a separate charge for the Commandant's time.

I started to ask how much eight thousand pesos came to in dollars—then shut up, realizing that I had not the slightest idea of the buying power of a dollar in this new world we had been dumped into.

Margrethe discussed the billing with Lieutenant Sanz, who looked embarrassed. There was much expostulation and waving of hands. She listened, then told me, "Alec, it isn't Anibal's idea and it is not even the fault of the Commandant. The tariffs on these services—rescue at sea, use of the *aeroplano*, and so forth—are set from *el Distrito Real*, the Royal District—that's the same as Mexico City, I believe. Lieutenant Sanz tells me that there is an economy drive on at the top level, with great pressure on everyone to make all public services self-supporting. He says that, if the Commandant did not charge us for our rescue and the Inspector Royal ever found out about it, it would be deducted from the Commandant's pay. Plus whatever punitive measures a royal commission found appropriate. And Anibal wants you to know that he is devastated at this embarrassing situation. If he owned the *aeroplano* himself, we would simply be his guests. He will always look on you as his brother and me as his sister."

"Tell him I feel the same way about him and please make it at least as flowery as he made it."

"I will. And Roberto wants to be included."

"And the same goes for the Sergeant. But find out where and how to get to the American consul. We've got troubles."

Lieutenant Anibal Sanz was told to see to it that we appeared in court at four o'clock; with that we were dismissed. Sanz delegated Sergeant Roberto to escort us to the consul and back, expressed regret that his duty status kept him from escorting us personally—clicked his heels, bowed over Margrethe's hand, and kissed it. He got a lot of mileage out of that simple gesture; I could see that

Margrethe was pleased. But they don't teach that grace in Kansas. My loss.

Mazatlán is on a peninsula; the Coast Guard station is on the south shore not far from the lighthouse (tallest in the world—impressive!); the American consulate is about a mile away across town at the north shore, straight down *Avenida* Miguel Alemán its entire length—a pleasant walk, graced about halfway by a lovely fountain.

But Margrethe and I were barefooted.

Sergeant Dominguez did not suggest a taxi—and I could not.

At first being barefooted did not seem important. There were other bare feet on that boulevard and by no means all of them on children. (Nor did I have the only bare chest.) As a youngster I had regarded bare feet as a luxury, a privilege. I went barefooted all summer and put on shoes most reluctantly when school opened.

After the first block I was wondering why, as a kid, I had always looked forward to going barefooted. Shortly thereafter I asked Margrethe to ask Sergeant Roberto, please, to slow down and let me pick my way for maximum shade; this pesky sidewalk is frying my feet!

(Margrethe had not complained and did not—and I was a bit vexed with her that she had not. I benefited constantly from Margrethe's angelic fortitude—and found it hard to live up to.)

From there on I gave my full attention to pampering my poor, abused, tender pink feet. I felt sorry for myself and wondered why I had ever left God's country.

"I wept that I had no shoes, until I met a man who had no feet." I don't know who said that first, but it is part of our cultural heritage and should be.

It happened to me.

Not quite halfway, where Miguel Alemán crosses *Calle* Aquiles Serdan at the fountain, we encountered a street beggar. He looked up at us and grinned, held up a handful of pencils—"looked up" because he was riding a little wheeled dolly; he had no feet.

Sergeant Roberto called him by name and flipped him a coin; the beggar caught it in his teeth, flipped it into his pocket, called out, *"Gracias!"*—and turned his attention to me.

I said quickly, "Margrethe, will you please explain to him that I have no money whatever."

"Yes, Alec." She squatted down, spoke with him eye to eye. Then she straightened up. "Pepe says to tell you, that's all right; he'll catch you someday when you are rich."

"Please tell him that I will be back. I promise."

She did so. Pepe grinned at me, threw Margrethe a kiss, and saluted the Sergeant and me. We went on.

And I stopped being so finicky careful to coddle my feet. Pepe had forced me to reassess my situation. Ever since I had learned that the Mexican government did not regard rescuing me as a privilege but expected me to pay for it, I had been feeling sorry for myself, abused, put upon. I had been muttering to myself that my compatriots who complained that all Mexicans were blood-suckers, living on gringo tourists, were dead right! Not Roberto and the Lieutenant, of course—but the others. Lazy parasites, all of them!—with their hands out for the Yankee dollar.

Like Pepe.

I reviewed in my mind all the Mexicans I had met that day, each one I could remember, and asked forgiveness for my snide thoughts. Mexicans were simply fellow travelers on that long journey from dark to eternal darkness. Some carried their burdens well, some did not. And some carried very heavy burdens with gallantry and grace. Like Pepe.

Yesterday I had been living in luxury; today I was broke and in debt. But I have my health, I have my brain,

I have my two hands—and I have Margrethe. My burdens were light; I should carry them joyfully. Thank you, Pepe!

The door of the consulate had a small American flag over it and the Great Seal in bronze on it. I pulled the bell wire beside it.

After a considerable wait the door opened a crack and a female voice told us to go away (I needed no translation; her meaning was clear). The door started to close. Sergeant Roberto whistled loudly and called out. The crack widened; a dialogue ensued. Margrethe said, "He's telling her to tell *Don* Ambrosio that two American citizens are here who must see him at once because they must appear in court at four this afternoon."

Again we waited. After about twenty minutes the maid let us in and ushered us into a dark office. The consul came in, fixed my eye with his, and demanded to know how I dared to interrupt his siesta?

Then he caught sight of Margrethe and slowed down. To her it was: "How can I serve you? In the meantime will you honor my poor house by accepting a glass of wine? Or a cup of coffee?"

Barefooted and in a garish dress, Margrethe was a lady—I was riffraff. Don't ask me why this was so; it just was. The effect was most marked with men. But it worked with women, too. Try to rationalize it and you find yourself using words like "royal," "noble," "gentry," and "to the manner born"—all involving concepts anathema to the American democratic ideal. Whether this proves something about Margrethe or something about the democratic ideal I will leave as an exercise for the student.

Don Ambrosio was a pompous zero but nevertheless he was a relief because he spoke American—real American, not English; he had been born in Brownsville, Texas. I feel certain that the backs of his parents were wet. He had parlayed a talent for politics among his fellow Chicanos into a cushy sinecure, telling gringo travelers in the land of Montezuma why they could not have what they desperately needed.

Which he eventually told us.

I let Margrethe do most of the talking because she was obviously so much more successful at it than I was. She called us "Mr. and Mrs. Graham"—we had agreed on that name during the walk here. When we were rescued, she had used "Graham Hergensheimer" and had explained to me later that this let me choose: I could select "Hergensheimer" simply by asserting that the listener's memory had had a minor bobble; the name had been offered as "Hergensheimer Graham." No? Well, then *I* must have miscalled it—sorry.

I let it stay "Graham Hergensheimer" and thereby used the name "Graham" in order to keep things simple; to her I had always been "Graham" and I had been using the name myself for almost two weeks. Before I got out of the consulate I had told a dozen more lies, trying to keep our story believable. I did not want unnecessary complication; "Mr. and Mrs. Alec Graham" was easiest.

(Minor theological note: Many people seem to believe that the Ten Commandments forbid lying. Not at all! The prohibition is against bearing false witness against your neighbor—a specific, limited, and despicable sort of lie. But there is no Biblical rule forbidding simple untruth. Many theologians believe that no human social organization could stand up under the strain of absolute honesty. If you think their misgivings are unfounded, try telling your friends the ungarnished truth about what you think of their offspring—if you dare risk it.)

After endless repetitions (in which the *Konge Knut* shrank and became our private cruiser) *Don* Ambrosio said to me, "It's no use, Mr. Graham. I cannot issue you even a temporary document to substitute for your lost passport because you have offered me not one shred of proof that you are an American citizen."

I answered, *"Don* Ambrosio, I am astonished. I know that Mrs. Graham has a slight accent; we told you that she was born in Denmark. But do you honestly think that anyone not born amidst the tall corn could possibly have my accent?"

He gave a most Latin shrug. "I'm not an expert in mid-west accents. To my ear you could have been born to one of the harsher British accents, then have gone on the stage—and everybody knows that a competent actor can acquire the accent for any role. The People's Republic of England goes to any length these days to plant their sleepers in the States; you might be from Lincoln, England, rather than from somewhere near Lincoln, Nebraska."

"Do you really believe that?"

"What I believe is not the question. The fact is that I will not sign a piece of paper saying that you are an American citizen when I don't know that you are. I'm sorry. Is there anything more that I can do for you?"

(How can you do "more" for me when you haven't done anything yet?) "Possibly you can advise us."

"Possibly. I am not a lawyer."

I offered him our copy of the billing against us, explained it. "Is this in order and are these charges appropriate?"

He looked it over. "These charges are certainly legal both by their laws and ours. Appropriate? Didn't you tell me that they saved your lives?"

"No question about it. Oh, there's an outside chance that a fishing boat might have picked us up if the Coast Guard had not found us. But the Coast Guard did find us and did save us."

"Is your life—your two lives—worth less than eight thousand pesos? Mine is worth considerably more, I assure you."

"It isn't that, sir. We have no money, not a cent. It all went down with the boat."

"So send for money. You can have it sent care of the consulate. I'll go that far."

"Thank you. It will take time. In the meantime how can I get them off my neck? I was told that this judge will want cash and immediately."

"Oh, it's not that bad. It's true that they don't permit bankruptcy the way we do, and they do have a rather old-fashioned debtors-prison law. But they don't use it—just the threat of it. Instead the court will see that you get a job that will let you settle your indebtedness. *Don* Clemente is a humane judge; he will take care of you."

Aside from flowery nonsense directed at Margrethe, that ended it. We picked up Sergeant Roberto, who had been enjoying backstairs hospitality from the maid and the cook, and headed for the courthouse.

Don Clemente (Judge Ibañez) was as pleasant as *Don* Ambrosio had said he would be. Since we informed the clerk at once that we stipulated the debt but did not have the cash to pay it, there was no trial. We were simply seated in the uncrowded courtroom and told to wait while the judge disposed of cases on his docket. He handled several quickly. Some were minor offenses drawing fines; some were debt cases; some were hearings for later trial. I could not tell much about what was going on and whispering was frowned on, so Margrethe could not tell me much. But he was certainly no hanging judge.

The cases at hand were finished; at a word from the clerk we went out back with the "miscreants"—peasants, mostly—who owed fines or debts. We found ourselves lined up on a low platform, facing a group of men. Margrethe asked what this was—and was answered, *"La subasta."*

"What's that?" I asked her.

"Alec, I'm not sure. It's not a word I know."

Settlements were made quickly on the others; I gathered that most of them had been there before. Then there was just one man left of the group off the platform, just us on the platform. The man remaining looked sleekly prosperous. He smiled and spoke to me. Margrethe answered.

"What is he saying?" I asked.

"He asked you if you can wash dishes. I told him that you do not speak Spanish."

"Tell him that of course I can wash dishes. But that's hardly a job I want."

Five minutes later our debt had been paid, in cash, to the clerk of the court, and we had acquired a *patrón*, *Señor* Jaime Valera Guzman. He paid sixty pesos a day for Margrethe, thirty for me, plus our found. Court costs were twenty-five hundred pesos, plus fees for two non-resident work permits, plus war-tax stamps. The clerk figured our total indebtedness, then divided it out for us: In only a hundred and twenty-one days—four months—our obligation to our *patrón* would be discharged. Unless, of course, we spent some money during that time.

He also directed us to our *patrón*'s place of business, *Restaurante* Pancho Villa. Our *patrón* had already left in his private car. *Patrones* ride; *peones* walk.

XI

And Jacob served seven years for Rachel;
and they seemed unto him but a few days,
for the love he had to her.
Genesis 29:20

Sometimes, while washing dishes, I would amuse myself by calculating how high a stack of dishes I had washed since going to work for our *patrón, Don* Jaime. The ordinary plate used in Pancho Villa café stacked twenty plates to a foot. I arbitrarily decided that a cup and saucer, or two glasses, would count as one plate, since these items did not stack well. And so forth.

The great Mazatlán lighthouse is five hundred and fifteen feet tall, only forty feet shorter than the Washington Monument. I remember the day I completed my first "lighthouse stack." I had told Margrethe earlier that week that I was approaching my goal and expected to reach it by Thursday or early Friday.

And did so, Thursday evening—and left the scullery, stood in the door between the kitchen and the dining room, caught Margrethe's eye, raised my hands high and shook hands with myself like a pugilist.

Margrethe stopped what she was doing—taking orders from a family party—and applauded. This caused her to have to explain to her guests what was going on, and that resulted in her stopping by the scullery a few minutes later to pass to me a ten-peso note, a congratulatory gift from the father of that family. I asked her to thank him for me, and please tell him that I had just started my second lighthouse stack, which I was dedicating to him and his family.

Which in turn resulted in *Señora* Valera sending her husband, *Don* Jaime, to find out why Margrethe was wasting time and making a scene instead of paying attention to her work . . . which resulted in *Don* Jaime inquiring how much the diners had tipped me and then matching it.

The *Señora* had no reason to complain; Margrethe was not only her best waitress; she was her only bilingual waitress. The day we started to work for Sr. y Sra. Valera a sign painter was called in to paint a conspicuous sign: ENGLIS SPOKE HERE. Thereafter, in addition to being available for any English-speaking guests, Margrethe prepared menus in English (and the prices on the menus in English were about forty percent higher than the prices on the all-Spanish menus).

Don Jaime was not a bad boss. He was cheerful and, on the whole, kindly to his employees. When we had been there about a month, he told me that he would not have bid in my debt had it not been that the judge would not permit my contract to be separated from Margrethe's contract, we being a married couple (else I could have found myself a field hand able to see my wife only on rare occasions—as *Don* Ambrosio had told me, *Don* Clemente was a humane judge).

I told him that I was happy that the package included me but it simply showed his good judgment to want to hire Margrethe.

He agreed that that was true. He had attended the Wednesday labor auctions several weeks on end in search of a bilingual woman or girl who could be trained as a waitress, then had bid me in as well to obtain Margrethe—but he wished to tell me that he had not regretted it as he had never seen the scullery so clean, the dishes so immaculate, the silverware so shiny.

I assured him that it was my happy privilege to help

uphold the honor and prestige of *Restaurante* Pancho Villa and its distinguished *patrón, el Don* Jaime.

In fact it would have been difficult for me *not* to improve that scullery. When I took over, I thought at first that the floor was dirt. And so it was—you could have planted potatoes!—but under the filth, about a half inch down, was sound concrete. I cleaned and then kept it clean—my feet were still bare. Then I demanded roach powder.

Each morning I killed roaches and cleaned the floor. Each evening, just before quitting for the day, I sprinkled roach powder. It is impossible (I think) to conquer roaches, but it is possible to fight them to a draw, force them back and maintain a holding action.

As to the quality of my dishwashing, it could not be otherwise; my mother had a severe dirt phobia and, because of my placement in a large family, I washed or wiped dishes under her eye from age seven through thirteen (at which time I graduated through taking on a newspaper route that left me no time for dishwashing).

But just because I did it well, do not think I was enamored of dishwashing. It had bored me as a child; it bored me as a man.

Then why did I do it? Why didn't I run away?

Isn't that evident? Dishwashing kept me with Margrethe. Running away might be feasible for some debtors—I don't think much effort went into trying to track down and bring back debtors who disappeared some dark night—but running away was not feasible for a married couple, one of whom was a conspicuous blonde in a country in which any blonde is always conspicuous and the other was a man who could not speak Spanish.

While we both worked hard—eleven to eleven each day except Tuesday, with a nominal two hours off for siesta and a half hour each for lunch and dinner—we had the other twelve hours each day to ourselves, plus all day Tuesday.

Niagara Falls never supplied a finer honeymoon. We

had a tiny attic room at the back of the restaurant building. It was hot but we weren't there much in the heat of the day—by eleven at night it was comfortable no matter how hot the day had been. In Mazatlán most residents of our social class (zero!) did not have inside plumbing. But we worked and lived in a restaurant building; there was a flush toilet we shared with other employees during working hours and shared with no one the other twelve hours of each day. (There was also a Maw Jones out back, which I sometimes used during working hours—I don't think Margrethe ever used it.)

We had the use of a shower on the ground floor, back to back with the employees' toilet, and the needs of the scullery were such that the building had a large water heater. *Señora* Valera scolded us regularly for using too much hot water ("Gas costs money!"); we listened in silence and went right on using whatever amount of hot water we needed.

Our *patrón*'s contract with the state required him to supply us with food and shelter (and clothing, under the law, but I did not learn this until too late to matter), which is why we slept there, and of course we ate there— not the chef's specialties, but quite good food.

"Better is a dinner of herbs where love is, than a stalled ox and hatred therewith." We had only ourselves; it was enough.

Margrethe, because she sometimes received tips, especially from gringos, was slowly accumulating cash money. We spent as little of this as possible—she bought shoes for each of us—and she saved against the day when we would be free of our peonage and able to go north. I had no illusions that the nation north of us was the land of my birth . . . but it was this world's analog of it; English was spoken there and I was sure that its culture would have to be closer to what we had been used to.

Tips to Margrethe brought us into friction with *Señora* Valera the very first week. While *Don* Jaime was legally our *patrón*, she owned the restaurant—or so we were told by Amanda the cook. Jaime Valera had once been head-waiter there and had married the owner's daughter. This made him permanent *maître d'hôtel*. When his father-in-law died, he became the owner in the eyes of the public. But his wife retained the purse strings and presided over the cash register.

(Perhaps I should add that he was *"Don* Jaime" to us because he was our *patrón;* he was not a *Don* to the public. The honorific *"Don"* will not translate into English, but owning a restaurant does not make a man a *Don*—but, for example, being a judge does.)

The first time Margrethe was seen to receive a tip, the *Señora* told her to turn it over—at the end of each week she would receive her percentage.

Margrethe came straight to me in the scullery. "Alec, what shall I do? Tips were my main income in the *Konge Knut* and no one ever asked me to share them. Can she do this to me?"

I told her not to turn her tips over to the *Señora* but to tell her that we would discuss it with her at the end of the day.

There is one advantage to being a *peón:* You don't get fired over a disagreement with your boss. Certainly we could be fired . . . but that would simply lose the Valeras some ten thousand pesos they had invested in us.

By the end of the day I knew exactly what to say and how to say it—how Margrethe must say it, as it was another month before I soaked up enough Spanish to maintain a minimum conversation:

"Sir and Madam, we do not understand this ruling about gifts to me. We want to see the judge and ask him what our contract requires."

As I had suspected, they were not willing to see the judge about it. They were legally entitled to Margrethe's service but they had no claim on money given to her by a third party.

This did not end it. *Señora* Valera was so angry at being balked by a mere waitress that she had a sign posted: NO PROPINAS—NO TIPS, and the same notice was placed in the menus.

Peones can't strike. But there were five other waitresses, two of them Amanda's daughters. The day *Señora* Valera ordered no tipping she found that she had just one waitress (Margrethe) and no one in the kitchen. She gave up. But I am sure she never forgave us.

Don Jaime treated us as employees; his wife treated us as slaves. Despite that old cliché about "wage slaves," there is a world of difference. Since we both tried hard to be faithful employees while paying off our debt but flatly refused to be slaves, we were bound to tangle with *Señora* Valera.

Shortly after the disagreement over tips Margrethe became convinced that the *Señora* was snooping in our bedroom. If true, there was no way to stop her; there was no lock for the door and she could enter our room without fear of being caught any day while we were working.

I gave some thought to boobytraps until Margrethe vetoed the idea. She simply thereafter kept her money on her person. But it was a measure of what we thought of our "patroness" that Margrethe considered it necessary to take precautions against her stealing from us.

We did not let *Señora* Valera spoil our happiness. And we did not let our dubious status as a "married" couple spoil our somewhat irregular honeymoon. Oh, I would have spoiled it because I always have had this unholy itch to analyze matters I really do not know how to analyze. But Margrethe is much more practical than I am and simply did not permit it. I tried to rationalize our relationship to her by pointing out that polygamy was not forbidden by Holy Writ but solely by modern law and custom—and she chopped me off briskly by saying that she had no interest in how many wives or concubines King Solomon had and did not regard him or any Old Testament character as a model for her own behavior. If I did not want to live with her, speak up! Say so!

I shut up. Some problems are best let be, not chewed

over with words. This modern compulsion to "talk it out" is a mistake at least as often as it is a solution.

But her disdain for Biblical authority concerning the legality of one man having two wives was so sharp that I asked her about it later—not about polygamy; I stayed away from that touchy subject; I asked her how she felt about the authority of Holy Writ in general. I explained that the church I was brought up in believed in strict interpretation—"A whole Bible, not a Bible full of holes"—Scripture was the literal word of God . . . but that I knew that other churches felt that the spirit rather than the letter ruled . . . some being so liberal that they hardly bothered with the Bible. Yet all of them called themselves Christian.

"Margrethe my love, as deputy executive secretary of Churches United for Decency I was in daily contact with members of every Protestant sect in the country and in liaison association with many Roman Catholic clerics on matters where we could join in a united front. I learned that my own church did not have a monopoly on virtue. A man could be awfully mixed up in religious fundamentals and still be a fine citizen and a devout Christian."

I chuckled as I recalled something and went on, "Or to put it in reverse, one of my Catholic friends, Father Mahaffey, told me that even I could squeeze into Heaven, because the Good Lord in His infinite wisdom made allowances for the ignorance and wrongheadedness of Protestants."

This conversation took place on a Tuesday, our day off, the one day a week the restaurant did not open, and in consequence we were on top of *el Cerro de la Nevería*—Icebox Hill, but it sounds better in Spanish—and just finishing a picnic lunch. This hill was downtown, close to Pancho Villa café, but was a bucolic oasis; the citizens had followed the Spanish habit of turning hills into parks rather than building on them. A happy place—

"My dear, I would never try to proselytize you into my church. But I do want to know as much about you as possible. I find that I don't know much about churches in Denmark. Mostly Lutheran, I think—but does Denmark have its own established state church like some other European nations? Either way, which church is yours, and is it strict interpretationist or liberal—and again, either way, how do *you* feel about it? And remember what Father Mahaffey said—I agree with him. I don't think that my church has the only door into Heaven."

I was lying stretched out; Margrethe was seated with her knees drawn up and holding them and was faced west, staring out to sea. This placed her with her face turned away from me. She did not answer my query. Presently I said gently, "My dear, did you hear me?"

"I heard you."

Again I waited, then added, "If I have been prying where I should not pry, I'm sorry and I withdraw the question."

"No. I knew that I would have to answer it some day. Alec, I am not a Christian." She let go her knees, swung around, and looked me in the eye. "You can have a divorce as simply as we married, just by telling me so. I won't fight it; I will go quietly away. But, Alec, when you told me that you loved me, then later when you told me that we were married in the eyes of God, you did not ask me my religion."

"Margrethe."

"Yes, Alec?"

"First, wash out your mouth. Then ask my pardon."

"There may be enough wine left in the bottle to rinse out my mouth. But I cannot ask pardon for not telling you this. I would have answered truthfully at any time. You did not ask."

"Wash out your mouth for talking about divorce. Ask my pardon for daring to think that I would ever divorce you under any circumstances whatever. If you are ever naughty enough, I may beat you. But I would never put you away. For richer, for poorer, in sickness and health, now and forever. Woman, I love you! Get that through your head."

Suddenly she was in my arms, weeping for only the second time, and I was doing the only thing possible, namely, kissing her.

I heard a cheer behind me and turned my head. We had had the top of the hill to ourselves, it being a work day for most people. But I found that we had an audience of two streetwise urchins, so young that sex was unclear. Catching my eye, one of them cheered again, then made loud kissing noises.

"Beat it!" I called out. "Scram! *Vaya con Dios!* Is that what I wanted to say, Marga?"

She spoke to them and they did go away, after more high giggles. I needed the interruption. I had said to Margrethe what had to be said because she needed immediate reassurance after her silly, gallant speech. But nevertheless I was shaken to my depths.

I started to speak, then decided that I had said enough for one day. But Margrethe said nothing, too; the silence grew painful. I felt that matters could not be left so, balanced uncertainly on edge. "What is your faith, dear one? Judaism? I do remember now that there are Jews in Denmark. Not all Danes are Lutheran."

"Some Jews, yes. But barely one in a thousand. No, Alec. Uh— There are older Gods."

"Older than Jehovah? Impossible."

Margrethe said nothing—characteristically. If she disagreed, she usually said nothing. She seemed to have no interest in winning arguments, in which she must differ from 99 percent of the human race . . . many of whom appear willing to suffer any disaster rather than lose an argument.

So I found myself having to conduct both sides to keep the argument from dying through lack of nourishment. "I retract that. I should not have said, 'Impossible.' I was speaking from the accepted chronology as given by

Bishop Ussher. If one accepts his dating, then the world was created five thousand nine hundred and ninety-eight years ago this coming October. Of course that dating is not itself a matter of Holy Writ; Hales arrived at a different figure, uh, seven thousand four hundred and five, I think—I do better when I write figures down. And other scholars get slightly different answers.

"But they all agree that some four or five thousand years before Christ occurred the unique event, Creation. At that point Jehovah created the world and, in so doing, created time. Time cannot exist alone. As a corollary, nothing and no one and no god can be older than Jehovah, since Jehovah created time. You see?"

"I wish I'd kept quiet."

"My dear! I am simply trying to have an intellectual discussion; I did not and do not and never do and never will intend to hurt you. I said that was the case by the orthodox way of dating. Clearly you are using another way. Will you explain it to me?—and not jump all over poor old Alex every time he opens his mouth? I was schooled as a minister in a church that emphasizes preaching; discussion comes as naturally to me as swimming does to fish. But now you preach and I'll listen. Tell me about these older gods."

"You know of them. The oldest and greatest we celebrate tomorrow; the middle day of each week is his."

"Today is Tuesday, tomorrow— Wednesday! *Wotan!* He is your God?"

"Odin. 'Wotan' is a German distortion of Old Norse. Father Odin and his two brothers created the world. In the beginning there was void, nothing—then the rest of it reads much like Genesis, even to Adam and Eve—but called Askr and Embla rather than Adam and Eve."

"Perhaps it *is* Genesis, Margrethe."

"What do you mean, Alec?"

"The Bible is the Word of God, in particular the English translation known as the King James version because every word of that translation was sustained by prayer and the best efforts of the world's greatest schol-ars—any difference in opinion was taken directly to the Lord in prayer. So the King James Bible *is* the Word of God.

"But nowhere is it written that this can be the only Word of God. A sacred writing of another race at another time in another language can also be inspired history . . . *if* it is compatible with the Bible. And that is what you have just described, is it not?"

"Ah, just on Creation and on Adam and Eve, Alec. The chronology does not match at all. You said that the world was created about six thousand years ago?"

"About. Hales makes it longer. The Bible does not give dates; dating is a modern invention."

"Even that longer time—Hales?—is much too short. A hundred thousand years would be more like it."

I started to expostulate—after all, some things are just too much to be swallowed—then remembered that I had warned myself not to say anything that could cause Mar-grethe to shut up. "Go on, dear. Do your religious writ-ings tell what happened during all those millennia?"

"Almost all of it happened before writing was invented. Some was preserved in epic poems sung by skalds. But even that did not start until men learned to live in tribes and Odin taught them to sing. The longest period was ruled by the frost giants before mankind was more than wild animals, hunted for sport. But the real difference in the chronology is this, Alec. The Bible runs from Creation to Judgment Day, then Millennium—the Kingdom on Earth—then the War in Heaven and the end of the world. After that is the Heavenly City and Eternity—time has stopped. Is that correct?"

"Well, yes. A professional eschatologist would find that overly simplified but you have correctly described the main outlines. The details are given in Revelations—the Revelation of Saint John the Divine, I should say. Many prophets have witnessed the final things but Saint John is the only one with the complete story . . . because Christ

Himself delivered the Revelation to John to stop the elect from being deceived by false prophets. Creation, the Fall from Grace, the long centuries of struggle and trial, then the final battle, followed by Judgment and the Kingdom. What does your faith say, my love?"

"The final battle we call Ragnarok rather than Armageddon—"

"I can't see that terminology matters."

"Please, dear. The name does not matter but what happens does. In your Judgment Day the goats are separated from the sheep. The saved go to eternal bliss; the damned go to eternal punishment. Correct?"

"Correct—while noting for purposes of scientific accuracy that some authorities assert that, while bliss is eternal, God so loves the world that even the damned may eventually be saved; no soul is utterly beyond redemption. Other theologians regard this as heresy—but it appeals to me; I have never liked the idea of eternal damnation. I'm a sentimentalist, my dear."

"I know you are, Alec, and I love you for it. You should find the old religion appealing . . . as it does not have eternal damnation."

"It does not?"

"No. At Ragnarok the world as we know it will be destroyed. But that is not the end. After a long time, a time of healing, a new universe will be created, one better and cleaner and free from the evils of this world. It too will last for countless millennia . . . until again the forces of evil and cold contend against the forces of goodness and light . . . and again there is a time of rest, followed by a new creation and another chance for men. Nothing is ever finished, nothing is ever perfect, but over and over again the race of men gets another chance to do better than last time, ever and again without end."

"And this you believe, Margrethe?"

"I find it easier to believe than the smugness of the saved and the desperate plight of the damned in the Christian faith. Jehovah is said to be all powerful. If this

is true, then the poor damned souls in Hell are there because Jehovah planned it that way in every minute detail. Is this not so?"

I hesitated. The logical reconciliation of Omnipotence,
Omniscience, and Omnibenevolence is the thorniest
problem in theology, one causing even Jesuits to break
their teeth. "Margrethe, some of the mysteries of the Almighty are not easily explained. We mortals must accept
Our Father's benevolent intention toward us, whether or
not we always understand His works."

"Must a baby understand God's benevolent intention
when his brains are dashed out against a rock? Does he
then go straight to Hell, praising the Lord for His infinite
Wisdom and Goodness?"

"Margrethe! What in the world are you talking about?"

"I am talking about places in the Old Testament in
which Jehovah gives direct orders to kill babies, sometimes ordering that they be killed by dashing them
against rocks. See that Psalm that starts 'By the rivers of
Babylon—' And see the word of the Lord Jehovah in
Hosea: 'their infants shall be dashed in pieces, and their
women with child shall be ripped up.' And there is the
case of Elisha and the bears. Alec, do you believe in your
heart that your God caused bears to tear up little children merely because they made fun of an old man's bald
head?" She waited.

And I waited. Presently she said, "Is that story of the
she bears and the forty-two children the literal Word of
God?"

"Certainly it's the Word of God! But I don't pretend to
understand it fully. Margrethe, if you want detailed explanations of everything the Lord has done, pray to Him
for enlightenment. But don't crowd me about it."

"I did not intend to crowd you, Alec. I'm sorry."

"No need to be. I've never understood about those
bears but I don't let it shake my faith. Perhaps it's a parable. But look, dear, doesn't your Father Odin have a
pretty bloody history Himself?"

"Not on the same scale. Jehovah destroyed city after city, every man, woman, and child, down to the youngest baby. Odin killed only in combat against opponents his own size. But, most important difference of all, Father Odin is *not* all powerful and does *not* claim to be all wise."

(A theology that avoids the thorniest problem— But how can you call Him "God" if He is not omnipotent?)

She went on, "Alec my only love, I don't want to attack your faith. I don't enjoy it and never intended to—and hope that nothing like it will ever happen again. But you did ask me point blank whether or not I accepted the authority of 'Holy Writ'—by which you mean your Bible. I must answer just as point blank. I do not. The Jehovah or Yahweh of the Old Testament seems to me to be a sadistic, bloodthirsty, genocidal villain. I cannot understand how He can be identified with the gentle Christ of the New Testament. Even through a mystic Trinity."

I started to answer but she hurried on. "Dear heart, before we leave this subject I must tell you something I have been thinking about. Does your religion offer an explanation of the weird thing that has happened to us? Once to me, twice to you—this changed world?"

(It had been endlessly on my mind, too!) "No. I must confess it. I wish I had a Bible to search for an explanation. But I have been searching in my mind. I haven't been able to find anything that should have prepared me for this." I sighed. "It's a bleak feeling. But—" I smiled at her. "—Divine Providence placed you with me. No land is strange to me that has Margrethe in it."

"Dear Alec. I asked because the old religion does offer an explanation."

"What?"

"Not a cheerful one. At the beginning of this cycle Loki was overcome—do you know Loki?"

"Some. The mischief maker."

"'Mischief' is too mild a word; he works evil. For thousands of years he has been a prisoner, chained to a great rock. Alec, the end of every cycle in the story of man begins the same way. Loki manages to escape his bonds . . . and chaos results."

She looked at me with great sadness. "Alec, I am sorry . . . but I do believe that Loki is loose. The signs show it. Now *anything* can happen. We enter the Twilight of the Gods. Ragnarok comes. Our world ends."

XII

And in the same hour was there a great earthquake,
and the tenth part of the city fell, and in the
earthquake were slain of men seven thousand:
and the remnant were affrighted, and gave glory
to the God of Heaven.
Revelation 11:13

I washed another lighthouse stack of dishes while I pondered the things Margrethe had said to me that beautiful afternoon on Icebox Hill—but I never again mentioned the subject to Margrethe. And she did not speak of it to me; as Margrethe never argued about anything if she could reasonably keep silent.

Did I believe her theory about Loki and Ragnarok? Of course not! Oh, I had no objection to calling Armageddon by the name "Ragnarok." Jesus or Joshua or Jesu; Mary or Miriam or Maryam or Maria, Jehovah or Yahweh— any verbal symbol will do as long as speaker and listener agree on meaning. But Loki? Ask me to believe that a mythical demigod of an ignorant, barbarian race has wrought changes in the whole universe? Now, really!

I am a modern man, with an open mind—but not so empty that the wind blows through it. Somewhere in Holy Writ lay a rational explanation for the upsets that had happened to us. I need not look to ghost stories of long-dead pagans for explanation.

I missed not having a Bible at hand. Oh, no doubt there were Catholic Bibles at the basilica three blocks away . . .

in Latin or in Spanish. I wanted the King James version. Again no doubt there were copies of it somewhere in this city—but I did not know where. For the first time in my life I envied the perfect memory of Preachin' Paul (Rev. Paul Balonius) who tramped up and down the central states the middle of last century, preaching the Word without carrying the Book with him. Brother Paul was reputed to be able to quote from memory any verse cited by book, chapter, and number of verse, or, conversely, correctly place by book, chapter, and number any verse read to him.

I was born too late to meet Preachin' Paul, so I never saw him do this—but perfect memory is a special gift God bestows not too infrequently; I have no reason to doubt that Brother Paul had it. Paul died suddenly, somewhat mysteriously, and possibly sinfully—in the words of my mission studies professor, one should exercise great prudence in praying alone with a married woman.

I don't have Paul's gift. I can quote the first few chapters of Genesis and several of the Psalms and the Christmas story according to Luke, and some other passages. But for today's problem I needed to study in exact detail *all* the prophets, especially the prophecy known as the Revelation of Saint John the Divine.

Was Armageddon approaching? Was the Second Coming at hand? Would I myself still be alive in the flesh when the great Trump sounds?

A thrilling thought, and not one to be discarded too quickly. Many millions will be alive on that great day; that mighty host could include Alexander Hergensheimer. Would I hear His Shout and see the dead rise up and then myself "be caught up together with them in the clouds, to meet the Lord in the air" and then ever be with the Lord, as promised? The most thrilling passage in the Great Book!

Not that I had any assurance that I myself would be among those saved on that great day, even if I lived in the flesh to that day. Being an ordained minister of the Gospel does not necessarily improve one's chances. Clergymen are aware of this cold truth (if they are honest with themselves) but laymen sometimes think that men of the cloth have an inside track.

Not true! For a clergyman, there are no excuses. He can never claim that "he didn't know it was loaded," or cite youth and inexperience as a reason to ask for mercy, or claim ignorance of the law, or any of the other many excuses by which a layman might show a touch less than moral perfection but still be saved.

Knowing this, I was forced to admit that my own record lately did not suggest that I was among the saved. Certainly, I was born again. Some people seem to think that this is a permanent condition, like a college degree. Brother, don't count on it! I was only too aware that I had racked up quite a number of sins lately: Sinful pride. Intemperance. Greed. Lechery. Adultery. Doubt. And others.

Worse yet, I felt no contrition for the very worst of these.

If the record did not show that Margrethe was saved and listed for Heaven, then I had no interest in going there myself. God help me, that was the truth.

I worried about Margrethe's immortal soul.

She could not claim the second chance of all pre-Christian Era souls. She had been born into the Lutheran Church, not my church but ancestor to my church, ancestor to all Protestant churches, the first fruit of the Diet of Worms. (When I was a lad in Sunday school, "Diet of Worms" inspired mind pictures quite foreign to theology!)

The only way Margrethe could be saved would be by renouncing her heresy and seeking to be born again. But she must do this herself; I could not do it for her.

The most I could possibly do would be to urge her to seek salvation. But I would have to do it most carefully. One does not persuade a butterfly to light on one's hand

by brandishing a sword. Margrethe was not a heathen ignorant of Christ and needing only to be instructed. No,
she had been born into Christianity and had rejected it,
eyes open. She could cite Scripture as readily as I
could—at some time she had studied the Book most dili-
gently, far more than most laymen. When and why I
never asked, but I think it must have been at the time
when she began to contemplate leaving the Christian
faith. Margrethe was so serious and so *good* that I felt
certain that she would never take such a drastic step
without long, hard study.

How urgent was the problem of Margrethe? Did I have
thirty years or so to learn her mind and feel out the best
approach? Or was Armageddon so close upon us that
even a day's delay could doom her for eternity?

The pagan Ragnarok and the Christian Armageddon
have this in common: The final battle will be preceded by
great signs and portents. Were we experiencing such
omens? Margrethe thought so. Myself, I found the idea
that this world changing presaged Armageddon more attractive than the alternative, i.e., paranoia on my part.
Could a ship be wrecked and a world changed just to
keep me from checking a thumbprint? I had thought so at
the time but—oh, come now, Alex, you are not that important.

(Or was I?)

I have never been a Millenarianist. I am aware how
often the number one thousand appears in the Bible, especially in prophecy—but I have never believed that the
Almighty was constrained to work in even millennia—or
any other numbering patterns—just to please numer-
ologists.

On the other hand I know that many thousands of sen-
sible and devout people place enormous importance on
the forthcoming end of the Second Millennium, with
Judgment Day and Armageddon and all that must follow—expected at that time. They find their proofs in the

Bible and claim confirmation in the lines in the Great Pyramid and in a variety of Apocrypha.

But they differ among themselves as to the end of the millennium. 2000 A.D.? Or 2001 A.D.? Or is the correct dating 3 p.m. Jerusalem local time April 7, 2030 A.D.? If indeed scholars have the time and date of the Crucifixion—and the earthquake at the moment of His death—correctly figured against mundane time reckoning. Or should it be Good Friday 2030 A.D. as calculated by the lunar calendar? This is no trivial matter in view of what we are attempting to date.

But, if we take the birth of Christ rather than the date of the Crucifixion as the starting point from which to count the millennia, it is evident at once that neither the naive date of 2000 A.D. nor the slightly less naive date of 2001 can be the bimillenarian date *because Jesus was born in Bethlehem on Christmas Day year 5 B.C.*

Every educated person knows this and almost no one ever thinks about it.

How could the greatest event in all history, the birth of our Lord Incarnate, have been misdated by five years? Incredible!

Very easily. A sixth-century monk made a mistake in arithmetic. Our present dating ("Anno Domini") was not used until centuries after Christ was born. Anyone who has ever tried to decipher on a cornerstone a date written in Roman numerals can sympathize with the error of Brother Dionysius Exiguus. In the sixth century there were so few who could read at all that the error went undetected for many years—and by then it was too late to change all the records. So we have the ludicrous situation that Christ was born five years before Christ was born—an Irishism that can be resolved only by noting that one clause refers to fact and the other clause refers to a false-to-fact calendar.

For two thousand years the good monk's error was of little importance. But now it becomes of supreme importance. If the Millenarianists are correct, the end of the world can be expected *Christmas Day this year.*

Please note that I did not say "December 25th." The day and month of Christ's birth are unknown. Matthew notes that Herod was king; Luke states that Augustus was Caesar and that Cyrenius was governor of Syria, and we all know that Joseph and Mary had traveled from Nazareth to Bethlehem to be counted and taxed.

There are no other data, neither of Holy Writ nor of Roman civil records.

So there you have it. By Millenarianist theory the Final Judgment can be expected about thirty-five years from now . . . or later this afternoon!

Were it not for Margrethe this uncertainty would not keep me awake nights. But how can I sleep if my beloved is in immediate danger of being cast down into the Bottomless Pit, there to suffer throughout eternity?

What would *you* do?

Envision me standing barefooted on a greasy floor, washing dishes to pay off my indenture, while thinking deep thoughts of last and first things. A laughable sight! But dishwashing does not occupy all the mind; I was better off with hard bread for the mind to chew on.

Sometimes I contrasted my sorry state with what I had so recently been, while wondering if I would ever find my way back through the maze into the place I had built for myself.

Would I want to go back? Abigail was there—and, while polygamy was acceptable in the Old Testament, it was not accepted in the forty-six states. That had been settled once and for all when the Union Army's artillery had destroyed the temple of the antichrist in Salt Lake City and the Army had supervised the breaking up and diaspora of those immoral "families."

Giving up Margrethe for Abigail would be far too high a price to pay to resume the position of power and importance I had until recently held. Yet I had enjoyed my work and the deep satisfaction over worthwhile accomplishment that went with it. We had achieved our best year since the foundation was formed—I refer to the nonprofit corporation Churches United for Decency. "Nonprofit" does not mean that such an organization cannot pay appropriate salaries and even bonuses, and I had been taking a well-earned vacation after the best fundraising year of our history—primarily my accomplishment because, as deputy director, my first duty was to see that our coffers were kept filled.

But I took even greater satisfaction in our labors in the vineyards, as fund raising means nothing if our programs of spiritual welfare do not meet their goals.

The past year had seen the following positive accomplishments:

a) A federal law making abortion a capital offense;

b) A federal law making the manufacture, sale, possession, importation, transportation, and/or use of any contraceptive drug or device a felony carrying a mandatory prison sentence of not less than a year and a day but not more than twenty years for each offense—and eliminating the hypocritical subterfuge of "For Prevention of Disease Only";

c) A federal law that, while it did not abolish gambling, did make the control and licensing of it a federal jurisdiction. One step at a time—having built this foundation we could tackle those twin pits, Nevada and New Jersey, piece by piece. Divide and conquer!

d) A Supreme Court decision in which we had appeared as *amicus curiae* under which community standards of the typical or median-population community applied to all cities of each state (Tomkins v. Allied News Distributors);

e) Real progress in our drive to get tobacco defined as a prescription drug through the tactical device of separating snuff and chewing tobacco from the problem by inaugurating the definition "substances intended for burning and inhaling";

f) Progress at our annual national prayer meeting on several subjects in which I was interested. One was the matter of how to remove the tax-free status of any private school not affiliated with a Christian sect. Policy on this was not yet complete because of the thorny matter of Roman Catholic schools. Should our umbrella cover them? Or was it time to strike? Whether the Catholics were allies or enemies was always a deep problem to those of us out on the firing line.

At least as difficult was the Jewish problem—was a humane solution possible? If not, then what? Should we grasp the nettle? This was debated only *in camera*.

Another matter was a pet project of my own: the frustrating of astronomers. Few laymen realize what mischief astronomers are up to. I first noticed it when I was still in engineering school and took a course in descriptive astronomy under the requirements for breadth in each student's program. Give an astronomer a bigger telescope and turn him loose, leave him unsupervised, and the first thing he does is to come down with pestiferous, half-baked guesses denying the ancient truths of Genesis.

There is only one way to deal with this sort of nonsense: Hit them in the pocketbook! Redefine "educational" to exclude those colossal white elephants, astronomical observatories. Make the Naval Observatory the only one tax free, reduce its staff, and limit their activity to matters clearly related to navigation. (Some of the most blasphemous and subversive theories have come from tenured civil servants there who don't have enough legitimate work to keep them busy.)

Self-styled "scientists" are usually up to no good, but astronomers are the worst of the lot.

Another matter that comes up regularly at each annual prayer meeting I did not favor spending time or money on: "Votes for Women." These hysterical females styling themselves "suffragettes" are not a threat, can never win, and it just makes them feel self-important to pay attention to them. They should not be jailed and should not be displayed in stocks—never let them be martyrs! Ignore them.

There were other interesting and worthwhile goals that I kept off the agenda and did not suffer to be brought up from the floor in the sessions I moderated, but instead carried them on my "Maybe next year" list:

Separate schools for boys and girls.

Restoring the death penalty for witchcraft and satanism.

The Alaska option for the Negro problem.

Federal control of prostitution.

Homosexuals—what's the answer? Punishment? Surgery? Other?

There are endless good causes commending themselves to guardians of the public morals—the question is always how to pick and choose to the greater glory of God.

But all of these issues, fascinating as they are, I might never again pursue. A sculleryman who is just learning the local language (ungrammatically, I feel sure!) is not able to be a political force. So I did not worry about such matters and concentrated on my real problems: Margrethe's heresy and, more immediate but less important, getting legally free of peonage and going north.

We had served more than one hundred days when I asked *Don* Jaime to help me work out the exact date when we would have discharged the terms of our debt contract—a polite way of saying: Dear Boss, come the day, we are going to leave here like a scared rabbit. Plan on it.

I had figured on a total obligated time of one hundred and twenty-one days . . . and *Don* Jaime shocked me almost out of my Spanish by getting a result of one hundred and fifty-eight days.

More than six weeks to go when I figured that we would be free next week!

I protested, pointing out that our total obligation as listed by the court, divided by the auction value placed on our services (pesos sixty for Margrethe, half that for me, for each day), gave one hundred twenty-one days . . . of which we had served one hundred fifteen.

Not a hundred and fifteen—ninety-nine—he handed me a calendar and invited me to count. It was at that point that I discovered that our lovely Tuesdays did not reduce our committed time. Or so said our *patrón*.

"And besides that, Alexandro," he added, "you have failed to figure the interest on the unpaid balance; you haven't multiplied by the inflation factor; you haven't allowed for taxes, or even your contribution for Our Lady of Sorrows. If you fall ill, I should support you, eh?"

(Well, yes. While I had not thought about it, I did think a *patrón* had that duty toward his *peones.) "Don* Jaime, the day you bid in our debts, the clerk of the court figured the contract for me. He told me our obligation was one hundred and twenty-one days. He told me!"

"Then go talk to the clerk of the court about it." *Don* Jaime turned his back on me.

That chilled me. *Don* Jaime seemed as willing for me to take it up with the referee authority as he had been unwilling to discuss Margrethe's tips with the court. To me this meant that he had handled enough of these debt contracts to be certain how they worked and thus had no fear that the judge or his clerk might rule against him.

I was not able to speak with Margrethe about it in private until that night. "Marga, how could I be so mistaken about this? I thought the clerk worked it out for us before he had us countersign the assignment of debt. One hundred and twenty-one days. Right?"

She did not answer me at once. I persisted, "Isn't that what you told me?"

"Alec, despite the fact that I now usually think in English—or in Spanish, lately—when I must do arithmetic, I work it in Danish. The Danish word for sixty is *'tres'*— and that is also the Spanish word for three. Do you see how easily I could get mixed up? I don't know now whether I said to you, *'Ciento y veintiuno'* or *'Ciento y sesentiuno'*—because I remember numbers in Danish, not in English, not in Spanish. I thought you did the division yourself."

"Oh, I did. Certainly the clerk didn't say, 'A hundred and twenty-one.' He didn't use any English that I recall. And at that time I did not know any Spanish. *Señor* Muñoz explained it to you and you translated for me and later I did the arithmetic again and it seemed to confirm what he had said. Or you had said. Oh, shucks, I don't know!"

"Then why don't we forget it until we can ask *Señor* Muñoz?"

"Marga, doesn't it upset you to find that we are going to have to slave away in this dump an extra five weeks?"

"Yes, but not very much. Alec, I've always had to work. Working aboard ship was harder work than teaching school—but I got to travel and see strange places. Waiting tables here is a little harder than cleaning rooms in the *Konge Knut*—but I have you with me here and that more than makes up for it. I want to go with you to your homeland . . . but it's not my homeland, so I'm not as eager to leave here as you are. To me, today, where you are is my homeland."

"Darling, you are so logical and reasonable and civilized that you sometimes drive me right straight up the wall."

"Alec, I don't mean to do that. I just want us to stop worrying about it until we can see *Señor* Muñoz. But right this minute I want to rub your back until you relax."

"Madame, you've convinced me! But only if I have the privilege of rubbing your poor tired feet before you rub my back."

We did both. "Ah, wilderness were paradise enow!"

Beggars can't be choosy. I got up early the next morning, saw the clerk's runner, was told that I could not see
the clerk until court adjourned for the day, so I made a
semi-appointment for close-of-court on Tuesday—"semi"
in that we were committed to show up; *Señor* Muñoz was
not. (But would be there, *Deus volent*.)

So on Tuesday we went on our picnic outing as usual,
as we could not see *Señor* Muñoz earlier than about 4
p.m. But we were Sunday-go-to-meeting rather than
dressed for a picnic—meaning that we both wore our
shoes, both had had baths that morning, and I had
shaved, and I wore my best clothes, handed down from
Don Jaime but clean and fresh, rather than the tired
Coast Guard work pants I wore in the scullery. Margrethe
wore the colorful outfit she had acquired our first day in
Mazatlán.

Then we both endeavored not to get too sweaty or
dusty. Why we thought it mattered I cannot say. But
somehow each of us felt that propriety called for one's
best appearance in visiting a court.

As usual we walked over to the fountain to see our
friend Pepe before swinging back to climb our hill. He
greeted us in the intimate mode of friends and we exchanged graceful amenities of the sort that fit so well in
Spanish and are almost never encountered in English.
Our weekly visit with Pepe had become an important
part of our social life. We knew more about him now—
from Amanda, not from him—and I respected him more
than ever.

Pepe had not been born without legs (as I had once
thought); he had formerly been a teamster, driving lorries over the mountains to Durango and beyond. Then
there had been an accident and Pepe had been pinned
under his rig for two days before he was rescued. He was
brought in to Our Lady of Sorrows apparently D.O.A.

Pepe was tougher than that. Four months later he was
released from hospital; someone passed the hat to buy

him his little cart; he received his mendicant's license, and he took up his pitch by the fountain—friend to streetwalkers, friend to *Dons*, and a merry grin for the worst that fate could hand him.

When, after a decent interval for conversation and inquiries as to health and welfare and that of mutual acquaintances, we turned to leave, I offered our friend a one-peso note.

He handed it back. "Twenty-five centavos, my friend. Do you not have change? Or did you wish me to make change?"

"Pepe our friend, it was our intention and our wish that you keep this trivial gift."

"No no no. From tourists I take their teeth and ask for more. From you, my friend, twenty-five centavos."

I did not argue. In Mexico a man has his dignity, or he is dead.

El Cerro de la Nevería is one hundred meters high; we climbed it very slowly, with me hanging back because I wanted to be certain not to place any strain on Margrethe. From signs I was almost certain that she was in a family way. But she had not seen fit to discuss it with me and of course I could not raise the subject if she did not.

We found our favorite place, where we enjoyed shade from a small tree but nevertheless had a full view all around, three hundred and sixty degrees—northwest into the Gulf of California, west into the Pacific and what might or might not be clouds on the horizon capping a peak at the tip of Baja California two hundred miles away, southwest along our own peninsula to *Cerro Vigía* (Lookout Hill) with beautiful *Playa de las Olas Altas* between us and *Cerro Vigía*, then beyond it *Cerro Creston*, the site of the giant lighthouse, the *"Faro"* itself commanding the tip of the peninsula—south right across town to the Coast Guard landing. On the east and northeast were the mountains that concealed Durango a hundred and fifty miles away . . . but today the air was so clear that it felt as if we could reach out and touch those peaks.

Mazatlán was spread out below like a toy village. Even the basilica looked like an architect's scale model from up here, rather than a most imposing church—for the umpteenth time I wondered how the Catholics, with their (usually) poverty-stricken congregations, could build such fine churches while their Protestant opposite numbers had such a time raising the mortgages on more modest structures.

"Look, Alec!" said Margrethe. "Anibal and Roberto have their new *aeroplano!*" She pointed.

Sure enough, there were now *two aeroplanos* at the Coast Guard mooring. One was the grotesque giant dragonfly that had rescued us; the new one was quite different. At first I thought it had sunk at its moorings; the floats on which the older craft landed on the water were missing from this structure.

Then I realized that this new craft was literally a flying boat. The body of the *aeroplano* itself was a float, or a boat—a watertight structure. The propelling engines of this craft were mounted above the wings.

I was not sure that I trusted these radical changes. The homely certainties of the craft we had ridden in were more to my taste.

"Alec, let's go call on them next Tuesday."

"All right."

"Do you suppose that Anibal would possibly offer us a ride in his new *aeroplano?*"

"Not if the Commandant knows about it." I did not say that the newfangled rig did not look safe to me; Margrethe was always fearless. "But we'll call on them and ask to see it. Lieutenant Anibal will like that. Roberto, too. Let's eat."

"Piggy piggy," she answered, and spread out a *servilleta,* started covering it with food from a basket I had carried. Tuesdays gave Margrethe an opportunity to vary Amanda's excellent Mexican cooking with her own

Danish and international cooking. Today she had elected to make Danish open-face sandwiches so much enjoyed by all Danes—and by anyone else who has ever had a chance to enjoy them. Amanda allowed Margrethe to do what she liked in the kitchen, and *Señora* Valera did not interfere—she never came into the kitchen, under some armed truce arrived at before we joined the staff. Amanda was a woman of firm character.

Today's sandwiches featured heavily the tender, tasty shrimp for which Mazatlán is famous, but the shrimp were just a starter. I remember ham, turkey, crumbled crisp bacon, mayonnaise, three sorts of cheese, several sorts of pickle, little peppers, unidentified fish, thin slices of beef, fresh tomato, tomato paste, three sorts of lettuce, what I think was deep-fried eggplant. But thank goodness it is not necessary to understand food in order to enjoy it—Margrethe placed it in front of me; I happily chomped away, whether I knew what I was eating or not.

An hour later I was belching and pretending not to. "Margrethe, have I told you today that I love you?"

"Yes, but not lately."

"I do. You are not only beautiful, fair to see and of gainly proportions, you are also a fine cook."

"Thank you, sir."

"Do you wish to be admired for your intellectual excellence as well?"

"Not necessarily. No."

"As you wish. If you change your mind, let me know. Quit fiddling with the remnants; I'll tidy up later. Lie down here beside me and explain to me why you continue to live with me. It can't be for my cooking. Is it because I am the best dishwasher on the west coast of Mexico?"

"Yes." She went right on tidying things, did not stop until our picnic site was perfectly back in order, with all that was left back in the basket, ready to be returned to Amanda.

Then she lay down beside me, slid her arm under my neck—then raised her head. "What's that?"

"What's—" Then I heard it. A distant rumble increasing in volume, like a freight train coming 'round the bend. But the nearest railway, the line north to Chihuahua and south to Guadalajara, was distant, beyond the peninsula of Mazatlán.

The rumble grew louder; the ground started to sway. Margrethe sat up. "Alec, I'm frightened."

"Don't be afraid, dear; I'm here." I reached up and pulled her down to me, held her tight while the solid ground bounced up and down under us and the roaring rumble increased to unbelievable volume.

If you've ever been in an earthquake, even a small one, you know what we were feeling better than my words can say. If you have never been in one, you won't believe me—and the more accurately I describe it, the more certain you are not to believe me.

The worst part about a quake is that there is nothing solid to cling to anywhere . . . but the most startling thing is the noise, the infernal racket of every sort—the crash of rock grinding together under you, the ripping, rending sounds of buildings being torn apart, the screams of the frightened, the cries of the hurt and the lost, the howling and wailing of animals caught by disaster beyond their comprehension.

And none of it will stop.

This went on for an endless time—then the main earthquake hit us and the city fell down.

I could hear it. The noise that could not increase suddenly doubled. I managed to get up on one elbow and look. The dome of the basilica broke like a soap bubble. "Oh, Marga, look! No, don't—this is terrible."

She half sat up, said nothing and her face was blank. I kept my arm around her and looked down the peninsula past *Cerro Vigía* and at the lighthouse.

It was leaning.

While I watched it broke about halfway up, then slowly and with dignity collapsed to the ground.

Past the city I caught sight of the moored *aeroplanos* of the Coast Guard. They were dancing around in a frenzy; the new one dipped one wing; the water caught it—then I lost sight of it as a cloud rose up from the city, a cloud of dust from thousands and thousands of tons of shattered masonry.

I looked for the restaurant, and found it: EL RESTAU-RANTE PANCHO VILLA. Then while I watched, the wall on which the sign was painted crumpled and fell into the street. Dust rose up and concealed where it had been.

"Margrethe! It's gone. The restaurant. El Pancho Villa." I pointed.

"I don't see anything."

"It's gone, I tell you. Destroyed. Oh, thank the Lord that Amanda and the girls were not there today!"

"Yes. Alec, won't it ever stop?"

Suddenly it did stop—much more suddenly than it started. Miraculously the dust was gone; there was no racket, no screams of the hurt and dying, no howls of animals.

The lighthouse was back where it belonged.

I looked to the left of it, checking on the moored *aeroplanos*—nothing. Not even the driven piles to which they should be tied. I looked back at the city—all serene. The basilica was unhurt, beautiful. I looked for the Pancho Villa sign.

I could not find it. There was a building on what seemed the proper corner, but its shape was not quite right and it had different windows. "Marg— Where's the restaurant?"

"I don't know. Alec, what is happening?"

"They're at it again," I said bitterly. "The world changers. The earthquake is over but this is not the city we were in. It looks a lot like it but it's not the same."

I was only half right. Before we could make up our

minds to start down the hill, the rumble started up again. Then the swaying . . . then the greatly increased noise and violent movement of the land, and *this* city was destroyed. Again I saw our towering lighthouse crack and fall. Again the church fell in on itself. Again the dust clouds rose and with it the screams and howls.

I raised my clenched fist and shook it at the sky. "God damn it! *Stop!* Twice is too much."

I was not blasted.

XIII

*I have seen all the works that are done under the sun; and,
behold, all is vanity and vexation of the spirit.*
Ecclesiastes 1:14

I am going to skip over the next three days, for there
was nothing good about them. "There was blood in the
streets and dust." Survivors, those of us who were not
hurt, not prostrate with grief, not dazed or hysterical
beyond action—few of us, in short—worked at the rubble
here and there trying to find living creatures under the
bricks and stones and plaster. But how much can you do
with your naked fingers against endless tons of rock?

And how much can you do when you do dig down and
discover that you were too late, that indeed it was too
late before you started? We heard this mewling, something like a kitten, so we dug most carefully, trying not to
put any pressure on whatever was underneath, trying not
to let the stones we shifted dislodge anything that would
cause more grief underneath—and found the source. An
infant, freshly dead. Pelvis broken, one side of its head
bashed. "Happy shall he be, that taketh and dasheth thy
little ones against the stones." I turned my head away
and threw up. Never will I read Psalm 137 again.

That night we spent on the lower slopes of Icebox Hill.
When the sun went down, we perforce stopped trying.
Not only did the darkness make it impossible to work but
there was looting going on. I had a deep conviction that
any looter was a potential rapist and murderer. I was

prepared to die for Margrethe should it become necessary—but I had no wish to die gallantly but futilely, in a
confrontation that could have been avoided.

Early the following afternoon the Mexican Army arrived. We had accomplished nothing useful in the meantime—more of the same picking away at rubble. Never
mind what we found. The soldiers put a stop even to that;
all civilians were herded back up the peninsula, away
from the ruined city, to the railroad station across the
river. There we waited—new widows, husbands freshly
bereaved, lost children, injured on make-do stretchers,
walking wounded, some with no marks on them but with
empty eyes and no speech. Margrethe and I were of the
lucky ones; we were merely hungry, thirsty, dirty, and
covered with bruises from head to foot from lying on the
ground during the earthquake. Correction: during two
earthquakes.

Had anyone else experienced *two* earthquakes?

I hesitated to ask. I seemed to be the unique observer to
this world-changing—save that, twice, Margrethe had
come with me because I was holding her at the instant.
Were there other victims around? Had there been others
in *Konge Knut* who had kept their mouths shut about it as
carefully as I had? How do you ask? Excuse me, amigo,
but is this the same city it was yesterday?

When we had waited at the railroad station about two
hours an army water cart came through—a tin cup of
water to each refugee and a soldier with a bayonet to enforce order in the queues.

Just before sundown the cart came back with more
water and with loaves of bread; Margrethe and I were
rationed a quarter of a loaf between us. A train backed
into the station about then and the army people started
loading it even as supplies were being unloaded. Marga
and I were lucky; we were pushed into a passenger car—
most rode in freight cars.

The train started north. We weren't asked whether or

not we wanted to go north; we weren't asked for money for fares; all of Mazatlán was being evacuated. Until its water system could be restored, Mazatlán belonged to the rats and the dead.

No point in describing the journey. The train moved; we endured. The railway line leaves the coast at Guaymas and goes straight north across Sonora to Arizona—beautiful country but we were in no shape to appreciate it. We slept as much as we could and pretended to sleep the rest of the time. Every time the train stopped, some left it—unless the police herded them back on. By the time we reached Nogales, Sonora, the train was less than half full; the rest seemed headed for Nogales, Arizona, and of course we were.

We reached the international gate early afternoon three days after the quake.

We were herded into a detention building just over the line, and a man in a uniform made a speech in Spanish: "Welcome, amigos! The United States is happy to help its neighbors in their time of trial and the U.S. Immigration Service has streamlined its procedures so that we can take care of all of you quickly. First we must ask you all to go through delousing. Then you'll be issued green cards outside of quota so that you can work at any job anywhere in the States. But you will find labor agents to help you as you leave the compound. And a soup kitchen! If you are hungry, stop and have your first meal here as guests of Uncle Sam. Welcome to *los Estados Unidos!*"

Several people had questions to ask but Margrethe and I headed for the door that led to the delousing setup. I resented the name assigned to this sanitary routine—a requirement that you take delousing is a way of saying that you are lousy. Dirty and mussed we certainly were, and I had a three-day beard. But lousy?

Well, perhaps we were. After a day of picking through the ruins and two days crowded in with other unwashed in a railroad car that was not too clean when we boarded it, could I honestly assert that I was completely free of vermin?

Delousing wasn't too bad. It was mostly a supervised shower bath with exhortations in Spanish to scrub the hairy places thoroughly with a medicated soft soap. In the meantime my clothes went through some sort of sterilization or fumigation—autoclave, I think—then I had to wait, bare naked, for twenty minutes to reclaim them, while I grew more and more angry with each passing minute.

But once I was dressed again, I got over my anger, realizing that no one was intentionally pushing me around; it was simply that any improvised procedure for handling crowds of people in an emergency is almost certain to be destructive of human dignity. (The Mexican refugees seemed to find it offensive; I heard mutterings.)

Then again I had to wait, for Margrethe.

She came out the exit door from the distaff side, caught my eye, and smiled, and suddenly everything was all right. How could she come out of a delousing chamber and look as if she had just stepped out of a bandbox?

She came up to me and said, "Did I keep you waiting, dear? I'm sorry. There was an ironing board in there and I seized the chance to touch up my dress. It looked a sorry sight when it came out of the washer."

"I didn't mind waiting," I fibbed. "You're beautiful." (No fib!) "Shall we go to dinner? Soup kitchen dinner, I'm afraid."

"Isn't there some paper work we have to go through?"

"Oh. I think we can hit the soup kitchen first. We don't want green cards; they are for Mexican nationals. Instead I must explain about our lost passports." I had worked this out in my head and had explained it to Margrethe on the train. This is what I would say had happened to us: We were tourists, staying in *Hotel de las Olas Altas* on the beach. When the earthquake hit, we were on the beach. So we lost our clothes, our money, our passports, everything, as our hotel had been destroyed. We were lucky to be alive, and the clothes we were wearing had been given to us by Mexican Red Cross.

This story had two advantages: *Hotel de las Olas Altas* had indeed been destroyed, and the rest of the story had no easy way to be checked.

I found that we had to go through the green-card queue in order to reach the soup kitchen. Eventually we got as far as the table. A man there shoved a file card in front of me, saying in Spanish: "Print your name, last name first. List your address. If it was destroyed in the quake, say so, and give some other address—cousin, father, priest, somebody whose home was not destroyed."

I started my spiel. The functionary looked up and said, "Amigo, you're holding up the line."

"But," I said, "I don't need a green card. I don't want a green card. I'm an American citizen returning from abroad and I'm trying to explain why I don't have my passport. And the same for my wife."

He drummed on the table, "Look," he said, "your accent says that you're native American. But I can't do anything about your lost passport and I've got three hundred and fifty refugees still to process, and another trainload just pulling in. I won't get to bed before two. Why don't you do us both a favor and accept a green card? It won't poison you and it'll get you in. Tomorrow you can fight with the State Department about your passport—but not with me. Okay?"

I'm stupid but not stubborn. "Okay." For my Mexican accommodation address I listed *Don* Jaime; I figured he owed me that much. His address had the advantage of being in another universe.

The soup kitchen was what you would expect from a charity operation. But it was gringo cooking, the first I had had in months—and we were hungry. The Stark's Delicious apple I had for dessert was indeed delicious. It was still short of sundown when we were out on the

streets of Nogales—free, bathed, fed, and inside the
United States legally or almost. We were at least a thousand percent better off than those two naked survivors
who had been picked up out of the ocean seventeen weeks
ago.

But we were still orphans of fate, no money at all, no
place to rest, no clothes but those we were wearing, and
my three-day beard and the shape my clothes were in
after going through an autoclave or whatever made me
look like a skid row derelict.

The no-money situation was particularly annoying because we *did* have money, Margrethe's hoarded tips. But
the paper money said *"Reino"* where it should have read
"República" and the coins did not have the right faces.
Some of the coins may have contained enough silver to
have some minor intrinsic value. But, if so, there was no
easy way to cash it in at once. And any attempt to spend
any of this money would simply get us into major trouble.

How much had we lost? There are no interuniversal exchange rates. One might make a guess in terms of equivalent purchasing power—so many dozens of eggs, or so
many kilos of sugar. But why bother? Whatever it was,
we had lost it.

This paralleled a futility I had run into in Mazatlán. I
had attempted, while lord of the scullery, to write to a)
Alexander Hergensheimer's boss, the Reverend Dr.
Dandy Danny Dover, D.D., director of Churches United
for Decency, and b) Alec Graham's lawyers in Dallas.

Neither letter was answered; neither came back. Which
was what I had expected, as neither Alec nor Alexander
came from a world having flying machines, *aeroplanos*.

I would try both again—but with small hope; I already
knew that this world would feel strange both to Graham
and to Hergensheimer. How? Nothing that I had noticed
until we reached Nogales. But here, in that detention
hall, was (hold tight to your chair) *television*. A handsome
big box with a window in one side, and in that window

living pictures of people . . . and sounds coming out of it of those selfsame people talking.

Either you have this invention and are used to it and take it for granted, or you live in a world that does not have it—and you don't believe me. Learn from me, as I have been forced to believe unbelievable things. There *is* such an invention; there is a world where it is as common as bicycles, and its name is television—or sometimes teevee or telly or video or even "idiot box"—and if you were to hear some of the purposes for which this great wonder is used, you would understand the last tag.

If you ever find yourself flat broke in a strange city and no one to turn to, and you do not want to turn yourself in at a police station and don't want to be mugged, there is just one best answer for emergency help. You will usually find it in the city's tenderloin, near skid row:

The Salvation Army.

Once I laid hands on a telephone book it took me no time at all to get the address of the Salvation Army mission (although it did take me a bit of time to recognize a telephone when I saw one—warning to interworld travelers: Minor changes can be even more confusing than major changes).

Twenty minutes and one wrong turn later Margrethe and I were at the mission. Outside on the sidewalk four of them—French horn, big drum, two tambourines—were gathering a crowd. They were working on "Rock of Ages" and doing well, but they needed a baritone and I was tempted to join them.

But a couple of store fronts before we reached the mission Margrethe stopped and plucked at my sleeve. "Alec . . . must we do this?"

"Eh? What's the trouble, dear? I thought we had agreed."

"No, sir. You simply told me."

"Mmm— Perhaps I did. You don't want to go to the Salvation Army?"

She took a deep breath and sighed it out. "Alec . . . I have not been inside a church since—since I left the Lutheran Church. To go to one now— I think it would be sinful."

(Dear Lord, what can I do with this child? She is apostate not because she is heathen . . . but because her rules are even more strict than Yours. Guidance, please—and do hurry it up!) "Sweetheart, if it feels sinful to you, we won't do it. But tell me what we are to do now; I've run out of ideas."

"Ah— Alec, are there not other institutions to which a person in distress may turn?"

"Oh, certainly. In a city this size the Roman Catholic Church is bound to have more than one refuge. And there will be other Protestant ones. Probably a Jewish one. And—"

"I meant, 'Not connected with a church.'"

"Ah, so. Margrethe, we both know that this is not really my home country; you probably know as much about how it works as I do. There may be refuges for the homeless here that are totally unconnected with a church. I'm not sure, as churches tend to monopolize the field—nobody else wants it. If it were early in the day instead of getting dark, I would try to find something called united charities or community chest or the equivalent, and look over the menu; there might be something. But now— Finding a policeman and asking for help is the only other thing I can think of this time of day . . . and I can tell you ahead of time what a cop in this part of town would do if you told him you had nowhere to sleep. He would point you toward the mission right there. Old Sal."

"In København—or Stockholm or Oslo—I would go straight to the main police station. You just ask for a place to sleep; they give it to you."

"I have to point out that this is not Denmark or Sweden or Norway. Here they might let us stay—by locking me in the drunk tank and locking you up in the holding pen for prostitutes. Then tomorrow morning we might or might not be charged with vagrancy. I don't know."

"Is America really so evil?"

"I don't know, dear—this isn't my America. But I don't want to find out the hard way. Sweetheart . . . if I *worked* for whatever they give us, could we spend a night with the Salvation Army without your feeling sinful about it?"

She considered it solemnly—Margrethe's greatest lack was a total absence of sense of humor. Good nature—loads. A child's delight in play, yes. Sense of humor? "Life is real and life is earnest—"

"Alec, if that can be arranged, I would not feel wrong in entering. I will work, too."

"Not necessary, dear; it will be my profession that is involved. When they finish feeding the derelicts tonight, there will be a high stack of dirty dishes—and you are looking at the heavyweight champion dishwasher in all of Mexico and *los Estados Unidos.*"

So I washed dishes. I also helped spread out hymn-books and set up the evening services. And I borrowed a safety razor and a blade from Brother Eddie McCaw, the adjutant. I told him how we happened to be there—vacationing on the Mexican Riviera, sunbathing on the beach when the big one hit—all the string of lies I had prepared for the Immigration Service and hadn't been able to use. "Lost it all. Cash, travelers checks, passports, clothes, ticket home, the works. But just the same, we were lucky. We're alive."

"The Lord had His arms around you. You tell me that you are born again?"

"Years back."

"It will do our lost sheep good to rub shoulders with you. When it comes time for witnessing, will you tell them all about it? You're the first eyewitness. Oh, we felt it here but it just rattled the dishes."

"Glad to."

"Good. Let me get you that razor."

So I witnessed and gave them a truthful and horrendous description of the quake, but not as horrid as it really was—I never want to see another rat—or another dead baby—and I thanked the Lord publicly that Margrethe and I had not been hurt and found that it was the most sincere prayer I had said in years.

The Reverend Eddie asked that roomful of odorous outcasts to join him in a prayer of thanks that Brother and Sister Graham had been spared, and he made it a good rousing prayer that covered everything from Jonah to the hundredth sheep, and drew shouts of *"Amen!"* from around the room. One old wino came forward and said that he had at last seen God's grace and God's mercy and he was now ready to give his life to Christ.

Brother Eddie prayed over him, and invited others to come forward and two more did—a natural evangelist, he saw in our story a theme for his night's sermon and used it, hanging it on Luke fifteen, ten, and Matthew six, nineteen. I don't know that he had prepared from those two verses—probably not, as any preacher worth his salt can preach endlessly from either one of them. Either way, he could think on his feet and he made good use of our unplanned presence.

He was pleased with us, and I am sure that is why he told me, as we were cleaning up for the night, after the supper that followed the service, that while of course they didn't have separate rooms for married couples— they didn't often get married couples—still, it looked like Sister Graham would be the only one in the sisters' dormitory tonight, so why didn't I doss down in there instead of in the men's dormitory? No double bed, just stacked bunks—sorry! But at least we could be in the same room.

I thanked him and we happily went to bed. Two people can share a very narrow bed if they really want to sleep together.

The next morning Margrethe cooked breakfast for the

derelicts. She went into the kitchen and volunteered and soon was doing it all as the regular cook did not cook breakfast; it was the job of whoever had the duty. Breakfast did not require a graduate chef—oatmeal porridge, bread, margarine, little valencia oranges (culls?), coffee. I left her there to wash dishes and to wait until I came back.

I went out and found a job.

I knew, from listening to wireless (called "radio" here) while washing dishes the night before, that there was unemployment in the United States, enough to be a political and social problem.

There is always work in the Southwest for agricultural labor but I had dodged that sort of work yesterday. I'm not too proud for that work; I had followed the harvest for several years from the time I was big enough to handle a pitchfork. But I could not take Margrethe into the fields.

I did not expect to find a job as a clergyman; I hadn't even told Brother Eddie that I was ordained. There is always an unemployment problem for preachers. Oh, there are always empty pulpits, true—but ones in which a church mouse would starve.

But I had a second profession.

Dishwasher.

No matter how many people are out of work, there are always dishwashing jobs going begging. Yesterday, in walking from the border gate to the Salvation Army mission, I had noticed three restaurants with "Dishwasher Wanted" signs in their windows—noticed them because I had had plenty of time on the long ride from Mazatlán to admit to myself that I had no other salable skill.

No salable skill. I was not ordained in this world; I would not *be* ordained in this world as I could not show graduation from seminary or divinity school—or even the backing of a primitive sect that takes no mind of schools but depends on inspiration by the Holy Ghost.

I was certainly not an engineer.

I could not get a job teaching even those subjects I knew well because I no longer could show any formal preparation—I couldn't even show that I had graduated from middle school!

In general I was no salesman. True, I had shown an unexpected talent for the complex skills that make up a professional money-raiser . . . but here I had no record, no reputation. I might someday do this again—but we needed cash *today*.

What did that leave? I had looked at the help-wanted ads in a copy of the Nogales *Times* someone had left in the mission. I was not a tax accountant. I was not any sort of a mechanic. I did not know what a software designer was but I was not one, nor was I a "computer" anything. I was not a nurse or any sort of health care professional.

I could go on indefinitely listing the things I was not, and could not learn overnight. But that is pointless. What I could do, what would feed Margrethe and me while we sized up this new world and learned the angles, was what I had been forced to do as a *peón*.

A competent and reliable dishwasher never starves. (He's more likely to die of boredom.)

The first place did not smell good and its kitchen looked dirty; I did not linger. The second place was a major-chain hotel, with several people in the scullery. The boss looked me over and said, "This is a Chicano job; you wouldn't be happy here." I tried to argue; he shut me off.

But the third was okay, a restaurant only a little bigger than the Pancho Villa, with a clean kitchen and a manager no more than normally jaundiced.

He warned me, "This job pays minimum wage and there are no raises. One meal a day on the house. I catch you sneaking anything, even a toothpick, and out you go that instant—no second chance. You work the hours I set and I change 'em to suit me. Right now I need you for noon to four, six to ten, five days a week. Or you can work six days but no overtime scale for it. Overtime scale if I require you to work more than eight hours in one day, or more than forty-eight hours in one week."

"Okay."

"All right, let's see your Social Security card."

I handed him my green card.

He handed it back. "You expect me to pay you twelve dollars and a half an hour on the basis of a green card? You're no Chicano. You trying to get me in trouble with the government? Where did you get that card?"

So I gave him the song and dance I had prepared for the Immigration Service. "Lost everything. I can't even phone and tell somebody to send me money; I have to get home first before I can shake any assets loose."

"You could get public assistance."

"Mister, I'm too stinkin' proud." (I don't know how and I can't prove I'm me. Just don't quiz me and let me wash dishes.)

"Glad to hear it. 'Stinking proud,' I mean. This country could use more like you. Go over to the Social Security office and get them to issue you a new one. They will, even if you can't recall the number of your old one. Then come back here and go to work. Mmm— I'll start you on payroll right now. But you must come back and put in a full day to collect."

"More than fair. Where is the Social Security office?"

So I went to the Federal Building and told my lies over again, embroidering only as necessary. The serious young lady who issued the card insisted on giving me a lecture on Social Security and how it worked, a lecture she had apparently memorized. I'll bet you she never had a "client" (that's what she called me) who listened so carefully. It was all new to me.

I gave the name "Alec L. Graham." This was not a conscious decision. I had been using that name for weeks, answered with it by reflex—then was not in a good position to say, "Sorry, Miss, my name is actually Hergensheimer."

I started work. During my four-to-six break I went back to the mission—and learned that Margrethe had a job, too.

It was temporary, three weeks—but three weeks at just the right time. The mission cook had not had a vacation in over a year and wanted to go to Flagstaff to visit her daughter, who had just had a baby. So Margrethe had her job for the time being—and her bedroom, also for the time being.

So Brother and Sister Graham were in awfully good shape—for the time being.

XIV

*I returned, and saw under the sun, that the race
is not to the swift, nor the battle to the strong,
neither yet bread to the wise, nor yet riches to men of
understanding, nor yet favour to men of skill;
but time and chance happeneth to them all.*
Ecclesiastes 9:11

Pray tell me why there is not a dishwashing school of philosophy? The conditions would seem ideal for indulging in the dear delights of attempting to unscrew the inscrutable. The work keeps the body busy while demanding almost nothing of the brain. I had eight hours every day in which to try to find answers to questions.

What questions? *All* questions. Five months earlier I had been a prosperous and respected professional in the most respected of professions, in a world I understood thoroughly—or so I thought. Today I was sure of nothing and had nothing.

Correction—I had Margrethe. Wealth enough for any man, I would not trade her for all the riches of Cathay. But even Margrethe represented a solemn contract I could not yet fulfill. In the eyes of the Lord I had taken her to wife . . . but I was not supporting her.

Yes, I had a job—but in truth she was supporting herself. When Mr. Cowgirl hired me, I had not been daunted by "minimum wage and no raises." Twelve dollars and fifty cents per hour struck me as a dazzling sum—why, many a married man in Wichita (*my* Wichita, in another universe) supported a family on twelve and a half dollars per *week*.

What I did not realize was that here $12.50 would not buy a tuna sandwich in that same restaurant—not a fancy restaurant, either; cheap, in fact. I would have had less trouble adjusting to the economy in this strange-but-familiar world if its money had been described in unfamiliar terms—shillings, shekels, soles, anything but dollars. I had been brought up to think of a dollar as a substantial piece of wealth; the idea that a hundred dollars a day was a poverty-level minimum wage was not one I could grasp easily.

Twelve-fifty an hour, a hundred dollars a day, five hundred a week, twenty-six thousand dollars a year— *Poverty* level? Listen carefully. In the world in which I grew up, that was riches beyond dreams of avarice.

Getting used to price and wage levels in dollars that weren't really dollars was simply the most ubiquitous aspect of a strange economy; the main problem was how to cope, how to stay afloat, how to make a living for me and my wife (and our children, with one expected all too soon if I had guessed right) in a world in which I had no diplomas, no training, no friends, no references, no track record of any sort. Alex, what in God's truth *are* you good for? . . . other than dishwashing!

I could easily wash a lighthouse stack of dishes while worrying that problem alone. It *had* to be solved. Today I washed dishes cheerfully . . . but soon I must do better for my beloved. Minimum wage was not enough.

Now at last we come to the prime question: Dear Lord God Jehovah, what mean these signs and portents Thou hast placed on me Thy servant?

There comes a time when a faithful worshiper must get up off his knees and deal with his Lord God in blunt and practical terms. Lord, *tell* me what to believe! Are these the deceitful great signs and wonders of which You warned, sent by antichrist to seduce the very elect?

Or are these true signs of the final days? Will we hear Your Shout?

Or am I as mad as Nebuchadnezzar and all of these appearances merely vapors in my disordered mind?

If one of these be true, then the other two are false. How am I to choose? Lord God of Hosts, how have I offended Thee?

In walking back to the mission one night I saw a sign that could be construed as a direct answer to my prayers: MILLIONS NOW LIVING WILL NEVER DIE. The sign was carried by a man and with him was a small child handing out leaflets.

I contrived not to accept one. I had seen that sign many times throughout my life, but I had long tended to avoid Jehovah's Witnesses. They are so stiff-necked and stubborn that it is impossible to work with them, whereas Churches United for Decency is necessarily an ecumenical association. In fund raising and in political action one must (while of course shunning heresy) avoid arguments on fiddling points of doctrine. Word-splitting theologians are the death of efficient organization. How can you include a sect in practical labor in the vineyards of the Lord if that sect asserts that they alone know the Truth, the whole Truth, and nothing but the Truth and all who disagree are heretics, destined for the fires of Hell?

Impossible. So we left them out of C.U.D.

Still— Perhaps this time they were right.

Which brings me to the most urgent of all questions: How to lead Margrethe back to the Lord before the Trump and the Shout.

But "how" depends on "when." Premillenarian theologians differ greatly among themselves as to the date of the Last Trump.

I rely on the scientific method. On any disputed point there is always one sure answer: Look it up in the Book.

And so I did, now that I was living at the Salvation Army mission and could borrow a copy of the Holy Bible. I looked it up again and again and again . . . and learned why premillenarians differed so on their dates.

The Bible is the literal Word of God; let there be no mistake about that. But nowhere did the Lord promise us that it would be easy to read.

Again and again Our Lord and His incarnation as the Son, Jesus of Nazareth, the Messiah, promises His disciples that their generation (i.e., first century A.D.) will see His return. Elsewhere, and again many times, He promises that He will return after a thousand years have passed . . . or is it two thousand years . . . or is it some other period, after the Gospel has been preached to all mankind in every country?

Which is true?

All are true, if you read them right. Jesus did indeed return in the generation of His twelve disciples; He did so at the first Easter, His resurrection. That was His first return, the utterly necessary one, the one that proved to all that He was indeed the Son of God and God Himself. He returned again after a thousand years and, in His infinite mercy, ruled that His children be given yet another grant of grace, a further period of trial, rather than let sinners be consigned forthwith to the fiery depths of Hell. His Mercy is infinite.

These dates are hard to read, and understandably so, as it was never His intention to encourage sinners to go on sinning because the day of reckoning had been postponed. What is precise, exact, and unmistakable, repeated again and again, is that He expects every one of His children to live every day, every hour, every heart beat, as if this one were the last. When is the end of this age? When is the Shout and the Trump? When is the Day of Judgment? *Now!* You will be given no warning whatever. No time for deathbed contrition. You must live in a state of grace . . . or, when the instant comes, you will be cast down into the Lake of Fire, there to burn in agony throughout all eternity.

So reads the Word of God.

And to me, so sounds the voice of doom. I had *no* period of grace in which to lead Margrethe back into the fold . . . as the Shout may come this very day.

What to do? What to do?

For mortal man, with any problem too great, there is only one thing to do: Take it to the Lord in prayer.

And so I did, again and again and again. Prayer is always answered. But it is necessary to recognize the answer . . . and it may not be the answer you want.

In the meantime one must render unto Caesar the things that are Caesar's. Of course I elected to work six days a week rather than five ($31,200 a year!)—as I needed every shekel I could garner. Margrethe needed everything!—and so did I. Especially we needed shoes. The shoes we had been wearing when disaster struck in Mazatlán had been quite good shoes—for peasants in Mazatlán. But they had been worn during two days of digging through rubble after the quake, then had been worn continuously since then; they were ready for the trash bin. So we needed shoes, at least two pairs each, one pair for work, one for Sunday-go-to-meeting.

And many other things. I don't know what all a woman needs, but it is more complex than what a man needs. I had to put money into Margrethe's hands and encourage her to buy what she needed. I could pig it with nothing much more than shoes and a pair of dungarees (to spare my one good outfit)—although I did buy a razor, and got a haircut at a barber's college near the mission, one where a haircut was only two dollars if one was willing to accept the greenest apprentice, and I was. Margrethe looked at it and said gently that she thought she could do as well herself, and save us that two dollars. Later she took scissors and straightened out what that untalented apprentice had done to me . . . and thereafter I never again spent money on barbers.

But saving two dollars did not offset a greater damage. I had honestly thought, when Mr. Cowgirl hired me, that I was going to be paid a hundred dollars every day I worked.

He didn't pay me that much and he didn't cheat me. Let me explain.

I finished that first day of work tired but happy. Happier than I had been since the earthquake struck, I mean—happiness is relative. I stopped at the cashier's stand where Mr. Cowgirl was working on his accounts, Ron's Grill having closed for the day. He looked up. "How did it go, Alec?"

"Just fine, sir."

"Luke tells me that you are doing okay." Luke was a giant blackamoor, head cook and my nominal boss. In fact he had not supervised me other than to show me where things were and make sure that I knew what to do.

"That's pleasant to hear. Luke's a good cook." That one-meal-a-day bonus over minimum wage I had eaten at four o'clock as breakfast was ancient history by then. Luke had explained to me that the help could order anything on the menu but steaks or chops, and that today I could have all the seconds I wanted if I chose either the stew or the meat loaf.

I chose the meat loaf because his kitchen smelled and looked clean. You can tell far more about a cook by his meat loaf than you can from the way he grills a steak. I took seconds on the meat loaf—with no catsup.

Luke was generous in the slab of cherry pie he cut for me, then he added a scoop of vanilla ice cream . . . which I did not rate, as it was an either/or, not both.

"Luke seldom says a good word about white boys," my employer went on, "and never about a Chicano. So you must be doing okay."

"I hope so." I was growing a mite impatient. We are all

the Lord's children but it was the first time in my life that a blackamoor's opinion of my work had mattered. I simply wanted to be paid so that I could hurry home to Margrethe—to the Salvation Army mission, that is.

Mr. Cowgirl folded his hands and twiddled his thumbs. "You want to be paid, don't you?"

I controlled my annoyance. "Yes, sir."

"Alec, with dishwashers I prefer to pay by the week."

I felt dismay and I am sure my face showed it.

"Don't misunderstand me," he added. "You're an hourly-rate employee, so you are paid at the end of each day if that's what you choose."

"Then I do choose. I need the money."

"Let me finish. The reason I prefer to pay dishwashers weekly instead of daily is that, all too often, if I hire one and pay him at the end of the day, he goes straight out and buys a jug of muscatel, then doesn't show up for a couple of days. When he does, he wants his job back. Angry at me. Ready to complain to the Labor Board. Funny part about it is that I may even be able to give him his job back—for another one-day shot at it—because the bum I've hired in his place has gone and done the same thing.

"This isn't likely to happen with Chicanos as they usually want to save money to send back to Mexico. But I've yet to see the Chicano who could handle the scullery to suit Luke . . . and I need Luke more than I need a particular dishwasher. Negras—Luke can usually tell me whether a spade is going to work out, and the good ones are better than a white boy any time. But the good ones are always trying to improve themselves . . . and if I don't promote them to pantry boy or assistant cook or whatever, soon they go across the street to somebody who will. So it's always a problem. If I can get a week's work out of a dishwasher, I figure I've won. If I get two weeks, I'm jubilant. Once I got a full month. But that's once in a lifetime."

"You're going to get three full weeks out of me," I said. "Now can I have my pay?"

"Don't rush me. If you elect to be paid once a week, I go for a dollar more on your hourly rate. That's forty dollars more at the end of the week. What do you say?"

(No, that's forty-eight more per week, I told myself. Almost $34,000 per year just for washing dishes. Whew!) "That's forty-eight dollars more each week," I answered.

"Not forty. As I'm going for that six-days-a-week option. I do need the money."

"Okay. Then I pay you once a week."

"Just a moment. Can't we start it tomorrow? I need some cash today. My wife and I haven't anything, anything at all. I've got the clothes I'm standing in, nothing else. The same for my wife. I can sweat it out a few more days. But there are things a woman just has to have."

He shrugged. "Suit yourself. But you don't get the dollar-an-hour bonus for today's work. And if you are one minute late tomorrow, I'll assume you're sleeping it off and I put the sign back in the window."

"I'm no wino, Mr. Cowgirl."

"We'll see." He turned to his bookkeeping machine and did something to its keyboard. I don't know what because I never understood it. It was an arithmetic machine but nothing like a Babbage Numerator. It had keys on it somewhat like a typewriting machine. But there was a window above that where numbers and letters appeared by some sort of magic.

The machine whirred and tinkled and he reached into it and brought out a card, handed it to me. "There you are."

I took it and examined it, and again felt dismay.

It was a piece of pasteboard about three inches wide and seven long, with numerous little holes punched in it and with printing on it that stated that it was a draft on Nogales Commercial and Savings Bank by which Ron's

Grill directed them to pay to Alec L. Graham— No, not one hundred dollars.

Fifty-one dollars and twenty-seven cents.

"Something wrong?" he asked.

"Uh, I had expected twelve-fifty an hour."

"That's what I paid you. Eight hours at minimum wage. You can check the deductions yourself. That's not my arithmetic; this is an IBM 1990 and it's instructed by IBM software, *Paymaster Plus* . . . and IBM has a standing offer of ten thousand dollars to any employee who can show that this model IBM and this mark of their software fouled up a pay check. Look at it. Gross pay, one hundred dollars. Deductions all listed. Add 'em up. Subtract them. Check your answer against IBM's answer. But don't blame me. I didn't write those laws—and I like them even less than you do. Do you realize that almost every dishwasher that comes in here, whether wetback or citizen, wants me to pay him in cash and forget the deductions? Do you know what the fine is if they catch me doing it just once? What happens if they catch me a second time? Don't look sour at me—go talk to the government."

"I just don't understand it. It's new to me, all of it. Can you tell me what these deductions mean? This one that says 'Admin,' for example."

"That stands for 'administration fee' but don't ask me why you have to pay it, as I am the one who has to do the bookkeeping and I certainly don't get paid to do it."

I tried to check the other deductions against the fine-print explanations. "SocSec" turned out to be "Social Security." The young lady had explained that to me this morning . . . but I had told her at the time that, while it was certainly an excellent idea, I felt that I would have to wait until later before subscribing to it; I could not afford it just yet. "MedIns" and "HospIns" and "DentIns" were simple enough but I could not afford them now, either. But what was "PL217?" The fine print simply referred to a date and page in "PubReg." What about "DepEduc" and "UNESCO?"

And what in the world was "Income Tax?"

"I still don't understand it. It's all new to me."

"Alec, you're not the only one who doesn't understand it. But why do you say it is new to you? It has been going on all your life ... and your daddy's and your grand-daddy's, at least."

"I'm sorry. What is 'Income Tax'?"

He blinked at me. "Are you sure you don't need to see a shrink?"

"What is a 'shrink'?"

He sighed. "Now I need to see one. Look, Alec. Just take it. Discuss the deductions with the government, not with me. You sound sincere, so maybe you were hit on the head when you got caught in the Mazatlán quake. I just want to go home and take a Miltown. So take it, please."

"All right. I guess. But I don't know anyone who would cash this for me."

"No problem. Endorse it back to me and I'll pay you cash. But keep the stub, as the IRS will insist on seeing all your deduction stubs before paying you back any overpayment."

I didn't understand that, either, but I kept the stub.

Despite the shock of learning that almost half my pay was gone before I touched it, we were better off each day, as, between us, Margrethe and I had over four hundred dollars a week that did not have to be spent just to stay alive but could be converted into clothing and other necessities. Theoretically she was being paid the same wages as had been the cook she replaced, or twenty-two dollars an hour for twenty-four hours a week, or $528/week.

In fact she had the same sort of deductions I had, which caused her net pay to come to just under $290/week. Again theoretically. But $54/week was checked off for lodging—fair enough, I decided, when I found out what rooming houses were charging. More than fair, in fact. Then we were assessed $105/week for meals. Brother McCaw at first had put us down for $140/week for meals and had offered to show by his books that Mrs. Owens, the regular cook, had always paid, by checkoff, $10 each day for her meals . . . so the two of us should be assessed $140/week.

I agreed that that was fair (having seen the prices on the menu at Ron's Grill)—fair in theory. But I was going to have my heaviest meal of the day where I worked. We compromised on ten a day for Marga, half that for me.

So Margrethe wound up with a hundred and thirty-one a week out of a gross of five hundred and twenty-eight.

If she could collect it. Like most churches, the Salvation Army lives from hand to mouth . . . and sometimes the hand doesn't quite reach the mouth.

Nevertheless we were well off and better off each week. At the end of the first week we bought new shoes for Margrethe, first quality and quite smart, for only $279.90, on sale at J. C. Penney's, marked down from $350.

Of course she fussed at getting new shoes for her before buying shoes for me. I pointed out that we still had over a hundred dollars toward shoes for me—next week—and would she please hold it for us so that I would not be tempted to spend it. Solemnly she agreed.

So the following Monday we got shoes for me even cheaper—Army surplus, good, stout comfortable shoes that would outlast anything bought from a regular shoe store. (I would worry about dress shoes for me after I had other matters under control. There is nothing like being barefoot broke to adjust one's mundane values.) Then we went to the Goodwill retail store and bought a dress and a summer suit for her, and dungaree pants for me.

Margrethe wanted to get more clothes for me—we still had almost sixty dollars. I objected.

"Why not, Alec? You need clothes every bit as badly as I do . . . yet we have spent almost all that you have saved on *me*. It's not fair."

I answered, "We've spent it where it was needed. Next week, if Mrs. Owens comes back on time, you'll be out of a job and we'll have to move. I think we should move on. So let's save what we can for bus fare."

"Move on where, dear?"

"To Kansas. This is a world strange to each of us. Yet it is familiar, too—same language, same geography, some of the same history. Here I'm just a dishwasher, not earning enough to support you. But I have a strong feeling that Kansas—Kansas in this world—will be so much like the Kansas I was born in that I'll be able to cope better."

"Whither thou goest, beloved."

The mission was almost a mile from Ron's Grill; instead of trying to go "home" at my four-to-six break, I usually spent my free time, after eating, at the downtown branch library, getting myself oriented. That, and newspapers that customers sometimes left in the restaurant, constituted my principal means of reeducation.

In this world Mr. William Jennings Bryan had indeed been President and his benign influence had kept us out of the Great European War. He then had offered his services for a negotiated peace. The Treaty of Philadelphia had more or less restored Europe to what it had been before 1913.

I didn't recognize any of the Presidents after Bryan, either from my own world or from Margrethe's world. Then I became utterly bemused when I first ran across the name of the current President: His Most Christian Majesty, John Edward the Second, Hereditary President of the United States and Canada, Duke of Hyannisport, Comte de Québec, Defender of the Faith, Protector of the Poor, Marshal in Chief of the Peace Force.

I looked at a picture of him, laying a cornerstone in Alberta. He was tall and broad-shouldered and blandly handsome and was wearing a fancy uniform with enough medals on his chest to ward off pneumonia. I studied his face and asked myself, "Would you buy a used car from this man?"

But the more I thought about it, the more logical it seemed. Americans, all during their two and a quarter centuries as a separate nation, had missed the royalty they had shucked off. They slobbered over European royalty whenever they got the chance. Their wealthiest citizens married their daughters to royalty whenever possible, even to Georgian princes—a "prince" in Georgia being a farmer with the biggest manure pile in the neighborhood.

I did not know where they had hired this royal dude. Perhaps they had sent to Estoril for him, or even had him shipped in from the Balkans. As one of my history profs had pointed out, there are always out-of-work royalty around, looking for jobs. When a man is out of work, he can't be fussy, as I knew too well. Laying cornerstones is probably no more boring than washing dishes. But the hours are longer. I think. I've never been a king. I'm not sure that I would take a job in the kinging business if it were offered to me; there are obvious drawbacks and not just the long hours.

On the other hand—

Refusing a crown that you know will never be offered to you is sour grapes, by definition. I searched my heart and concluded that I probably would be able to persuade myself that it was a sacrifice I should make for my fellow men. I would pray over it until I was convinced that the Lord *wanted* me to accept this burden.

Truly I am not being cynical. I know how frail men can be in persuading themselves that the Lord wants them to do something they wanted to do all along—and I am no better than my brethren in this.

But the thing that stonkered me was the idea of Canada united with us. Most Americans do not know why Canadians dislike us (I do not), but they do. The idea that Canadians would ever vote to unite with us boggles the mind.

I went to the library desk and asked for a recent general history of the United States. I had just started to study it when I noted by the wall clock that it was almost four o'clock . . . so I had to check it back in and hustle to get back to my scullery on time. I did not have library loan privileges as I could not as yet afford the deposit required of nonresidents.

More important than the political changes were technical and cultural changes. I realized almost at once that this world was more advanced in physical science and technology than my own. In fact I realized it almost as quickly as I saw a "television" display device.

I never did understand how televising takes place. I tried to learn about it in the public library and at once bumped into a subject called "electronics." (Not "electrics" but "electronics.") So I tried to study up about electronics and encountered the most amazing mathematical gibberish. Not since thermodynamics had caused me to decide that I had a call for the ministry have I seen such confusing and turgid equations. I don't think Rolla Tech could ever cope with such amphigory—at least not Rolla Tech when I was an undergraduate there.

But the superior technology of this world was evident in many more things than television. Consider "traffic lights." No doubt you have seen cities so choked with traffic that it is almost impossible to cross major streets other than through intervention by police officers. Also no doubt you have sometimes been annoyed when a policeman charged with controlling traffic has stopped the flow in your direction to accommodate some very important person from city hall or such.

Can you imagine a situation in which traffic could be controlled in great volume *with no police officers whatever* at hand—just an impersonal colored light?

Believe me, that is exactly what they had in Nogales.

Here is how it works:

At every busy intersection you place a minimum of twelve lights, four groups of three, a group facing each of the cardinal directions and so screened that each group can be seen only from its direction. Each group has one red light, one green light, one amber light. These lights are served by electrical power and each shines brightly enough to be seen at a distance of a mile, more or less, even in bright sunlight. These are not arc lights; these are very powerful Edison lamps—this is important because these lights must be turned on and off every few moments and must function without fail hours on end, even days on end, twenty-four hours a day.

These lights are placed up high, on telegraph poles, or suspended over intersections, so that they may be seen by teamsters or drivers or cyclists from a distance. When the green lights shine, let us say, north and south, the red lights shine east and west—traffic may flow north and south, while east and west traffic is required to stand and wait *exactly as if a police officer had blown his whistle and held up his hands, motioning traffic to move north and south while restraining traffic from moving east and west.*

Is that clear? The lights replace the policeman's hand signals.

The amber lights replace the policeman's whistle; they warn of an imminent change in the situation.

But what is the advantage?—since someone, presumably a policeman, must switch the lights on and off, as needed. Simply this: The switching is done *automatically* from a distance (even miles!) at a central switchboard.

There are many other marvels about this system, such as electrical counting devices to decide how long each light burns for best handling of the traffic, special lights for controlling left turns or to accommodate people on foot . . . but the truly great marvel is this: People *obey* these lights.

Think about it. With no policemen anywhere around people obey these blind and dumb bits of machinery *as if they were policemen.*

Are people here so sheeplike and peaceful that they can be controlled this easily? No. I wondered about it and found some statistics in the library. This world has a higher rate of violent crime than does the world in which I was born. Caused by these strange lights? I don't think so. I think that the people here, although disposed to violence against each other, accept obeying traffic lights as a logical thing to do. Perhaps.

As may be, it is passing strange.

Another conspicuous difference in technology lies in air traffic. Not the decent, cleanly, safe, and silent dirigible airships of my home world— No, no! These are more like the *aeroplanos* of the Mexicano world in which Margrethe and I sweated out our indentures before the great quake that destroyed Mazatlán. But they are so much bigger, faster, noisier, and fly so much higher than the *aeroplanos* we knew that they are almost another breed—or are indeed another breed, perhaps, as they are called "jet planes." Can you imagine a vehicle that flies eight miles above the ground? Can you imagine a giant car that moves faster than sound? Can you imagine a screaming whine so loud that it makes your teeth ache?

They call this "progress." I long for the comfort and graciousness of LTA *Count von Zeppelin*. Because you can't get away from these behemoths. Several times a day one of these things goes screaming over the mission, fairly low down, as it approaches a grounding at the flying field north of the city. The noise bothers me and makes Margrethe very nervous.

Still, most of the enhancements in technology really are progress—better plumbing, better lighting indoors and out, better roads, better buildings, many sorts of machinery that make human labor less onerous and more productive. I am never one of those back-to-nature freaks who sneer at engineering; I have more reason than most people to respect engineering. Most people who sneer at technology would starve to death if the engineering infrastructure were removed.

We had been in Nogales just short of three weeks when I was able to carry out a plan that I had dreamed of for nearly five months . . . and had actively plotted since our arrival in Nogales (but had to delay until I could afford it). I picked Monday to carry it out, that being my day off. I told Margrethe to dress up in her new clothes as I was taking my best girl out for a treat, and I dressed up, too— my one suit, my new shoes, and a clean shirt . . . and shaved and bathed and nails clean and trimmed.

It was a lovely day, sunny and not too hot. We both felt cheerful because, first, Mrs. Owens had written to Brother McCaw saying that she was staying on another week if she could be spared, and second, we now had enough money for bus fares for both of us to Wichita, Kansas, although just barely—but the word from Mrs. Owens meant that we could squirrel away another four hundred dollars for eating money on the way and still arrive not quite broke.

I took Margrethe to a place I had spotted the day I looked for a job as a dishwasher—a nice little place outside the tenderloin, an old-fashioned ice cream parlor.

We stopped outside it. "Best girl, see this place? Do you remember a conversation we had when we were floating on the broad Pacific on a sunbathing mat and not really expecting to live much longer?—at least I was not."

"Beloved, how could I forget?"

"I asked you what you would have if you could have anything in the world that you wanted. Do you remember what you answered?"

"Of course I do! It was a hot fudge sundae."

"Right! Today is your unbirthday, dear. You are about to have that hot fudge sundae."

"Oh, Alec!"

"Don't blubber. Can't stand a woman who cries. Or you can have a chocolate malt. Or a sawdust sundae. Whatever your heart desires. But I did make sure that this place always has hot fudge sundaes before I brought you here."

"We can't afford it. We should save for the trip."

"We *can* afford it. A hot fudge sundae is five dollars.

Two for ten dollars. And I'm going to be a dead game sport and tip the waitress a dollar. Man does not live by bread alone. Nor does woman, Woman. Come along!"

We were shown to a table by a pretty waitress (but not as pretty as my bride). I seated Margrethe with her back to the street, holding the chair for her, and then sat down opposite her. "I'm Tammy," the waitress said as she offered us a menu. "What would you folks like this lovely day?"

"We won't need the menu," I said. "Two hot fudge sundaes, please."

Tammy looked thoughtful. "All right, if you don't mind waiting a few minutes. We may have to make up the hot sauce."

"A few minutes, who cares? We've waited much longer than that."

She smiled and went away. I looked at Marga. "We've waited *much* longer. Haven't we?"

"Alec, you're a sentimentalist and that's part of why I love you."

"I'm a sentimental slob and right now I'm slavering at the thought of hot fudge sundae. But I wanted you to see this place for another reason, too. Marga, how would you like to run such a place as this? Us, that is. Together. You'd be boss, I'd be dishwasher, janitor, handyman, bouncer, and whatever was needed."

She looked very thoughtful. "You are serious?"

"Quite. Of course we couldn't go into business for ourselves right away; we will have to save some money first. But not much, the way I plan it. A dinky little place, but bright and cheerful—after I paint it. A soda fountain, plus a very limited menu. Hot dogs. Hamburgers. Danish open-face sandwiches. Nothing else. Soup, maybe. But canned soups are no problem and not much inventory."

Margrethe looked shocked. "Not canned soups. I can serve a real soup . . . cheaper and better than anything out of a tin."

"I defer to your professional judgment, Ma'am. Kansas

has half a dozen little college towns; any of them would welcome such a place. Maybe we pick a shop already existing, a mom-and-pop place—work for them a year, then buy them out. Change the name to The Hot Fudge Sundae. Or maybe Marga's Sandwiches."

"The Hot Fudge Sundae. Alec, do you really think we can do this?"

I leaned toward her and took her hand. "I'm sure we can, darling. And without working ourselves to death, too." I moved my head. "That traffic light is staring me right in the eye."

"I know. I can see it reflected in your eye every time it changes. Want to swap seats? It won't bother me."

"It doesn't bother me. It just has a somewhat hypnotic effect." I looked down at the table, looked back at the light. "Hey, it's gone out."

Margrethe twisted her neck to look. "I don't see it. Where?"

"Uh . . . pesky thing has disappeared. Looks like."

I heard a male voice at my elbow. "What'll it be for you two? Beer or wine; we're not licensed for the hard stuff."

I looked around, saw a waiter. "Where's Tammy?"

"Who's Tammy?"

I took a deep breath, tried to slow my heart, then said, "Sorry, brother; I shouldn't have come in here. I find I've left my wallet at home." I stood up. "Come, dear."

Wide-eyed and silent, Margrethe came with me. As we walked out, I looked around, noting changes. I suppose it was a decent enough place, as beer joints go. But it was not our cheerful ice cream parlor.

And not our world.

XV

Boast not thyself of tomorrow; for
thou knowest not what a day may bring forth.
Proverbs 27:1

Outside, without planning it, I headed us toward the Salvation Army mission. Margrethe kept quiet and held tight to my arm. I should have been frightened; instead I was boiling angry. Presently I muttered, "Damn them! Damn them!"

"Damn who, Alec?"

"I don't know. That's the worst of it. Whoever is doing this to us. Your friend Loki, maybe."

"He is not my friend, any more than Satan is your friend. I dread and fear what Loki is doing to our world."

"I'm not afraid, I'm angry. Loki or Satan or whoever, this last is too much. No sense to it. Why couldn't they wait thirty minutes? That hot fudge sundae was practically under our nose—and they snatched it away! Marga, that's not right, that's not fair! That's sheer, unadulterated cruelty. Senseless. On a par with pulling wings off flies. I despise them. Whoever."

Instead of continuing with useless talk about matters we could not settle, Margrethe said, "Dear, where are we going?"

"Eh?" I stopped short. "Why, to the mission, I suppose."

"Is this the right way?"

"Why, yes, cert—" I paused to look around. "I don't

173

know." I had been walking automatically, my attention fully on my anger. Now I found that I was unsure of any landmarks. "I guess I'm lost."

"I know I am."

It took us another half hour to get straightened out. The neighborhood was vaguely familiar but nothing was quite right. I found the block where Ron's Grill should be, could not find Ron's Grill. Eventually a policeman directed us to the mission . . . which was now in a different building. To my surprise, Brother McCaw was there. But he did not recognize us, and his name was now McNabb. We left, as gracefully as possible. Not very, that is.

I walked us back the way we had come—slowly, as I wasn't going anywhere. "Marga, we're right back where we were three weeks ago. Better shoes, that's all. A pocket full of money—but money we can't spend, as it is certain to be funny money here . . . good for a quiet rest behind bars if I tried to pass any of it."

"You're probably right, dear one."

"There is a bank on that corner just ahead. Instead of trying to spend any of it, I could walk in and simply ask whether or not it was worth anything."

"There couldn't be any harm in that. Could there?"

"There shouldn't be. But our friend Loki could have another practical joke up his sleeve. Uh, we've got to know. Here—you take everything but one bill. If they arrest me, you pretend not to know me."

"No!"

"What do you mean, 'No'? There is no point in both of us being in jail."

She looked stubborn and said nothing. How can you argue with a woman who won't talk? I sighed. "Look, dear, the only other thing I can think of is to look for another job washing dishes. Maybe Brother McNabb will let us sleep in the mission tonight."

"I'll look for a job, too. I can wash dishes. Or cook. Or something."

"We'll see. Come inside with me, Marga; we'll go to jail together. But I think I've figured out how to handle this without going to jail." I took out one treasury note, crumpled it, and tore one corner. Then we went into the bank together, me holding it in my hand as if I had just picked it up. I did not go to a teller's window; instead I went to that railing behind which bank officials sit at their desks.

I leaned on the railing and spoke to the man nearest to it; his desk sign marked him as assistant manager. "Excuse me, sir! Can you answer a question for me?"

He looked annoyed but his reply did not show it. "I'll try. What's on your mind?"

"Is this really money? Or is it stage money, or something?"

He looked at it, then looked more closely. "Interesting. Where did you get this?"

"My wife found it on a sidewalk. Is it money?"

"Of course it's not money. Whoever heard of a twenty-dollar note? Stage money, probably. Or an advertising promotion."

"Then it's not worth anything?"

"It's worth the paper it's printed on, that's all. I doubt that it could even be called counterfeit, since there has been no effort to make it look like the real thing. Still, the Treasury inspectors will want to see it."

"All right. Can you take care of it?"

"Yes. But they'll want to talk to you, I'm sure. Let's get your name and address. And your wife's, of course, since she found it."

"Okay. I want a receipt for it." I gave our names as "Mr. and Mrs. Alexander Hergensheimer" and gave the address—but not the name—of Ron's Grill. Then I solemnly accepted a receipt.

Once out on the sidewalk I said, "Well, we're no worse off than we thought we were. Time for me to look for some dirty dishes."

"Alec—"

"Yes, beloved?"

"We were going to Kansas."

"So we were. But our bus-fare money is not worth the paper it is printed on. I'll have to earn some more. I can. I did it once, I can do it again."

"Alec. Let us now go to Kansas."

A half hour later we were walking north on the highway to Tucson. Whenever anyone passed us, I signalled our hope of being picked up.

It took us three hitches simply to reach Tucson. At Tucson it would have made equal sense to head east toward El Paso, Texas, as to continue on Route 89, as 89 swings west before it goes north to Phoenix. It was settled for us by the chance that the first lift we were able to beg out of Tucson was with a teamster who was taking a load north.

This ride we were able to pick up at a truckers' stop at the intersection of 89 and 80, and I am forced to admit that the teamster listened to our plea because Margrethe is the beauty she is—had I been alone I might still be standing there. I might as well say right now that this whole trip depended throughout on Margrethe's beauty and womanly charm quite as much as it depended on my willingness to do any honest work whatever, no matter how menial, dirty, or difficult.

I found this fact unpleasant to face. I held dark thoughts of Potiphar's wife and of the story of Susanna and the Elders. I found myself being vexed with Margrethe when her only offense lay in being her usual gracious, warm, and friendly self. I came close to telling her not to smile at strangers and to keep her eyes to herself.

That temptation hit me sharpest that first day at sundown when this same trucker stopped at a roadside oasis centered around a restaurant and a fueling facility. "I'm going to have a couple of beers and a sirloin steak," he announced. "How about you, Maggie baby? Could you use a rare steak? This is the place where they just chase the cow through the kitchen."

She smiled at him. "Thank you, Steve. But I'm not hungry."

My darling was telling an untruth. She knew it, I knew it—and I felt sure that Steve knew it. Our last meal had been breakfast at the mission, eleven hours and a universe ago. I had tried to wash dishes for a meal at the truckers' stop outside Tucson, but had been dismissed rather abruptly. So we had had nothing all day but water from a public drinking faucet.

"Don't try to kid your grandmother, Maggie. We've been on the road four hours. You're hungry."

I spoke up quickly to keep Margrethe from persisting in an untruth—told, I felt certain, on my behalf. "What she means, Steve, is that she doesn't accept dinner invitations from other men. She expects me to provide her dinner." I added, "But I thank you on her behalf and we both thank you for the ride. It's been most pleasant."

We were still seated in the cab of his truck, Margrethe in the middle. He leaned forward and looked around her. "Alec, you think I'm trying to get into Maggie's pants, don't you?"

I answered stiffly that I did not think anything of the sort while thinking privately that that was exactly what I thought he had been trying to accomplish all along . . . and I resented not only his unchivalrous overtures but also the gross language he had just used. But I had learned the hard way that rules of polite speech in the world in which I had grown up were not necessarily rules in another universe.

"Oh, yes, you do think so. I wasn't born yesterday and a lot of my life has been spent on the road, getting my illusions knocked out. You think I'm trying to lay your woman because every stud who comes along tries to put the make on her. But let me clue you in, son. I don't knock when there's nobody at home. And I can always tell. Maggie ain't having any. I checked that out hours ago. And congratulations; a faithful woman is good to find. Isn't that true?"

"Yes, certainly," I agreed grudgingly.

"So get your feathers down. You're about to take your wife to dinner. You've already said thank you to me for the ride but why don't you really thank me by inviting me to dinner?—so I won't have to eat alone."

I hope that I did not look dismayed and that my instant of hesitation was not noticeable. "Certainly, Steve. We owe you that for your kindness. Uh, will you excuse me while I make some arrangements?" I started to get out of the cab.

"Alec, you don't lie any better than Maggie does."

"Excuse me?"

"You think I'm blind? You're broke. Or, if you aren't absolutely stony, you are so near flat you can't afford to buy me a sirloin steak. Or even the blueplate special."

"That is true," I answered with—I hope—dignity. "The arrangements I must make are with the restaurant manager. I hope to exchange dishwashing for the price of three dinners."

"I thought so. If you were just ordinary broke, you'd be riding Greyhound and you'd have some baggage. If you were broke but not yet hungry broke, you'd hitchhike to save your money for eating but you would have some sort of baggage. A kiester each, or at least a bindle. But you've got no baggage . . . and you're both wearing suits—in the desert, for God's sake! The signs all spell disaster."

I remained mute.

"Now look," he went on. "Possibly the owner of this joint would let you wash dishes. More likely he's got three wetbacks pearl-diving this very minute and has turned down at least three more already today; this is on the main north-south route of *turistas* coming through holes in the Fence. In any case I can't wait while you wash dishes; I've got to herd this rig a lot of miles yet tonight. So I'll make you a deal. You take me to dinner but I lend you the money."

"I'm a poor risk."

"Nope, you're a good risk. What the bankers call a

character loan, the very best risk there is. Sometime, this coming year, or maybe twenty years from now, you'll run across another young couple, broke and hungry. You'll buy them dinner on the same terms. That pays me back. Then when they do the same, down the line, that pays you back. Get it?"

"I'll pay you back sevenfold!"

"Once is enough. After that you do it for your own pleasure. Come on, let's eat."

Rimrock Restop restaurant was robust rather than fancy—about on a par with Ron's Grill in another world. It had both counter and tables. Steve led us to a table and shortly a fairly young and rather pretty waitress came over.

"Howdy, Steve! Long time."

"Hi, Babe! How'd the rabbit test come out?"

"The rabbit died. How about your blood test?" She smiled at me and at Margrethe. "Hi, folks! What'll you have?"

I had had time to glance at the menu, first down the right-hand side, of course—and was shocked at the prices. Shocked to find them back on the scale of the world I knew best, I mean. Hamburgers for a dime, coffee at five cents, *table d'hôte* dinners at seventy-five to ninety cents—these prices I understood.

I looked at it and said, "May I have a cheese super-burger, medium well?"

"Sure thing, Ace. How about you, dear?"

Margrethe took the same, but medium rare.

"Steve?" the waitress inquired.

"That'll be three beers—*Coors*—and three sirloin steaks, one rare, one medium rare, one medium. With the usual garbage. Baked potato, fried promises, whatever. The usual limp salad. Hot rolls. All the usual. Dessert later. Coffee."

"Gotcha."

"Wantcha to meet my friends. Maggie, this is Hazel. That's Alec, her husband."

"You lucky man! Hi, Maggie; glad to know you. Sorry to see you in such company, though. Has Steve tried to sell you anything?"

"No."

"Good. Don't buy anything, don't sign anything, don't bet with him. And be glad you're safely married; he's got wives in three states."

"Four," Steve corrected.

"Four now? Congratulations. Ladies' restroom is through the kitchen, Maggie; men go around behind." She left moving fast, with a swish of her skirt.

"That's a fine broad," Steve said. "You know what they say about waitresses, especially in truckers' joints. Well, Hazel is probably the only hash-slinger on this highway who *ain't* sellin' it. Come on, Alec." He got up and led me outdoors and around to the men's room. I followed him. By the time I understood what he had said, it was too late to resent his talking that way in a lady's presence. Then I was forced to admit that Margrethe had not resented it—had simply treated it as information. As praise of Hazel, in fact. I think my greatest trouble with all these worrisome world changes had to do, not with economics, not with social behavior, not with technology, but simply with language, and the *mores* and taboos thereto.

Beer was waiting for us when we returned, and so was Margrethe, looking cool and refreshed.

Steve toasted us. "Skoal!"

We echoed *"Skaal!"* and I took a sip and then a lot more—just what I needed after a long day on a desert highway. My moral downfall in S.S. *Konge Knut* had included getting reacquainted with beer, something I had not touched since my days as an engineering student, and very little then—no money for vices. This was excellent beer, it seemed to me, but not as good as the Danish Tuborg served in the ship. Did you know that there is not one word against beer in the Bible? In fact the word "beer" in the Bible means "fountain" or "well."

The steaks were delicious.

Under the mellowing influence of beer and good food I found myself trying to explain to Steve how we happened to be down on our luck and accepting the charity of strangers . . . without actually saying anything. Presently Margrethe said to me, "Alec. Tell him."

"You think I should?"

"I think Steve is entitled to know. And I trust him."

"Very well. Steve, we are strangers from another world."

He neither laughed nor smiled; he just looked interested. Presently he said, "Flying saucer?"

"No. I mean another universe, not just another planet. Although it seems like the same planet. I mean, Margrethe and I were in a state called Arizona and a city called Nogales just earlier today. Then it changed. Nogales shrank down and nothing was quite the same. Arizona looks about the same, although I don't know this state very well."

"Territory."

"Excuse me?"

"Arizona is a territory, not a state. Statehood was voted down."

"Oh. That's the way it was in my world, too. Something about taxes. But we didn't come from my world. Nor from Marga's world. We came from—" I stopped. "I'm not telling this very well." I looked across at Margrethe. "Can you explain it?"

"I can't *explain* it," she answered, "because I don't understand it. But, Steve, it's true. I'm from one world, Alec is from another world, we've lived in still another world, and we were in yet again another world this morning. And now we are here. That is why we don't have any money. No, we do have money but it's not money of this world."

Steve said, "Could we take this one world at a time? I'm getting dizzy."

I said, "She left out two worlds."

"No, dear—three. You may have forgotten the iceberg world."

"No, I counted that. I— Excuse me, Steve. I'll try to take it one world at a time. But it isn't easy. This morning— We went into an ice cream parlor in Nogales because I wanted to buy Margrethe a hot fudge sundae. We sat down at a table, across from each other like right now, and that put me facing a set of traffic lights—"

"A set of what?"

"A set of traffic signal lights, red, green, and amber. That's how I spotted that we had changed worlds again. This world doesn't have signal lights, or at least I haven't seen any. Just traffic cops. But in the world we got up in this morning, instead of traffic cops, they do it with signal lights."

"Sounds like they do it with mirrors. What's this got to do with buying Maggie a hot fudge sundae?"

"That was because, when we were shipwrecked and floating around in the ocean, Margrethe wanted a hot fudge sundae. This morning was my first chance to buy one for her. When the traffic lights disappeared, I knew we had changed worlds again—and that meant that my money wasn't any good. So I could not buy her a hot fudge sundae. And could not buy her dinner tonight. No money. No spendable money, I mean. You see?"

"I think I fell off three turns back. What happened to your money?"

"Oh." I dug into my pocket, hauled out our carefully hoarded bus-fare money, picked out a twenty-dollar bill, handed it to Steve. "Nothing happened to it. Look at this."

He looked at it carefully. "'Lawful money for all debts public and private.' That sounds okay. But who's this joker with his picture on it? And when did they start printing twenty-dollar treasury notes?"

"Never, in your world. I guess. The picture is of William Jennings Bryan, President of the United States from 1913 to 1921."

"Not at Horace Mann School in Akron, he wasn't. Never heard of him."

"In my school he was elected in 1896, not sixteen years later. And in Margrethe's world Mr. Bryan was never president at all. Say! Margrethe! This just might be your world!"

"Why do you think so, dear?"

"Maybe, maybe not. As we came north out of Nogales I didn't notice a flying field or any signs concerning one. And I just remembered that I haven't heard or seen a jet plane all day long. Or any sort of a flying machine. Have you?"

"No. No, I haven't. But I haven't been thinking about them." She added, "I'm almost certain there haven't been any near us."

"There you have it! Or maybe this is my world. Steve, what's the situation on aeronautics here?"

"Arrow what?"

"Flying machines. Jet planes. Aeroplanes of any sort. And dirigibles—do you have dirigibles?"

"None of those things rings any bells with me. You're talking about flying, real flying, up in the air like a bird?"

"Yes, yes!"

"No, of course not. Or do you mean balloons? I've seen a balloon."

"Not balloons. Oh, a dirigible is a sort of a balloon. But it's long instead of round—sort of cigar-shaped. And it's propelled by engines something like your truck and goes a hundred miles an hour and more—and usually fairly high, one or two thousand feet. Higher over mountains."

For the first time Steve showed surprise rather than interest. "God A'mighty! You've actually *seen* something like that?"

"I've ridden in them. Many times. First when I was only twelve years old. You went to school in Akron? In my world Akron is world famous as the place where they build the biggest, fastest, and best dirigible airships in all the world."

Steve shook his head. "When the parade goes by, I'm out for a short beer. That's the story of my life. Maggie, you've seen airships? Ridden in them?"

"No. They are not in my world. But I've ridden in a flying machine. An *aeroplano*. Once. It was terribly exciting. Frightening, too. But I would like to do it again."

"I betcha would. Me, I reckon it would scare the tar out of me. But I would take a ride in one, even if it killed me. Folks, I'm beginning to believe you. You tell it so straight. That and this money. If it *is* money."

"It *is* money," I insisted, "from another world. Look at it closely, Steve. Obviously it's not money of your world. But it's not play money or stage money either. Would anybody bother to make steel engravings that perfect just for stage money? The engraver who made the plates expected that note to be accepted as money . . . yet it isn't even a correct denomination—that's the first thing you noticed. Wait a moment." I dug into another pocket. "Yup! Still here." I took out a ten-peso note—from the Kingdom of Mexico. I had burned most of the useless money we had accumulated before the quake—Margrethe's tips at El Pancho Villa—but I had saved a few souvenirs. "Look at this, too. Do you know Spanish?"

"Not really. TexMex. *Cantina* Spanish." He looked at the Mexican money. "This looks okay."

"Look more closely," Margrethe urged him. "Where it says '*Reino*.' Shouldn't that read '*República*'? Or is Mexico a kingdom in this world?"

"It's a republic . . . partly because I helped keep it that way. I was an election judge there when I was in the Marines. It's amazing what a few Marines armed to their eyebrows can do to keep an election honest. Okay, pals; you've sold me. Mexico is not a kingdom and hitchhikers who don't have the price of dinner on them ought not to be carrying around Mexicano money that says it *is* a kingdom. Maybe I'm crazy but I'm inclined to throw in with you. What's the explanation?"

"Steve," I said soberly, "I wish I knew. The simplest explanation is that I've gone crazy and that it's all imaginary—you, me, Marga, this restaurant, this world—all products of my brain fever."

"You can be imaginary if you want to, but leave Maggie and me out of it. Do you have any other explanations?"

"Uh . . . that depends. Do you read the Bible, Steve?"

"Well, yes and no. Being on the road, lots of times I find myself wide awake in bed with nothing around to read but a Gideon Bible. So sometimes I do."

"Do you recall Matthew twenty-four, twenty-four?"

"Huh? Should I?"

I quoted it for him. "That's one possibility, Steve. These world changes may be signs sent by the Devil himself, intended to deceive us. On the other hand they may be portents of the end of world and the coming of Christ into His kingdom. Hear the Word:

"'Immediately after the tribulation of those days shall the sun be darkened, and the moon shall not give her light, and the stars shall fall from heaven, and the powers of the heavens shall be shaken:

"'And then shall appear the sign of the Son of man in heaven: and then shall all the tribes of the earth mourn, and they shall see the Son of man coming in the clouds of heaven with power and great glory.

"'And he shall send his angels with a great sound of a trumpet, and they shall gather together his elect from the four winds, from one end of heaven to the other.'

"That's what it adds up to, Steve. Maybe these are the false signs of the tribulations before the end, or maybe these wonders foretell the Parousia, the coming of Christ. But, either way, we are coming to the end of the world. Are you born again?"

"Mmm, I can't rightly say that I am. I was baptized a long time ago, when I was too young to have much say in the matter. I'm not a churchgoer, except sometimes to see my friends married or buried. If I was washed clean once, I guess I'm a little dusty by now. I don't suppose I qualify."

"No, I'm certain that you do not. Steve, the end of the world is coming and Christ is returning soon. The most urgent business you have—that anyone has!—is to take your troubles to Jesus, be washed in His Blood, and be born again in Him. Because you will receive no warning. The Trump will sound and you will either be caught up into the arms of Jesus, safe and happy forevermore, or you will be cast down into the fire and brimstone, there to suffer agonies through all eternity. You must be ready."

"Cripes! Alec, have you ever thought about becoming a preacher?"

"I've thought about it."

"You should do more than think about it, you should be one. You said all that just like you believed every word of it."

"I do."

"Thought maybe. Well, I'll pay you the respect of giving it some hard thought. But in the meantime I hope they don't hold Kingdom Come tonight because I've still got this load to deliver. Hazel! Let me have the check, dear; I've got to get the show on the road."

Three steak dinners came to $3.90; six beers was another sixty cents, for a total of $4.50. Steve paid with a half eagle, a coin I had never seen outside a coin collection—I wanted to look at this one but had no excuse.

Hazel picked it up, looked at it. "Don't get much gold around here," she remarked. "Cartwheels are the usual thing. And some paper, although the boss doesn't like paper money. Sure you can spare this, Steve?"

"I found the Lost Dutchman."

"Go along with you; I'm not going to be your fifth wife."

"I had in mind just a temporary arrangement."

"Not that either—not for a five-dollar gold piece." She dug into an apron pocket, took out a silver half dollar. "Your change, dear."

He pushed it back toward her. "What'll you do for fifty cents?"

She picked it up, pocketed it. "Spit in your eye. Thanks. Night, folks. Glad you came in."

During the thirty-five miles or so on into Flagstaff Steve asked questions of us about the worlds we had seen but made no comments. He talked just enough to keep us talking. He was especially interested in my descriptions of airships, jet planes, and *aeroplanos*, but anything technical fascinated him. Television he found much harder to believe than flying machines—well, so did I. But Margrethe assured him that she had seen television herself, and Margrethe is hard to disbelieve. Me, I might be mistaken for a con man. But not Margrethe. Her voice and manner carry conviction.

In Flagstaff, just short of Route 66, Steve pulled over to the side and stopped, left his engine running. "All out," he said, "if you insist on heading east. If you want to go north, you're welcome."

I said, "We've got to get to Kansas, Steve."

"Yes, I know. While you can get there either way, Sixty-Six is your best bet . . . though why anyone should want to go to Kansas beats me. It's that intersection ahead, there. Keep right and keep going; you can't miss it. Watch out for the Santa Fe tracks. Where you planning to sleep tonight?"

"I don't have any plans. We'll walk until we get another ride. If we don't get an all-night ride and we get too sleepy, we can sleep by the side of the road—it's warm."

"Alec, you listen to your Uncle Dudley. You're not going to sleep on the desert tonight. It's warm now; it'll be freezing cold by morning. Maybe you haven't noticed but we've been climbing all the way from Phoenix. And if the Gila monsters don't get you, the sand fleas will. You've got to rent a cabin."

"Steve, I can't rent a cabin."

"The Lord will provide. You believe that, don't you?"

"Yes," I answered stiffly, "I believe that." (But He also helps those who help themselves.)

"So let the Lord provide. Maggie, about this end-of-the-world business, do you agree with Alec?"

"I certainly don't disagree!"

"Mmm. Alec, I'm going to give it a lot of thought . . . starting tonight, by reading a Gideon Bible. This time I don't want to miss the parade. You go on down Sixty-Six, look for a place saying 'cabins.' Not 'motel,' not 'roadside inn,' not a word about Simmons mattresses or private baths—just 'cabins.' If they ask more than two dollars, walk away. Keep dickering and you might get it for one."

I wasn't listening very hard as I was growing quite angry. Dicker with *what?* He knew that I was utterly without funds—didn't he believe me?

"So I'll say good-bye," Steve went on. "Alec, can you get that door? I don't want to get out."

"I can get it." I opened it, stepped down, then remembered my manners. "Steve, I want to thank you for everything. Dinner, and beer, and a long ride. May the Lord watch over you and keep you."

"Thank you and don't mention it. Here." He reached into a pocket, pulled out a card. "That's my business card. Actually it's my daughter's address. When you get to Kansas, drop me a card, let me know how you made out."

"I'll do that." I took the card, then started to hand Margrethe down.

Steve stopped her. "Maggie! Aren't you going to kiss ol' Steve good-bye?"

"Why, certainly, Steve!" She turned back and half faced him on the seat.

"That's better. Alec, you'd better turn your back."

I did not turn my back but I tried to ignore it, while watching out the corner of my eye.

If it had gone on one half-second longer, I would have dragged her out of that cab bodily. Yet I am forced to admit that Margrethe was not having attentions forced on her; she was cooperating fully, kissing him in a fashion no married woman should ever kiss another man.

I endured it.

At last it ended. I handed her down, and closed the door. Steve called out, "'Bye, kids!" and his truck moved forward. As it picked up speed he tooted his horn twice.

Margrethe said, "Alec, you are angry with me."

"No. Surprised, yes. Even shocked. Disappointed. Saddened."

"Don't sniff at me!"

"Eh?"

"Steve drove us two hundred and fifty miles and bought us a fine dinner and didn't laugh when we told him a preposterous story. And now you get hoity-toity and holier-than-thou because I kissed him hard enough to show that I appreciated what he had done for me *and* my husband. I won't stand for it, do you hear?"

"I just meant that—"

"Stop it! I won't listen to explanations. Because you're wrong! And now *I* am angry and I shall stay angry until you realize you are wrong. So think it over!" She turned and started walking rapidly toward the intersection of 66 with 89.

I hurried to catch up. "Margrethe!"

She did not answer and increased her pace.

"Margrethe!" Eyes straight ahead—

"Margrethe darling! I was wrong. I'm sorry, I apologize."

She stopped abruptly, turned and threw her arms around my neck, started to cry. "Oh, Alec, I love you so and you're such a fub!"

I did not answer at once as my mouth was busy. At last I said, "I love you, too, and what is a fub?"

"You are."

"Well— In that case I'm your fub and you're stuck with me. Don't walk away from me again."

"I won't. Not ever." We resumed what we had been doing.

After a while I pulled my face back just far enough to whisper: "We don't have a bed to our name and I've never wanted one more."

"Alec. Check your pockets."

"Huh?"

"While he was kissing me, Steve whispered to me to tell you to check your pockets and to say, 'The Lord will provide.'"

I found it in my left-hand coat pocket: a gold eagle. Never before had I held one in my hand. It felt warm and heavy.

XVI

*Shall mortal man be more just than God? shall a
man be more pure than his maker?*
Job 4:17

*Teach me, and I will hold my tongue: and cause
me to understand wherein I have erred.*
Job 6:24

At a drugstore in downtown Flagstaff I exchanged that gold eagle for nine cartwheels, ninety-five cents in change, and a bar of Ivory soap. Buying soap was Margrethe's idea. "Alec, a druggist is not a banker; changing money is something he may not want to do other than as part of a sale. We need soap. I want to wash your underwear and mine, and we both need baths . . . and I suspect that, at the sort of cheap lodging Steve urged us to take, soap may not be included in the rent."

She was right on both points. The druggist raised his eyebrows at the ten-dollar gold piece but said nothing. He took the coin, let it ring on the glass top of a counter, then reached behind his cash register, fetched out a small bottle, and subjected the coin to the acid test.

I made no comment. Silently he counted out nine silver dollars, a half dollar, a quarter, and two dimes. Instead of pocketing the coins at once, I stood fast, and subjected each coin to the same ringing test he had used, using his glass counter. Having done so, I pushed one cartwheel back at him.

Again he made no comment—he had heard the dull

ring of that putatively silver coin as well as I. He rang up "No Sale," handed me another cartwheel (which rang clear as a bell), and put the bogus coin somewhere in the back of the cash drawer. Then he turned his back on me.

At the outskirts of town, halfway to Winona, we found a place shabby enough to meet our standards. Margrethe conducted the dicker, in Spanish. Our host asked five dollars. Marga called on the Virgin Mary and three other saints to witness what was being done to her. Then she offered him five pesos.

I did not understand this maneuver; I knew she had no pesos on her. Surely she would not be intending to offer those unspendable "royal" pesos I still carried?

I did not find out, as our host answered with a price of three dollars and that is final, *Señora*, as God is my witness.

They settled on a dollar and a half, then Marga rented clean sheets and a blanket for another fifty cents—paid for the lot with two silver dollars but demanded pillows and clean pillow-cases to seal the bargain. She got them but the *patrón* asked something for luck. Marga added a dime and he bowed deeply and assured us that his house was ours.

At seven the next morning we were on our way, rested, clean, happy, and hungry. A half hour later we were in Winona and much hungrier. We cured the latter at a little trailer-coach lunchroom: a stack of wheat cakes, ten cents; coffee, five cents—no charge for second cup, no limit on butter or syrup.

Margrethe could not finish her hot cakes—they were lavish—so we swapped plates and I salvaged what she had left.

A sign on the wall read: CASH WHEN SERVED — NO TIPPING — ARE YOU READY FOR JUDGMENT DAY? The cook-waiter (and owner, I think) had a copy of *The Watch Tower* propped up by his range. I asked, "Brother, do you have any late news on when to expect Judgment Day?"

"Don't joke about it. Eternity is a long time to spend in the Pit."

I answered, "I was not joking. By the signs and portents I think we are in the seven-year period prophesied in the eleventh chapter of Revelation, verses two and three. But I don't know how far we are into it."

"We're already well into the second half," he answered. "The two witnesses are now prophesying and the antichrist is abroad in the land. Are you in a state of grace? If not, you had better get cracking."

I answered, "'Therefore be ye also ready: for such an hour as ye think not the Son of man cometh.'"

"You'd better believe it!"

"I do believe it. Thanks for a good breakfast."

"Don't mention it. May the Lord watch over you."

"Thank you. May He bless you and keep you." Marga and I left.

We headed east again. "How is my sweetheart?"

"Full of food and happy."

"So am I. Something you did last night made me especially happy."

"Me, too. But you always do, darling man. Every time."

"Uh, yes, there's that. Me, too. Always. But I meant something you said, earlier. When Steve asked if you agreed with me about Judgment Day and you told him you did agree. Marga, I can't tell you how much it has worried me that you have not chosen to be received back into the arms of Jesus. With Judgment Day rushing toward us and no way to know the hour—well, I've worried. I do worry. But apparently you are finding your way back to the light but had not yet discussed it with me."

We walked perhaps twenty paces while Margrethe did not say anything.

At last she said quietly, "Beloved, I would put your mind at rest. If I could. I cannot."

"So? I do not understand. Will you explain?"

"I did not tell Steve that I agreed with you. I said to him that I did not disagree."

"But that's the same thing!"

"No, darling. What I did not say to Steve but could have said in full honesty is that I will *never* publicly disagree with my husband about anything. Any disagreement with you I will discuss with you in private. Not in Steve's presence. Not anyone's."

I chewed that over, let several possible comments go unsaid—at last said, "Thank you, Margrethe."

"Beloved, I do it for my own dignity as well as for yours. All my life I have hated the sight of husband and wife disagreeing—disputing—quarreling in public. If you say that the sun is covered with bright green puppy dogs, I will not disagree in public."

"Ah, but it is!"

"Sir?" She stopped, and looked startled.

"My good Marga. Whatever the problem, you always find a gentle answer. If I ever do see bright green puppy dogs on the face of the sun, I will try to remember to discuss it with you in private, not face you with hard decisions in public. I love you. I read too much into what you said to Steve because I really do worry."

She took my hand and we walked a bit farther without talking.

"Alec?"

"Yes, my love?"

"I do not willingly worry you. If I am wrong and you are going to the Christian Heaven, I do want to go with you. If this means a return to faith in Jesus—and it seems that it does—then that is what I want. I will try. I cannot promise it, as faith is not a matter of simple volition. But I will try."

I stopped to kiss her, to the amusement of a carload of men passing by. "Darling, more I cannot ask. Shall we pray together?"

"Alec, I would rather not. Let me pray alone—and I

will! When it comes time to pray together, I will tell you."

Not long after that we were picked up by a ranch couple who took us into Winslow. They dropped us there without asking any questions and without us offering any information, which must set some sort of record.

Winslow is much larger than Winona; it is a respectable town as desert communities go—seven thousand at a guess. We found there an opportunity to carry out something Steve had indirectly suggested and that we had discussed the night before.

Steve was correct; we were not dressed for the desert. True, we had had no choice, as we had been caught by a world change. But I did not see another man wearing a business suit in the desert. Nor did we see Anglo women dressed in women's suits. Indian women and Mexican women wore skirts, but Anglo women wore either shorts or trousers—slacks, jeans, cutoffs, riding pants, something. Rarely a skirt, never a suit.

Furthermore our suits were not right even as city wear. They looked as out of place as styles of the Mauve Decade would look. Don't ask me how as I am no expert on styles, especially for women. The suit that I wore had been both smart and expensive when worn by my *patrón*, *Don* Jaime, in Mazatlán in another world . . . but on me, in the Arizona desert in this world, it was something out of skid row.

In Winslow we found just the shop we needed: SECOND WIND — A Million Bargains — All Sales Cash, No Guarantees, No Returns — All Used Clothing Sterilized Before Being Offered For Sale. Above this were the same statements in Spanish.

An hour later, after much picking over of their stock and some heavy dickering by Margrethe, we were dressed for the desert. I was wearing khaki pants, a shirt to match, and a straw hat of vaguely western style. Margrethe was wearing considerably less: shorts that were both short and tight—indecently so—and an upper garment that was less than a bodice but slightly more than a brassière. It was termed a "halter."

When I saw Marga in this outfit, I whispered to her, "I positively will not permit you to appear in public in that shameless costume."

She answered, "Dear, don't be a fub so early in the day. It's too hot."

"I'm not joking. I forbid you to buy that."

"Alec, I don't recall asking your permission."

"Are you defying me?"

She sighed. "Perhaps I am. I don't want to. Did you get your razor?"

"You saw me!"

"I have your underpants and socks. Is there anything more you need now?"

"No. Margrethe! Quit evading me!"

"Darling, I told you that I will not quarrel with you in public. This outfit has a wrap-around skirt; I was about to put it on. Let me do so and settle the bill. Then we can go outside and talk in private."

Fuming, I went along with what she proposed. I might as well admit that, under her careful management, we came out of that bazaar with more money than we had had when we came in. How? That suit from my *patrón,* *Don* Jaime, that looked so ridiculous on me, looked just right on the owner of the shop—in fact he resembled *Don* Jaime. He had been willing to swap, even, for what I needed—khaki shirt and pants and straw hat.

But Margrethe insisted on something to boot. She demanded five dollars, got two.

I learned, as she settled our bill, that she had wrought similar magic in getting rid of that tailored suit she no longer needed. We entered the shop with $7.55; we left it with $8.80 . . . and desert outfits for each of us, a comb (for two), a toothbrush (also for two), a knapsack, a safety razor, plus a minimum of underwear and socks—all secondhand but alleged to be sterilized.

I am not good at tactics, not with women. We were outside and down the highway to an open place where we could talk privately before Margrethe would talk to me—and I did not realize that I had already lost.

Without stopping, she said, "Well, dear? You had something to discuss."

"Uh, with that skirt in place your clothing is acceptable. Barely. But you are not to appear in public in those shorts. Is that understood?"

"I intended to wear just the shorts. If the weather is warm. As it is."

"But, Margrethe, I told you not to—" She was unsnapping the skirt, taking it off. "You are defying me!"

She folded it up neatly. "May I place this in the knapsack? Please?"

"You are deliberately disobeying me!"

"But, Alec, I don't have to obey you and you don't have to obey me."

"But— Look, dear, be reasonable. You know I don't usually give orders. But a wife must obey her husband. Are you my wife?"

"You told me so. So I am until you tell me otherwise."

"Then it is your duty to obey me."

"No, Alec."

"But that is a wife's first duty!"

"I don't agree."

"But— This is madness! Are you leaving me?"

"No. Only if you divorce me."

"I don't believe in divorce. Divorce is wrong. Against Scripture."

She made no answer.

"Margrethe . . . *please* put your skirt on."

She said softly, "Almost you persuade me, dearest. Will you explain why you want me to do so?"

"What? Because those shorts, worn alone, are indecent!"

"I don't see how an article of clothing can be indecent, Alec. A person, yes. Are you saying that *I* am indecent?"

"Uh— You're twisting my words. When you wear those shorts—without a skirt—in public, you expose so much of yourself that the spectacle is indecent. Right now, walking this highway, your limbs are fully exposed . . . to the people in that car that just passed, for example. They saw you. I saw them staring!"

"Good. I hope they enjoyed it."

"What?"

"You tell me that I am beautiful. But you could be prejudiced. I hope that my appearance is pleasing to other people as well."

"Be serious, Margrethe; we're speaking of your naked limbs. Naked."

"You're saying my legs are bare. So they are. I prefer them bare when the weather is warm. What are you frowning at, dear? Are my legs ugly?"

("Thou art all fair, my love; there is no spot in thee!") "Your limbs are beautiful, my love; I have told you so many times. But I have no wish to share your beauty."

"Beauty is not diminished by being shared. Let's get back to the subject, Alec; you were explaining how my legs are indecent. If you can explain it. I don't think you can."

"But, Margrethe, nakedness is indecent by its very nature. It inspires lewd thoughts."

"Really? Does seeing my legs cause you to get an erection?"

"Margrethe!"

"Alec, stop being a fub! I asked a simple question."

"An improper question."

She sighed. "I don't see how that question can possibly be improper between husband and wife. And I will never concede that my legs are indecent. Or that nakedness is indecent. I have been naked in front of hundreds of people—"

"Margrethe!"

She looked surprised. "Surely you know that?"

"I did not know it and I am shocked to hear it."

"Truly, dear? But you know how well I swim."

"What's that got to do with it? I swim well, too. But I don't swim naked; I wear a bathing suit." (But I was remembering most sharply the pool in *Konge Knut*—of course my darling was used to nude swimming. I found myself out on a limb.)

"Oh. Yes, I've seen such suits, in Mazatlán. And in Spain. But, darling, we're going astray again. The problem is wider than whether or not bare legs are indecent or whether I should have kissed Steve good-bye or even whether I must obey you. You are expecting me to be what I am not. I want to be your wife for many years, for all my life—and I hope to share Heaven with you if Heaven is your destination. But, darling, I am not a child, I am not a slave. Because I love you I wish to please you. But I will not obey an order simply because I am a wife."

I could say that I overwhelmed her with the brilliance of my rebuttal. Yes, I could say that, but it would not be true. I was still trying to think of an answer when a car slowed down as it overtook us. I heard a whistle of the sort called "wolf." The car stopped beyond us and backed up. "Need a ride?" a voice called out.

"Yes!" Margrethe answered, and hurried. Perforce, I did, too.

It was a station wagon with a woman behind the wheel, a man riding with her. Both were my age or older. He reached back, opened the rear door. "Climb in!"

I handed Margrethe in, followed her and closed the door. "Got room enough?" he asked. "If not, throw that junk on the floor. We never sit in the back seat, so stuff sort o' gravitates to it. We're Clyde and Bessie Bulkey."

"He's Bulkey; I'm just well fed," the driver added.

"You're supposed to laugh at that; I've heard it before." He was indeed bulky, the sort of big-boned beefy man who is an athlete in school, then puts on weight later. His wife had correctly described both of them; she was not fat but carried some extra padding.

"How do you do, Mrs. Bulkey, Mr. Bulkey. We're Alec and Margrethe Graham. Thank you for picking us up."

"Don't be so formal, Alec," she answered. "How far you going?"

"Bessie, *please* keep one eye on the road."

"Clyde, if you don't like the way I'm herding this heap, I'll pull over and let you drive."

"Oh, no, no, you're doing fine!"

"Pipe down then, or I invoke rule K. Well, Alec?"

"We're going to Kansas."

"Coo! We're not going that far; we turn north at Chambers. That's just a short piece down the road, about ninety miles. But you're welcome to that much. What are you going to do in Kansas?"

(What was I going to do in Kansas? Open an ice cream parlor . . . bring my dear wife back to the fold . . . prepare for Judgment Day—) "I'm going to wash dishes."

"My husband is too modest," Margrethe said quietly. "We're going to open a small restaurant and soda fountain in a college town. But on our way to that goal we are likely to wash dishes. Or almost any work."

So I explained what had happened to us, with variations and omissions to avoid what they wouldn't believe. "The restaurant was wiped out, our Mexican partners were dead, and we lost everything we had. I said 'dishwashing' because that is the one job I can almost always find. But I'll take a swing at 'most anything."

Clyde said, "Alec, with that attitude you'll be back on your feet before you know it."

"We lost some money, that's all. We're not too old to start over again." (Dear Lord, will You hold off Judgment Day long enough for me to do it? Thy will be done. Amen.)

Margrethe reached over and squeezed my hand. Clyde noticed it. He had turned around in his seat so that he faced us as well as his wife. "You'll make it," he said. "With your wife backing you, you're bound to make it."

"I think so. Thank you." I knew why he was turned to

face us: to stare at Margrethe. I wanted to tell him to keep his eyes to himself but, under the circumstances, I could not. Besides that, it was clear that Mr. and Mrs. Bulkey saw nothing wrong with the way my beloved was dressed; Mrs. Bulkey was dressed the same way, only more so. Or less so. Less costume, more bare skin. I must admit, too, that, while she was not the immortal beauty Margrethe is, she was quite comely.

At Painted Desert we stopped, got out, and stared at the truly unbelievable natural beauty. I had seen it once before; Margrethe had never seen it and was breathless. Clyde told me that they always stopped, even though they had seen it hundreds of times.

Correction: I had seen it once before . . . in another world. Painted Desert tended to prove what I had strongly suspected: It was not Mother Earth that changed in these wild changes; it was man and his works—and even those only in part. But the only obvious explanation seemed to lead straight to paranoia. If so, I must not surrender to it; I must take care of Margrethe.

Clyde bought us hot dogs and cold drinks and brushed aside my offer to pay. When we got back into their car, Clyde took the wheel and invited Margrethe to ride up front with him. I was not pleased but could not show it, as Bessie promptly said, "Poor Alec! Has to put up with the old bag. Don't sulk, dear; it's only twenty-three miles to the turn-off for Chambers . . . or less than twenty-three minutes the way Clyde drives."

This time Clyde took thirty minutes. But he waited and made sure that we had a ride to Gallup.

We reached Gallup long before dark. Despite $8.80 in our pockets, it seemed time to look for dirty dishes. Gallup has almost as many motels and cabin courts as it has Indians and almost half of these hostelries have restaurants. I checked a baker's dozen before I found one that needed a dishwasher.

Fourteen days later we were in Oklahoma City. If you think that is slow time, you are correct; it is less than fifty miles a day. But plenty had happened and I was feeling decidedly paranoid—world change after world change and always timed to cause me maximum trouble.

Ever seen a cat play with a mouse? The mouse never has a chance. If he has even the brains the good Lord gives a mouse, he knows that. Nevertheless the mouse keeps on trying . . . and is hauled back every time.

I was the mouse.

Or we were the mice, for Margrethe was with me . . . and she was all that kept me going. She didn't complain and she didn't quit. So I couldn't quit.

Example: I had figured out that, while paper money was never any good after a world change, hard money, gold and silver, would somehow be negotiable, as bullion if not as coin. So, when I got a chance to lay hands on hard money, I was stingy with it and refused to take paper money in change for hard money.

Smart boy. Alec, you're a real brain.

So on our third day in Gallup Marga and I took a nap in a room paid for by dishwashing (me) and by cleaning rooms (Margrethe). We didn't intend to go to sleep; we simply wanted to rest a bit before eating; it had been a long, hard day. We lay down on top of the bedspread.

I was just getting relaxed when I realized that something hard was pressing against my spine. I roused enough to figure out that our hoarded silver dollars had slipped out of my side pocket when I had turned over. So I eased my arm out from under Marga's head, retrieved the dollars, counted them, added the loose change, and placed it all on the bedside table a foot from my head, then got horizontal again, slid my arm under Marga's head and fell right to sleep.

When I woke up it was pitch dark.

I came wide awake. Margrethe was still snoring softly on my arm. I shook her a little "Honey. Wake up."

"Mrrrf?"

"It's late. We may have missed dinner."

She came quickly awake. "Can you switch on the bed lamp?"

I fumbled at the bedside table, nearly fell out of bed. "Can't find the pesky thing. It's dark as the inside of a pile of coal. Wait a sec, I'll get the overhead light."

I got cautiously off the bed, headed for the door, stumbled over a chair, could not find the door—groped for it, did find it, groped some more and found a light switch by it. The overhead light came on.

For a long, dismal moment neither of us said anything. Then I said, inanely and unnecessarily, "They did it again."

The room had the characterless anonymity of any cheap motel room anywhere. Nevertheless it was different in details from the room in which we had gone to sleep.

And our hoarded silver dollars were gone.

Everything but the clothes we were wearing was gone—knapsack, clean socks, spare underwear, comb, safety razor, everything. I inspected, made certain.

"Well, Marga, what now?"

"Whatever you say, sir."

"Mmm. I don't think they'll know me in the kitchen. But they still might let me wash dishes."

"Or they may need a waitress."

The door had a spring lock and I had no key, so I left it an inch ajar. The door led directly outdoors and looked across a parking court at the office—a corner room with a lighted sign reading OFFICE—all commonplace except that it did not match the appearance of the motel in which we had been working. In that establishment the manager's office had been in the front end of a central building, the rest of that central building being the coffee shop.

Yes, we had missed dinner.

And breakfast. This motel did not have a coffee shop.

"Well, Marga?"

"Which way is Kansas?"

"That way . . . I think. But we have two choices. We can go back into the room, go to bed properly, and sleep until daylight. Or we can get out there on the highway and try to thumb a ride. In the dark."

"Alec, I see only *one* choice. If we go back inside and go to bed, we'll get up at daylight, some hours hungrier and no better off. Maybe worse off, if they catch us sleeping in a room we didn't pay for—"

"I washed an awful lot of dishes!"

"Not here, you didn't. Here they might send for the police."

We started walking.

That was typical of the persecution we suffered in trying to get to Kansas. Yes, I said "persecution." If paranoia consists in believing that the world around you is a conspiracy against you, I had become paranoid. But it was either a "sane" paranoia (if you will pardon the Irishism), or I was suffering from delusions so monumental that I should be locked up and treated.

Maybe so. If so, Margrethe was part of my delusions— an answer I could not accept. It could not be *folie à deux;* Margrethe was sane in any world.

It was the middle of the day before we got anything to eat, and by then I was beginning to see ghosts where a healthy man would see only dust devils. My hat had gone where the woodbine twineth and the New Mexico sun on my head was not helping my state.

A carload of men from a construction site picked us up and took us into Grants, and bought us lunch before they left us there. I may be certifiably insane but I am not stupid; we owe that ride and that meal to the fact that Margrethe in shorts indecently tight is a sight that attracts the attention of men. That gave me plenty to think about while I enjoyed (and I did enjoy it!) that lunch they bought us. But I kept my ruminations to myself.

After they left us I said, "East?"

"Yes, sir. But first I would like to check the public library. If there is one."

"Oh, yes! Surely." Earlier, in the world of our friend Steve, the lack of any sort of air travel had caused me to suspect that Steve's world might be the world where Margrethe was born (and therefore the home of "Alec Graham" as well). In Gallup we had checked on this at the public library—I had looked up American history in an encyclopedia while Marga checked on Danish history. It took us each about five minutes to determine that Steve's world was not the world Marga was born in. I found that Bryan had been elected in 1896 but had died in office, succeeded by his vice president, Arthur Sewall—and that was all I needed to know; I then simply raced through presidents and wars I had never heard of.

Margrethe had finished her line of investigation with her nose twitching with indignation. Once outside where we didn't have to whisper I asked her what was troubling her. "This isn't your world, dear; I made sure of that."

"It certainly isn't!"

"But we didn't have anything but a negative to go on. There may be many worlds that have no aeronautics of any sort."

"I'm glad this isn't my world! Alec, in this world *Denmark is part of Sweden*. Isn't that terrible?"

Truthfully I did not understand her upset. Both countries are Scandinavian, pretty much alike—or so it seemed to me. "I'm sorry, dear. I don't know much about such things." (I had been to Stockholm once, liked the place. It didn't seem a good time to tell her so.)

"And that silly book says that Stockholm is the capital and that Carl Sixteenth is king. Alec, he isn't even royal! And now they tell me he's *my* king!"

"But, sweetheart, he's not your king. This isn't even your world."

"I know. Alec? If we have to settle here—if the world doesn't change again—couldn't I be naturalized?"

"Why, yes. I suppose so."

She sighed. "I don't want to be a Swede."

I kept quiet. There were some things I couldn't help her with.

So in Grants we again went to a public library to see what the latest changes had done to the world. Since we had seen no *aeroplanos* and no dirigibles, again it was possible that we were in Margrethe's world. This time I looked first under "Aeronautics"—did not find dirigibles but did find flying machines . . . invented by Dr. Alberto Santos-Dumont of Brazil early in this century—and I was bemused by the inventor's name, as, in my world, he had been a pioneer in dirigibles second only to Count von Zeppelin. Apparently the doctor's aerodynes were primitive compared with jet planes, or even *aeroplanos;* they seemed to be curiosities rather than commercial vehicles. I dropped it and turned to American history, checking first on William Jennings Bryan.

I couldn't find him at all. Well, I had known that this was not my world.

But Marga was all smiles, could hardly wait to get outside the no-talking area to tell me about it. "In this world Scandinavia is all one big country . . . and København is its capital!"

"Well, good!"

"Queen Margrethe's son Prince Frederik was crowned King Eric Gustav—no doubt to please the outlanders. But he is true Danish royalty and a Dane right down to his skull bone. This is as it should be!"

I tried to show her that I was happy, too. Without a cent between us, with no idea where we would sleep that night, she was delighted as a child at Christmas . . . over an event that I could not see mattered at all.

Two short rides got us into Albuquerque and I decided that it was prudent to stay there a bit—it's a big place—even if we had to throw ourselves on Salvation Army charity. But I quickly found a job as a dishwasher in the coffee shop of the local Holiday Inn and Margrethe went to work as a waitress in the same shop.

We had been working there less than two hours when she came back to the scullery and slid something into my hip pocket while I was bent over a sink. "A present for you, dear!"

I turned around. "Hi, Gorgeous." I checked my pocket—a safety razor of the travel sort—handle unscrews, and razor and handle and blades all fit into a waterproof case smaller than a pocket Testament, and intended to be carried in a pocket. "Steal it?"

"Not quite. Tips. Got it at the lobby notions stand. Dear, at your first break I want you to shave."

"Let me clue you, doll. You get hired for your looks. I get hired for my strong back, weak mind, and docile disposition. They don't care how I look."

"But I do."

"Your slightest wish is my command. Now get out of here; you're slowing up production."

That night Margrethe explained why she had bought me a razor ahead of anything else. "Dear, it's not just because I like your face smooth and your hair short—although I do! These Loki tricks have kept on and each time we have to find work at once just to eat. You say that nobody cares how a dishwasher looks . . . but *I* say looking clean and neat helps in getting hired for *any* job, and can't possibly hurt.

"But there is another reason. As a result of these changes, you've had to let your whiskers grow once, twice—I can count five times, once for over three days. Dearest, when you are freshly shaved, you stand tall and look happy. And that makes me happy."

Margrethe made for me a sort of money belt—actually a cloth pocket and a piece of cloth tape—which she wanted me to wear in bed. "Dear, we've lost anything we didn't have on us whenever a shift took place. I want you to put your razor and our hard money into this when you undress for bed."

"I don't think we can outwit Satan that easily."

"Maybe not. We can try. We come through each change with the clothes we are wearing at the time and with whatever we have in our pockets. This seems to fit the rules."

"Chaos does not have rules."

"Perhaps this is not chaos. Alec, if you won't wear this to bed, do you mind if I do?"

"Oh, I'll wear it. It won't stop Satan if he really wants to take it away from us. Nor does it really worry me. Once he dumped us mother naked into the Pacific and we pulled out of it—remember? What *does* worry me is— Marga, have you noticed that every time we have gone through a change we've been holding each other? At least holding hands?"

"I've noticed."

"Change happens in the blink of an eye. What happens if we're not together, holding each other? At least touching? Tell me."

She kept quiet so long that I knew she did not intend to answer.

"Uh huh," I said. "Me, too. But we *can't* be Siamese twins, touching all the time. We have to work. My darling, my life, Satan or Loki or whatever bad spirit is doing this to us, can separate us forever simply by picking any instant when we are not touching."

"Alec."

"Yes, my love?"

"Loki has been able to do this to us at any moment for a long time. It has not happened."

"So it may happen the next second."

"Yes. But it may not happen at all."

We moved on, and suffered more changes. Margrethe's precautions did seem to work—although in one change they seemed to work almost too well; I barely missed a jail sentence for unlawful possession of silver coins. But a quick change (the quickest we had seen) got rid of the charge, the evidence, and the complaining witness. We found ourselves in a strange courtroom and were quickly evicted for lacking tickets entitling us to remain there.

But the razor stayed with me; no cop or sheriff or marshal seemed to want to confiscate that.

We were moving on by our usual method (my thumb and Margrethe's lovely legs; I had long since admitted to myself that I might as well enjoy the inevitable) and had been dropped in a pretty part of—Texas, it must have been—by a trucker who had turned north off 66 on a side road.

We had come out of the desert into low green hills. It was a beautiful day but we were tired, hungry, sweaty, and dirty, for our persecutors—Satan or whoever—had outdone themselves: three changes in thirty-six hours.

In one day I had had two dishwashing jobs in the same town at the same address . . . and had collected nothing. It is difficult to collect from The Lonesome Cowboy Steak House when it turns into Vivian's Grill in front of your eyes. The same was true three hours later when Vivian's Grill melted into a used-car lot. The only thing good about these shocks was that by great good fortune (or conspiracy?) Margrethe was with me each time—in one case she had come to get me and was waiting with me while my boss was figuring my time, in the other she had been working with me.

The third change did us out of a night's lodging that had already been paid for in kind by Margrethe's labor.

So when that trucker dropped us, we were tired and hungry and dirty and my paranoia had reached a new high.

We had been walking a few hundred yards when we came to a sweet little stream, a sight in Texas precious beyond all else.

We stopped on the culvert bridging it. "Margrethe, how would you like to wade in that?"

"Darling, I'm going to do more than wade in it, I'm going to bathe in it."

"Hmm— Yes, go under the fence, along the stream about fifty, seventy-five yards, and I don't think anyone could see us from the road."

"Sweetheart, they can line up and cheer if they want to; I'm going to have a bath. And— That water looks clean. Would it be safe to drink?"

"The upstream side? Certainly. We've taken worse chances every day since the iceberg. Now if we had something to eat— Say, your hot fudge sundae. Or would you prefer scrambled eggs?" I held up the lower wire of the fence to let her crawl under.

"Will you settle for an Oh Henry bar?"

"Make that a Milky Way," I answered, "if I have my druthers."

"I'm afraid you don't, dear. An Oh Henry bar is all there is." She held the wire for me.

"Maybe we'd better stop talking about food we don't have," I said, and crawled under—straightened up and added, "I'm ready to eat raw skunk."

"Food we do have, dear man. I have an Oh Henry in my tote."

I stopped abruptly. "Woman, if you're joking, I'm going to beat you."

"I'm not joking."

"In Texas it is legal to correct a wife with a stick not thicker than one's thumb." I held up my thumb. "Do you see one about this size?"

"I'll find one."

"Where did you get a candy bar?"

"That roadside stop where Mr. Facelli treated us to coffee and doughnuts."

Mr. Facelli had been our middle-of-the-night ride just before the truck that had just dropped us. Two small cake doughnuts each and the sugar and cream for coffee had been our only calories for twenty-four hours.

"The beating can wait. Woman, if you stole it, tell me

about it later. You really do have a real live Oh Henry? Or am I getting feverish?"

"Alec, do you think I would steal a candy bar? I bought it from a coin machine while you and Mr. Facelli were in the men's room after we ate."

"How? We don't have any money. Not from this world."

"Yes, Alec. But there was a dime in my tote, from two changes back. Of course it was not a good dime, strictly speaking. But I couldn't see any real harm if the machine would take it. And it did. But I put it out of sight before you two got back . . . because I didn't have three dimes and could not offer a candy bar to Mr. Facelli." She added anxiously, "Do you think I cheated? Using that dime?"

"It's a technicality I won't go into . . . as long as I get to share in the proceeds of the crime. And that makes me equally guilty. Uh . . . eat first, or bathe first?"

We ate first, a picnic banquet washed down by delicious creek water. Then we bathed, with much splashing and laughing—I remember it as one of the happiest times of my life. Margrethe had soap in her tote bag, too, and I supplied the towel, my shirt. First I wiped Margrethe with it, then I wiped me with it. The dry, warm air finished the job.

What happened immediately after was inevitable. I had never in my life made love outdoors, much less in bright daylight. If anyone had asked me, I would have said that for me it would be a psychological impossibility; I would be too inhibited, too aware of the indecency involved.

I am amazed and happy to say that, while keenly aware of the circumstances, I was untroubled at the time and quite able . . . perhaps because of Margrethe's bubbling, infectious enthusiasm.

I have never slept naked on grass before, either. I think we slept about an hour.

When we woke up, Margrethe insisted on shaving me. I

could not shave myself very well as I had no mirror, but she could and did, with her usual efficiency. We stood knee-deep in the water; I worked up soapsuds with my hands and slathered my face. She shaved and I renewed the lather as needed.

"There," she said at last, and gave me a sign-off kiss, "you'll do. Rinse off now and don't forget your ears. I'll find the towel. Your shirt." She climbed onto the bank while I leaned far over and splashed water on my face.

"Alec—"

"I can't hear you; the water's running."

"Please, dear!"

I straightened up, wiped the water out of my eyes, looked around.

Everything we owned was gone, everything but my razor.

XVII

Margrethe said, "What did you do with the soap?"

I took a deep breath, sighed it out. "Did I hear you correctly? You're asking what I did with the soap?"

"What would you rather I said?"

"Uh— I don't know. But not that. A miracle takes place . . . and you ask me about a bar of soap."

"Alec, a miracle that takes place again and again and again is no longer a miracle; it's just a nuisance. Too many, too much. I want to scream or break into tears. So I asked about the soap."

I had been halfway to hysteria myself when Margrethe's statement hit me like a dash of cold water. Margrethe? She who took icebergs and earthquakes in her stride, she who never whimpered in adversity . . . *she* wanted to scream?

"I'm sorry, dear. I had the soap in my hands when you were shaving me. I did not have it in my hands when I rinsed my face. I suppose I laid it on the bank. But I don't recall. Does it matter?"

"Not really, I suppose. Although that cake of Camay, used just once, would be half our worldly goods if I could

213

find it, this razor being the other half. You may have placed it on the bank, but I don't see it."

"Then it's gone. Marga, we've got urgent things to worry about before we'll be dirty enough to need soap again. Food, clothing, shelter." I scrambled up onto the bank. "Shoes. We don't even have *shoes*. What do we do now? I'm stumped. If I had a wailing wall, I'd wail."

"Steady, dear, steady."

"Is it all right if I just whimper a little?"

She came close, put her arms around me, and kissed me. "Whimper all you want to, dear, whimper for both of us. Then let's decide what to do."

I can't stay depressed with Margrethe's arms around me. "Do you have any ideas? I can't think of anything but picking our way back to the highway and trying to thumb a ride . . . which doesn't appeal to me in the state I'm in. Not even a fig leaf. Do you see a fig tree?"

"Does Texas have fig trees?"

"Texas has everything. What do we do now?"

"We go back to the highway and start walking."

"Barefooted? Why not stand still and wave our thumbs? We can't go far enough barefooted to matter. My feet are tender."

"They'll toughen up. Alec, we *must* keep moving. For our morale, love. If we give up, we'll die. I know it."

Ten minutes later we were moving slowly east on the highway. But it was not the highway we had left. This one was four lanes instead of two, with wide paved shoulders. The fence marking the right of way, instead of three strands of barbed wire, was chain-link steel as high as my head. We would have had a terrible time reaching the highway had it not been for the stream. By going back into the water and holding our breaths, we managed to slither under the fence. This left us sopping wet again (and no towel-shirt) but the warm air corrected that in a few minutes.

There was much more traffic on this highway than there had been on the one we had left, both freight and what seemed to be passenger cars. And it was *fast*. How fast I could not guess, but it seemed at least twice as fast as any ground transportation I had ever seen. Perhaps as fast as transoceanic dirigibles.

There were big vehicles that had to be freight movers but looked more like railroad boxcars than they looked like lorries. And even longer than boxcars. But as I stared I figured out that each one was at least three cars, articulated. I figured this out by attempting to count wheels. Sixteen per car? Six more on some sort of locomotive up front, for a total of fifty-four wheels. Was this possible?

These behemoths moved with no sound but the noise of air rushing past them, plus a whoosh of tires against pavement. My dynamics professor would have approved.

In the lane nearest us were smaller vehicles that I assumed to be passenger cars, although I could not see anyone inside. Where one would expect windows appeared to be mirrors or burnished steel. They were long and low and as sleekly shaped as an airship.

And now I saw that this was not *one* highway, but *two*. All the traffic on the pavement nearest us was going east; at least a hundred yards away another stream of traffic was going west. Still farther away, seen only in glimpses, was a limit fence for the northern side of the widest right of way I have ever seen.

We trudged along on the edge of the shoulder. I began to feel gloomy about the chances of being picked up. Even if they could see us (which seemed uncertain), how could they stop quickly enough to pick up someone on the highway? Nevertheless I waved the hitchhikers' sign at each car.

I kept my misgivings to myself. After we had been walking a dismal time, a car that had just passed us dropped out of the traffic lane onto the shoulder, stopped at least a quarter mile ahead of us, then backed toward us at a speed I would regard as too fast if I were going forward. We got hastily off the shoulder.

It stopped alongside us. A mirrored section a yard wide

and at least that high lifted up like a storm-cellar door, and I found myself looking into the passenger compartment. The operator looked out at us and grinned. "I don't believe it!"

I tried to grin back. "I don't believe it myself. But here we are. Will you give us a ride?"

"Could be." He looked Margrethe up and down. "My, aren't you the purty thing! What happened?"

Margrethe answered, "Sir, we are lost."

"Looks like. But how did you manage to lose your clothes, too? Kidnapped? Or what? Never mind, that can wait. I'm Jerry Farnsworth."

I answered, "We're Alec and Margrethe Graham."

"Good to meet you. Well, you don't look armed—except for that thing in your hand, Miz Graham. What is it?"

She held it out to him. "A razor."

He accepted it, looked at it, handed it back. "Durned if it isn't. Haven't seen one like that since I was too young to shave. Well, I don't see how you can highjack me with that. Climb in. Alec, you can have the back seat; your sister can sit up here with me." Another section of the shell swung upward.

"Thank you," I answered, thinking sourly about beggars and choosers. "Marga is not my sister, she's my wife."

"Lucky man! Do you object to your wife riding with me?"

"Oh, of course not!"

"I think that answer would cause a tension meter to jingle. Dear, you'd better get back there with your husband."

"Sir, you invited me to sit with you and my husband voiced his approval." Margrethe slipped into the forward passenger seat. I opened my mouth and closed it, having found I had nothing to say. I climbed into the back seat, discovered that the car was bigger inside than out; the seat was roomy and comfortable. The doors closed down; the "mirrors" now were windows.

"I'm about to put her back into the flow," our host said, "so don't fight the safeties. Sometimes this buggy bucks like a Brahma bull, six gees or better. No, wait a sec. Where are you two going?" He looked at Margrethe.

"We're going to Kansas, Mr. Farnsworth."

"Call me Jerry, dear. In your skin?"

"We have no clothing, sir. We lost it."

I added, "Mr. Farnsworth—Jerry—we're in a distressed state. We lost everything. Yes, we are going to Kansas, but first we must find clothes somewhere—Red Cross, maybe, I don't know. And I've got to find a job and make us some money. Then we'll go to Kansas."

"I see. I think I do. Some of it. How are you going to get to Kansas?"

"I had in mind continuing straight on to Oklahoma City, then north. Stick to the main highways. Since we're hitchhiking."

"Alec, you really are lost. See that fence? Do you know the penalty for a pedestrian caught inside that fence?"

"No, I don't."

"Ignorance is bliss. You'll be much better off on the small side roads where hitching is still legal, or at least tolerated. If you're for Oke City, I can help you along. Hang on." He did something at controls in front of him. He didn't touch the wheel because there wasn't any wheel to touch. Instead there were two hand grips.

The car vibrated faintly, then jumped sideways. I felt as if I had fallen into soft mush and my skin tingled as with static electricity. The car bucked like a small boat in a heavy sea, but that "soft mush" kept me from being battered about. Suddenly it quieted down and only that faint vibration continued. The landscape was streaking past.

"Now," said Mr. Farnsworth, "tell me about it."

"Margrethe?"

"Of course, dearest. You must."

"Jerry . . . we're from another world."

"Oh, no!" He groaned. "Not another flying saucer! That makes four this week. That's your story?"

"No, no. I've never seen a flying saucer. We're from earth, but . . . different. We were hitchhiking on Highway Sixty-Six, trying to reach Kansas—"

"Wait a minute. You said, 'Sixty-Six.'"

"Yes, of course."

"That's what they used to call this road before they rebuilt it. But it hasn't been called anything but Interstate Forty for, oh, over forty years, maybe fifty. Hey. *Time* travelers! Are you?"

"What year is this?" I asked.

"Nineteen-ninety-four."

"That's our year, too. Wednesday the eighteenth of May. Or was this morning. Before the change."

"It still is. But— Look, let's quit jumping around. Start at the beginning, whenever that was, and tell me how you wound up inside the fence, bare naked."

So I told him.

Presently he said, "That fire pit. Didn't burn you?"

"One small blister."

"Just a blister. I reckon you would be safe in Hell."

"Look, Jerry, they really do walk on live coals."

"I know, I've seen it. In New Guinea. Never hankered to try it. That iceberg— Something bothers me. How does an iceberg crash into the *side* of a vessel? An iceberg is dead in the water, always. Certainly a ship can bump into one but damage should be to the *bow*. Right?"

"Margrethe?"

"I don't know, Alec. What Jerry says sounds right. But it *did* happen."

"Jerry, I don't know either. We were in a forward stateroom; maybe the whole front end was crushed in. But, if Marga doesn't know, I surely do not, as I got banged on the head and went out like a light. Marga kept me afloat—I told you."

Farnsworth looked thoughtfully at me. He had swiveled his seat around to face both of us while I talked, and he had showed Margrethe how to unlock her chair so that it would turn, also, which brought us three into an intimate circle of conversation, knees almost touching—and left him with his back to the traffic. "Alec, what became of this Hergensheimer?"

"Maybe I didn't make that clear—it's not too clear to me, either. It's *Graham* who is missing. *I* am Hergensheimer. When I walked through the fire and found myself in a different world, I found myself in Graham's place, as I said. Everybody called me Graham and seemed to think that I *was* Graham—and Graham was missing. I guess you could say I took the easy way out . . . but there I was, thousands of miles from home, no money, no ticket, and nobody had ever heard of Alexander Hergensheimer." I shrugged and spread my hands helplessly. "I sinned. I wore his clothes, I ate at his table, I answered to his name."

"I still don't get the skinny of this. Maybe you look enough like Graham to fool almost anyone . . . but your wife would know the difference. Margie?"

Margrethe looked into my eyes with sadness and love, and answered steadily, "Jerry, my husband is confused. A strange amnesia. He is Alec Graham. There is no Alexander Hergensheimer. There never was."

I was left speechless. True, Margrethe and I had not discussed this matter for many weeks; true, she had never flatly admitted that I was not Alec Graham. I was learning again (again and again!) that one never won an argument with Margrethe. Any time I thought I had won, it always turned out that she had simply shut up.

Farnsworth said to me, "Maybe that knock in the head, Alec?"

"Look, that knock in the head was nothing—a few minutes unconsciousness, nothing more. And no gaps in my memory. Anyhow it happened two weeks *after* the fire walk. Jerry, my wife is a wonderful woman . . . but I *must* disagree with her on this. She wants to believe that I am Alec Graham because she fell in love with Graham before she ever met me. She believes it because she needs to believe it. But of course I know who I am: Hergensheimer. I admit that amnesia can have some funny effects . . . but there was one clue that I could not have faked, one that said emphatically that I, Alexander Hergensheimer, was not Alec Graham."

I slapped my stomach, where a bay window had been. "Here is the proof: I wore Graham's clothes, I told you. But his clothes did not fit me perfectly. At the time of the fire walk I was rather plump, too heavy, carrying a lot of flab right here." I slapped my stomach again. "Graham's clothes were too tight around the middle for me. I had to suck in hard and hold my breath to fasten the waistband on any pair of his trousers. That could not happen in the blink of an eye, while walking through a fire pit. Nor did it. Two weeks of rich food in a cruise ship gave me that bay window . . . and it proves that I am not Alec Graham."

Margrethe not only kept quiet, her expression said nothing. But Farnsworth insisted. "Margie?"

"Alec, you were having exactly that trouble with your clothes *before* the fire walk. For the same reason. Too much rich food." She smiled. "I'm sorry to contradict you, my beloved . . . but I'm awfully glad you're you."

Jerry said, "Alec, many is the man who would walk through fire to get a woman to look at him that way just once. When you get to Kansas, you had better go see the Menningers; you've got to get that amnesia untangled. Nobody can fool a woman about her husband. When she's lived with him, slept with him, given him enemas and listened to his jokes, a substitution is impossible no matter how much the ringer may look like him. Even an identical twin could not do it. There are all those little things a wife knows and the public never sees."

I said, "Marga, it's up to you."

She answered, "Jerry, my husband is saying that I must refute that—in part—myself. At that time I did not know Alec as well as a wife knows her husband. I was not his wife then; I was his lover—and I had been such only a few days." She smiled. "But you're right in essence; I recognized him."

Farnsworth frowned. "I'm getting mixed up again. We're talking about either one man or two. This Alexander Hergensheimer— Alec, tell me about him."

"I'm a Protestant preacher, Jerry, ordained in the Brothers of the Apocalypse Christian Church of the One Truth—the Apocalypse Brethren as you hear us referred to. I was born on my grandfather's farm outside Wichita on May twenty-second—"

"Hey, you've got a birthday this week!" Jerry remarked. Marga looked alert.

"So I have. I've been too busy to think about it. —in nineteen-sixty. My parents and grandparents are dead; my oldest brother is still working the family farm—"

"That's why you're going to Kansas? To find your brother?"

"No. That farm is in another world, the one I grew up in."

"Then why are you going to Kansas?"

I was slow in answering. "I don't have a logical answer. Perhaps it's the homing instinct. Or it may be something like horses running back into a burning barn. I don't know, Jerry. But I have to go back and try to find my roots."

"That's a reason I can understand. Go on."

I told him about my schooling, not hiding the fact that I had failed to make it in engineering—my switch to the seminary and my ordination on graduation, then my association with C.U.D. I did not mention Abigail, I did not mention that I hadn't been too successful as a parson largely (in my private opinion) because Abigail did not like people and my parishioners did not like Abigail. Impossible to put all details into a short biography—but the fact is that I could not mention Abigail at all without throwing doubt on the legitimacy of Margrethe's status . . . and this I could not do.

"That's about it. If we were in my native world, you could phone C.U.D. national headquarters in Kansas City, Kansas, and check on me. We had had a successful year and I was on vacation. I took a dirigible, the *Count von Zeppelin* of North American Airlines, from Kansas City airport to San Francisco, to Hilo, to Tahiti, and there I joined the Motor Vessel *Konge Knut* and that about brings us up to date, as I've told you the rest."

"You sound kosher, you talk a good game—are you born again?"

"Certainly! I'm afraid I'm not in a state of grace now . . . but I'm working on it. We're in the Last Days, brother; it's urgent. Are *you* born again?"

"Discuss it later. What's the second law of thermodynamics?"

I made a wry face. "Entropy always increases. That's the one that tripped me."

"Now tell me about Alec Graham."

"Not much I can tell. His passport showed that he was born in Texas, and he gave a law firm in Dallas as an address. For the rest you had better ask Margrethe; she knew him, I didn't." (I did not mention an embarrassing million dollars. I could not explain it, so I left it out . . . and Marga had only my word for it; she had never seen it.)

"Margie? Can you fill us in on Alec Graham?"

She was slow in answering. "I'm afraid I can't add anything to what my husband has told you."

"Hey! You're letting me down. Your husband gave a detailed description of Dr. Jekyll; can't you describe Mr.

Hyde? So far, he's a zero. A mail drop in Dallas, nothing more."

"Mr. Farnsworth, I'm sure you've never been a shipboard stewardess—"

"Nope, I haven't. But I was a room steward in a cargo liner—two trips when I was a kid."

"Then you'll understand. A stewardess knows many things about her passengers. She knows how often they bathe. She knows how often they change their clothes. She knows how they smell—and everyone does smell, some good, some bad. She knows what sort of books they read—or don't read. Most of all she knows whether or not they are truly gentlefolk, honest, generous, considerate, warmhearted. She knows everything one could need to know to judge a person. Yet she may not know a passenger's occupation, home town, schooling, or any of those details that a friend would know.

"Before the day of the fire walk I had been Alec Graham's stewardess for four weeks. For the last two of those weeks I was his mistress and was ecstatically in love with him. After the fire walk it was many days before his amnesia let us resume our happy relationship—and then it did, and I was happy again. And now I have been his wife for four months—months of some adversity but the happiest time of my whole life. And it still is and I think it always will be. And that is all I know about my husband Alec Graham." She smiled at me and her eyes were brimming with tears, and I found that mine were, too.

Jerry sighed and shook his head. "This calls for a Solomon. Which I am not. I believe both your stories— and one of them can't be correct. Never mind. My wife and I practice Muslim hospitality, something I learned in the late war. Will you accept our hospitality for a night or two? You had better say yes."

Marga glanced at me; I said, "Yes!"

"Good. Now to see if the boss is at home." He swiveled

around to face forward, touched something. A few moments later a light came on and something went *beep!* once. His face lighted up and he spoke: "Duchess, this is your favorite husband."

"Oh, Ronny, it's been so *long.*"

"No, no. Try again."

"Albert? Tony? George, Andy, Jim—"

"Once more and get it right; I have company with me."

"Yes, Jerry?"

"Company for dinner and overnight and possibly more."

"Yes, my love. How many and what sexes and when will you be home?"

"Let me ask Hubert." Again he touched something. "Hubert says twenty-seven minutes. Two guests. The one seated by me is about twenty-three, give or take a bit, blonde, long, wavy hair, dark blue eyes, height about five seven, mass about one twenty, other basics I have not checked but about those of our daughter. Female. I am certain she is female as she is not wearing so much as a G-string."

"Yes, dear. I'll scratch her eyes out. After I've fed her, of course."

"Good. But she's no menace as her husband is with her and is watching her closely. Did I say that he is naked, too?"

"You did not. Interesting."

"Do you want his basic statistic? If so, do you want it relaxed or at attention?"

"My love, you are a dirty old man, I am happy to say. Quit trying to embarrass your guests."

"There is madness in my method, Duchess. They are naked because they have no clothes at all. Yet I suspect that they do embarrass easily. So please meet us at the gate with clothing. You have her statistics, except— Margie, hand me a foot." Marga promptly put a foot up high, without comment. He felt it. "A pair of your sandals will fit, I think. Zapatos for him. Of mine."

"His other sizes? Never mind the jokes."

"He's about my height and shoulders, but I am twenty pounds heavier, at least. So something from my skinny rack. If Sybil has a houseful of her junior barbarians, please use extreme prejudice to keep them away from the gate. These are gentle people; we'll introduce them after they have a chance to dress."

"Roger Wilco, Sergeant Bilko. But it is time that you introduced them to *me*."

"*Mea culpa.* My love, this is Margrethe Graham, Mrs. Alec Graham."

"Hello, Margrethe, welcome to our home."

"Thank you, Mrs. Farnsworth—"

"Katherine, dear. Or Kate."

"'Katherine.' I can't tell you how much you are doing for us . . . when we were so miserable!" My darling started to cry.

She stopped it abruptly. "And this is my husband, Alec Graham."

"Howdy, Mrs. Farnsworth. And thank you."

"Alec, you bring that girl straight here. I want to welcome her. Both of you."

Jerry cut in. "Hubert says twenty-two minutes, Duchess."

"*Hasta la vista.* Sign off and let me get busy."

"End." Jerry turned his seat around. "Kate will find you a pretty to wear, Margie . . . although in your case there ought to be a law. Say, are you cold? I've been yacking so much I didn't think of it. I keep this buggy cool enough for me, in clothes. But Hubert can change it to suit."

"I am a Viking, Jerry; I never get cold. Most rooms are too warm to suit me."

"How about you, Alec?"

"I'm warm enough," I answered, fibbing only a little.

"I believe—" Jerry started to say—

—as the heavens opened with the most brilliant light imaginable, outshining day, and I was gripped by sudden grief, knowing that I failed to lead my beloved back to grace.

XVIII

Then Satan answered the Lord, and said,
Doth Job fear God for nought?
Job 1:7

Canst thou by searching find out God? canst thou
find out the Almighty unto perfection?
Job 11:7

I waited for the Shout.

My feelings were mixed. Did I want the Rapture? Was I ready to be snatched up into the loving arms of Jesus? Yes, dear Lord. Yes! Without Margrethe? No, no! Then you choose to be cast down into the Pit? Yes—no, but— Make up your mind!

Mr. Farnsworth looked up. "See that baby go!"

I looked up through the roof of the car. There was a second sun directly overhead. It seemed to shrink and lose brilliance as I watched it.

Our host went on, "Right on time! Yesterday we had a hold, missed the window, and had to reslot. When you're sitting on the pad, and single-H is boiling away, even a hold for one orbit can kill your profit margin. And yesterday wasn't even a glitch; it was a totally worthless recheck ordered by a Nasa fatbottom. Figures."

He seemed to be talking English.

Margrethe said breathlessly, "Mr. Farnsworth—Jerry —what was it?"

"Eh? Never seen a lift-off before?"

"I don't know what a lift-off is."

"Mm . . . yes. Margie, the fact that you and Alec are from another world—or worlds—hasn't really soaked through my skull yet. Your world doesn't have space travel?"

"I'm not sure what you mean but I don't think we do."

I was fairly sure what he meant so I interrupted. "Jerry, you're talking about flying to the moon, aren't you? Like Jules Verne."

"Yes. Close enough."

"That was an ethership? Going to the moon? Golly Moses!" The profanity just slipped out.

"Slow down. That was not an ethership, it was an unmanned freight rocket. It is not going to Luna; it is going only as far as Leo—low Earth orbit. Then it comes back, ditches off Galveston, is ferried back to North Texas Port, where it will lift again sometime next week. But some of its cargo will go on to Luna City or Tycho Under—and some may go as far as the Asteroids. Clear?"

"Uh . . . not quite."

"Well, in Kennedy's second term—"

"Who?"

"John F. Kennedy. President. Sixty-one to sixty-nine."

"I'm sorry. I'm going to have to relearn history again. Jerry, the most confusing thing about being bounced around among worlds is not new technology, such as television or jet planes—or even space-travel ships. It is different history."

"Well— When we get home, I'll find you an American history, and a history of space travel. A lot of them around the house; I'm in space up to my armpits— started with model rockets as a kid. Now, besides Diana Freight Lines, I've got a piece of Jacob's Ladder and the Beanstalk, both—just a tax loss at present but—"

I think he caught sight of my face. "Sorry. You skim through the books I'll dig out for you, then we'll talk."

Farnsworth looked back at his controls, punched something, blinked at it, punched again, and said, "Hubert says that we'll have the sound in three minutes twenty-one seconds."

When the sound did arrive, I was disappointed. I had expected a thunderclap to match that incredible light. Instead it was a rumble that went on and on, then faded away without a distinct end.

A few minutes later the car left the highway, swung right in a large circle and went under the highway through a tunnel and came out on a smaller highway. We stayed on this highway (83, I noted) about five minutes, then there was a repeated beeping sound and a flash of lights. "I hear you," Mr. Farnsworth said. "Just hold your horses." He swung his chair around and faced forward, grasped the two hand grips.

The next several minutes were interesting. I was reminded of something the Sage of Hannibal said: "If it warn't for the honor, I'd druther uv walked." Mr. Farnsworth seemed to regard any collision avoided by a measurable distance as less than sporting. Again and again that "soft mush" saved us from bruises if not broken bones. Once that signal from the machinery went *Bee-bee-bee-beep!* at him; he growled in answer: "Pipe down! You mind your business; I'll mind mine," and subjected us to another near miss.

We turned off onto a narrow road, private I concluded, as there was an arch over the entrance reading FARNSWORTH'S FOLLY. We went up a grade. At the top, lost among trees, was a high gate that snapped out of the way as we approached it.

There we met Katie Farnsworth.

If you have read this far in this memoir, you know that I am in love with my wife. That is a basic, like the speed of light, like the love of God the Father. Know ye now that I learned that I could love another person, a woman, without detracting from my love for Margrethe, without wishing to take her from her lawful mate, without lusting to possess her. Or at least not much.

In meeting her I learned that five feet two inches is the perfect height for a woman, that forty is the perfect age, and that a hundred and ten pounds is the correct weight, just as for a woman's voice contralto is the right register. That my own beloved darling is none of these is irrelevant; Katie Farnsworth makes them perfect for *her* by being herself content with what *she* is.

But she startled me first by the most graceful gesture of warm hospitality I have ever encountered.

She knew from her husband that we were utterly without clothes; she knew also from him that he felt that we were embarrassed by our state. So she had fetched clothing for each of us.

And she herself was naked.

No, that's not right; *I* was naked, she was unclothed. That's not quite right, either. Nude? Bare? Stripped? Undressed? No, she was dressed in her own beauty, like Mother Eve before the Fall. She made it seem so utterly appropriate that I wondered how I had ever acquired the delusion that freedom from clothing equals obscenity.

Those clamshell doors lifted; I got out and handed Margrethe out. Mrs. Farnsworth dropped what she was carrying, put her arms around Margrethe and kissed her. "Margrethe! Welcome, dear."

My darling hugged her back and sniffled again.

Then she offered me her hand. "Welcome to you, too, Mr. Graham. Alec." I took her hand, did not shake it. Instead I handled it like rare china and bowed over it. I felt that I should kiss it but I had never learned how.

For Margrethe she had a summer dress the shade of Marga's eyes. Its styling suggested the Arcadia of myth; one could imagine a wood nymph wearing it. It hung on the left shoulder, was open all the way down on the right but wrapped around with generous overlap. Both sides of this simple garment ended in a long sash ribbon; the end that went under passed through a slot, which permitted both ends to go all the way around Marga's waist, then to tie at her right side.

It occurred to me that this was a fit-anyone dress. It would be tight or loose on any figure depending on how it was tied.

Katie had sandals for Marga in blue to match her dress. For me she had Mexican sandals, zapatos, of the cut-leather openwork sort that are almost as fit-anyone as that dress, simply by how they are tied. She offered me trousers and shirt that were superficially equivalent to those I had bought in Winslow at the SECOND WIND— but these were tailormade of summer-weight wool rather than mass-produced from cheap cotton. She also had for me socks that fitted themselves to my feet and knit shorts that seemed to be my size.

When she had dressed us, there was still clothing on the grass—hers. I then realized that she had walked to the gate dressed, stripped down there, and waited for us—"dressed" as we were.

That's politeness.

Dressed, we all got into the car. Mr. Farnsworth waited a moment before starting up his driveway. "Katie, our guests are Christians."

Mrs. Farnsworth seemed delighted. "Oh, how very interesting!"

"So I thought. Alec? *Verb. sap.* Not many Christians in these parts. Feel free to speak your mind in front of Katie and me . . . but when anyone else is around, you may be more comfortable not discussing your beliefs. Understand me?"

"Uh . . . I'm afraid I don't." My head was in a whirl and I felt a ringing in my ears.

"Well . . . being a Christian isn't against the law here; Texas has freedom of religion. Nevertheless Christians aren't at all popular and Christian worship is mostly underground. Uh, if you want to get in touch with your own people, I suppose we could manage to locate a catacomb. Kate?"

"Oh, I'm sure we could find someone who knows. I can put out some feelers."

"If Alec says to, dear. Alec, you're in no danger of being stoned; this country isn't some ignorant redneck backwoods. Or not much danger. But I don't want you to be discriminated against or insulted."

Katie Farnsworth said, "Sybil."

"Oh, oh! Yes. Alec, our daughter is a good girl and as civilized as one can expect in a teenager. But she is an apprentice witch, a recent convert to the Old Religion— and, being both a convert and a teenager, dead serious about it. Sybil would not be rude to a guest—Katie brought her up properly. Besides, she knows I would skin her alive. But it would be a favor to me if you will avoid placing too much strain on her. As I'm sure you know, every teenager is a time bomb waiting to go off."

Margrethe answered for me: "We will be most careful. This 'Old Religion'—is this the worship of Odin?"

I felt a chill . . . when I was already discombobulated beyond my capacity. But our host answered, "No. Or at least I don't think so. You could ask Sybil. If you are willing to risk having your ear talked off; she'll try to convert you. Very intense."

Katie Farnsworth added, "I have never heard Sybil mention Odin. Mostly she speaks just of 'the Goddess.' Don't Druids worship Odin? Truly I don't know. I'm afraid Sybil considers us so hopelessly old-fashioned that she doesn't bother to discuss theology with us."

"And let's not discuss it now," Jerry added, and started us up the drive.

The Farnsworth mansion was long, low, and rambling, with a flavor of lazy opulence. Jerry swung us under a *porte-cochère;* we all got out. He slapped the top of his car as one might slap the neck of a horse. It moved away and turned the corner of the house as we went inside.

I'm not going to say much about their house as, while it was beautiful and Texas lavish, it would not necessarily appear any one way long enough to justify describing it; most of what we saw Jerry called "hollow grams." How can I describe them? Frozen dreams? Three-dimensional pictures? Let me put it this way: Chairs were solid. So were table tops. Anything else in that house, better touch it cautiously and find out, as it might be as beautifully *there* as a rainbow . . . and just as insubstantial.

I don't know how these ghosts were produced. I think it is possible that the laws of physics in that world were somewhat different from those of the Kansas of my youth.

Katie led us into what Jerry called their "family room" and Jerry stopped abruptly. "Bloody Hindu whorehouse!"

It was a very large room with ceilings that seemed impossibly high for a one-storey ranch house. Every wall, arch, alcove, soffit, and beam was covered with sculptured figures. But such figures! I found myself blushing. These figures had apparently been copied from that notorious temple cavern in southern India, the one that depicts every possible vice of venery in obscene and blatant detail.

Katie said, "Sorry, dear! The youngsters were dancing in here." She hurried to the left, melted into one sculpture group and disappeared. "What will you have, Gerald?"

"Uh, Remington number two."

"Right away."

Suddenly the obscene figures disappeared, the ceiling lowered abruptly and changed to a beam-and-plaster construction, one wall became a picture window looking out at mountains that belonged in Utah (not Texas), the wall opposite it now carried a massive stone fireplace with a goodly fire crackling in it, the furniture changed to the style sometimes called "mission" and the floor changed to flagstones covered with Amerindian rugs.

"That's better. Thank you, Katherine. Sit down, friends—pick a spot and squat."

I sat down, avoiding what was obviously the "papa" chair—massive and leather upholstered. Katie and

Marga took a couch together. Jerry sat in that papa chair.
"My love, what will you drink?"

"Campari and soda, please."

"Sissy. And you, Margie?"

"Campari and soda would suit me, too."

"Two sissies. Alec?"

"I'll go along with the ladies."

"Son, I'll tolerate that in the weaker sex. But not from
a grown man. Try again."

"Uh, Scotch and soda."

"I'd horsewhip you, if I had a horse. Podnuh, you have
just one more chance."

"Uh . . . bourbon and branch?"

"Saved yourself. Jack Daniel's with water on the side.
Other day, man in Dallas tried to order *Irish* whisky.
Rode him out o' town on a rail. Then they apologized to
him. Turned out he was a Yankee and didn't know any
better." All this time our host was drumming with his
fingertips on a small table at his elbow. He stopped this
fretful drumming and, suddenly, at the table by my chair
appeared a Texas jigger of brown liquid and a tumbler of
water. I found that the others had been served, too. Jerry
raised his glass. "Save your Confederate money! *Salud!*"

We drank and he went on, "Katherine, do you know
where our rapscallion is hiding?"

"I think they are all in the pool, dear."

"So." Jerry resumed that nervous drumming. Suddenly
there appeared in the air in front of our host, seated on a
diving board that jutted out of nowhere, a young female.
She was in bright sunlight although the room we were in
was in cool shadow. Drops of water sprinkled on her. She
faced Jerry, which placed her back toward me. "Hi, Pip-
squeak."

"Hi, Daddy. Kiss kiss."

"In a pig's eye. When was the last time I spanked you?"

"My ninth birthday. When I set fire to Aunt Minnie.
What did I do now?"

"By the great golden gawdy greasy gonads of God, what do you *mean* by leaving that vulgar, bawdy, pornic program running in the family room?"

"Don't give me that static, Daddy doll; I've seen your books."

"Never mind what I have in my private library; answer my question."

"I forgot to turn it off, Daddy. I'm sorry."

"That's what the cow said to Mrs. Murphy. But the fire burned on. Look, my dear, you know you are free to use the controls to suit yourself. But when you are through, you must put the display back the way you found it. Or, if you don't know how, you must put it back to zero for the default display."

"Yes, Daddy. I just *forgot.*"

"Don't go squirming around like that; I'm not through chewing you out. By the big brass balls of Koshchei, *where* did you get *that* program?"

"At campus. It was an instruction tape in my tantric yoga class."

"'Tantric yoga'? Swivel hips, you don't need such a course. Does your mother know about this?"

Katherine moved in smoothly: "I urged her to take it, dear one. Sybil is talented, as we know. But raw talent is not enough; she needed tutoring."

"So? I'll never argue with your mother on this subject, so I withdraw to a previously prepared position. That tape. How did you come by it? You are familiar with the applicable laws concerning copyrighted material; we both remember the hooraw over that *Jefferson Starship* tape—"

"Daddy, you're worse than an elephant! Don't you *ever* forget anything?"

"Never, and much worse. You are warned that anything you say may be taken down in writing and held against you at another time and place. How say you?"

"I demand to see an attorney!"

"Oh, so you *did* pirate it!"

"Don't you wish I had! So you could gloat. I'm sorry, Daddy, but I paid the catalog fee, in full, in cash, and the campus library service copied it for me. So there. Smarty."

"Smarty yourself. You wasted your money."

"I don't think so. I like it."

"So do I. But you wasted your money. You should have asked *me* for it."

"Huh!"

"Gotcha! I thought at first you had been picking locks in my study or working a spell on 'em. Pleased to hear that you were merely extravagant. How much?"

"Uh . . . forty-nine fifty. That's at student's discount."

"Sounds fair; I paid sixty-five. All right. But if it shows up on your semester billing, I'll deduct it from your allowance. Just one thing, sugar plum— I brought two nice people home, a lady and a gentleman. We walk into the parlor. What had been the parlor. And these two gentlefolk are faced with the entire Kama Sutra, in panting, quivering color. What do you think of that?"

"I didn't *mean* to."

"So we'll forget it. But it is never polite to shock people, especially guests, so let's be more careful next time. Will you be at dinner?"

"Yes. If I can be excused early and run, run, run. Date, Daddy."

"What time will you be home?"

"Won't. All-night gathering. Rehearsal for Midsummer Night. Thirteen covens."

He sighed. "I suppose that I should thank the Three Crones that you are on the pill."

"Pill shmill. Don't be a cube, Daddy; nobody ever gets pregnant at a Sabbat; everybody knows that."

"Everybody but me. Well, let us offer thanks that you are willing to have dinner with us." Suddenly she shrieked as she fell forward off the board. The picture followed her down.

She splashed, then came up spouting water. "Daddy! You pushed me!"

"How could you say such a thing?" he answered in self-righteous tones. The living picture suddenly vanished.

Katie Farnsworth said conversationally, "Gerald keeps trying to dominate his daughter. Hopelessly, of course. He should take her to bed and discharge his incestuous yearnings. But they are both too prissy for that."

"Woman, remind me to beat you."

"Yes, dearest. You wouldn't have to force her. Make your intentions plain and she will burst into tears and surrender. Then both of you will have the best time of your lives. Wouldn't you say so, Margrethe?"

"I would say so."

By then I was too numb to be shocked by Margrethe's words.

Dinner was a gourmet's delight and a social confusion. It was served in the formal dining hall, i.e., that same family room with a different program controlling the hollow grams. The ceiling was higher, the windows were tall, evenly spaced, framed by floor-length drapes, and they looked out on formal gardens.

One piece of furniture wheeled itself in, and was not a hollow gram—or not much so. It was a banquet table that (so far as I know) was, in itself, pantry, stove, icebox—all of a well-equipped kitchen. That's a conclusion, subject to refutation. All I can say is that I never saw a servant and never saw our hostess do any work. Nevertheless her husband congratulated her on her cooking—as well he might, and so did we.

Jerry did a little work; he carved a roast (prime rib, enough for a troop of hungry Boy Scouts) and he served the plates, serving them at his place. Once a plate was loaded, it went smoothly around to the person for whom it was intended, like a toy train on a track—but there was no train and no track. Machinery concealed by hollow grams? I suppose so. But that simply covers one mystery with another.

(I learned later that a swank Texas household in that world would have had human servants conspicuously in sight. But Jerry and Katie had simple tastes.)

There were six of us at the table, Jerry at one end, Katie at the other; Margrethe sat on Jerry's right, his daughter Sybil on his left; I was at the right of my hostess, and at her left was Sybil's young man, her date. This put him opposite me, and I had Sybil on my right.

The young man's name was Roderick Lyman Culverson III; he did not manage to catch my name. I have long suspected that the male of our species, in most cases, should be raised in a barrel and fed through the bung-hole. Then, at age eighteen, a solemn decision can be made: whether to take him out of the barrel, or to drive in the bung.

Young Culverson gave me no reason to change my opinion—and I would have voted to drive in the bung.

Early on, Sybil made clear that they were at the same campus. But he seemed to be as much a stranger to the Farnsworths as he was to us. Katie asked, "Roderick, are you an apprentice witch, too?"

He looked as if he had sniffed something nasty, but Sybil saved him from having to answer such a crude question. "Mothuh! Rod received his athame *ages* ago."

"Sorry I goofed," Katie said tranquilly. "Is that a diploma you get when you finish your apprenticeship?"

"It's a sacred knife, Mama, used in ritual. It can be used to—"

"*Sybil!* There are gentiles present." Culverson frowned at Sybil, then glared at me. I thought how well he would look with a black eye but I endeavored to keep my thoughts out of my face.

Jerry said, "Then you're a graduate warlock, Rod?"

Sybil broke in again. "Daddy! The correct word is—"

"Pipe down, sugar plum! Let him answer for himself. Rod?"

"That word is used only by the ignorant—"

"Hold it! I am uninformed on some subjects, and then I seek information, as I am now doing. But you don't sit at my table and call me ignorant. Now, can you answer me without casting asparagus?"

Culverson's nostrils spread but he took a grip on himself. "'Witch' is the usual term for both male and female adepts in the Craft. 'Wizard' is an acceptable term but is not technically exact; it means 'sorcerer' or 'magician' ... but not all magicians are witches and not all witches practice magic. But 'warlock' is considered to be offensive as well as incorrect because it is associated with Devil worship—and the Craft is *not* Devil worship—and the word itself by its derivation means 'oath breaker'— and witches do not break oaths. Correction: The Craft forbids the breaking of oaths. A witch who breaks an oath, even to a gentile, is subject to discipline, even expulsion if the oath is that major. So I am not a 'graduate warlock.' The correct designation for my present status is 'Accepted Craftsman,' that is to say: 'witch.'"

"Well stated! Thank you. I ask forgiveness for using the term 'warlock' to you and about you—" Jerry waited.

A long moment later Culverson said hastily, "Oh, certainly! No offense meant and none taken."

"Thank you. To add to your comments about derivations, 'witch' derives from 'wicca' meaning 'wise,' and from 'wicce' meaning 'woman' ... which may account for most witches being female and suggests that our ancestors may have known something that we don't. In any case 'the Craft' is the short way of saying 'the Craft of Wisdom.' Correct?"

"Eh? Oh, certainly! Wisdom. That's what the Old Religion is all about."

"Good. Son, listen to me carefully. Wisdom includes not getting angry unnecessarily. The Law ignores trifles and the wise man does, too. Such trifles as a young girl

defining an athame among gentiles—knowledge that isn't
all that esoteric anyhow—and an old fool using a word
inappropriately. Understand me?"

Again Jerry waited. Then he said very softly, "I said,
'Do you understand me?'"

Culverson took a deep breath. "I understood you. A
wise man ignores trifles."

"Good. May I offer you another slice of the roast?"

Culverson kept quiet for some time then. As did I. As
did Sybil. Katie and Jerry and Margrethe kept up a flow
of polite chitchat that ignored the fact that a guest had
just been thoroughly and publicly spanked. Presently
Sybil said, "Daddy, are you and Mama expecting me to
attend fire worship Friday?"

"'Expect' is hardly the word," Jerry answered, "when
you have picked another church of your own. 'Hope'
would be closer."

Katie added, "Sybil, tonight you feel that your coven is
all the church you will ever need. But that could change
. . . and I understand that the Old Religion does not forbid its members to attend other religious services."

Culverson put in, "That reflects centuries, millennia, of
persecution, Mrs. Farnsworth. It is still in our laws that
each member of a coven must also belong publicly to
some socially approved church. But we no longer try too
hard to enforce it."

"I see," agreed Katie. "Thank you, Roderick. Sybil,
since your new church encourages membership in another church, it might be prudent to attend fairly regularly just to protect your Brownie points. You may need
them."

"Exactly," agreed her father. "'Brownie points.' Ever
occur to you, hon, that your pop being a stalwart pillar of
the congregation, with a fast checkbook, might have
something to do with the fact that he also sells more Cadillacs than any other dealer in Texas?"

"Daddy, that sounds utterly shameless."

"It sure is. It also sells Cadillacs. And don't call it fire worship; you know it is not. It is not the flame we worship, but what it stands for."

Sybil twisted her serviette and, for the moment, looked a troubled thirteen instead of the mature woman her body showed her to be. "Papa, that's just it. All my life that flame has meant to me healing, cleansing, life everlasting—until I studied the Craft. Its history. Daddy, to a witch . . . *fire means the way they kill us!*"

I was shocked almost out of breathing. I think it had not really sunk into me emotionally that these two, obnoxious but commonplace young punk, and pretty and quite delightful young girl . . . daughter of Katie, daughter of Jerry, our two Good Samaritans without equal— that these two were *witches*.

Yes, yes, I know: Exodus twenty-two verse eighteen, "Thou shalt not suffer a witch to live." As solemn an injunction as the Ten Commandments, given to Moses directly by God, in the presence of all the children of Israel—

What was I doing breaking bread with witches?

Mark me for a coward. I did not stand up and denounce them. I sat tight.

Katie said, "Darling, darling! That was clear back in the middle ages! Not today, not now, not here."

Culverson said, "Mrs. Farnsworth, every witch knows that the terror can start up again any time. Even a season of bad crops could touch it off. And Salem wasn't very long ago. Nor very far away." He added, "There are still Christians around. They would set the fires if they could. Just like Salem."

This was a great chance to keep my mouth shut. I blurted out, "No witch was burned at Salem."

He looked at me. "What do you know about it?"

"The burnings were in Europe, not here. In Salem witches were hanged, except one who was pressed to death." (Fire should never have been used. The Lord God ordered us not to suffer them to live; He did *not* tell us to put them to death by torture.)

He eyed me again. "So? You seem to approve of the hangings."

"I never said anything of the sort!" (Dear God, forgive me!)

Jerry cut in. "I rule this subject out of order! There will be no further discussion of it at the table. Sybil, we don't want you to attend if it upsets you or reminds you of tragic occasions. Speaking of hanging, what shall we do about the backfield of the Dallas Cowboys?"

Two hours later Jerry Farnsworth and I were again seated in that room, this time it being Remington number three: a snow storm against the windows, an occasional cold draft across the floor, and once the howl of a wolf—a roaring fire felt good. He poured coffee for us, and brandy in huge snifters, big enough for goldfish. "You hear of noble brandy," he said. "Napoleon, or Carlos Primero. But this is royal brandy—so royal it has hemophilia."

I gulped; I did not like the joke. I was still queasy from thinking about witches, dying witches. With a jerk of the heels, or dancing on flames. And all of them with Sybil's sweet face.

Does the Bible define "witch" somewhere? Could it be that these modern members of the Craft were not at all what Jehovah meant by "witch"?

Quit dodging, Alex! Assume that "witch" in Exodus means exactly what "witch" means here in Texas today. You're the judge and she has confessed. *Can you sentence Katie's teenager to hang? Will you spring the trap?* Don't dodge it, boy; you've been dodging all your life.

Pontius Pilate washed his hands.

I will not sentence a witch to die! So help me, Lord, I can do no other.

Jerry said, "Here's to the success of your venture, yours and Margie's. Sip it slowly and it will not intoxicate; it will simply quiet your nerves while it sharpens your wits. Alec, tell me now why you expect the end of the world."

For the next hour I went over the evidence, pointing out that it was not just one prophecy that agreed on the signs, but many: Revelations, Daniel, Ezekiel, Isaiah, Paul in writing to the Thessalonians, and again to the Corinthians, Jesus himself in all four of the Gospels, again and again in each.

To my surprise Jerry had a copy of the Book. I picked out passages easy for laymen to understand, wrote down chapter and verse so that he could study them later. One Thessalonians 4:15–17 of course, and the 24th chapter of the Gospel according to Saint Matthew, all fifty-one verses of it, and the same prophecies in Saint Luke, chapter twenty-one—and Luke 21:32 with its clue to the confusion of many as to "this generation." What Christ actually said was that the generation which sees these signs and portents will live to see His return, hear the Shout, experience Judgment Day. The message is plain if you read *all* of it; the errors have arisen from picking out bits and pieces and ignoring the rest. The parable of the fig tree explains this.

I also picked out for him, in Isaiah and Daniel and elsewhere, the Old Testament prophecies that parallel the New Testament prophecies.

I handed him this list of prophecies and urged him to study them carefully, and, if he encountered difficulties, simply read more widely. And take it to God. "'Ask, and it shall be given you; seek, and ye shall find.'"

He said, "Alec, I can agree with one thing. The news for the past several months has looked to me like Armageddon. Say tomorrow afternoon. Might as well be the end of the world and Judgment Day, as there won't be enough left to salvage after this one." He looked sad. "I used to worry about what kind of a world Sybil would grow up in. Now I wonder if she'll grow up."

"Jerry. Work on it. Find your way to grace. Then lead your wife and daughter. You don't need me, you don't need anyone but Jesus. He said, 'Behold, I stand at the door and knock; if anyone hears My voice, I will come in to him.' Revelations three, twenty."

"You believe."

"I do."

"Alec, I wish I could go along with you. It would be comforting, the world being what it is today. But I can't see proof in the dreams of long-dead prophets; you can read anything into them. Theology is never any help; it is searching in a dark cellar at midnight for a black cat that isn't there. Theologians can persuade themselves of anything. Oh, my church, too—but at least mine is honestly pantheistic. Anyone who can worship a trinity and insist that his religion is a monotheism can believe anything— just give him time to rationalize it. Forgive me for being blunt."

"Jerry, in religion bluntness is necessary. 'I know that my Redeemer liveth, and that He shall stand at the latter day upon the earth.' That's Job again, chapter nineteen. He's your Redeemer, too, Jerry—I pray that you find Him."

"Not much chance, I'm afraid." Jerry stood up.

"You haven't found Him *yet*. Don't quit. I'll pray for you."

"Thank you, and thanks for trying. How do the shoes feel?"

"Comfortable, quite."

"If you insist on hitting the road tomorrow, you must have shoes that won't give you bunions between here and Kansas. You're sure?"

"I'm sure. And sure that we must leave. If we stayed another day, you'd have us so spoiled we would never hit the road again." (The truth that I could not tell him was that I was so upset by witchcraft and fire worship that I had to leave. But I could not load my weakness onto him.)

"Let me show you to your bedroom. Quietly, as Margie

may be asleep. Unless our ladies have stayed up even later than we have."

At the bedroom door he put out his hand. "If you're right and I'm wrong, you tell me that it's possible that even you can slip."

"True. I'm not in a state of grace, not now. I've got to work on it."

"Well, good luck. But if you do slip, look me up in Hell, will you?"

So far as I could tell, Jerry was utterly serious. "I don't know that it is permitted."

"Work on it. And so will I. I promise you"—he grinned—"some hellacious hospitality. Really warm!"

I grinned back. "It's a date."

Again my darling had fallen asleep without undressing. I smiled at her without making a sound, then got beside her and pillowed her head on my shoulder. I would let her wake up slowly, then undress the poor baby and put her to bed. Meanwhile I had a thousand—well, dozens—of thoughts to get untangled.

Presently I noticed that it was getting light. Then I noticed how scratchy and lumpy the bed was. The light increased and I saw that we were sprawled over bales of hay, in a barn.

XIX

And Ahab said to Elijah, Hast thou found me,
O mine enemy? And he answered, I have found thee:
because thou hast sold thyself to work evil
in the sight of the Lord.
1 Kings 21:20

We did the last ninety miles down 66 from Clinton to Oklahoma City pushing hard, ignoring the fact that we were flat broke again, nothing to eat, nowhere to sleep.

We had seen a dirigible.

Of course this changed everything. For months I had been nobody from nowhere, penniless, dishwashing my only trade, and a tramp in fact. But back in my own world— A well-paying job, a respected position in the community, a fat bank account. And an end to this truly infernal bouncing around between worlds.

We were riding into Clinton middle of the morning, guests of a farmer taking a load of produce into town. I heard Margrethe gasp. I looked where she was staring— and there she was!—silvery and sleek and beautiful. I could not make out her name, but her logo told me that she was Eastern Airlines.

"Dallas–Denver Express," our host remarked, and hauled a watch out of his overalls. "Six minutes late. Unusual."

I tried to cover my excitement. "Does Clinton have an airport?"

"Oh, no. Oklahoma City, nearest. Goin' to give up hitchhiking and take to the air?"

"Would be nice."

"Wouldn't it, though. Beats farmin'."

I kept the conversation on inanities until he dropped us outside the city market a few minutes later. But, once Margrethe and I were alone, I could hardly contain myself. I started to kiss her, then suddenly stopped myself. Oklahoma is every bit as moral as Kansas; most communities have stiff laws about public lallygagging.

I wondered how hard I was going to find it to readjust, after many weeks in many worlds not one of which had the high moral standards of my home world. It could be difficult to stay out of trouble when (admit it!) I had grown used to kissing my wife in public and to other displays, innocent in themselves, but never seen in public in moral communities. Worse, could I keep my darling out of trouble? I had been born here and could slip back into its ways . . . but Marga was as affectionate as a collie pup and had no sense of shame whatever about showing it.

I said, "Sorry, dear, I was about to kiss you. But I must not."

"Why not?"

"Uh, I can't kiss you in public. Not here. Only in private. It's— It's a case of 'When in Rome, one must do as the Romans do.' But never mind that now. Darling, we're home! My home, and now it's your home. You saw the dirigible."

"That was an airship truly?"

"Really and truly . . . and the happiest sight I've seen in months. Except— Don't get your hopes up too high, too fast. We know how some of these shifting worlds strongly resemble each other in many ways. I suppose there is an outside possibility that this is a world with dirigibles . . . but not *my* world. Oh, I don't believe that— but let's not get too excited."

(I did not notice that Margrethe was not at all excited.)

"How will you tell that this is your world?"

"We could check just as we have before, at public libraries. But in this case there is something faster and better. I want to find the Bell Telephone office—I'll ask at that grocery store."

I wanted the telephone office rather than a public telephone because I wanted to consult telephone books before making telephone calls—was it my world?

Yes, it was! The office had telephone books for all of Oklahoma and also books from major cities in other states—including a most familiar telephone book for Kansas City, Kansas. "See, Margrethe?" I pointed to the listing for Churches United for Decency, National Office.

"I see."

"Isn't it exciting? Doesn't it make you want to dance and sing?"

"I am very happy for you, Alec."

(She made it sound like: "Doesn't he look natural? And so many lovely flowers.")

We had the alcove where the telephone books were to ourselves. So I whispered urgently, "What's the trouble, dear? This is a happy occasion. Don't you understand? Once I get on that phone we'll have money. No more menial jobs, no more wondering how we will eat or where we will sleep. We'll go straight home by Pullman—no, by dirigible! You'll like that, I know you will! The ultimate in luxury. Our honeymoon, darling— the honeymoon we could never afford."

"You will not take me to Kansas City."

"What do you mean?"

"Alec . . . your wife is there."

Believe me when I say that I had not thought once about Abigail in many, many weeks. I had become convinced that I would never see her again (regaining my home world was totally unexpected) and I now had a wife, all the wife any man could ever want: Margrethe.

I wonder if that first shovelful of dirt hits a corpse with the same shock.

I pulled out of it. Some. "Marga, here's what we'll do.

Yes, I have a problem, but we can solve it. Of course you go to Kansas City with me! You must. But there, because of Abigail, I must find a quiet place for you to stay while I get things straightened out." (Straightened out? Abigail was going to scream bloody murder.) "First I must get at my money. Then I must see a lawyer." (Divorce? In a state where there was only one legal ground and that one granted divorce only to the injured party? Margrethe the other woman? Impossible. Let Margrethe be exposed in stocks? Be ridden out of town on a rail if Abigail demanded it? Never mind what would be done to me, never mind that Abigail would strip me of every cent—Margrethe must not be subjected to the Scarlet Letter laws of my home world. No!)

"Then we will go to Denmark." (No, it can't be divorce.)

"We will?"

"We will. Darling, you are my wife, now and forever. I can't leave you here while I get things worked out in Kay See; the world might shift and I would lose you. But we can't go to Denmark until I lay hands on my money. All clear?" (What if Abigail has cleaned out my bank account?)

"Yes, Alec. We will go to Kansas City."

(That settled part of it. But it did not settle Abigail. Never mind, I would burn that bridge when I came to it.)

Thirty seconds later I had more problems. Certainly the girl in charge would place a call for me long distance collect. Kansas City? For Kansas City, either Kansas or Missouri, the fee to open the trunk line for query was twenty-five cents. Deposit it in the coin box, please, when I tell you. Booth two.

I went to the booth and dug into my pocket for coins, laid them out:

A twenty-cent piece;

Two threepenny coppers;

A Canadian quarter, with the face of the Queen (queen?);

A half dollar;

Three five-cent pieces that were *not* nickels, but smaller.

And not one of these coins carried the familiar "God Is Our Fortress" motto of the North American Union.

I stared at that ragbag collection and tried to figure out when this last change had taken place. Since I last was paid evidently, which placed it later than yesterday afternoon but earlier than the hitch we had gotten just after breakfast. While we slept last night? But we had not lost our clothes, had not lost our money. I even had my razor, a lump in my breast pocket.

Never mind—any attempt to understand all the details of these changes led only to madness. The shift had indeed taken place; I was here in my native world . . . and it had left me with no money. With no legal money.

By Hobson's choice, that Canadian quarter looked awfully good. I did not try to tell myself that the Eighth Commandment did not apply to big corporations. Instead I did promise myself that I would pay it back. I picked it up and took the receiver off the hook.

"Number, please."

"Please place a collect call to Churches United for Decency in Kansas City, Kansas. The number is State Line 1224J. I'll speak to anyone who answers."

"Deposit twenty-five cents, please." I deposited that Canadian quarter and held my breath—heard it go *ting-thunk-thunk*. Then Central said, "Thank you. Do not hang up. Please wait."

I waited. And waited. And waited.

"On your call to Kansas City— Churches United for Decency reports that they do not accept collect calls."

"Hold it! Please tell them that the Reverend Alexander Hergensheimer is calling."

"Thank you. Please deposit twenty-five cents."

"Hey! I didn't get any use out of that first quarter. You hung up too soon."

"We did not disconnect; the party in Kansas City hung up."

"Well, call them back, please, and this time tell them not to hang up."

"Yes, sir. Please deposit twenty-five cents."

"Central, would I be calling collect if I had plenty of change on me? Get them on the line and tell them who I am. Reverend Alexander Hergensheimer, Deputy Executive Director."

"Please wait on the line."

So I waited again. And waited.

"Reverend? The party in Kansas City says to tell you that they do not accept collect calls from—I am quoting exactly—Jesus Christ Himself."

"That's no way to talk on the telephone. Or anywhere."

"I quite agree. There was more. This person said to tell you that he had never heard of you."

"Why, that—" I shut up, as I had no way to express myself within the dignity of the cloth.

"Yes, indeed. I tried to get his name. He hung up on me."

"Young man? Old man? Bass, tenor, baritone?"

"Boy soprano. I gathered an impression that it was the office boy, answering the phone during the lunch hour."

"I see. Well, thank you for your efforts. Above and beyond the call of duty, in my opinion."

"A pleasure, Reverend."

I left there, kicking myself. I did not explain to Margrethe until we were clear of the building. "Hoist by my own petard, dear one. I wrote that 'No Collect Calls' order myself. An analysis of the telephone log proved to me beyond any possible doubt that collect calls to our office were never for the benefit of the association. Nine out of ten are begging calls . . . and Churches United for Decency is not a charity. It collects money; it does not give it away. The tenth call is either from a troublemaker or a crank. So I set this firm rule and enforced it . . . and it paid off at once. Saved hundreds of dollars a year just in telephone tolls." I managed to smile. "Never dreamed that I would be caught in my own net."

"What are your plans now, Alec?"

"Now? Get out on Highway Sixty-Six and start waving my thumb. I want us to reach Oklahoma City before five o'clock. It should be easy; it's not very far."

"Yes, sir. Why five o'clock, may I ask?"

"You can always ask anything and you know it. Knock off the Patient Griselda act, sweetheart; you've been moping ever since we saw that dirigible. Because there is a district office of C.U.D. in Oklahoma City and I want to be there before they close. Wait'll you see them roll out the red carpet, hon! Get to Oke City and our troubles are over."

That afternoon reminded me of wading through sorghum. January sorghum. We had no trouble getting rides—but the rides were mostly short distances. We averaged about twenty miles an hour on a highway that permitted sixty miles per hour. We lost fifty-five minutes for a good reason: a free meal. For the umpteenth time a trucker bought us something to eat when he ate . . . for the reason that there is almost no man alive who can stop to eat, and fail to invite Margrethe to eat if she is there. (Then I get fed, too, simply because I'm her property. I'm not complaining.)

We ate in twenty minutes, then he spent thirty minutes and endless quarters playing pinball machines . . . and I stood there and seethed and Margrethe stood beside him and clapped her hands and squealed when he made a good score. But her social instincts are sound; he then drove us all the rest of the way to Oklahoma City. There he went through town when he could have taken a bypass, and at four-twenty he dropped us at 36th and Lincoln, only two blocks from the C.U.D. district office.

I walked that two blocks whistling. Once I said, "Smile, hon! A month from now—or sooner—we'll eat in the Tivoli."

"Truly?"

"Truly. You've told me so much about it that I can't wait. There's the building!"

Our suite is on the second floor. It warmed the cockles to see the door with lettering on the glass: CHURCHES UNITED FOR DECENCY — Enter.

"After you, my love!" I grabbed the knob, to open for her.

The door was locked.

I banged on it, then spotted a doorbell and rang it. Then I alternated knocking and ringing. And again.

A blackamoor carrying a mop and a pail came down the corridor, started to pass us. I called, "Hey, Uncle! Do you have a key to this suite?"

"Sure don't, Captain. Ain't nobody in there now. They most generally locked up and gone by four o'clock."

"I see. Thanks."

"A pleasure, Captain."

Out on the street again, I grinned sheepishly at Margrethe. "Red carpet treatment. Closing at four. When the cat is away, the mice will play. Some heads will roll, I promise you. I can't think of another cliché to fit the situation. Oh, yes, I can. Beggars can't be choosers. Madam, would you like to sleep in the park tonight? Warm night, no rain expected. Chiggers and mosquitoes, no extra charge."

We slept in Lincoln Park, on the golf course, on a green that was living velvet—alive with chiggers.

It was a good night's sleep despite chiggers. We got up when the first early golfers showed up, and we got off the golf course with nothing worse than dirty looks. We made use of public washrooms in the park, and rejoined much neater, feeling fresher, me with a fresh shave, and both of us filled with free water for breakfast. On the whole I felt cheerful. It was too early to expect those self-appointed playboys at C.U.D. to show up, so, when we ran across a policeman, I asked the location of the public library, then I added, "By the way, where is the airport?"

"The what?"

"The dirigible flying field."

The cop turned to Margrethe. "Lady, is he sick?"

I did feel sick a half hour later when I checked the directory in the building we had visited the afternoon before . . . I felt sick but unsurprised to find no Churches United for Decency among its tenants. But to make certain I walked up to the second floor. That suite was now occupied by an insurance firm.

"Well, dear, let's go to the public library. Find out what kind of world we are in."

"Yes, Alec." She was looking cheerful. "Dearest, I'm sorry you are disappointed . . . but I am so relieved. I— I was frightened out of my wits at the thought of meeting your wife."

"You won't. Not ever. Promise. Uh, I'm sort of relieved, too. And hungry."

We walked a few more steps. "Alec. Don't be angry."

"I'll do no more than give you a fat lip. What is it?"

"I have five quarters. Good ones."

"At this point I am supposed to say, 'Daughter, were you a good girl in Philadelphy?' Out with it. Whom did you kill? Much blood?"

"Yesterday. Those pinball games. Every time Harry won free games he gave me a quarter. 'For luck,' he said."

I decided not to beat her. Of course they were not "good quarters" but they turned out to be good enough. Good enough, that is, to fit coin machines. We had passed a penny arcade; such places usually have coin-operated food dispensers and this one did. The prices were dreadfully high—fifty cents for a skimpy stale sandwich; twenty-five cents for a bare mouthful of chocolate. But it was better than some breakfasts we had had on the road. And we certainly did not steal, as the quarters from my world were real silver.

Then we went to the public library to find out what sort of world we must cope with now.

We found out quickly:

Marga's world.

XX

*The wicked flee when no man pursueth: but the
righteous are bold as a lion.*
Proverbs 28:1

Margrethe was as elated as I had been the day before.
She bubbled, she smiled, she looked sixteen. I looked
around for a private place—back of book stacks or somewhere—where I could kiss her without worrying about a
proctor. Then I remembered that this was Margrethe's
world where nobody cared . . . and grabbed her where
she stood and bussed her properly.

And got scolded by a librarian.

No, not for what I had done, but because we had been
somewhat noisy about it. Public kissing did not in itself
disturb that library's decorum. Hardly. I noticed, while I
was promising to keep quiet and apologizing for the
breach, a display rack by that librarian's desk:

New Titles INSTRUCTIONAL PORNOGRAPHY —
Ages 6 to 12

Fifteen minutes later I was waving my thumb again on
Highway 77 to Dallas.

Why Dallas? A law firm: O'Hara, Rigsbee, Crumpacker,
and Rigsbee.

As soon as we were outside the library, Marga had
started talking excitedly about how she could now end
our troubles: her bank account in Copenhagen.

I said, "Wait a minute, darling. Where's your check-book? Where's your identification?"

What it came to was that Margrethe could possibly draw on her assets in Denmark after several days at a highly optimistic best or after several weeks at a more probable estimate . . . and that even the longer period involved quite a bit of money up front for cablegrams. Telephone across the Atlantic? Marga did not think such a thing existed. (And even if it did, I thought it likely that cablegrams were cheaper and more certain.)

Even after all arrangements had been made, it was possible that actual payment might involve postal delivery from Europe—in a world that had no airmail.

So we headed for Dallas, I having assured Marga that, at the very worst, Alec Graham's lawyers would advance Alec Graham enough money to get him (us) off the street, and, with luck, we would come at once into major assets.

(Or they might fail to recognize me as Alec Graham and prove that I was not he—by fingerprints, by signature, by something—and thereby lay the ghost of "Alec Graham" in Margrethe's sweet but addled mind. But I did not mention this to Margrethe.)

It is two hundred miles from Oklahoma City to Dallas; we arrived there at 2 p.m., having picked up a ride at the intersection of 66 and 77, and kept it clear into the Texas metropolis. We were dropped where 77 crosses 80 at the Trinity River, and we walked to the Smith Building; it took us half an hour.

The receptionist in suite 7000 looked like something out of the sort of stage show that C.U.D. has spent much time and money to suppress. She was dressed but not very much, and her makeup was what Marga calls "high style." She was nubile and pretty and, with my newly learned toleration, I simply enjoyed the sinful sight. She smiled and said, "May I help you?"

"This is a fine day for golf. Which of the partners is still in the office?"

"Only Mr. Crumpacker, I'm afraid."

"He's the one I want to see."

"And whom shall I say is calling?"

(First hurdle— I missed it. Or did she?) "Don't you recognize me?"

"I'm sorry. Should I?"

"How long have you been working here?"

"Just over three months."

"That accounts for it. Tell Crumpacker that Alec Graham is here."

I could not hear what Crumpacker said to her but I was watching her eyes; I think they widened—I feel sure of it. But all she said was, "Mr. Crumpacker will see you." Then she turned to Margrethe. "May I offer you a magazine while you wait? And would you like a reefer?"

I said, "She's coming with me."

"But—"

"Come along, Marga." I headed quickly for the inner offices.

Crumpacker's door was easy to find; it was the one with the squawking issuing from it. This shut off as I opened the door and held it for Margrethe. As I followed her in, he was saying, "Miss, you'll have to wait outside!"

"No," I denied, as I closed the door behind me. "Mrs. Graham stays."

He looked startled. "Mrs. Graham?"

"Surprised you, didn't I? Got married since I saw you last. Darling, this is Sam Crumpacker, one of my attorneys." (I had picked his first name off his door.)

"How do you do, Mr. Crumpacker?"

"Uh, glad to meet you, Mrs. Graham. Congratulations. Congratulations to you, Alec—you always could pick 'em."

I said, "Thanks. Sit down, Marga."

"Just a moment, folks! Mrs. Graham can't stay—really she can't! You know that."

"I know no such thing. This time I'm going to have a witness." No, I did not know that he was crooked. But I had learned long ago, in dealing with legislators, that anyone who tries to keep you from having a witness is bad news. So C.U.D. always had witnesses and always stayed within the law; it was cheaper that way.

Marga was seated; I sat down beside her. Crumpacker had jumped up when we came in; he remained standing. His mouth worked nervously. "I ought to call the Federal prosecutor."

"Do that," I agreed. "Pick up the phone there and call him. Let's *both* of us go see him. Let's tell him *everything*. With witnesses. Let's call in the press. All of the press, not just the tame cats."

(What did I know? Nothing. But when it's necessary to bluff, always bluff big. I was scared. This rat could turn and fight like a cornered mouse—a rabid one.)

"I should."

"Do it, do it! Let's name names, and tell who did what and who got paid. I want to get *everything* out into the open . . . before somebody slips cyanide into my soup."

"Don't talk that way."

"Who has a better right? Who pushed me overboard? *Who?*"

"Don't look at me!"

"No, Sammie, I don't think you did it; you weren't there. But it could be your godson. Eh?" Then I smiled my biggest right-hand-of-fellowship smile. "Just joking, Sam. My old friend would not want me dead. But you can tell me some things and help me out. Sam, it's not convenient to be dumped way off on the other side of the world—so you owe me." (No, I still knew nothing . . . nothing save the evident fact that here was a man with a guilty conscience—so crowd him.)

"Alec, let's not do anything hasty."

"I'm in no hurry. But I've got to have explanations. And money."

"Alec, I tell you on my word of honor all I know about what happened to you is that this squarehead ship came into Portland and you ain't aboard. And I have to go all the way to Oregon f' God's sake to witness them breaking into your strong-box. And there's only a hundred thousand in it; the rest is missing. Who got it, Alec? Who got to you?"

He had his eyes on me; I hope my face didn't show anything. But he had hulled me. Was this true? This shyster would lie as easily as he talked. Had my friend the purser, or the purser and the captain in cahoots, looted that lockbox?

As a working hypothesis, always prefer the simpler explanation. This man was more likely to lie than the purser was to steal. And it was likely—no, certain—that the captain would have to be present before the purser would force his way into the lockbox of a missing passenger. If these two responsible officers, with careers and reputations to lose, nevertheless combined to steal, why would they leave a hundred thousand behind? Why not take it all and be blandly ignorant about the contents of my lockbox?—as indeed they should be. Something fishy here.

"What are you implying was missing?"

"Huh?" He glanced at Margrethe. "Uh— Well, damn it, there should have been nine hundred grand more. The money you didn't pass over in Tahiti."

"Who says I didn't?"

"What? Alec, don't make things worse. Mr. Z. says so. You tried to drown his bagman."

I looked at him and laughed. "You mean those tropical gangsters? They tried to get the boodle without identifying themselves and without giving receipts. I told them an emphatic no—so the clever boy had his muscle throw me into the pool. Hmm— Sam, I see it now. Find out who came aboard the *Konge Knut* in Papeete."

"Why?"

"That's your man. He not only got the boodle; he pushed me overboard. When you know, don't bother to try to get him extradited, just tell me his name. I'll arrange the rest myself. Personally."

"Damn it, we want that million dollars."

"Do you think you can get it? It wound up in Mr. Z.'s hands . . . but you got no receipt. And I got a lot of grief from asking for a receipt. Don't be silly, Sam; the nine hundred thousand is gone. But not my fee. So pass over that hundred grand. Now."

"*What?* The Federal prosecutor in Portland kept that, impounded it as evidence."

"Sam, Sam boy, don't try to teach your grandmother how to steal sheep. As evidence for *what?* Who is charged? Who is indicted? What crime is alleged? Am I charged with stealing something out of my own lockbox? What crime?"

"'What crime?' Somebody stole that nine hundred grand, that's what!"

"Really? Who's the complainant? Who asserts that there ever was nine hundred thousand in that lockbox? I certainly never told anyone that—so *who says?* Pick up that phone, Sam; call the Federal prosecutor in Portland. Ask him why he held that money—on whose complaint? Let's get to the bottom of this. Pick it up, Sam. If that Federal clown has my money, I want to shake it loose from him."

"You're almighty anxious to talk to prosecutors! Strange talk from *you.*"

"Maybe I've had an acute attack of honesty. Sam, your unwillingness to call Portland tells me all I need to know. You were called out there to act on my behalf, as my attorney. American passenger lost overboard, ship of foreign registry, you betcha they get hold of the passenger's attorney to inventory his assets. Then they pass it all over to his attorney and he gives a receipt for it. Sam, what did you do with my clothes?"

"Eh? Gave 'em to the Red Cross. Of course."

"You did, eh?"

"After the prosecutor released 'em, I mean."

"Interesting. The Federal attorney keeps the money, although no one has complained that any money is missing

... but lets the clothes out of his hands *when the only probable crime is murder.*"

"*Huh?*"

"Me, I mean. Who pushed me and who hired him to? Sam, we both know where the money is." I stood up, pointed. "In that safe. That's where it logically has to be. You wouldn't bank it; there would be a record. You wouldn't hide it at home; your wife might find it. And you certainly didn't split with your partners. Sam, open it. I want to see whether there is a hundred thousand in there . . . or a million."

"You're out of your mind!"

"Call the Federal prosecutor. Let him be our witness."

I had him so angry he couldn't talk. His hands trembled. It isn't safe to get a little man too angry—and I topped him by six inches, weight and other measurements to match. He wouldn't attack me himself—he was a lawyer—but I would need to be careful going through doorways, and such.

Time to try to cool him— "Sam, Sam, don't take it so seriously. You were leaning on me pretty heavily . . . so I leaned back. The good Lord alone knows why prosecutors do anything—the gonif most likely has stolen it by now . . . in the belief that I am dead and will never complain. So I'll go to Portland and lean on him, hard."

"There's paper out on you there."

"Really? What charges?"

"Seduction under promise of marriage. A female crewman of that ship." He had the grace to look apologetically at Margrethe. "Sorry, Mrs. Graham. But your husband asked me."

"Quite all right," she answered crisply.

"I do get around, don't I? What does she look like? Is she pretty? What's her name?"

"I never saw her; she wasn't there. Her name? Some Swede name. Let me think. Gunderson, that was it. Margaret S. Gunderson."

Margrethe, bless her heart, never let out a peep—not

even at being called a Swede. I said in wonderment, "I'm accused of seducing this woman . . . aboard a foreign-flag vessel, somewhere in the South Seas. So there's a warrant out for me in Portland, Oregon. Sam, what kind of a lawyer are you? To let a client have paper slapped on him on that sort of charge."

"I'm a smart lawyer, that's the kind I am. Just as you said, no telling what a Federal attorney will do; they take their brains out when they appoint 'em. It simply wasn't important enough to talk about, you being dead, or so we all thought. I'm just looking out for your interests, letting you know about it before you step in it. Gimme some time, I'll get it quashed—*then* you go to Portland."

"Sounds reasonable. There aren't any charges outstanding on me here, are there?"

"No. Well, yes and no. You know the deal; we assured them that you would not be coming back, so they turned the blind eye when you left. But here you are, back. Alec, you can't afford to be seen here. Or elsewhere in Texas. Or anywhere in the States, actually. Word gets around, and they'll dig up those old charges."

"I was innocent!"

He shrugged. "Alec, all my clients are innocent. I'm talking like a father, in your own interest. Get out of Dallas. If you go as far as Paraguay, so much the better."

"How? I'm broke. Sam, I've *got* to have some dough."

"Have I ever let you down?" He got out his wallet, counted out five one-hundred-dollar bills, laid them in front of me.

I looked at them. "What's that? A tip?" I picked them up, pocketed them. "That much won't get us to Brownsville. Now let's see some money."

"See me tomorrow."

"Don't play games, Sam. Open that safe and get me some real money. Or I don't come here tomorrow; I go see the Federal man and sing like the birdies. After I get square with him—and I will; the Feds love a state's witness, it's the only way they ever win a case—then I go to Oregon and pick up that hundred grand."

"Alec, are you threatening me?"

"You play games, I play games. Sam, I need a car and I don't mean a beat-up Ford. A Cadillac. Doesn't have to be new, but a cream puff, clean, and a good engine. A Cadillac and a few grand and we'll be in Laredo by midnight, and in Monterrey by morning. I'll call you from Mexico City and give you an address. If you really want me to go to Paraguay and stay there, you send the money to D.F. for me to do it."

It did not work out quite that way, but I settled for a used Pontiac and left with six thousand dollars in cash, and instructions to go to a particular used-car lot and accept the deal offered me—Sam would call and set it up. He agreed also to call the Hyatt and get us the bridal suite, and would see that they held it. Then I was to come back at ten the next morning.

I refused to get up that early. "Make that eleven. We're still on our honeymoon."

Sam chuckled, slapped me on the back, and agreed.

Out in the corridor we headed toward the elevators but went ten feet farther and I opened the door to the fire-escape trunk. Margrethe followed me without comment but once inside the staircase trunk and out of earshot of others she said, "Alec, that man is not your friend."

"No, he's not."

"I am afraid for you."

"I'm afraid for me, too."

"Terribly afraid. I fear for your life."

"My love, I fear for my life, too. And for yours. You are in danger as long as you are with me."

"I will *not* leave you!"

"I know. Whatever this is, we are in it together."

"Yes. What are our plans now?"

"Now we go to Kansas."

"Oh, good! Then we are not driving to Mexico?"

"Hon, I don't even know how to drive a car."

We came out in a basement garage and walked up a ramp to a side street. There we walked several blocks away from the Smith Building, picked up a cruising taxi, rode it to the Texas & Pacific Station, there picked up a taxi at the taxi rank, and rode it to Fort Worth, twenty-five miles west. Margrethe was very quiet on the trip. I did not ask her what she was thinking about because I knew: It can't be happy-making to discover that a person you fell in love with was mixed up in some shenanigan that smelled of gangsters and rackets. I made myself a solemn promise never to mention the matter to her.

In Fort Worth I had the hackie drop us on its most styl-ish shopping street, letting him pick it. Then I said to Marga, "Darling, I'm about to buy you a heavy gold chain."

"Goodness, darling! I don't need a gold chain."

"We need it. Marga, the first time I was in this world—with you, in *Konge Knut*—I learned that here the dollar was soft, not backed by gold, and every price I have seen today confirms that. So, if change comes again—and we never know—even the hard money of this world, quarters and half dollars and dimes, won't be worth anything be-cause they're not really silver. As for the paper money I got from Crumpacker—waste paper!

"Unless I change it into something else. We'll start with that gold chain and from here on you wear it to bed, you even wear it to bathe—unless you hang it around my neck."

"I see. Yes."

"We'll buy some heavy gold jewelry for each of us, then I'm going to try to find a coin dealer—buy some silver cartwheels, maybe some gold coins. But my purpose is to get rid of most of this paper money in the next hour—all but the price of two bus tickets to Wichita, Kansas, three hundred and fifty miles north of here. Could you stand to

ride a bus all night tonight? I want to get us out of
Texas."

"Certainly! Oh, dear, I do want to get out of Texas!
Truly, I'm still frightened."

"Truly, you are not alone."

"But—"

"'But' what, dear? And quit looking sad."

"Alec, I haven't had a bath for *four days.*"

We found the jewelry shop, we found the coin shop; I
spent about half that fiat money and saved the rest for
bus fare and other purposes in this world—such as dinner, which we ate as soon as the shops started to close. A
hamburger we had eaten in Gainesville seemed an
awfully long way off in time and space. Then I deter-
mined that there was a bus going north—Oklahoma City,
Wichita, Salina—at ten o'clock that evening. I bought
tickets and paid an extra dollar on each ticket to reserve
seats. Then I threw money away like a drunken sailor—
took a room in a hotel across from the bus station, knowing that we would be checking out in less than two hours.

It was worth it. Hot baths for each of us, taking turns,
each of us remaining fully dressed and carrying the
other's clothing, jewelry, and all the money while the
other was naked and wet. And carrying my razor, which
had become a talisman of how to outwit Loki's playful
tricks.

And new, clean underwear for each of us, purchased in
passing while we were converting paper money into val-
uta.

I had hoped for time enough for love—but no; by the
time I was clean and dry we had to dress and check out
to catch that bus. Never mind, there would be other
times. We climbed into the bus, put the backrests back,
put Marga's head on my shoulder. As the bus headed
north we fell asleep.

I woke up sometime later because the road was so
rough. We were seated right behind the driver, so I

leaned forward and asked, "Is this a detour?" I could not recall a rough stretch when we had ridden south on this same road about twelve hours earlier.

"No," he said. "We've crossed into Oklahoma, that's all. Not much pavement in Oklahoma. Some near Oke City and a little between there and Guthrie."

The talk had wakened Margrethe; she straightened up. "What is it, dear?"

"Nothing. Just Loki having fun with us. Go back to sleep."

XXI

What are these which are arrayed in white robes? and
whence came they? And I said unto him, Sir, thou knowest.
And he said unto me, These are they which came out
of great tribulation, and have washed their robes,
and made them white in the blood of the Lamb.
Therefore are they before the throne of God,
and serve Him day and night in His temple.
Revelation 8:13–15

I was driving a horse and buggy and not enjoying it.
The day was hot, the dust kicked up by horse's hooves
stuck to sweaty skin, flies were bad, there was no breeze.
We were somewhere near the corner of Missouri, Kansas,
and Oklahoma, but I was not sure where. I had not seen a
map for days and the roads were no longer marked with
highway signs for the guidance of automobilists—there
were no automobiles.

The last two weeks (more or less—I had lost track of
the days) had been endless torments of Sisyphus, one ridiculous frustration after another. Sell silver dollars to a
local dealer in exchange for that world's paper?—no
trouble; I did it several times. But it didn't always help.
Once I had sold silver for local paper money and we had
ordered dinner—when, boom, another world change and
we went hungry. Another time I was cheated out-
rageously and when I complained, I was told: "Neighbor,
possession of that coin is illegal and you know it. I've of-

fered you a price anyhow because I like you. Will you take it? Or shall I do my plain duty as a citizen?"

I took it. The paper money he gave us for five ounces of silver would not buy dinner for Marga and me at a back-woods gourmet spot called "Mom's Diner."

That was in a charming community called (by a sign at its outskirts):

THE TEN COMMANDMENTS
A Clean Community
Blackamoors, Kikes, Papists
Keep Moving!

We kept moving. That whole two weeks had been spent trying to travel the two hundred miles from Oklahoma City to Joplin, Missouri. I had been forced to give up the notion of avoiding Kansas City. I still had no intention of staying in or near Kansas City, not when a sudden change of worlds could land us in Abigail's lap. But I had learned in Oklahoma City that the fastest and indeed the only practical route to Wichita was a long detour through Kansas City. We had retrogressed to the horse-and-buggy era.

When you consider the total age of the earth, from Creation in 4004 B.C. to the year of Our Lord 1994, or 5998 years—call it 6000—in a period of 6000 years, 80 or 90 years is nothing much. And that is how short a time it has been since the horse-and-buggy day in my world. My father was born in that day (1909) and my paternal grandfather not only never owned an automobile but refused to ride in one. He claimed that they were spawn of the Devil, and used to quote passages from Ezekiel to prove it. Perhaps he was right.

But the horse-and-buggy era does have shortcomings. There are obvious ones such as no inside plumbing, no air conditioning, no modern medicine. But for us there was an unobvious but major one; where there are no trucks and no cars there is effectively no hitchhiking. Oh, it is sometimes possible to hitch rides on farm wagons—but the difference in speed between a human's walk and a horse's walk is not great. We rode when we could but, either way, fifteen miles was a good day's progress—too good; it left no time to work for meals and a place to sleep.

There is an old paradox, Achilles and the Tortoise, in which the remaining distance to your goal is halved at each step. The question is: How long does it take to reach your goal? The answer is: You can't get there from here.

That is the way we "progressed" from Oklahoma City to Joplin.

Something else compounded my frustration: I became increasingly persuaded that we were indeed in the latter days, and we could expect the return of Jesus and the Final Judgment at any moment—and my darling, my necessary one, was not yet back in the arms of Jesus. I refrained from nagging her about it, although it took all my will power to respect her wish to handle it alone. I began to sleep badly through worrying about her.

I became a bit crazy, too (in addition to my paranoid belief that these world changes were aimed at me personally)—crazy in that I acquired an unfounded but compelling belief that finishing this journey was essential to the safety of my darling's immortal soul. Just let us get as far as Kansas, dear Lord, and I will pray without ceasing until I have converted her and brought her to grace. O Lord God of Israel, grant me this boon!

I continued to look for dishwashing jobs (or anything) even while we still had silver and gold to trade for local money. But motels disappeared entirely; hotels became scarce and restaurants decreased in numbers and size to fit an economy in which travel was rare and almost all meals were eaten at home.

It became easier to find jobs cleaning stalls in livery stables. I preferred dishwashing to shoveling horse manure—especially as I had only one pair of shoes. But I stuck to the rule of take any honest work but *keep moving!*

You may wonder why we did not shift to hitching rides on freight trains. In the first place I did not know how, never having done it. Still more important, I could not guarantee Marga's safety. There were the hazards of mounting a moving freight car. But worse were dangers from people: railroad bulls and road kids—hobos, tramps, bindlestiffs, bums. No need to discuss those grisly dangers, as I kept her away from rail lines and hobo jungles.

And I worried. While abiding strictly by her request not to be pressured, I did take to praying aloud every night and in her presence, on my knees. And at last, to my great joy, my darling joined me, on her knees. She did not pray aloud and I stopped vocalizing myself, save for a final: "In Jesus' name, Amen." We still did not talk about it.

I wound up driving this horse and buggy (goodness, what a hot day!—"Cyclone weather," my grandmother Hergensheimer would have called it) as a result of a job cleaning stalls in a livery stable. As usual I had quit after one day, telling my temporary employer that my wife and I had to move on to Joplin; her mother was ill.

He told me that he had a rig that needed to be returned to the next town up the road. What he meant was that he had too many rigs and nags on hand, his own and others, or he would have waited until he could send it back by renting it to a passing drummer.

I offered to return it for one day's wages at the same extremely low rate that he had paid me to shovel manure and curry nags.

He pointed out that he was doing me a favor, since my wife and I had to get to Joplin.

He had both logic and strength of position on his side; I agreed. But his wife did put up a lunch for us, as well as giving us breakfast after we slept in their shed.

So I was not too unhappy driving that rig, despite the weather, despite the frustrations. We were getting a few miles closer to Joplin every day—and now my darling was praying. It was beginning to look like "Home Free!" after all.

We had just reached the outskirts of this town (Lowell? Racine? I wish I could remember) when we encountered something right straight out of my childhood: a camp meeting, an old-time revival. On the left side of the road was a cemetery, well kept but the grass was drying; facing it on the right was the revival tent, pitched in a pasture. I wondered whether the juxtaposition of graveyard and Bible meeting was accidental, or planned?—if the Reverend Danny had been involved, I would know it was planned; most people cannot see gravestones without thinking about the long hereafter.

Crowded ranks of buggies and farm wagons stood near the tent, and a temporary corral lay beyond them. Picnic tables of the plank-and-sawhorse type were by the tent on the other side; I could see remains of lunch. This was a serious Bible meeting, one that started in the morning, broke for lunch, carried on in the afternoon—would no doubt break for supper, then adjourn only when the revivalist judged that there were no more souls to be saved that day.

(I despise these modern city preachers with their five-minute "inspirational messages." They say Billy Sunday could preach for seven hours on only a glass of water—then do it again in the evening *and* the next day. No wonder heathen cults have spread like a green bay tree!)

There was a two-horse caravan near the tent. Painted on its side was: Brother "Bible" Barnaby. Out front was a canvas sign on guys and stays:

> That Old-Time Religion!
> Brother "Bible" Barnaby
> Healing Every Session

10a.m. — 2p.m. — 7p.m.
Every Day from Sunday June 5th till
!!!JUDGMENT DAY!!!

I spoke to the nag and pulled on the reins to let her know that I wanted to stop. "Darling, look at that!"

Margrethe read the sign, made no comment.

"I admire his courage," I said. "Brother Barnaby is betting his reputation that Judgment Day will arrive before it's time to harvest wheat . . . which could be early this year, hot as it is."

"But you think Judgment Day is soon."

"Yes, but I'm not betting a professional reputation on it . . . just my immortal soul and hope of Heaven. Marga, every Bible student reads the prophecies slightly differently. Or very differently. Most of the current crop of premillenarians don't expect the Day earlier than the year two thousand. I want to hear how Brother Barnaby reasons. He might have something. Do you mind if we stay here an hour?"

"We will stay however long you wish. But— Alec, you wish me to go in? Must I?"

"Uh—" (Yes, darling, I certainly do want you to go inside.) "You would rather wait in the buggy?"

Her silence was answer enough. "I see. Marga, I'm not trying to twist your arm. Just one thing— We have not been separated except when utterly necessary for several weeks. And you know why. With the changes coming almost every day, I would hate to have one hit while you were sitting out here and I was inside, quite a way off. Uh, we could stand outside the tent. I see they have the sides rolled up."

She squared her shoulders. "I was being silly. No, we will go inside. Alec, I do need to hold your hand; you are right: Change comes fast. But I will not ask you to stay away from a meeting of your coreligionists."

"Thank you, Marga."

"And, Alec— I will *try!*"

"Thank you. Thank you loads! Amen!"

"No need to tank me. If you go to your Heaven, I want to go, too!"

"Let's go inside, dear."

I put the buggy at the far end of a rank, then led the mare to the corral, Marga with me. As we came back to the tent I could hear:

"—the corner where you are!
"Brighten the corner where you are!
"Someone far from harbor you may guide across the bar!
"So—"

I chimed in: "—brighten the corner where you are!"
It felt good.

Their instrumental music consisted of a foot-pumped organ and a slide trombone. The latter surprised me but pleased me; there is no other instrument that can get right down and rassle with *The Holy City* the way a trombone can, and it is almost indispensable for *The Son of God Goes Forth to War*.

The congregation was supported by a choir in white angel robes—a scratch choir, I surmised, as the white robes were homemade, from sheets. But what that choir may have lacked in professionalism it made up for in zeal. Church music does not have to be good as long as it is sincere—and loud.

The sawdust trail, six feet wide, led straight down the middle, benches on each side. It dead-ended against a chancel rail of two-by-fours. An usher led us down the trail in answer to my hope for seats down front. The place was crowded but he got people to squeeze over and we wound up on the aisle in the second row, me outside. Yes, there were still seats in the back, but every preacher despises people—their name is legion!—who sit clear at the back when there are seats open down front.

As the music stopped, Brother Barnaby stood up and

came to the pulpit, placed his hand on the Bible. "It's all in the Book," he said quietly, almost in a whisper. The congregation became dead still.

He stepped forward, looked around. "Who loves you?"

"Jesus loves me!"

"Let Him hear you."

"JESUS LOVES ME!"

"How do you know that?"

"IT'S IN THE BOOK!"

I became aware of an odor I had not smelled in a long time. My professor of homiletics pointed out to us once in a workshop session that a congregation imbued with religious fervor has a strong and distinctive odor ("stink" is the word he used) compounded of sweat and both male and female hormones. "My sons," he told us, "if your assembled congregation smells too sweet, you aren't getting to them. If you can't make 'em sweat, if they don't break out in their own musk like a cat in rut, you might as well quit and go across the street to the papists. Religious ecstasy is the strongest human emotion; when it's there, you can smell it!"

Brother Barnaby got to them.

(And, I must confess, I never did. That's why I wound up as an organizer and money-raiser.)

"Yes, it's in the Book. The Bible is the Word of God, not just here and there, but every word. Not as allegory, but as literal truth. You shall know the truth and the truth will make you free. I read to you now from the Book: 'For the Lord Himself will descend from Heaven with a shout, with the voice of the archangel, and with the Trump of God: and the dead in Christ shall rise first.'

"That last line is great news, my brothers and sisters: '—the dead in Christ shall rise first.' What does that say? It does not say that the dead shall rise first; it says that the *dead in Christ* shall rise first. Those who were washed in the blood of the Lamb, born again in Jesus, and then have died in a state of grace *before* His second coming, they will not be forgotten, they will be *first*. Their graves

will open, they will be miraculously restored to life and
health and physical perfection and will lead the parade
to Heaven, there to dwell in happiness by the great white
throne forevermore!"

Someone shouted, "Hallelujah!"

"Bless you, sister. Ah, the good news! All the dead in
Christ, every one! Sister Ellen, taken from her family by
the cruel hand of cancer, but who died with the name of
Jesus on her lips, *she* will help lead the procession. Asa's
beloved wife, who died giving birth but in a state of
grace, she will be there! All your dear ones who died in
Christ will be gathered up and you will see them in
Heaven. Brother Ben, who lived a sinful life, but found
God in a foxhole before an enemy bullet cut him down, *he*
will be there . . . and his case is specially good news, witnessing that God can be found anywhere. Jesus is present
not only in churches—in fact there are fancy-Dan
churches where His Name is rarely heard—"

"You can say that again!"

"And I will. God is everywhere; He can hear you when
you speak. He can hear you more easily when you are
ploughing a field, or down on your knees by your bed,
than He can in some ornate cathedral surrounded by the
painted and perfumed. He is here *now*, and He promises
you, 'I will never desert you, nor will I ever forsake you. I
stand at the door and knock, if anyone hears My voice
and opens the door, I will come in to him, and will dine
with him, and he with Me.' That's His promise, dearly
beloved, in plain words. No obscurities, no highfalutin
'interpretation,' no so-called 'allegorical meanings.'
Christ Himself is waiting for you, if only you will ask.

"And if you do ask, if you are born again in Jesus, if He
washes away your sins and you reach that state of grace
. . . what then? I read you the first half of God's promise
to the faithful. You will hear the Shout, you will hear the
great Trumpet sounding His advent, as He promised, and
the dead in Christ shall rise again. Those dry bones will
rise again and be covered with living, healthy flesh.

"*Then* what?

"Hear the words of the Lord: 'Then we which are alive'— That's you and me, brothers and sisters; God is talking about *us*. 'Then we which are alive and remain shall be caught up together with them in the clouds, to meet the Lord in the air and so shall we ever be with the Lord'!

"So shall we ever be! So shall we *ever* be! With the Lord in Heaven!"

"Hallelujah!"

"Bless His Name!"

"Amen! Amen!"

(I found that I was one of those saying "Amen!")

"But there's a price. There are no free tickets to Heaven. What happens if you *don't* ask Jesus to help you? What if you ignore His offer to be washed free of sin and reborn in the blood of the Lamb? What then? Well? Answer me!"

The congregation was still save for heavy breathing, then a voice from the back said, not loudly, "Hellfire."

"Hellfire and damnation! Not for just a little while but through all eternity! Not some mystical, allegorical fire that singes only your peace of mind and burns no more than a Fourth of July sparkler. This is the real thing, a raging fire, as real as this." Brother Barnaby slapped the pulpit with a crack that could be heard throughout the tent. "The sort of fire that makes a baseburner glow cherry red, then white. And you are *in* that fire, Sinner, and the ghastly pain goes on and on, and it never stops. Never! There's no hope for you. No use asking for a second chance. You've *had* your second chance . . . and your millionth chance. And more. For two thousand years sweet Jesus has been begging you, *pleading* with you, to accept from Him that for which He died in agony on the Cross to give you. So, once you are burning in that fiery Pit and trying to cough up the brimstone—that's sulfur, plain ordinary sulfur, burning and stinking, and it will burn your lungs and blister your sinful hide!—when you're roasting deep in the Pit for your sins, don't go whining about how dreadful it hurts and how you didn't know it would be like that. Jesus knows all about pain; He died on the Cross. He died for *you*. But you wouldn't listen and now you're down in the Pit and whining.

"And there you'll *stay*, suffering burning agony throughout eternity! Your whines can't be heard from down in the Pit; they are drowned out by the screams of billions of other sinners!"

Brother Barnaby lowered his voice to conversational level. "Do you want to burn in the Pit?"

"No!" — "Never!" — "Jesus save us!"

"Jesus will save you, if you ask Him to. Those who died in Christ are saved, we read about them. Those alive when He returns will be saved if they are born again and remain in that state of grace. He promised us that He would return, and that Satan would be chained for a thousand years while He rules in peace and justice here on earth. That's the Millennium, folks, that's the great day at hand. After that thousand years Satan will be loosed for a little while and the final battle will be fought. There'll be war in Heaven. The Archangel Michael will be the general for our side, leading God's angels against the Dragon—that's Satan again—and his host of fallen angels. And Satan lost—will lose, that is, a thousand years from now. And nevermore will he be seen in Heaven.

"But that's a thousand years from now, dear friends. You will live to see it . . . *if* you accept Jesus and are born again before that Trumpet blast that signals His return. When will that be? Soon, soon! What does the Book say? In the Bible God tells you not once but many times, in Isaiah, in Daniel, in Ezekiel, and in all four of the Gospels, that you will *not* be told the exact hour of His return. Why? So you can't sweep the dirt under the rug, that's why! If He told you that He would arrive New Year's Day the year two thousand, there are those who would spend the next five and a half years consorting with lewd women, worshiping strange gods, breaking every one of the Ten Commandments . . . then, sometime Christmas Week nineteen ninety-nine you would find them in church, crying repentance, trying to make a deal.

"No siree Bob! No cheap deals. It's the same price to everyone. The Shout and the Trump may be months away . . . or you may hear it before I can finish this sentence. It's up to you to be ready when it comes.

"But we know that it is coming soon. How? Again it's in the Book. Signs and portents. The first, without which the rest cannot happen, is the return of the Children of Israel to the Promised Land—see Ezekiel, see Matthew, see today's newspapers. They rebuild the Temple . . . and sure enough they have; it's in the *Kansas City Star*. There be other signs and portents, wonders of all sorts—but the greatest are tribulations, trials to test the souls of men the way Job was tested. Can there be a better word to describe the twentieth century than 'tribulations'?

"Wars and terrorists and assassinations and fires and plagues. And more wars. Never in history has mankind been tried so bitterly. But endure as Job endured and the end is happiness and eternal peace—the peace of God, which passeth all understanding. He offers you His hand, He loves you, He will save you."

Brother Barnaby stopped and wiped his forehead with a large handkerchief that was already soggy from such use. The choir (perhaps at a signal from him) started singing softly, "We shall gather at the river, the beautiful, beautiful river, that flows by the throne of God—" and presently segued into:

"Just as I am, without one plea—"

Brother Barnaby got down on one knee and held out his arms to us. "Please! Won't you answer Him? Come, accept Jesus, let Him gather you in His arms—"
The choir continued softly with:

"But that Thy blood was shed for me,

"And Thou bidd'st me come to Thee,
"O Lamb of God, I come, I come!"

And the Holy Ghost descended.

I felt Him overpower me and the joy of Jesus filled my heart. I stood up and stepped out into the aisle. Only then did I remember that I had Margrethe with me. I turned and saw her staring back at me, her face filled with a sweet and deeply serious look. "Come, darling," I whispered, and led her into the aisle. Together we went down the sawdust trail to God.

There were others ahead of us at the chancel rail. I found us a place, pushed some crutches and a truss aside, and knelt down. I placed my right hand on the rail, rested my forehead on it, while I continued to hold Marga's hand with my left. I prayed Jesus to wash away our sins and receive us into His arms.

One of Brother Barnaby's helpers was whispering into my ear. "How is it with you, brother?"

"I'm fine," I said happily, "and so is my wife. Help someone who needs it."

"Bless you, brother." He moved on. A sister farther down was writhing and speaking in tongues; he stopped to comfort her.

I bowed my head again, then became aware of neighing and loud squeals of frightened horses and a great flapping and shaking of the canvas roof above us. I looked up and saw a split start and widen, then the canvas blew away. The ground trembled, the sky was dark.

The Trump shook my bones, the Shout was the loudest ever heard, joyous and triumphant. I helped Margrethe to her feet and smiled at her. "It's *now*, darling!"

We were swept up.

We were tumbled head over heels and tossed about by a funnel cloud, a Kansas twister. I was wrenched away from Marga and tried to twist back, but could not. You can't swim in a twister; you go where it takes you. But I knew she was safe.

The storm turned me upside down and held me there for a long moment, about two hundred feet up. The horses had broken out of the corral, and some of the people, not caught up, were milling about. The force of the twister turned me again and I stared down at the cemetery.

The graves were opening.

XXII

When the morning stars sang together,
and all the sons of God shouted for joy.
Job 38:7

The wind whipped me around, and I saw no more of the graves. By the time I was faced down again the ground was no longer in sight—just a boiling cloud glowing inside with a great light, amber and saffron and powder blue and green gold. I continued to search for Margrethe, but few people drifted near me and none was she. Never mind, the Lord would protect her. Her temporary absence could not dismay me; we had taken the only important hurdle together.

I thought about that hurdle. What a near thing! Suppose that old mare had thrown a shoe and the delay had caused us to reach that point on the road an hour later than we did? Answer: We would never have reached it. The Last Trump would have sounded while we were still on the road, with neither of us in a state of grace. Instead of being caught up into the Rapture, we would have gone to Judgement unredeemed, then straight to Hell.

Do I believe in predestination?

That is a good question. Let's move on to questions I can answer. I floated above those clouds for a time unmeasured by me. I sometimes saw other people but no one came close enough for talk. I began to wonder when I would see our Lord Jesus—He had promised specifically that He would meet us "in the air."

I had to remind myself that I was behaving like a little child who demands that Mama do it *now* and is answered, "Be patient, dear. Not yet." God's time and mine were not the same; the Bible said so. Judgment Day had to be a busy time and I had no concept of what duties Jesus had to carry out. Oh, yes, I did know of one; those graves opening up reminded me. Those who had died in Christ (millions? billions? more?) were to go *first* to meet our Father Who art in Heaven, and of course the Lord Jesus would be with them on that glorious occasion; He had promised them that.

Having figured out the reason for the delay, I relaxed. I was willing to wait my turn to see Jesus . . . and when I did see Him, I would ask Him to bring Margrethe and me together.

No longer worried, no longer hurried, utterly comfortable, neither hot nor cold, not hungry, not thirsty, floating as effortlessly as a cloud, I began to feel the bliss that had been promised. I slept.

I don't know how long I slept. A long time—I had been utterly exhausted; the last three weeks had been grinding. Running a hand across my face told me that I had slept a couple of days or more; my whiskers had reached the untidy state that meant at least two days of neglect. I touched my breast pocket—yes, my trusty Gillette, gift of Marga, was still buttoned safely inside. But I had no soap, no water, no mirror.

This irritated me as I had been awakened by a bugle call (not the Great Trumpet—probably just one wielded by an angel on duty), a call that I knew without being told meant, "Wake up there! It is now your turn."

It was indeed—so when the "roll was called up yonder" I showed up with a two-day beard. Embarrassing!

Angels handled us like traffic cops, herding us into the formations they wanted. I knew they were angels; they wore wings and white robes and were heroic in size—one that flew near me was nine or ten feet tall. They did not flap their wings (I learned later that wings were worn only for ceremony, or as badges of authority). I discovered that I could move as these traffic cops directed. I had not been able to control my motions earlier; now I could move in any direction by volition alone.

They brought us first into columns, single file, stretched out for miles (hundreds of miles? thousands?). Then they brought the columns into ranks, twelve abreast—these were stacked in layers, twelve deep. I was, unless I miscounted, number four in my rank, which was stacked three layers down. I was about two hundred places back in my column—estimated while forming up—but I could not guess how long the column was.

And we flew past the Throne of God.

But first an angel positioned himself in the air about fifty yards off our left flank. His voice carried well. "Now hear this! You will pass in review in this formation. Hold your position at all times. Guide on the creature on your left, the creature under you, and the one ahead of you. Leave ten cubits between ranks and between layers, five cubits elbow to elbow in ranks. No crowding, no breaking out of ranks, no slowing down as we pass the Throne. Anybody breaking flight discipline will be sent to the tail end of the flight . . . and I'm warning you now, the Son might be gone by then, with nobody but Peter or Paul or some other saint to receive the parade. Any questions?"

"How much is a cubit?"

"Two cubits is one yard. Any creature in this cohort who does not know how long a yard is?"

No one spoke up. The angel added, "Any more questions?"

A woman to my left and above me called out, "Yes! My daughter didn't have her cough medicine with her. So I fetched it. Can you take it to her?"

"Creature, please accept my assurance that any cough your daughter manages to take with her to Heaven will be purely psychosomatic."

"But her doctor said—"

"And in the meantime shut up and let's get on with this parade. Special requests can be filed after arriving in Heaven."

There were more questions, mostly silly, confirming an opinion I had kept to myself for years: Piety does not imply horse sense.

Again the trumpet sounded; our cohort's flightmaster called out, *"Forward!"* Seconds later there was a single blast; he shouted, *"Fly!"* We moved forward.

(Note: I call this angel "he" because he seemed male. Ones that seemed to be female I refer to as "she." I never have been sure about sex in an angel. If any. I think they are androgynous but I never had a chance to find out. Or the courage to ask.)

(Here's another one that bothers me. Jesus had brothers and sisters; is the Virgin Mary still a virgin? I have never had the courage to ask that question, either.)

We could see His throne for many miles ahead. This was not the great white Throne of God the Father in Heaven; this was just a field job for Jesus to use on this occasion. Nevertheless it was magnificent, carved out of a single diamond with its myriad facets picking up Jesus' inner light and refracting it in a shower of fire and ice in all directions. And that is what I saw best, as the face of Jesus shines with such blazing light that, without sunglasses, you can't really see His features.

Never mind; you knew Who He was. One could not help knowing. A feeling of overpowering awe grabbed me when we were still at least twenty-five miles away. Despite my professors of theology, for the first time in my life I understood (felt) that single emotion that is described in the Bible by two words used together: love and fear. I loved/feared the Entity on that throne, and now I knew why Peter and James had abandoned their nets and followed Him.

And of course I did not make my request to Him as we passed closest (about a hundred yards). In my life on earth I had addressed (prayed to) Jesus by name thousands of times; when I saw Him in the Flesh I simply reminded myself that the angel herding us had promised us a chance to file personal requests when we reached Heaven. Soon enough. In the meantime it pleased me to think about Margrethe, somewhere in this parade, seeing the Lord Jesus on His throne . . . and if I had not intervened, she might never have seen Him. It made me feel warm and good, on top of the ecstatic awe I felt in staring at His blinding light.

Some miles past the throne the column swung up and to the right, and we left the neighborhood first of earth and then of the solar system. We headed straight for Heaven and picked up speed.

Did you know that earth looks like a crescent moon when you look back at it? I wondered whether or not any flat-earthers had managed to attain the Rapture. It did not seem likely, but such ignorant superstition is not totally incompatible with believing in Christ. Some superstitions are absolutely forbidden—astrology, for example, and Darwinism. But the flat-earth nonsense is nowhere forbidden that I know of. If there were any flat-earthers with us, how did they feel to look back and *see* that the earth was round as a tennis ball?

(Or would the Lord in His mercy let them perceive it as flat? Can mortal man ever understand the viewpoint of God?)

It seemed to take about two hours to reach the neighborhood of Heaven. I say "seemed to" because it might have been any length of time; there was no human scale by which to judge. In the same vein, the total period of the Rapture seemed to me to be about two days . . . but I had reason later to believe that it may have been seven years—at least by some reckoning. Measures of time and space become very slippery when one lacks mundane clocks and yardsticks.

As we approached the Holy City our guides had us slow

down and then make a sightseeing sweep around it before going in through one of the gates.

This was no minor jaunt. New Jerusalem (Heaven, the
Holy City, Jehovah's capital) is laid out foursquare like
the District of Columbia, but it is enormously bigger, one
thousand three hundred and twenty miles on a side, five
thousand two hundred and eighty miles around it, and
that gives an area of one million seven hundred and
forty-two thousand four hundred square miles.

This makes cities like Los Angeles or New York look
tiny.

In solemn truth the Holy City covers an area more than
six times as big as all of Texas! At that, it's crowded. But
they are expecting only a few more after us.

It's a walled city, of course, and the walls are two hundred and sixteen feet high, and the same wide. The tops
of the wall are laid out in twelve traffic lanes—and no
guard rails. Scary. There are twelve gates, three in each
wall, the famous pearly gates (and they are); these normally stand open—will not be closed, we were told, until
the Final Battle.

The wall itself is of iridescent jasper but it has a dozen
footings in horizontal layers that are more dazzling than
the wall itself: sapphire, chalcedony, emerald, sardonyx,
chrysolite, beryl, topaz, amethyst—I may have missed
some. New Jerusalem is so dazzling everywhere that it is
hard for a human to grasp it—impossible to grasp it all
at once.

When we finished the sweep around the Holy City, our
cohort's flightmaster herded us into a holding pattern
like dirigibles at O'Hare and kept us there until he received a signal that one of the gates was free—and I was
hoping to get at least a glimpse of Saint Peter, but no—
his office is at the main gate, the Gate of Judah, whereas
we went in by the opposite gate, named for Asher, where
we were registered by angels deputized to act for Peter.

•   •   •

Even with all twelve gates in use and dozens of Peter-deputized clerks at each gate and examination waived (since we all were caught up at the Rapture—guaranteed saved) we had to queue up quite a long time just to get registered in, receive temporary identifications, temporary bunking assignments, temporary eating assignments—

("Eating"?)

Yes, I thought so, too, and I asked the angel who booked me about it. He/she looked down at me. "Refection is optional. It will do you no harm never to eat and not to drink. But many creatures and some angels enjoy eating, especially in company. Suit yourself."

"Thank you. Now about this berthing assignment. It's a single. I want a double, for me and my wife. I want—"

"Your former wife, you mean. In Heaven there is no marriage or giving in marriage."

"Huh? Does that mean we can't live together?"

"Not at all. But both of you must apply, together, at Berthing General. See the office of Exchange and Readjustments. Be sure, each of you, to fetch your berthing chit."

"But that's the problem! I got separated from my wife. How do I find her?"

"Not part of my M.O.S. Ask at the information booth. In the meantime use your singles apartment in Gideon Barracks."

"But—"

He (she?) sighed. "Do you realize how many thousands of hours I have been sitting here? Can you guess how complex it is to provide for millions of creatures at once, some alive and never dead, others newly incarnate? This is the first time we have had to install plumbing for the use of fleshly creatures—do you even suspect how inconvenient *that* is? I say that, when you install plumbing, you are bound to get creatures who *need* plumbing—and there goes the neighborhood! But did they listen to me? Hunh! Pick up your papers, go through that door, draw a robe and a halo—harps are optional. Follow the green line to Gideon Barracks."

"No!"

I saw his (her) lips move; she (he) may have been praying. "Do you think it is proper to run around Heaven looking the way you do? You are quite untidy. We aren't used to living-flesh creatures. Uh . . . Elijah is the last I recall, and I must say that you look almost as disreputable as he did. In addition to discarding those rags and putting on a decent white robe, if I were you I would do something about that dandruff."

"Look," I said tensely. "Nobody knows the trouble I've seen, nobody knows but Jesus. While you've been sitting around in a clean white robe and a halo in an immaculate city with streets of gold, I've been struggling with Satan himself. I know I don't look very neat but I didn't choose to come here looking this way. Uh— Where can I pick up some razor blades?"

"Some what?"

"Razor blades. Gillette double-edged blades, or that type. For this." I took out my razor, showed it to her/him. "Preferably stainless steel."

"Here everything is stainless. But what in Heaven is *that?*"

"A safety razor. To take this untidy beard off my face."

"Really? If the Lord in His wisdom had intended His male creations not to have hair on their faces, He would have created them with smooth features. Here, let me dispose of that." He-she reached for my razor.

I snatched it back. "Oh, no, you don't! Where's that information booth?"

"To your left. Six hundred and sixty miles." She-he sniffed.

I turned away, fuming. Bureaucrats. Even in Heaven. I didn't ask any more questions there because I spotted a veiled meaning. Six hundred and sixty miles is a figure I recalled from our sightseeing tour: the exact distance from a center gate (such as Asher Gate, where I was) to the center of Heaven, i.e., the Great White Throne of the Lord God Jehovah, God the Father. He (she) was telling me, none too gently, that if I did not like the way I was being treated, I could take my complaints to the Boss— i.e., "Get lost!"

I picked up my papers and backed away, looked around for someone else in authority.

The one who organized this gymkhana, Gabriel or Michael or whoever, had anticipated that there would be lots of creatures milling around, each with problems that didn't quite fit the system. So scattered through the crowd were cherubs. Don't think of Michelangelo or Luca della Robbia; these were not bambinos with dimpled knees; these were people a foot and a half taller than we newcomers were—like angels but with little cherub wings and each with a badge reading "STAFF."

Or maybe they were indeed angels; I never have been sure about the distinction between angels and cherubim and seraphim and such; the Book seems to take it for granted that you know such things without being told. The papists list *nine* different classes of angels! By whose authority? It's not in the Book!

I found only two distinct classes in Heaven: angels and humans. Angels consider themselves superior and do not hesitate to let you know it. And they are indeed superior in position and power and privilege. Saved souls are second-class citizens. The notion, one that runs all through Protestant Christianity and maybe among papists as well, that a saved soul will practically sit in the lap of God—well, it ain't so! So you're saved and you go to Heaven—you find at once that you are the new boy on the block, junior to everybody there.

A saved soul in Heaven occupies much the position of a blackamoor in Arkansas. And it's the angels who really rub your nose in it.

I never met an angel I liked.

And this derives from how they feel about us. Let's look at it from the angelic viewpoint. According to Daniel there are a hundred million angels in Heaven. Before the Resurrection and the Rapture, Heaven must have been uncrowded, a nice place to live and offering a good career—some messenger work, some choral work, an occasional ritual. I'm sure the angels liked it.

Along comes a great swarm of immigrants, many millions (billions?), and some of them aren't even housebroken. All of them require nursemaiding. After untold eons of beatific living, suddenly the angels find themselves working overtime, running what amounts to an enormous orphan asylum. It's not surprising that they don't like us.

Still . . . I don't like them, either. Snobs!

I found a cherub (angel?) with a STAFF badge and asked the location of the nearest information booth. He hooked a thumb over his shoulder. "Straight down the boulevard six thousand furlongs. It's by the River that flows from the Throne."

I stared down the boulevard. At that distance God the Father on His Throne looked like a rising sun. I said, "Six thousand furlongs is over six hundred miles. Isn't there one in this neighborhood?"

"Creature, it was done that way on purpose. If we had placed a booth on each corner, every one of them would have crowds around it, asking silly questions. This way, a creature won't make the effort unless it has a truly important question to ask."

Logical. And infuriating. I found that I was again possessed by unheavenly thoughts. I had always pictured Heaven as a place of guaranteed beatitude—not filled with the same silly frustration so common on earth. I counted to ten in English, then in Latin. "Uh, what's the flight time? Is there a speed limit?"

"Surely you don't think that you would be allowed to *fly* there, do you?"

"Why not? Just earlier today I flew here and then all the way around the City."

"You just thought you did. Actually, your cohort leader did it all. Creature, let me give you a tip that may keep you out of trouble. When you get your wings—*if* you ever do get wings—don't try to fly over the Holy City. You'll be grounded so fast your teeth will ache. And your wings stripped away."

"Why?"

"Because you don't rate it, that's why. You Johnny-Come-Latelies show up here and think you own the place. You'd carve your initials in the Throne if you could get that close to it. So let me put you wise. Heaven operates by just one rule: R.H.I.P. Do you know what that means?"

"No," I answered, not entirely truthfully.

"Listen and learn. You can forget the Ten Commandments. Here only two or three of them still apply and you'll find you can't break those even if you were to try. The golden rule everywhere in Heaven is: Rank Hath Its Privileges. At this eon you are a raw recruit in the Armies of the Lord, with the lowest rank possible. And the least privilege. In fact the only privilege I can think of that you rate is being here, just being here. The Lord in His infinite wisdom has decreed that you qualify to enter here. But that's all. Behave yourself and you will be allowed to stay. Now as to the traffic rule you asked about. Angels and nobody else fly over the Holy City. When on duty or during ceremonies. That does not mean you. Not even if you get wings. If you do. I emphasize this because a surprising number of you creatures have arrived here with the delusion that going to Heaven automatically changes a creature into an angel. It doesn't. It can't. Creatures *never* become angels. A saint sometimes. Though seldom. An angel, never."

I counted ten backwards, in Hebrew. "If you don't mind, I'm still trying to reach that information booth. Since I am not allowed to fly, how *do* I get there?"

"Why didn't you say that in the first place? Take the bus."

• • •

Sometime later I was seated in a chariot bus of the Holy City Transit Lines and we were rumbling toward the distant Throne. The chariot was open, boat-shaped, with an entrance in the rear, and had no discernible motive power and no teamster or conductor. It stopped at marked chariot stops and that is how I got aboard. I had not yet found out how to get it to stop.

Apparently everyone in the City rode these buses (except V.I.P.s who rated private chariots). Even angels. Most passengers were humans dressed in conventional white and wearing ordinary halos. But a few were humans in costumes of various eras and topped off by larger and fancier halos. I noticed that angels were fairly polite to these creatures in the fancier halos. But they did not sit with them. Angels sat in the front of the car, these privileged humans in the middle part, and the common herd (including yours truly) in the rear.

I asked one of my own sort how long it took to reach the Throne.

"I don't know," I was answered. "I don't go nearly that far."

This soul seemed to be female, middle-aged, and friendly, so I used a commonplace opener. "That's a Kansas accent, is it not?"

She smiled. "I don't think so. I was born in Flanders."

"Really? You speak very fluent English."

She shook her head gently. "I never learned English."

"But—"

"I know. You are a recent arrival. Heaven is not affected by the Curse of Babel. Here the Confusion of Tongues never took place . . . and a good thing for me as I have no skill in languages—a handicap before I died. Not so here." She looked at me with interest. "May I ask where you died? And when?"

"I did not die," I told her. "I was snatched up alive in the Rapture."

Her eyes widened. "Oh, how thrilling! You must be very holy."

"I don't think so. Why do you say that?"

"The Rapture will come—came?—without warning. Or so I was taught."

"That's right."

"Then with no warning, and no time for confession, and no priest to help you . . . you were ready! As free from sin as Mother Mary. You came straight to Heaven. You *must* be holy." She added, "That's what I thought when I saw your costume, since saints—martyrs especially—often dress as they did on earth. I saw too that you are not wearing your saint's halo. But that's your privilege." She looked suddenly shy. "Will you bless me? Or do I presume?"

"Sister, I am not a saint."

"You will not grant me your blessing?"

(Dear Jesus, how did this happen to me?) "Having heard me say that, to the best of my knowledge and belief, I am not a saint, do you still want me to bless you?"

"If you will . . . holy father."

"Very well. Turn and lower your head a little—" Instead she turned fully and dropped to her knees. I put a hand on her head. "By authority vested in me as an ordained minister of the one true catholic church of Jesus Christ the Son of God the Father and by the power of the Holy Ghost, I bless this our sister in Christ. So mote it be!"

I heard echoes of "Amen!" around us; we had had quite an audience. I felt embarrassed. I was not certain, and still am not certain, that I had any authority to bestow blessings in Heaven itself. But the dear woman had asked for it and I could not refuse.

She looked up at me with tears in her eyes. "I knew it, I knew it!"

"Knew what?"

"That you are a saint. Now you are wearing it!"

I started to say, "Wearing what?" when a minor miracle occurred. Suddenly I was looking at myself from outside: wrinkled and dirty khaki pants, Army-surplus shirt

with dark sweat stains in the armpits and a bulge of
razor in the left breast pocket, three-day growth of beard
and in need of a haircut . . . and, floating over my head, a
halo the size of a washtub, shining and sparkling!

"Up off your knees," I said instead, "and let's stop
being conspicuous."

"Yes, father." She added, "You should not be seated
back here."

"I'll be the judge of that, daughter. Now tell me about
yourself." I looked around as she resumed her seat, and
happened to catch the eye of an angel seated all alone, up
forward. (S)he gestured to me to come forward.

I had had my fill of the arrogance of angels; at first I
ignored the signal. But everyone was noticing and pretending not to, and my awe-struck companion was whispering urgently, "Most holy person, the angelic one
wants to see you."

I gave in—partly because it was easier, partly because
I wanted to ask the angel a question. I got up and went to
the front of the bus.

"You wanted me?"

"Yes. You know the rules. Angels in front, creatures in
back, saints in the middle. If you sit in back with creatures, you are teaching them bad habits. How can you
expect to maintain your saintly privileges if you ignore
protocol? Don't let it happen again."

I thought of several retorts, all unheavenly. Instead I
said, "May I ask a question?"

"Ask."

"How much longer until this bus reaches the River
from the Throne?"

"Why do you ask? You have all eternity before you."

"Does that mean that you don't know? Or that you
won't tell?"

"Go sit down in your proper section. At once!"

I went back and tried to find a seat in the after space.
But my fellow creatures had closed in and left me no
room. No one said anything and they would not meet my

eye, but it was evident that no one would aid me in defying the authority of an angel. I sighed and sat down in the mid-section, in lonely splendor, as I was the only saint aboard. If I was a saint.

I don't know how long it took to reach the Throne. In Heaven the light doesn't vary and the weather does not change and I had no watch. It was simply a boringly long time. Boring? Yes. A gorgeous palace constructed of precious stones is a wonderful sight to see. A dozen palaces constructed of jewels can be a dozen wonderful sights, each different from the other. But a hundred miles of such palaces will put you to sleep, and six hundred miles of the same is deadly dull. I began to long for a used-car lot, or a dump, or (best yet) a stretch of green and open countryside.

New Jerusalem is a city of perfect beauty; I am witness to that. But that long ride taught me the uses of ugliness.

I never have found out who designed the Holy City. That God authorized the design and construction is axiomatic. But the Bible does not name the architect(s), or the builder(s). Freemasons speak of "the Great Architect," meaning Jehovah—but you won't find that in the Bible. Just once I asked an angel, "Who designed this city?" He didn't sneer at my ignorance, he didn't scold me—he appeared to be unable to conceive it as a question. But it remains a question to me: Did God create (design and build) the Holy City Himself, right down to the smallest jewel? Or did He farm it out to subordinates?

Whoever designed it, the Holy City has a major shortcoming, in my opinion—and never mind telling me that my presumption in passing judgment on God's design is blasphemous. It *is* a lack, a serious one.

It lacks a public library.

One reference librarian who had devoted her life to answering any and all questions, trivial and weighty, would be more use in Heaven than another cohort of arrogant angels. There must be plenty of such ladies in Heaven, as it takes a saintly disposition and the patience of Job to be a reference librarian and to stick with it for forty years. But to carry on their vocation they would need books and files and so forth, the tools of their profession. Given a chance, I'm sure they would set up the files and catalog the books—but where would they get the books? Heaven does not seem to have a book-publishing industry.

Heaven doesn't have industry. Heaven doesn't have an economy. When Jehovah decreed, after the expulsion from Eden, that we descendants of Adam must gain our bread by the sweat of our faces, He created economics and it has been operating ever since for ca. 6000 years.

But not in Heaven.

In Heaven He giveth us our daily bread *without* the sweat of our faces. In truth you don't need daily bread; you can't starve, you won't even get hungry enough to matter—just hungry enough to enjoy eating if you want to amuse yourself by stopping in any of the many restaurants, refectories, and lunchrooms. The best hamburger I ever ate in my life was in a small lunchroom off the Square of the Throne on the banks of the River. But again, I'm ahead of my story.

Another lack, not as serious for my taste but serious, is gardens. No gardens, I mean, except the grove of the Tree of Life by the River near the Throne, and a few, a very few, private gardens here and there. I think I know why this is so and, if I am right, it may be self-correcting. Until we reached Heaven (the people of the Rapture and the resurrected dead-in-Christ) almost all citizens of the Holy City were angels. The million or so exceptions were martyrs for the faith, children of Israel so holy that they made it without ever having personally experienced Christ (i.e., mostly before 30 A.D.), and another group from unenlightened lands—souls virtuous without ever knowing of Christ. So 99 percent of the citizens of the Holy City were angels.

Angels don't seem to be interested in horticulture. I

suppose that figures—I can't imagine an angel down on his/her knees, mulching the soil around a plant. They just aren't the dirty-fingernails sort needed to grow prize roses.

Now that angels are outnumbered by humans by at least ten to one I expect that we will see gardens—gardens, garden clubs, lectures on how to prepare the soil, and so forth. All the endless ritual of the devoted gardener. Now they will have time for it.

Most humans in Heaven do what they want to do without the pressure of need. That nice lady (Suzanne) who wanted my blessing was a lacemaker in Flanders; now she teaches it in a school open to anyone who is interested. I have gathered a strong impression that, for most humans, the real problem of an eternity of bliss is how to pass the time. (Query: Could there be something to this reincarnation idea so prevalent in other religions but so firmly rejected by Christianity? Could a saved soul be rewarded, eventually, by being shoved back into the conflict? If not on earth, then elsewhere? I've got to lay hands on a Bible and do some searching. To my utter amazement, here in Heaven Bibles seem to be awfully hard to come by.)

The information booth was right where it was supposed to be, close to the bank of the River of the Water of Life that flows from the Throne of God and winds through the grove of the Tree of Life. The Throne soars up from the middle of the grove but you can't see it very well that close to its base. It's like looking up at the tallest of New York skyscrapers while standing on the sidewalk by it. Only more so. And of course you can't see the Face of God; you are looking straight up one thousand four hundred and forty cubits. What you see is the Radiance . . . and you can feel the Presence.

The information booth was as crowded as that cherub had led me to expect. The inquirers weren't queued up; they were massed a hundred deep around it. I looked at that swarm and wondered how long it would take me to work my way up to the counter. Was it possible to work my way there other than by the nastiest of bargain-day tactics, stepping on corns, jabbing with elbows, all the things that make department stores so uninviting to males?

I stood back and looked at that mob and tried to figure out how to cope. Or was there some other way to locate Margrethe without stepping on corns?

I was still standing there when a STAFF cherub came up to me. "Holy one, are you trying to reach the information booth?"

"I surely am!"

"Come with me. Stay close behind me." He was carrying a long staff of the sort used by riot police. "Gangway! Make way for a saint! Step lively there!" In nothing flat I reached the counter of the booth. I don't think anyone was injured but there must have been some hurt feelings. I don't approve of that sort of action; I think that treatment should be even-handed for everyone. But, where R.H.I.P. is the rule, being even a corporal is vastly better than being a private.

I turned to thank the cherub; he was gone. A voice said, "Holy one, what do you want?" An angel back of the counter was looking down at me.

I explained that I wanted to locate my wife. He drummed on the counter. "That's not ordinarily a service we supply. There is a co-op run by creatures called 'Find Your Friends and Loved Ones' for that sort of thing."

"Where is it?"

"Near Asher Gate."

"*What?* I just came from there. That's where I registered in."

"You should have asked the angel who checked you in. You registered recently?"

"Quite recently; I was caught up in the Rapture. I did ask the angel who registered me . . . and got a fast brushoff. He, she, uh, that angel told me to come here."

"Mrf. Lemme see your papers."

I passed them over. The angel studied them, slowly and carefully, then called to another angel, who had stopped servicing the mob to watch. "Tirl! Look at this."

So the second angel looked over my papers, nodded sagely, handed them back—glanced at me, shook his head sadly. "Is something wrong?" I asked.

"No. Holy one, you had the misfortune to be serviced, if that is the word, by an angel who wouldn't help his closest friend, if he had one, which he doesn't. But I'm a bit surprised that she was so abrupt with a saint."

"I wasn't wearing this halo at the time."

"That accounts for it. You drew it later?"

"I did not draw it. I acquired it miraculously, on the way from Asher Gate to here."

"I see. Holy one, it's your privilege to put Khromitycinel on the report. On the other hand I could use the farspeaker to place your inquiry for you."

"I think that would be better."

"So do I. In the long run. For you. If I make my meaning clear."

"You do."

"But before I call that co-op let's check with Saint Peter's office and make sure your wife has arrived. When did she die?"

"She didn't die. She was caught up in the Rapture, too."

"So? That means a quick and easy check, no searching of old rolls. Full name, age, sex if any, place and date of— no, we don't need that. Full name first."

"Margrethe Svensdatter Gunderson."

"Better spell that."

I did so.

"That's enough for now. If Peter's clerks can spell. You can't wait here; we don't have a waiting room. There is a little restaurant right opposite us—see the sign?"

I turned and looked. " 'The Holy Cow'?"

"That's it. Good cooking, if you eat. Wait there; I'll send word to you."

"Thank you!"

"You are welcome—" She glanced again at my papers, then handed them back. "—Saint Alexander Hergensheimer."

The Holy Cow was the most homey sight I had seen since the Rapture: a small, neat lunchroom that would have looked at home in Saint Louis or Denver. I went inside. A tall blackamoor whose chef's hat stuck up through his halo was at the grill with his back to me. I sat down at the counter, cleared my throat.

"Just hold your horses." He finished what he was doing, turned around. "What can I— Well, well! Holy man, what can I fix for you? Name it, just name it!"

"Luke! It's good to see you!"

He stared at me. "We have met?"

"Don't you remember me? I used to work for you. Ron's Grill, Nogales. Alec. Your dishwasher."

He stared again, gave a deep sigh. "You sure fooled me . . . Saint Alec."

"Just 'Alec' to my friends. It's some sort of administrative mistake, Luke. When they catch it, I'll trade this Sunday job for an ordinary halo."

"Beg to doubt—Saint Alec. They don't make mistakes in Heaven. Hey! Albert! Take the counter. My friend Saint Alec and I are going to sit in the dining room. Albert's my sous-chef."

I shook hands with a fat little man who was almost a parody of what a French chef should look like. He was wearing a *Cordon Bleu* hat as well as his halo. Luke and I went through a side door into a small dining room, sat down at a table. We were joined by a waitress and I got another shock.

Luke said, "Hazel, I want you to meet an old friend of

mine, Saint Alec—he and I used to be business associates. Hazel is hostess of The Holy Cow."

"I was Luke's dishwasher," I told her. "Hazel, it's wonderful to see you!" I stood up, started to shake hands, then changed my mind for the better, put my arms around her.

She smiled up at me, did not seem surprised. "Welcome, Alec! 'Saint Alec' now, I see. I'm not surprised."

"I am. It's a mistake."

"Mistakes don't happen in Heaven. Where is Margie? Still alive on earth?"

"No." I explained how we had been separated. "So I'm waiting here for word."

"You'll find her." She kissed me, quickly and warmly—which reminded me of my four-day beard. I seated her, sat down with my friends. "You are sure to find her quickly, because that is a promise we were made and is precisely carried out. Reunion in Heaven with friends and loved ones. 'We shall gather by the River—' and sure enough, there it is, right outside the door. Steve— Saint Alec, you do remember Steve? He was with you and Margie when we met."

"How could I forget him? He bought us dinner and gave us a gold eagle when we were stony. Do I remember Steve!"

"I'm happy to hear you say that . . . because Steve credits you with converting him—born-again conversion—and getting him into Heaven. You see, Steve was killed on the Plain of Meggido, and I was killed in the War, too, uh, that was about five years after we met you—"

"*Five years?*"

"Yes. I was killed fairly early in the War; Steve lasted clear to Armageddon—"

"Hazel . . . it hasn't been much over a month since Steve bought us that dinner at Rimrock."

"That's logical. You were caught up in the Rapture and that touched off the War. So you spent the War years up in the air, and that makes it work out that Steve and I are here first even though you left first. You can discuss it with Steve; he'll be in soon. By the way, I'm his concubine now—his wife, except that here there is no marrying or giving in marriage. Anyhow Steve went back into the Corps when war broke out and got up to captain before they killed him. His outfit landed at Haifa and Steve died battling for the Lord at the height of Armageddon. I'm real proud of him."

"You should be. Luke, did the War get you, too?"

Luke gave a big grin. "No, sir, Saint Alec. They hanged me."

"You're joking!"

"No joke. They hanged me fair and square. You remember when you quit me?"

"I didn't quit you. A miracle intervened. That's how I met Hazel. And Steve."

"Well . . . you know more about miracles than I do. Anyway, we had to get another dishwasher right fast, and we had to take a Chicano. Man, he was a real bad ass, that one. Pulled a knife on me. That was his mistake. Pull a knife on a cook in his own kitchen? He cut me up some, I cut him up proper. Jury mostly his cousins, I think. Anyhow the D.A. said it was time for an example. But it was all right. I had been baptized long before that; the prison chaplain helped me be born again. I spoke a sermon standing on that trap with the noose around my neck. Then I said, 'You can do it now! Send me to Jesus! Hallelujah!' And they did. Happiest day of my life!"

Albert stuck his head in. "Saint Alec, there's an angel here looking for you."

"Coming!"

The angel was waiting just outside for the reason that he was taller than the doorway and not inclined to stoop. "You are Saint Alexander Hergensheimer?"

"That's me."

"Your inquiry concerning a creature designated Margrethe Svensdatter Gunderson: The report reads: Subject was not caught up in the Rapture, and has not shown up in any subsequent draft. This creature, Margrethe Svensdatter Gunderson, is not in Heaven and is not expected. That is all."

XXIII

I cry unto Thee, and Thou dost not hear me:
I stand up, and Thou regardest me not.
Job 30:20

So of course I eventually wound up in Saint Peter's office at the Gate of Judah—having chased all over Heaven first. On Hazel's advice I went back to the Gate of Asher and looked up that co-op "Find Your Friends and Loved Ones."

"Saint Alec, angels don't pass out misinformation and the records they consult are accurate. But they may not have consulted the right records, and, in my opinion, they would not have searched as deeply as you would search if you were doing it yourself—angels being angels. Margie might be listed under her maiden name."

"That was what I gave them!"

"Oh. I thought you asked them to search for 'Margie Graham'?"

"No. Should I go back and ask them to?"

"No. Not yet. And when you do—if you must—don't ask again at this information booth. Go directly to St. Peter's office. There you'll get personal attention from other humans, not from angels."

"That's for me!"

"Yes. But try first at 'Find Your Friends and Loved Ones.' That's not a bureaucracy; it's a co-op made up of volunteers, all of them people who really care. That's how Steve found me after he was killed. He didn't know

303

my family name and I hadn't used it for years, anyhow. He didn't know my date and place of death. But a little old lady at 'Find Your Friends' kept right on searching females named Hazel until Steve said 'Bingo!' If he had just checked at the main personnel office—Saint Peter's—they would have reported 'insufficient data, no identification.'"

She smiled and went on, "But the co-op uses imagination. They brought Luke and me together, even though we hadn't even met before we died. After I got tired of loafing I decided that I wanted to manage a little restaurant—it's a wonderful way to meet people and make friends. So I asked the co-op and they set their computers on 'cook,' and after a lot of false starts and wrong numbers it got Luke and me together and we formed a partnership and set up the Holy Cow. A similar search got us Albert."

Hazel, like Katie Farnsworth, is the sort of woman who heals just by her presence. But she's practical about it, too, like my own treasure. She volunteered to launder my dirty clothes and lent me a robe of Steve's to wear while my clothes dried. She found me a mirror and a cake of soap; at long last I tackled a five-day (seven-year?) beard. My one razor blade was closer to being a saw than a knife by then, but a half hour's patient honing using the inside of a glass tumbler (a trick I had learned in seminary) restored it to temporary usefulness.

But now I needed a proper shave even though I had shaved—tried to shave—a couple of hours ago. I did not know how long I had been on this hunt but I did know that I had shaved four times . . . with cold water, twice without soap, and once by Braille—no mirror. Plumbing had indeed been installed for us fleshly types . . . but not up to *American Standard* quality. Hardly surprising, since angels don't use plumbing and don't need it, and since the overwhelming majority of the fleshly ones have little or no experience with inside plumbing.

The people who man the co-op were as helpful as Hazel

said they would be (and I don't think my fancy halo had anything to do with it) but nothing they turned up gave me any clue to Margrethe, even though they patiently ran computer searches on every combination I could think of.

I thanked them and blessed them and headed for Judah Gate, all the way across Heaven, thirteen hundred and twenty miles away. I stopped only once, at the Square of the Throne, for one of Luke's heavenburgers and a cup of the best coffee in New Jerusalem, and some encouraging words from Hazel. I continued my weary search feeling much bucked up.

The Heavenly Bureau of Personnel occupies two colossal palaces on the right as you come through the gate. The first and smaller is for B.C. admissions; the second is for admissions since then, and includes Peter's office suite, on the second floor. I went straight there.

A big double door read SAINT PETER — Walk In, so I did. But not into his office; here was a waiting room big enough for Grand Central Station. I pushed through a turnstile that operated by pulling a ticket out of a slot, and a mechanical voice said, "Thank you. Please sit down and wait to be called."

My ticket read "2013" and the place was crowded; I decided, as I looked around for an empty seat, that I was going to need another shave before my number would come up.

I was still looking when a nun bustled up to me, and ducked a knee in a quick curtsy. "Holy one, may I serve you?" I did not know enough about the costumes worn by Roman Catholic orders to know what sisterhood she belonged to, but she was dressed in what I would call "typical"—long black dress down to her ankles and to her wrists, white starched deal over her chest and around her neck and covering her ears, a black headdress covering everything else and giving her the silhouette of a sphinx, a *big* rosary hanging around her neck . . . and an ageless, serene face topped off by a lopsided pince-nez. And, of course, her halo.

The thing that impressed me most was that she was here. She was the first proof I had seen that papists can be saved. In seminary we used to argue about that in late-night bull sessions . . . although the official position of my church was that certainly they could be saved, as long as they believed as we did and were born again in Jesus. I made a mental note to ask her when and how she had been born again—it would be, I was sure, an inspiring story.

I said, "Why, thank you, Sister! That's most kind of you. Yes, you can help me—that is, I hope you can. I'm Alexander Hergensheimer and I'm trying to find my wife. This is the place to inquire, is it not? I'm new here."

"Yes, Saint Alexander, this is the place. But you did want to see Saint Peter, did you not?"

"I'd like to pay my respects. If he's not too busy."

"I'm sure he will want to see you, Holy Father. Let me tell my Sister Superior." She picked up the cross on her rosary, appeared to whisper into it, then looked up. "Is that spelled H,E,R,G,E,N,S,H,E,I,M,E,R, Saint Alexander?"

"Correct, Sister."

She spoke again to the rosary. Then she added, to me, "Sister Marie Charles is secretary to Saint Peter. I'm her assistant and general gopher." She smiled. "Sister Mary Rose."

"It is good to meet you, Sister Mary Rose. Tell me about yourself. What order are you?"

"I'm a Dominican, Holy Father. In life I was a hospital administrator in Frankfurt, Germany. Here, where there is no longer a need for nursing, I do this work because I like to mingle with people. Will you come with me, sir?"

The crowd parted like the waters of the Red Sea, whether in deference to the nun or to my gaudy halo, I cannot say. Maybe both. She took me to an unmarked side door and straight in, and I found myself in the office of her boss, Sister Marie Charles. She was a tall nun, as tall as I am, and handsome—or "beautiful" may be more accurate. She seemed younger than her assistant . . . but how is one to tell with nuns? She was seated at a big flattop desk piled high and with an old-style Underwood typewriter swung out from its side. She got up quickly, faced me, and dropped that odd curtsy.

"Welcome, Saint Alexander! We are honored by your call. Saint Peter will be with you soon. Will you be seated? May we offer you refreshment? A glass of wine? A Coca-Cola?"

"Say, I would really enjoy a Coca-Cola! I haven't had one since I was on earth."

"A Coca-Cola, right away." She smiled. "I'll tell you a secret. Coca-Cola is Saint Peter's one vice. So we always have them on ice here."

A voice came out of the air above her desk—a strong, resonant baritone of the sort I think of as a good preaching voice—a voice like that of "Bible" Barnaby, may his name be blessed. "I heard that, Charlie. Let him have his Coke in here; I'm free now."

"Were you eavesdropping again, Boss?"

"None of your lip, girl. And fetch one for me, too."

Saint Peter was up and striding toward the door with his hand out as I was ushered in. I was taught in church history that he was believed to have been about ninety when he died. Or when he was executed (crucified?) by the Romans, if he was. (Preaching has always been a chancy vocation, but in the days of Peter's ministry it was as chancy as that of a Marine platoon sergeant.)

This man looked to be a strong and hearty sixty, or possibly seventy—an outdoor man, with a permanent suntan and the scars that come from sun damage. His hair and beard were full and seemed never to have been cut, streaked with gray but not white, and (to my surprise) he appeared to have been at one time a redhead. He was well muscled and broad shouldered, and his hands were calloused, as I learned when he gripped my hand. He was dressed in sandals, a brown robe of coarse wool, a halo like mine, and a dinky little skullcap resting in the middle of that fine head of hair.

I liked him on sight.

He led me around to a comfortable chair near his desk chair, seated me before he sat back down. Sister Marie Charles was right behind us with two Cokes on a tray, in the familiar pinchwaist bottles and with not-so-familiar (I had not seen them for years) Coke glasses with the tulip tops and the registered trademark. I wondered who had the franchise in Heaven and how such business matters were handled.

He said, "Thanks, Charlie. Hold all calls."

"Even?"

"Don't be silly. Beat it." He turned to me. "Alexander, I try to greet each newly arrived saint personally. But somehow I missed you."

"I arrived in the middle of a mob, Saint Peter. Those from the Rapture. And not at this gate. Asher Gate."

"That accounts for it. A busy day, that one, and we still aren't straightened out. But a saint should be escorted to the main gate . . . by twenty-four angels and two trumpets. I'll have to look into this."

"To be frank, Saint Peter," I blurted out, "I don't think I *am* a saint. But I can't get this fancy halo off."

He shook his head. "You are one, all right. And don't let your misgivings gnaw at you; no saint *ever* knows that he is one, he has to be told. It is a holy paradox that anyone who thinks he is a saint never is. Why, when I arrived here and they handed me the keys and told me I was in charge, I didn't believe it. I thought the Master was playing a joke on me in return for a couple of japes I pulled on Him back in the days when we were barnstorming around the Sea of Galilee. Oh, no! He meant it. Rabbi Simon bar Jona the old fisherman was gone and I've been Saint Peter ever since. As you are Saint Alexander, like it or not. And you will like it, in time."

He tapped on a fat file folder lying on his desk. "I've

been reading your record. There is no doubt about your sanctity. Once I reviewed your record I recalled your trial. Devil's Advocate against you was Thomas Aquinas; he came up to me afterwards and told me that his attack was *pro forma*, as there had never been any doubt in his mind but what you qualified. Tell me, that first miracle, ordeal by fire—did your faith ever waver?"

"I guess it did. I got a blister out of it."

Saint Peter snorted. "One lonely blister! And you don't think you qualify. Son, if Saint Joan had had faith as firm as yours, she would have quenched the fire that martyred her. I know of—"

Sister Marie Charles' voice announced, "Saint Alexander's wife is here."

"Show her in!" To me he added, "Tell you later."

I hardly heard him; my heart was bursting.

The door opened; in walked Abigail.

I don't know how to describe the next few minutes. Heartbreaking disappointment coupled with embarrassment summarizes it.

Abigail looked at me and said severely, "Alexander, what in the world are you doing wearing that preposterous halo? Take it off instantly!"

Saint Peter rumbled, "Daughter, you are not 'in the world'; you are in my private office. You will not speak to Saint Alexander that way."

Abigail turned her gaze to him, and sniffed. "You call *him* a saint? And didn't your mother teach you to stand up for ladies? Or are saints exempt from such niceties?"

"I do stand up, for *ladies*. Daughter, you will address me with respect. And you will speak to your husband with the respect a wife owes her husband."

"He's not my husband!"

"Eh?" Saint Peter looked from her to me, then back. "Explain yourself."

"Jesus said, 'For in the resurrection they neither marry, nor are given in marriage, but are as the angels.' So there! And He said it again in Mark twelve, twenty-three."

"Yes," agreed Saint Peter, "I heard Him say it. To the Sadducees. By that rule you are no longer a wife."

"Yes! Hallelujah! Years I have waited to be rid of that clod—be rid of him without sinning."

"I'm unsure about the latter. But not being a wife does not relieve you of the duty to speak politely to this saint who was once your husband." Peter turned again to me. "Do you wish her to stay?"

"Me? No, no! There's been a mistake."

"So it appears. Daughter, you may go."

"Now you just wait! Having come all this way, I have things I've been planning to tell you. Perfectly scandalous goings-on I have seen around here. Why, without the slightest sense of decency—"

"Daughter, I dismissed you. Will you walk out on your own feet? Or shall I send for two stalwart angels and have you thrown out?"

"Why, the very idea! I was just going to say—"

"You are not going to say!"

"Well, I certainly have as much right to speak my mind as anyone!"

"Not in this office. Sister Marie Charles!"

"Yes, sir!"

"Do you still remember the judo they taught you when you were working with the Detroit police?"

"I do!"

"Get this yenta out of here."

The tall nun grinned and dusted her hands together. What happened next happened so fast that I can't describe it. But Abigail left very suddenly.

Saint Peter sat back down, sighed, and picked up his Coke. "That woman would try the patience of Job. How long were you married to her?"

"Uh, slightly over a thousand years."

"I understand you. Why did you send for her?"

"I didn't. Well, I didn't intend to." I started to try to explain.

He stopped me. "Of course! Why didn't you say that you were searching for your concubine? You misled Mary Rose. Yes, I know whom you mean: the zaftig shiksa who runs all through the latter part of your dossier. Very nice girl, she seemed to me. You are looking for her?"

"Yes, surely. The day of the Trump and the Shout we were snatched up together. But that whirlwind, a real Kansas twister, was so violent that we were separated."

"You inquired about her before. An inquiry relayed from the information booth by the River."

"That's right."

"Alexander, that inquiry is the last entry in your file. I can order the search repeated . . . but I can tell you ahead of time that it will be useful only to assure you. The answer will be the same: She is not here."

He stood up and came around to put a hand on my shoulder. "This is a tragedy that I have seen repeated endlessly. A loving couple, confident of eternity together: One comes here, the other does not. What can I do? I wish I could do something. I can't."

"Saint Peter, there has been a mistake!"

He did not answer.

"Listen to me! I know! She and I were side by side, kneeling at the chancel rail, praying . . . and just before the Trump and the Shout the Holy Ghost descended on us and we were in a perfect state of grace and were snatched up together. *Ask* Him! Ask *Him!* He will listen to *you.*"

Peter sighed again. "He will listen to anyone, in any of His Aspects. But I will inquire." He picked up a telephone instrument so old-fashioned that Alexander Graham Bell could have assembled it. "Charlie, give me the Spook. Okay, I'll wait. *Hi!* This is Pete, down at the main gate. Heard any new ones? No? Neither have I. Listen, I got a problem. Please run Yourself back to the day of the Shout and the Trump, when You, in Your aspect as Junior, caught up alive all those incarnate souls who were at that moment in a state of grace. Place Yourself outside a wide place in the road called Lowell, Kansas—that's in North America—and at a tent meeting, a revival under canvas. Are You there? Now, at least a few femtoseconds before the Trump, it is alleged by one Alexander Hergensheimer, now canonized, that You descended on him and his beloved concubine Margrethe. She is described as about three and a half cubits tall, blonde, freckled, eighty mina— Oh, You do? Oh. Too late, huh? I was afraid of that. I'll tell him."

I interrupted, whispering urgently, "Ask Him where she is!"

"Boss, Saint Alexander is in agony. He wants to know where she is. Yes, I'll tell him." Saint Peter hung up. "Not in Heaven, not on earth. You can figure out the answer for yourself. And I'm sorry."

I must state that Saint Peter was endlessly patient with me. He assured me that I could talk with any One of the Trinity . . . but reminded me that, in consulting the Holy Ghost we had consulted all of Them. Peter had fresh searches made of the Rapture list, the graves-opened list, and of the running list of all arrivals since then—while telling me that no computer search could conceivably deny the infallible answers of God Himself speaking as the Holy Ghost . . . which I understood and agreed with, while welcoming new searches.

I said, "But how about on earth? Could she be alive somewhere there? Maybe in Copenhagen?"

Peter answered, "Alexander, He is as omniscient on earth as He is in Heaven. Can't you see that?"

I gave a deep sigh. "I see that. I've been dodging the obvious. All right, how do I get from here to Hell?"

"Alec! Don't talk that way!"

"The hell I won't talk that way! Peter, an eternity here without her is not an eternity of bliss; it is an eternity of boredom and loneliness and grief. You think this damned gaudy halo means anything to me when I *know*—yes, you've convinced me!—that my beloved is burning in the Pit? I didn't ask much. Just to be allowed to live with her. I was willing to wash dishes forever if only I could see her smile, hear her voice, touch her hand! She's been shipped on a technicality and you know it! Snobbish, bad-tempered angels get to live here without ever doing one lick to deserve it. But my Marga, who is a real angel if one ever lived, gets turned down and sent to Hell to everlasting torture on a childish twist in the rules. You can tell the Father and His sweet-talking Son and that sneaky Ghost that they can take their gaudy Holy City and shove it! If Margrethe has to be in Hell, that's where *I* want to be!"

Peter was saying, "Forgive him, Father; he's feverish with grief—he doesn't know what he is saying."

I quieted down a little. "Saint Peter, I know exactly what I am saying. I don't want to stay here. My beloved is in Hell, so that is where I want to be. Where I *must* be."

"Alec, you'll get over this."

"What you don't see is that I don't *want* to get over this. I want to be with my love and share her fate. You tell me she's in Hell—"

"No, I told you that it is certain that she is not in Heaven and not on earth."

"Is there a fourth place? Limbo, or some such?"

"Limbo is a myth. I know of no fourth place."

"Then I want to leave here at once and look all over Hell for her. How?"

Peter shrugged.

"Damn it, don't give me a run-around! That's all I've been handed since the day I walked through the fire—one run-around after another. Am I a prisoner?"

"No."

"Then tell me how to go to Hell."

"Very well. You can't wear that halo to Hell. They wouldn't let you in."

"I never wanted it. Let's go!"

Not long after that I stood on the threshold of Judah Gate, escorted there by two angels. Peter did not say good-bye to me; I guess he was disgusted. I was sorry about that; I liked him very much. But I could not make him understand that Heaven was not Heaven to me without Margrethe.

I paused at the brink. "I want you to take one message back to Saint Peter—"

They ignored me, grabbed me from both sides, and tossed me over.

I fell.

And fell.

XXIV

Oh that I knew where I might find him!
that I might come even to his seat!
I would order my cause before him,
and fill my mouth with arguments.
Job 23:3–4

And still I fell.

For modern man one of the most troubling aspects of
eternity lies in getting used to the slippery quality of
time. With no clocks and no calendars and lacking even
the alternation of day and night, or the phases of the
moon, or the pageant of seasons, duration becomes sub-
jective and "What time is it?" is a matter of opinion, not
of fact.

I think I fell longer than twenty minutes; I do not think
that I fell as long as twenty years.

But don't risk any money on it either way.

There was nothing to see but the insides of my eyeballs.
There was not even the Holy City receding in the distance.

Early on, I tried to entertain myself by reliving in
memory the happiest times in my life—and found that
happy memories made me sad. So I thought about sad
occasions and that was worse. Presently I slept. Or I
think I did. How can you tell when you are totally cut off
from sensation? I remember reading about one of those
busybody "scientists" building something he called a
"sensory deprivation chamber." What he achieved was a

thrill-packed three-ring circus compared with the meager delights of falling from Heaven to Hell.

My first intimation that I was getting close to Hell was the stink. Rotten eggs. H_2S. Hydrogen sulfide. The stench of burning brimstone.

You don't die from it, but small comfort that may be, since those who encounter this stench are dead when they whiff it. Or usually so; I am not dead. They tell of other live ones in history and literature—Dante, Aeneas, Ulysses, Orpheus. But weren't all of those cases fiction? Am I the first living man to go to Hell, despite all those yarns?

If so, how long will I stay alive and healthy? Just long enough to hit the flaming surface of the Lake?—there to go *psst!* and become a rapidly disappearing grease spot? Had my Quixotic gesture been just a wee bit hasty? A rapidly disappearing grease spot could not be much help to Margrethe; perhaps I should have stayed in Heaven and bargained. A saint in full-dress halo picketing the Lord in front of His Throne might have caused Him to reverse His decision . . . since *His* decision it had to be, L. G. Jehovah being omnipotent.

A bit late to think of it, boy! You can see the red glow on the clouds now. That must be boiling lava down there. How far down? Not far enough! How fast am I falling? Too fast!

I can see what the famous Pit is now: the caldera of an incredibly enormous volcano. Its walls are all around me, miles high, yet the flames and the molten lava are still a long, long way below me. But coming up fast! How are your miracle-working powers today, Saint Alec? You coped with that other fire pit with only a blister; think you can handle this one? The difference is only a matter of degree.

"With patience and plenty of saliva the elephant deflowered the mosquito." That job was just a matter of degree, too; can you do as well as that elephant? Saint Alec, that was not a saintly thought; what has happened to your piety? Maybe it's the influence of this wicked neighborhood. Oh, well, you no longer need worry about sinful thoughts; it is too late to worry about any sin. You no longer risk going to Hell for your sins; you are now entering Hell—you are now *in* Hell. In roughly three seconds you are going to be a grease spot. 'Bye, Marga my own! I'm sorry I never managed to get you that hot fudge sundae. Satan, receive my soul; Jesus is a fink—

They netted me like a butterfly. But a butterfly would have needed asbestos wings to have been saved the way I was saved; my pants were smoldering. They threw a bucket of water over me when they had me on the bank.

"Just sign this chit."

"What chit?" I sat up and looked out at the flames.

"This chit." Somebody was holding a piece of paper under my nose and offering me a pen.

"Why do you want me to sign it?"

"You have to sign it. It acknowledges that we saved you from the burning Pit."

"I want to see a lawyer. Meanwhile I won't sign anything." The last time I was in this fix it got me tied down, washing dishes, for four months. This time I couldn't spare four months; I had to get busy at once, searching for Margrethe.

"Don't be stupid. Do you want to be tossed back into *that* stuff?"

A second voice said, "Knock it off, Bert. Try telling him the truth."

("Bert?" I thought that first voice was familiar!) "Bert! What are *you* doing here?" My boyhood chum, the one who shared my taste in literature. Verne and Wells and Tom Swift—"garbage," Brother Draper had called it.

The owner of the first voice looked at me more closely. "Well, I'll be a buggered baboon. Stinky Hergensheimer!"

"In the flesh."

"I'll be eternally damned. You haven't changed much.

Rod, get the net spread again; this is the wrong fish. Stinky, you've cost us a nice fee; we were fishing for Saint Alexander."

"Saint who?"

"Alexander. A Mick holy man who decided to go slumming. Why he didn't come in by a Seven-Forty-Seven God only knows; we don't usually get carriage trade here at the Pit. As may be, you've probably cost us a major client by getting in the way just when this saint was expected . . . and you ought to pay us for that."

"How about that fin you owe me?"

"Boy, do you have a memory! That's outlawed by the statute of limitations."

"Show it to me in Hell's law books. Anyhow, limitations can't apply; you never answered me when I tried to collect. So it's five bucks, compounded quarterly at six percent, for . . . how many years?"

"Discuss it later, Stinky. I've got to keep an eye out for this saint."

"Bert."

"Later, Stinky."

"Do you recall my right name? The one my folks gave me?"

"Why, I suppose— *Alexander!* Oh, no, Stinky, it can't be! Why, you almost flunked out of that backwoods Bible college, after you did flunk out of Rolla." His face expressed pain and disbelief. "Life can't be that unfair."

"'The Lord moves in mysterious ways, His wonders to perform.' Meet Saint Alexander, Bert. Would you like me to bless you? In lieu of a fee, I mean."

"We insist on cash. Anyhow, I don't believe it."

"I believe it," the second man, the one Bert had called "Rod," put in. "And I'd like your blessing, father; I've never been blessed by a saint before. Bert, there's nothing showing on the distant-warning screen and, as you know, only one ballistic arrival was projected for this watch— so this *has* to be Saint Alexander."

"Can't be. Rod, I know this character. If he's a saint,

I'm a pink monkey—" There was a bolt of lightning out of a cloudless sky. When Bert picked himself up, his clothes hung on him loosely. But he did not need them, as he was now covered with pink fur.

The monkey looked up at me indignantly. "Is that any way to treat an old pal?"

"Bert, I didn't do it. Or at least I did not intend to do it. Around me, miracles just happen; I don't do them on purpose."

"Excuses. If I had rabies, I'd bite you."

Twenty minutes later we were in a booth at a lakefront bar, drinking beer and waiting for a thaumaturgist reputed to be expert in shapes and appearances. I had been telling them why I was in Hell. "So I've got to find her. First I've got to check the Pit; if she's in there it's *really* urgent."

"She's not in there," said Rod.

"Huh? I hope you can prove that. How do you know?"

"There's never anyone in the Pit. That's a lot of malarkey thought up to keep the peasants in line. Sure, a lot of the hoi polloi arrive ballistically, and a percentage of them used to fall into the Pit until the manager set up this safety watch Bert and I are on. But falling into the Pit doesn't do a soul any harm . . . aside from scaring him silly. It burns, of course, so he comes shooting out even faster than he went in. But he's not damaged. A fire bath just cleans up his allergies, if any."

(Nobody in the Pit! No "burning in Hell's fires throughout eternity"—what a shock that was going to be to Brother "Bible" Barnaby . . . and a lot of others whose stock in trade depended on Hell's fires. But I was not here to discuss eschatology with two lost souls; I was here to find Marga.) "This 'manager' you speak of. Is that a euphemism for the Old One?"

The monkey—Bert, I mean—squeaked, "If you mean Satan, say so!"

"That's who I mean."

"Naw. Mr. Ashmedai is city manager; Satan never does any work. Why should he? He owns this planet."

"This is a planet?"

"You think maybe it's a comet? Look out that window. Prettiest planet in this galaxy. And the best kept. No snakes. No cockroaches. No chiggers. No poison ivy. No tax collectors. No rats. No cancer. No preachers. Only two lawyers."

"You make it sound like Heaven."

"Never been there. You say you just came from there; you tell us."

"Well . . . Heaven's okay, if you're an angel. It's not a planet; it's an artificial place, like Manhattan. I'm not here to plug Heaven; I'm here to find Marga. Should I try to see this Mr. Ashmedai? Or would I be better off going directly to Satan?"

The monkey tried to whistle, produced a mouselike squeak. Rod shook his head. "Saint Alec, you keep surprising me. I've been here since 1588, whenever that was, and I've never laid eyes on the Owner. I've never thought of trying to see him. I wouldn't know how to start. Bert, what do you think?"

"I think I need another beer."

"Where do you put it? Since that lightning hit you, you aren't big enough to put away one can of beer, let alone three."

"Don't be nosy and call the waiter."

The quality of discourse did not improve, as every question I asked turned up more questions and no answers. The thaumaturgist arrived and bore off Bert on her shoulder, Bert chattering angrily over her fee—she wanted half of all his assets and demanded a contract signed in blood before she would get to work. He wanted her to accept ten percent and wanted me to pay half of that.

When they left, Rod said it was time we found a pad for me; he would take me to a good hotel nearby.

I pointed out that I was without funds. "No problem, Saint Alec. All our immigrants arrive broke, but American Express and Diners Club and Chase Manhattan vie for the chance to extend first credit, knowing that whoever signs an immigrant first has a strong chance of keeping his business forever and six weeks past."

"Don't they lose a lot, extending unsecured credit that way?"

"No. Here in Hell, everybody pays up, eventually. Bear in mind that here a deadbeat can't even die to avoid his debts. So just sign in, and charge everything to room service until you set it up with one of the big three."

The Sans Souci Sheraton is on the Plaza, straight across from the Palace. Rod took me to the desk; I signed a registration card and asked for a single with bath. The desk clerk, a small female devil with cute little horns, looked at the card I had signed and her eyes widened. "Uh, *Saint* Alexander?"

"I'm Alexander Hergensheimer, just as I registered. I am sometimes called 'Saint Alexander,' but I don't think the title applies here."

She was busy not listening while she thumbed through her reservations. "Here it is, Your Holiness—the reservation for your suite."

"Huh? I don't need a suite. And I probably couldn't pay for it."

"Compliments of the management, sir."

XXV

And he had seven hundred wives, princesses, and three hundred concubines: and his wives turned away his heart.
1 Kings 11:3

Shall mortal man be more just than God? shall a man be more pure than his maker?
Job 4:17

"Compliments of the management!!" *How?* Nobody knew I was coming here until just before I was chucked out Judah Gate. Did Saint Peter have a hotline to Hell? Was there some sort of under-the-table cooperation with the Adversary? Brother, how that thought would scandalize the Board of Bishops back home!

Even more so, *why?* But I had no time to ponder it; the little devil—imp?—on duty slapped the desk bell and shouted, "Front!"

The bellhop who responded was human, and a very attractive youngster. I wondered how he had died so young and why he had missed going to Heaven. But it was none of my business so I did not ask. I did notice one thing: While he reminded me in his appearance of a Philip Morris ad, when he wa'ked in front of me, leading me to my suite, I was reminded of another cigarette ad—"So round, so firm, so fully packed." That lad had the sort of bottom that Hindu lechers write poetry about—could it have been that sort of sin that caused him to wind up here?

I forgot the matter when I entered that suite.

The living room was too small for football but large enough for tennis. The furnishings would be described as "adequate" by any well-heeled oriental potentate. The alcove called "the buttery" had a cold-table collation laid out ample for forty guests, with a few hot dishes on the end—roast pig with apple in mouth, baked peacock with feathers restored, a few such tidbits. Facing this display was a bar that was well stocked—the chief purser of *Konge Knut* would have been impressed by it.

My bellhop ("Call me 'Pat.'") was moving around, opening drapes, adjusting windows, changing thermostats, checking towels—all of those things bellhops do to encourage a liberal tip—while I was trying to figure out how to tip. Was there a way to charge a tip for a bellhop to room service? Well, I would have to ask Pat. I went through the bedroom (a Sabbath Day's journey!) and tracked Pat down in the bath.

Undressing. Trousers at half-mast and about to be kicked off. Bare bottom facing me. I called out, "Here, lad! *No!* Thanks for the thought . . . but boys are not my weakness."

"They're my weakness," Pat answered, "but I'm not a boy"—and turned around, facing me.

Pat was right; she was emphatically not a boy.

I stood there with my chin hanging down, while she took off the rest of her clothes, dumped them into a hamper. "There!" she said, smiling. "Am I glad to get out of that monkey suit! I've been wearing it since you were reported as spotted on radar. What happened, Saint Alec? Did you stop for a beer?"

"Well . . . yes. Two or three beers."

"I thought so. Bert Kinsey had the watch, did he not? If the Lake ever overflows and covers this part of town with lava, Bert will stop for a beer before he runs for it. Say, what are you looking troubled about? Did I say something wrong?"

324 | ROBERT A. HEINLEIN

"Uh, Miss. You are very pretty—but I didn't ask for a girl, either."

She stepped closer to me, looked up and patted my cheek. I could feel her breath on my chin, smell its sweetness. "Saint Alec," she said softly, "I'm not trying to seduce you. Oh, I'm available, surely; a party girl, or two or three, comes with the territory for all our luxury suites. But I can do a lot more than make love to you." She reached out, grabbed a bath towel, draped it around her hips. *"Ichiban* bath girl, too. Prease, you rike me wark arong spine?" She dimpled and tossed the towel aside. "I'm a number-one bartender, too. May I serve you a Danish zombie?"

"Who told you I liked Danish zombies?"

She had turned away to open a wardrobe. "Every saint I've ever met liked them. Do you like this?" She held up a robe that appeared to be woven from a light blue fog.

"It's lovely. How many saints have you met?"

"One. You. No, two, but the other one didn't drink zombies. I was just being flip. I'm sorry."

"I'm not; it may be a clue. Did the information come from a Danish girl? A blonde, about your size, about your weight, too. Margrethe, or Marga. Sometimes 'Margie.'"

"No. The scoop on you was in a printout I was given when I was assigned to you. This Margie—friend of yours?"

"Rather more than a friend. She's the reason I'm in Hell. On Hell. In?"

"Either way. I'm fairly certain I've never met your Margie."

"How does one go about finding another person here? Directories? Voting lists? What?"

"I've never seen either. Hell isn't very organized. It's an anarchy except for a touch of absolute monarchy on some points."

"Do you suppose I could ask Satan?"

She looked dubious. "There's no rule I know of that says you can't write a letter to His Infernal Majesty. But there is no rule that says He has to read it, either. I think it would be opened and read by some secretary; they wouldn't just dump it into the Lake. I don't think they would." She added, "Shall we go into the den? Or are you ready for bed?"

"Uh, I think I need a bath. I know I do."

"Good! I've never bathed a saint before. Fun!"

"Oh, I don't need help. I can bathe myself."

She bathed me.

She gave me a manicure. She gave me a pedicure, and *tsk-tsked* over my toenails—"disgraceful" was the mildest term she used. She trimmed my hair. When I asked about razor blades, she showed me a cupboard in the bath stocking eight or nine different ways of coping with beards. "I recommend that electric razor with the three rotary heads but, if you will trust me, you will learn that I am quite competent with an old-fashioned straight razor."

"I'm just looking for some Gillette blades."

"I don't know that brand but there are brand-new razors here to match all these sorts of blades."

"No, I want my own sort. Double-edged. Stainless."

"Wilkinson Sword, double-edged lifetime?"

"Maybe. Oh, here we are!—'Gillette Stainless — Buy Two Packs, Get One Free.'"

"Good. I'll shave you."

"No, I can do it."

A half hour later I settled back against pillows in a bed fit for a king's honeymoon. I had a fine Dagwood in my belly, a Danish zombie nightcap in my hand, and I was wearing brand-new silk pajamas in maroon and old gold. Pat took off that translucent peignoir in blue smoke that she had worn except while bathing me and got in beside me, placed a drink for herself, Glenlivet on rocks, where she could reach it.

(I said to myself, "Look, Marga, I didn't choose this. There is only this one bed. But it's a big bed and she's not trying to snuggle up. You wouldn't want me to kick her out, would you? She's a nice kid; I don't want to hurt her feelings. I'm tired; I'm going to drink this and go right to sleep.")

I didn't go right to sleep. Pat was not the least bit aggressive. But she was *very* cooperative. I found one part of my mind devoting itself intensely to what Pat had to offer (plenty!) while another part of my mind was explaining to Marga that this wasn't anything serious; I don't love her; I love you and only you and always will . . . but I haven't been able to sleep and—

Then we slept for a while. Then we watched a living hollow gram that Pat said was "X rated" and I learned about things I had never heard of, but it turned out that Pat had and could do them and could teach me, and this time I paused just long enough to tell Marga I was learning them for both of us, then I turned my whole attention to learning.

Then we napped again.

It was some time later that Pat reached out and touched my shoulder. "Turn over this way, dear; let me see your face. I thought so. Alec, I know you're carrying the torch for your sweetheart; that's why I'm here: to make it easier. But I can't if you won't try. What did she do for you that I haven't done and can't do? Does she have that famous left-hand thread? Or what? Name it, describe it. I'll either do it, or fake it, or send out for it. Please, dear. You're beginning to hurt my professional pride."

"You're doing just fine." I patted her hand.

"I wonder. More girls like me, maybe, in various flavors? Drown you in tits?—chocolate, vanilla, strawberry, tutti-frutti. 'Tutti-frutti'—hmm . . . Maybe you'd like a San Francisco sandwich? Or some other Sodom-and-Gomorrah fancy? I have a male friend from Berkeley who isn't all that male; he has a delicious, playful imagination; I've teamed with him many times. And he has on call others like him; he's a member of both Aleister Crowley Associates and Nero's Heroes and Zeroes. If you fancy a mob scene, Donny and I can cast it any way you like, and the Sans Souci will orchestrate it to suit your taste. Persian Garden, sorority house, Turkish harem, jungle drums with obscene rites, nunnery— 'Nunnery'— did I tell you what I did before I died?"

"I wasn't certain you had died."

"Oh, certainly. I'm not an imp faking human; I'm human. You don't think anyone could get a job like this without human experience, do you? You have to be human right down to your toes to please a fellow human most; that stuff about the superior erotic ability of succubi is just their advertising. I was a nun, Alec, from adolescence to death, most of it spent teaching grammar and arithmetic to children who didn't want to learn.

"I soon learned that my vocation had not been a true one. What I did not know was how to get out of it. So I stayed. At about thirty I discovered just how miserably awful my mistake had been; my sexuality reached maturity. Mean to say I got horny, Saint Alec, and stayed horny and got more so every year.

"The worst thing about my predicament was not that I was subjected to temptation but that I was *not* subjected to temptation—as I would have grabbed any opportunity. Fat chance! My confessor might have looked upon me with lust had I been a choir boy—as it was, he sometimes snored while I was confessing. Not surprising; my sins were dull, even to me."

"What were your sins, Pat?"

"Carnal thoughts, most of which I did not confess. Not being forgiven, they went straight into Saint Peter's computers. Blasphemous adulterous fornication."

"Huh? Pat, you have quite an imagination."

"Not especially, just horny. You probably don't know just how hemmed in a nun is. She is a bride of Christ; that's the contract. So even to *think* about the joys of sex makes of her an adulterous wife in the worst possible way."

"Be darned. Pat, I recently met two nuns, in Heaven. Both seemed like hearty wenches, one especially. Yet there they were."

"No inconsistency. Most nuns confess their sins regularly, are forgiven. Then they usually die in the bosom of their Family, with its chaplain or confessor at hand. So she gets the last rites with her sins all forgiven and she's shipped straight to Heaven, pure as Ivory soap.

"But not me!" She grinned. "I'm being punished for my sins and enjoying every wicked minute of it. I died a virgin in 1918, during the big flu epidemic, and so many died so fast that no priest got to me in time to grease me into Heaven. So I wound up here. At the end of my thousand-year apprenticeship—"

"Hold it! You died in 1918?"

"Yes. The great Spanish Influenza epidemic. Born in 1878, died in 1918, on my fourtieth birthday. Would you prefer for me to look forty? I can, you know."

"No, you look just fine. Beautiful."

"I wasn't sure. Some men— Lots of eager motherhumpers around here and most of them never got a chance to do it while they were alive. It's one of my easier entertainments. I simply lead you into hypnotizing yourself, you supply the data. Then I look and sound exactly like your mother. Smell like her, too. Everything. Except that I am available to you in ways that your mother probably was not. I—"

"Patty, I don't even *like* my mother!"

"Oh. Didn't that cause you trouble at Judgment Day?"

"No. That's not in the rules. It says in the Book that you must honor thy father and thy mother. Not one word about loving them. I honored her, all the full protocol. Kept her picture on my desk. A letter every week. Telephoned her on her birthday. Called on her in person as my duties permitted. Listened to her eternal bitching and to her poisonous gossip about her women friends. Never contradicted her. Paid her hospital bills. Followed her to her grave. But weep I did not. She didn't like me and I didn't like her. Forget my mother! Pat, I asked you a question and you changed the subject."

"Sorry, dear. Hey, look what I've found!"

"Don't change the subject again; just keep it warm in your hand while you answer my question. You said something about your 'thousand-year apprenticeship.'"

"Yes?"

"But you said also that you died in 1918. The Final Trump sounded in 1994—I know; I was there. That's only seventy-six years later than your death. To me that Final Trump seems like only a few days ago, about a month, no more. I ran across something that seemed to make it seven years ago. But that still isn't over nine hundred, the best part of a thousand years. I'm not a spirit, I'm a living body. And I'm not Methuselah." (Damn it, is Margrethe separated from me by a thousand years? This isn't fair!)

"Oh. Alec, in eternity a thousand years isn't any particular time; it is simply a long time. Long enough in this case to test whether or not I had both the talent and the disposition for the profession. That took quite a while because, while I was horny enough—and stayed that way; almost any guest can send me right through the ceiling—as you noticed—I had arrived here knowing nothing about sex. Nothing! But I did learn and eventually Mary Magdalene gave me high marks and recommended me for permanent appointment."

"Is *she* down *here?*"

"Oh. She's a visiting professor here; she's on the permanent faculty in Heaven."

"What does she teach in Heaven?"

"I have no idea but it can't be what she teaches here. Or I don't *think* so. Hmm. Alec, she's one of the eternal greats; she makes her own rules. But this time you changed the subject. I was trying to tell you that I don't know how long my apprenticeship lasted because time is whatever you want it to be. How long have you and I been in bed together?"

"Uh, quite a while. But not long enough. I think it must be near midnight."

"It's midnight if you want it to be midnight. Want me to get on top?"

The next morning, whenever that was, Pat and I had breakfast on the balcony looking out over the Lake. She was dressed in Marga's favorite costume, shorts tight and short, and a halter with her breasts tending to overflow their bounds. I don't know when she got her clothes, but my pants and shirt had been cleaned and repaired in the night and my underwear and socks washed—in Hell there seem to be busy little imps everywhere. Besides, they could have driven a flock of geese through our bedroom the latter part of the night without disturbing me.

I looked at Pat across the table, appreciating her wholesome, girl-scout beauty, with her sprinkle of freckles across her nose, and thought how strange it was that I had ever confused sex with sin. Sex can involve sin, surely—any human act can involve cruelty and injustice. But sex alone held no taint of sin. I had arrived here tired, confused, and unhappy—Pat had first made me happy, then caused me to rest, then left me happy this lovely morning.

Not any less anxious to find you, Marga my own—but in much better shape to push the search.

Would Margrethe see it that way?

Well, she had never seemed jealous of me.

How would I feel if she took a vacation, a sexual vacation, such as I had just enjoyed? That's a good question. Better think about it, boy—because sauce for the goose is not a horse of another color.

I looked out over the Lake, watched the smoke rise and the flames throwing red lights on the smoke . . . while right and left were green and sunny early summer sights, with snow-tipped mountains in the far distance. "Pat—"

"Yes, dear?"

"The Lake bank can't be more than a furlong from here. But I can't smell any brimstone."

"Notice how the breeze is blowing those banners? From anywhere around the Pit the wind blows toward the Pit. There it rises—incidentally slowing any soul arriving ballistically—and then on the far side of the globe there is a corresponding down draft into a cold pit where the hydrogen sulfide reacts with oxygen to form water and sulfur. The sulfur is deposited; the water comes out as water vapor, and returns. The two pits and this circulation control the weather here somewhat the way the moon acts as a control on earth weather. But gentler."

"I was never too hot at physical sciences . . . but that doesn't sound like the natural laws I learned in school."

"Of course not. Different Boss here. He runs this planet to suit himself."

Whatever I meant to answer got lost in a mellow gong played inside the suite. "Shall I answer, sir?"

"Sure, but how dare you call me 'sir'? Probably just room service. Huh?"

"No, dear Alec, room service will just come in when they see that we are through." She got up, came back quickly with an envelope. "Letter by Imperial courier. For you, dear."

"*Me?*" I accepted it gingerly, and opened it. An embossed seal at the top: the conventional Devil in red, horns, hooves, tail, pitchfork, and standing in flames. Below it:

Saint Alexander Hergensheimer
Sans Souci Sheraton
The Capital

Greetings:

    In response to your petition for an audience with His Infernal Majesty, Satan Mekratrig, Sovereign of Hell and His Colonies beyond, First of the Fallen Thrones, Prince of

Lies, I have the honour to advise you that His Majesty requires you to substantiate your request by supplying to this office a full and frank memoir of your life. When this has been done, a decision on your request will be made.

May I add to His Majesty's message this advice: Any attempt to omit, slur over, or color in the belief that you will thereby please His Majesty will *not* please Him.

I have the honour to remain,
Sincerely His,
(s) Beelzebub
Secretary to His Majesty

I read it aloud to Pat. She blinked her eyes and whistled. "Dear, you had better get busy!"

"I—" The paper burst into flames; I dropped it into the dirty dishes. "Does that always happen?"

"I don't know; it's the first time I've ever seen a message from Number One. And the first time I've heard of anyone being even conditionally granted an audience."

"Pat. I didn't ask for an audience. I planned to find out how to do so today. But I have not put in the request this answers."

"Then you must put in the request *at once*. It wouldn't do to let it stay unbalanced. I'll help dear—I'll type it for you."

The imps had been around again. In one corner of that vast living room I found that they had installed two desks, one a writing desk, with stacks of paper and a tumbler of pens, the other a more complex setup. Pat went straight to that one. "Dear, it looks like I'm still assigned to you. I'm your secretary now. The latest and best Hewlett-Packard equipment—this is going to be fun! Or do you know how to type?"

"I'm afraid not."

"Okay, you write it longhand; I'll put it into shape . . . and correct your spelling and your grammar—you just whip it out. Now I know why I was picked for this job. Not my girlish smile, dear—my typing. Most of my guild can't type. Many of them took up whoring because short-hand and typing were too much for them. Not me. Well, let's get to work; this job will run days, weeks, I don't know. Do you want me to continue to sleep here?"

"Do you want to leave?"

"Dear, that's the guest's decision. Has to be."

"I don't want you to leave." (Marga! Do please understand!)

"Good thing you said that, or I would have burst into tears. Besides, a good secretary should stick around in case something comes up in the night."

"Pat, that was an old joke when I was in seminary."

"It was an old joke before you were born, dear. Let's get to work."

Visualize a calendar (that I don't have), its pages ripping off in the wind. This manuscript gets longer and longer but Pat insists that Prince Beelzebub's advice must be taken literally. Pat makes two copies of all that I write; one copy stacks up on my desk, the other copy disappears each night. Imps again. Pat tells me that I can assume that the vanishing copy is going to the Palace, at least as far as the Prince's desk . . . so what I am doing so far must be satisfactory.

In less than two hours each day Pat types out and prints out what takes me all day to write. But I stopped driving so hard when a handwritten note came in:

> You are working too hard. Enjoy yourself. Take her to the theater. Go on a picnic. Don't be so wound up.
>
> (s) B.

The note self-destroyed, so I knew it was authentic. So I obeyed. With pleasure! But I am not going to describe the fleshpots of Satan's capital city.

This morning I finally reached that odd point where I was (am) writing now about what is going on now—and I hand my last page to Pat.

•   •   •

Less than an hour after I completed that line above the gong sounded; Pat went out into the foyer, hurried back. She put her arms around me. "This is good-bye, dear. I won't be seeing you again."

"*What!*"

"Just that, dear. I was told this morning that my assignment was ending. And I have something I must tell you. You will find, you are bound to learn, that I have been reporting on you daily. Please don't be angry about it. I am a professional, part of the Imperial security staff."

"Be damned! So every kiss, every sigh, was a fake."

"Not one was fake! Not one! And, when you find your Marga, please tell her that I said she is lucky."

"Sister Mary Patricia, is this another lie?"

"Saint Alexander, I have never lied to you. I've had to hold back some things until I was free to speak, that's all." She took her arms from around me.

"Hey! Aren't you going to kiss me good-bye?"

"Alec, if you really want to kiss me, you won't ask."

I didn't ask; I did it. If Pat was faking, she's a better actress than I think she is.

Two giant fallen angels were waiting to take me to the Palace. They were heavily armed and fully armored. Pat had packaged my manuscript and told me that I was expected to bring it with me. I started to leave—then stopped most suddenly. "My razor!"

"Check your pocket, dear."

"Huh? How'd it get there?"

"I knew you weren't coming back, dear."

Again I learned that, in the company of angels, I could fly. Out my own balcony, around the Sans Souci Sheraton, across the Plaza, and we landed on a third-floor balcony of Satan's Palace. Then through several corridors, up a flight of stairs with lifts too high to be comfortable for humans. When I stumbled, one of my escorts caught me, then steadied me until we reached the top, but said nothing—neither ever said anything.

Great brass doors, as complex as the Ghiberti Doors, opened. I was shoved inside.

And saw Him.

A dark and smoky hall, armed guards down both sides, a high throne, a Being on it, at least twice as high as a man . . . a Being that was the conventional Devil such as you see on a Pluto bottle or a deviled-ham tin—tail and horns and fierce eyes, a pitchfork in lieu of scepter, a gleam from braziers glinting off Its dark red skin, sleek muscles. I had to remind myself that the Prince of Lies could look any way He wished; this was probably to daunt me.

His voice rumbled out like a foghorn: "Saint Alexander, you may approach Me."

XXVI

I am a brother to dragons, and a companion to owls.
Job 30:29

I started up the steps leading to the throne. Again, the lifts were too high, the treads too wide, and now I had no one to steady me. I was reduced to crawling up those confounded steps while Satan looked down at me with a sardonic smile. From all around came music from an unseen source, death music, vaguely Wagnerian but nothing I could identify. I think it was laced with that below-sonic frequency that makes dogs howl, horses run away, and causes men to think of flight or suicide.

That staircase kept stretching.

I didn't count the number of steps when I started up, but the flight looked to be about thirty steps, no more. When I had been crawling up it for several minutes, I realized that it looked as high as ever. The Prince of Lies!

So I stopped and waited.

Presently that rumbling voice said, "Something wrong, Saint Alexander?"

"Nothing wrong," I answered, "because You planned it this way. If You really want me to approach You, You will turn off the joke circuit. In the meantime there is no point in my trying to climb a treadmill."

"You think I am doing that to you?"

"I *know* that You are. A game. Cat and mouse."

"You are trying to make a fool of Me, in front of My gentlemen."

"No, Your Majesty, I cannot make a fool of You. Only You can do that."

"Ah so. Do you realize that I can blast you where you stand?"

"Your Majesty, I have been totally in Your power since I entered Your realm. What do You wish of me? Shall I continue trying to climb Your treadmill?"

"Yes."

So I did, and the staircase stopped stretching and the treads reduced to a comfortable seven inches. In seconds I reached the same level as Satan—the level of His cloven feet, that is. Which put me much too close to Him. Not only was His Presence terrifying—I had to keep a close grip on myself—but also He *stank!* Of filthy garbage cans, of rotting meat, of civet and skunk, of brimstone, of closed rooms and gas from diseased gut—all that and worse. I said to myself, Alex Hergensheimer, if you let Him prod you into throwing up and thereby kill any chance of getting you and Marga back together—just don't do it! Control yourself!

"The stool is for you," said Satan. "Be seated."

Near the throne was a backless stool, low enough to destroy the dignity of anyone who sat on it. I sat.

Satan picked up a manuscript with a hand so big that the business-size sheets were like a deck of cards in His hand. "I've read it. Not bad. A bit wordy but My editors will cut it—better that way than too brief. We will need an ending for it . . . from you or by a ghost. Probably the latter; it needs more impact than you give it. Tell me, have you ever thought of writing for a living? Rather than preaching?"

"I don't think I have the talent."

"Talent shmalent. You should *see* the stuff that gets published. But you must hike up those sex scenes; today's cash customers demand such scenes *wet*. Never mind that now; I didn't call you here to discuss your literary style and its shortcomings. I called you in to make you an offer."

I waited. So did He. After a bit He said, "Aren't curious about the offer?"

"Your Majesty, certainly I am. But, if my race has learned one lesson concerning You, it is that a human should be extremely cautious in bargaining with You."

He chuckled and the foundations shook. "Poor little human, did you really think that I wanted to dicker for your scrawny soul?"

"I don't know what You want. But I'm not as smart as Dr. Faust, and not nearly as smart as Daniel Webster. It behooves me to be cautious."

"Oh, come! I don't want your soul. There's no market for souls today; there are far too many of them and quality is way down. I can pick them up at a nickel a bunch, like radishes. But I don't; I'm overstocked. No, Saint Alexander, I wish to retain your services. Your professional services."

(I was suddenly alarmed. What's the catch? Alex, this is loaded! Look behind you! What's He after?) "You need a dishwasher?"

He chuckled again, about 4.2 on the Richter scale. "No, no, Saint Alexander! Your vocation—not the exigency to which you were temporarily reduced. I want to hire you as a gospel-shouter, a Bible-thumper. I want you to work the Jesus business, just as you were trained to. You won't have to raise money or pass the collection plate; the salary will be ample and the duties light. What do you say?"

"I say You are trying to trick me."

"Now that's not very kind. No tricks, Saint Alexander. You will be free to preach exactly as you please, no restrictions. Your title will be personal chaplain to Me, and Primate of Hell. You can devote the rest of your time—as little or as much as you wish—to saving lost souls . . . and there are plenty of those here. Salary to be negotiated . . . but not less than the incumbent, Pope Alexander the Sixth, a notoriously greedy soul. You won't be pinched, I promise you. Well? How say you?"

(Who's crazy? The Devil, or me? Or am I having another of those nightmares that have been dogging me lately?) "Your Majesty, You have not mentioned anything I want."

"Ah so? Everybody needs money. You're broke; you can't stay in that fancy suite another day without finding a job." He tapped the manuscript. "This may bring in something, some day. Not soon. I'm not going to advance you anything on it; it might not sell. There are too many I-Was-a-Prisoner-of-the-Evil-King extravaganzas on the market already these days."

"Your Majesty, You have read my memoir; You *know* what I want."

"Eh? Name it."

"You know. My beloved. Margrethe Svensdatter Gunderson."

He looked surprised. "Didn't I send you a memo about that? She's not in Hell."

I felt like a patient who has kept his chin up right up to the minute the biopsy comes back . . . and then can't accept the bad news. "Are You *sure?*"

"Of course I am. Who do you think is in charge around here?"

(Prince of Liars, Prince of Lies!) "How can You be sure? The way I hear it, nobody keeps track. A person could be in Hell for years and You would never know, one way or the other."

"If that's the way you heard it, you heard wrong. Look, if you accept My offer, you'll be able to afford the best agents in history, from Sherlock Holmes to J. Edgar Hoover, to search all over Hell for you. But you'd be wasting your money; she is *not* in My jurisdiction. I'm telling you officially."

I hesitated. Hell is a big place; I could search it by myself throughout eternity and I might not find Marga. But plenty of money (how well I knew it!) made hard things easy and impossible things merely difficult.

However— Some of the things I had done as executive deputy of C.U.D. may have been a touch shoddy (meeting a budget isn't easy), but as an ordained minister I had never hired out to the Foe. Our Ancient Adversary. How can a minister of Christ be chaplain to Satan? Marga darling, I *can't.*

"No."

"I can't hear you. Let Me sweeten the deal. Accept and I will assign My prize female agent Sister Mary Patricia to you permanently. She'll be your slave—with the minor reservation that you must not sell her. However, you can rent her out, if you wish. How say you now?"

"No."

"Oh, come, come! You ask for one female; I offer you a better one. You can't pretend not to be satisfied with Pat; you've been shacked up with her for weeks. Shall I play back some of the sighs and moans?"

"You unspeakable cad!"

"Tut, tut, don't be rude to Me in My own house. You know and I know and we all know that there isn't any great difference between one female and another—save possibly in their cooking. I'm offering you one slightly better in place of the one you mislaid. A year from now you'll thank Me. Two years from now you'll wonder why you ever fussed. Better accept, Saint Alexander; it is the best offer you can hope for, because, I tell you solemnly, that Danish zombie you ask for is not in Hell. Well?"

"*No!*"

Satan drummed on the arm of his throne and looked vexed. "That's your last word?"

"Yes."

"Suppose I offered you the chaplain job *with* your ice maiden thrown in?"

"You said she wasn't in Hell!"

"I did not say that I did not know where she is."

"You can get her?"

"Answer My question. Will you accept service as My chaplain if the contract includes returning her to you?"

(Marga, Marga!) "No."

Satan said briskly, "Sergeant General, dismiss the guard. You come with me."

"Leftanright! . . . *Hace!* For'd! . . . *Harp!*"

Satan got down from His throne, went around behind it without further word to me. I had to hurry to catch up with His giant strides. Back of the throne was a long dark tunnel; I broke into a run when it seemed that He was getting away from me. His silhouette shrank rapidly against a dim light at the far end of the tunnel.

Then I almost stepped on His heels. He had not been receding as fast as I had thought; He had been changing in size. Or I had been. He and I were now much the same height. I skidded to a halt close behind Him as He reached a doorway at the end of the tunnel. It was barely lighted by a red glow.

Satan touched something at the door; a white fan light came on above the door. He opened it and turned toward me. "Come in, Alec."

My heart skipped and I gasped for breath. *"Jerry!* Jerry Farnsworth!"

XXVII

*For in much wisdom is much grief; and he that
increaseth knowledge increaseth sorrow.*
Ecclesiastes 1:18

*And Job spake, and said, Let the day
perish wherein I was born, and the night
in which it was said, There is a man
child conceived.*
Job 3:2–3

My eyes dimmed, my head started to spin, my knees
went rubbery. Jerry said sharply, "Hey, none of that!"—
grabbed me around the waist, dragged me inside,
slammed the door.

He kept me from falling, then shook me and slapped
my face. I shook my head and caught my breath. I heard
Katie's voice: "Let's get him in where he can lie down."

My eyes focused. "I'm okay. I was just taken all over
queer for a second." I looked around. We were in the
foyer of the Farnsworth house.

"You went into syncope, that's what you did. Not surprising, you had a shock. Come into the family room."

"All right. Hi, Katie. Gosh, it's good to see you."

"You, too, dear." She came closer, put her arms around
me, and kissed me. I learned again that, while Marga was
my be-all, Katie was my kind of woman, too. And Pat.
Marga, I wish you could have met Pat. (Marga!)

The family room seemed bare—unfinished furniture,
no windows, no fireplace. Jerry said, "Katie, give us

342

Remington number two, will you, please? I'm going to punch drinks."

"Yes, dear."

While they were busy, Sybil came tearing in, threw her arms around me (almost knocking me off my feet; the child is solid) and kissed me, a quick buss unlike Katie's benison. "Mr. Graham! You were terrific! I watched all of it. With Sister Pat. She thinks you're terrific, too."

The left wall changed into a picture window looking out at mountains; the opposite wall now had a field-stone fireplace with a brisk fire that looked the same as the last time I saw it. The ceiling now was low; furniture and floor and fixtures were all as I recalled "Remington number two." Katie turned away from the controls. "Sybil, let him be, dear. Alec, off your feet. Rest."

"All right." I sat down. "Uh . . . is this Texas? Or is it Hell?"

"Matter of opinion," Jerry said.

"Is there a difference?" asked Sybil.

"Hard to tell," said Katie. "Don't worry about it now, Alec. I watched you, too, and I agree with the girls. I was proud of you."

"He's a tough case," Jerry put in. "I didn't get a mite of change off him. Alec, you stubborn squarehead, I lost three bets on you." Drinks appeared at our places. Jerry raised his glass. "So here's to you."

"To Alec!"

"Right!"

"Here's to me," I agreed and took a big slug of Jack Daniel's. "Jerry? You're not *really*—"

He grinned at me. The tailored ranch clothes faded; the western boots gave way to cloven hooves, horns stuck up through His hair, His skin glowed ruddy red and oily over heavy muscles; in His lap a preposterously huge phallus thrust rampantly skyward.

Katie said gently, "I think You've convinced him, dear, and it's not one of Your prettier guises."

Quickly the conventional Devil faded and the equally

conventional Texas millionaire returned. "That's better,"
said Sybil. "Daddy, why do You use that corny one?"

"It's an emphatic symbol. But what I'm wearing now is
appropriate here. And you should be in Texas clothes,
too."

"Must I? I think Patty has Mr. Graham used to skin by
now."

"Her skin, not your skin. Do it before I fry you for
lunch."

"Daddy, You're a fraud." Sybil grew blue jeans and a
halter without moving out of her chair. "And I'm tired of
being a teenager and see no reason to continue the cha-
rade. Saint Alec knows he was hoaxed."

"Sybil, you talk too much."

"Dear One, she may be right," Katie put in quietly.

Jerry shook His head. I sighed and said what I had to
say. "Yes, Jerry, I know I've been hoaxed. By those who I
thought were my friends. And Marga's friends, too. *You*
have been behind it all? Then who am I? Job?"

"Yes and no."

"What does that mean . . . Your Majesty?"

"Alec, you need not call Me that. We met as friends. I
hope we will stay friends."

"How can we be friends? If I am Job. Your Majesty . . .
where is my wife!"

"Alec, I wish I knew. Your memoir gave Me some clues
and I have been following them. But I don't know as yet.
You must be patient."

"Uh . . . damn it, patient I'm not! *What* clues? Set me
on the trail! *Can't You see that I'm going out of my mind?*"

"No, I can't, because you're not. I've just been grilling
you. I pushed you to what should have been your breaking point. You can't be broken. However, you can't help
Me search for her, not at this point. Alec, you've got to
remember that you are human . . . and I am *not*. I have
powers that you can't imagine. I have limitations that
you cannot imagine, too. So hold your peace and listen.

"I am your friend. If you don't believe that I am, you

are free to leave My house and fend for yourself. There are jobs to be had down at the Lake front—if you can stand the reek of brimstone. You can search for Marga your own way. I don't owe you two anything as *I am not behind your troubles*. Believe Me."

"Uh . . . I *want* to believe You."

"Perhaps you'll believe Katie."

Katie said, "Alec, the Old One speaks sooth to you. He did not compass your troubles. Dear, did you ever bandage a wounded dog . . . and have the poor beastie, in its ignorance, gnaw away the dressing and damage itself still more?"

"Uh, yes." (My dog Brownie. I was twelve. Brownie died.)

"Don't be like that poor dog. Trust Jerry. If He is to help you, He must do things beyond your ken. Would you try to direct a brain surgeon? Or attempt to hurry one?"

I smiled ruefully and reached out to pat her hand. "I'll be good, Katie. I'll try."

"Yes, do try, for Marga's sake."

"I will. Uh, Jerry—stipulating that I'm merely human and can't understand everything, can You tell me *anything?*"

"What I can, I will. Where shall I start?"

"Well, when I asked if I was Job, You said, 'Yes and no.' What did You mean?"

"You are indeed another Job. With the original Job I was, I confess, one of the villains. This time I'm not.

"I'm not proud of the fashion in which I bedeviled Job. I'm not proud of the fashion in which I have so often let My Brother Yahweh maneuver Me into doing His dirty work—starting clear back with Mother Eve—and before that, in ways I cannot explain. And I've always been a sucker for a bet, any sort of a bet . . . and I'm not proud of that weakness, either."

Jerry looked at the fire and brooded. "Eve was a pretty one. As soon as I laid eyes on her I knew that Yahweh had finally cooked up a creation worthy of an Artist. Then I found out He had copied most of the design."

"Huh? But—"

"Man, do not interrupt. Most of your errors—this My Brother actively encourages—arise from believing that your God is solitary and all powerful. In fact My Brother—and I, too, of course—is no more than a corporal in the T.O. of the Commander in Chief. And, I must add, the Great One I think of as the C-in-C, the Chairman, the Final Power, may be a mere private to some higher Power I cannot comprehend.

"Behind every mystery lies another mystery. Infinite recession. But you don't need to know final answers—if there be such—and neither do I. You want to know what happened to you . . . and to Margrethe. Yahweh came to Me and offered the same wager We had made over Job, asserting that He had a follower who was even more stubborn than Job. I turned Him down. That bet over Job had not been much fun; long before it was concluded I grew tired of clobbering the poor schmo. So this time I told My Brother to take His shell games elsewhere.

"It was not until I saw you and Marga trudging along Interstate Forty, naked as kittens and just as helpless, that I realized that Yahweh had found someone else with whom to play His nasty games. So I fetched you here and kept you for a week or so—"

"What? Just one night!"

"Don't quibble. Kept you long enough to wring you dry, then sent you on your way . . . armed with some tips on how to cope, yes, but in fact you were doing all right on your own. You're a tough son of a bitch, Alec, so much so that I looked up the bitch you are the son of. A bitch she is and tough she was and the combo of that vixen and your sweet and gentle sire produced a creature able to survive. So I let you alone.

"I was notified that you were coming here; My spies are everywhere. Half of My Brother's personal staff are double agents."

"Saint Peter?"

"Eh? No, not Pete. Pete is a good old Joe, the most perfect Christian in Heaven or on earth. Denied his Boss thrice, been making up for it ever since. Utterly delighted to be on nickname terms with his Master in all three of His conventional Aspects. I like Pete. If he ever has a falling out with My Brother, he's got a job here.

"Then you showed up in Hell. Do you recall an invitation I extended to you concerning Hell?"

("—look me up. I promise you some hellacious hospitality.") "Yes!"

"Did I deliver? Careful how you answer; Sister Pat is listening."

"She's not listening," Katie denied. "Pat is a lady. Not much like some people. Darling, I can shorten this. What Alec wants to know is why he was persecuted, how he was persecuted, and what he can do about it now. Meaning Marga. Alec, the why is simple; you were picked for the same reason that a pit bull is picked to go into the pit and be torn to ribbons: because Yahweh thought you could win. The how is equally simple. You guessed right when you thought you were paranoid. Paranoid but not crazy; they were indeed conspiring against you. Every time you got close to the answer the razzle-dazzle started over again. That million dollars. Minor razzle-dazzle, that money existed only long enough to confuse you. I think that covers everything but what you can do. What you can do and all that you can do is to trust Jerry. He may fail—it's very dangerous—but He will try."

I looked at Katie with increased respect, and some trepidation. She had referred to matters I had never mentioned to Jerry. "Katie? Are you human? Or are you, uh, a fallen throne or something like that?"

She giggled. "First time anyone has suspected that. I'm human, all too human, Alec love. Furthermore I'm no stranger to you; you know lots about me."

"I do?"

"Think back. April of the year one thousand four hundred and forty-six years before the birth of Yeshua of Nazareth."

"I should be able to identify it that way? I'm sorry; I can't."

"Then try it this way: exactly forty years after the exodus from Egypt of the Children of Israel."

"The conquest of Canaan."

"Oh, pshaw! Try the Book of Joshua, chapter two. What's my name, what's my trade; was I mother, wife, or maid?"

(One of the best-known stories in the Bible. *Her?* I'm *talking* to her?) "Uh . . . *Rahab?*"

"The harlot of Jericho. That's me. I hid General Joshua's spies in my house . . . and thereby saved my parents and my brothers and sisters from the massacre. Now tell me I'm 'well preserved.'"

Sybil snickered. "Go ahead. I dare you."

"Gosh, Katie, you're well preserved! That's been over three thousand years, about thirty-four hundred. Hardly a wrinkle. Well, not many."

"'Not many'! No breakfast for you, young man!"

"Katie, you're beautiful and you know it. You and Margrethe tie for first place."

"Have you looked at *me?*" demanded Sybil. "I have my fans. Anyhow, Mom is over four thousand years old. A hag."

"No, Sybil, the parting of the Red Sea was in fourteen-ninety-one B.C. Add that to the date of the Rapture, nineteen-ninety-four A.D. Then add seven years—"

"Alec."

"Yes, Jerry?"

"Sybil is right. You just haven't noticed it. The thousand years of peace between Armageddon and the War in Heaven is half over. My Brother, wearing his Jesus hat, is now ruling on earth, and I am chained and cast down into the Pit for this entire thousand years."

"You don't look chained from here. Could I have some more Jack Daniel's?—I'm confused."

"I'm chained enough for this purpose; I've ceased 'going to and fro in the earth and walking up and down in it.' Yahweh has it all to Himself for the short time remaining before He destroys it. I won't bother His games." Jerry shrugged. "I declined to take part in Armageddon—I pointed out to Him that He had plenty of homegrown villains for it. Alec, with My Brother writing the scripts, I was always supposed to fight fiercely, like Harvard, then lose. It got monotonous. He's got me scheduled to take another dive at the end of this Millennium, to fulfill His prophecies. That 'War in Heaven' He predicted in the so-called Book of Revelation. I'm not going to go. I've told My angels that they can form a foreign legion if they want to, but I'm sitting this one out. What's the point in a battle if the outcome is predetermined thousands of years before the whistle?"

He was watching me while He talked. He stopped abruptly. "What's eating on you now?"

"Jerry . . . if it has been five hundred years since I lost Margrethe, it's hopeless. Isn't it?"

"Hey! Damnation, boy, haven't I told you not to try to understand things you can't understand? Would I be working on it if it were hopeless?"

Katie said, "Jerry, I had Alec all quieted down . . . and You got him upset again."

"I'm sorry."

"You didn't mean to. Alec, Jerry is blunt, but He's right. For you, acting alone, the search was always hopeless. But with Jerry's help, you may find her. Not certain, but a hope worth pursuing. But time isn't relevant, five hundred years or five seconds. You don't have to understand it, but do please believe it."

"All right. I will. Because otherwise there would be no hope, none."

"But there *is* hope; all you have to do now is be patient."

"I'll try. But I guess Marga and I will never have our soda fountain and lunch counter in Kansas."

"Why not?" asked Jerry.

"Five centuries? They won't even speak the same language. There will be no one who knows a hot fudge sundae from curried goat. Customs change."

"So you reinvent the hot fudge sundae and make a killing. Don't be a pessimist, son."

"Would you like one right now?" asked Sybil.

"I don't think he had better mix it with Jack Daniel's," Jerry advised.

"Thanks, Sybil . . . but I'd probably cry in it. I associate it with Marga."

"So don't. Son, crying in your drink is bad enough; crying into a hot fudge sundae is disgusting."

"Do I get to finish the story of my scandalous youth, or won't anybody listen?"

I said, "Katie, I'm listening. You made a deal with Joshua."

"With his spies. Alec love, to anyone whose love and respect I want—you, I mean—I need to explain something. Some people who know who I am—and even more who don't—class Rahab the harlot as a traitor. Treason in time of war, betrayal of fellow citizens, all that. I—"

"I never thought so, Katie. Jehovah had decreed that Jericho would fall. Since it was ordained, you couldn't change it. What you did was to save your father and mother and the other kids."

"Yes, but there is more to it, Alec. Patriotism is a fairly late concept. Back then, in the land of Canaan, any loyalty other than to one's family was personal loyalty to a chief of some sort—usually a successful warrior who dubbed himself 'king.' Alec, a whore doesn't—didn't—have that sort of loyalty."

"So? Katie, in spite of studying at seminary I don't really have any sharp concept of what life was like back then. I keep trying to see it in terms of Kansas."

"Not too different. A whore at that time and place was either a temple prostitute, or a slave, or a self-owned private contractor. I was a free woman. Oh, yeah? Whores don't fight city hall, they can't. An officer of the king comes in, he expects free tail and free drinks, same for the civic patrol—the cops. Same for any sort of politician. Alec, I tell you the truth; I gave away more tail than I sold—and often got a black eye as a bonus. No, I did not feel loyalty to Jericho; the Jews weren't any more cruel and they were *much* cleaner!"

"Katie, I don't know of any Protestant Christian who thinks anything bad of Rahab. But I have long wondered about one detail in her—your—story. Your house was on the city wall?"

"Yes. It was inconvenient for housekeeping—carrying water up all those steps—but convenient for business, and the rent was low. It was the fact that I lived on the wall that let me save General Joshua's agents. Used a clothesline; they went out the window. Didn't get my clothesline back, either."

"How high was that wall?"

"Hunh? Goodness, I don't know. It was *high*."

"Twenty cubits."

"Was it, Jerry?"

"I was there. Professional interest. First use of nerve warfare in combination with sonic weapons."

"The reason I ask about the height, Katie, is because it states in the Book that you gathered all your family into your house and stayed there, all during the siege."

"We surely did, seven horrid days. My contract with the Israelite spies required it. My place was only two little rooms, not big enough for three adults and seven kids. We ran out of food, we ran out of water, the kids cried, and my father complained. He happily took the money I brought in; with seven kids he needed it. But he resented having to stay under the same roof where I entertained johns, and he was especially bitter about having to use my bed. My workbench. But use it he did, and I slept on the floor."

"Then your family were all in your house when the walls came tumbling down."

"Yes, surely. We didn't dare leave it until they came for us, the two spies. My house was marked at the window with red string."

"Katie, your house was on the wall, thirty feet up. The Bible says the wall fell down flat. Wasn't anyone hurt?"

She looked startled. "Why, no."

"Didn't the house collapse?"

"No. Alec, it's been a long time. But I remember the trumpets and the shout, and then the earthquake rumble as the city wall fell. But my house wasn't hurt."

"Saint Alec!"

"Yes, Jerry?"

"You should know; you're a saint. A miracle. If Yahweh hadn't been throwing miracles right and left, the Israelites would never have conquered the Canaanites. Here this ragged band of Okies comes into a rich country of walled cities—and they never lose a battle. Miracles. Ask the Canaanites. If you can find one. My Brother pretty regularly had them all put to the sword, except some few cases where the young and pretty ones were saved as slaves."

"But it was the Promised Land, Jerry, and they were His Chosen People."

"They are indeed the Chosen People. Of course, being chosen by Yahweh is no great shakes. Do you know your Book well enough to know how many times He crossed 'em up? My Brother is a bit of a jerk."

I had had too much Jack Daniel's and too many shocks. But Jerry's casual blasphemy triggered me. "The Lord God Jehovah is a just God!"

"You never played marbles with Him. Alec, 'justice' is not a divine concept; it is a human illusion. The very basis of the Judeo-Christian code is injustice, the scapegoat system. The scapegoat sacrifice runs all through the Old Testament, then it reaches its height in the New Testament with the notion of the Martyred Redeemer. How can justice possibly be served by loading your sins on another? Whether it be a lamb having its throat cut ritually, or a Messiah nailed to a cross and 'dying for your sins.' Somebody should tell all of Yahweh's followers, Jews and Christians, that there is no such thing as a free lunch.

"Or maybe there is. Being in that catatonic condition called 'grace' at the exact moment of death—or at the Final Trump—will get you into Heaven. Right? You got to Heaven that way, did you not?"

"That's correct. I hit it lucky. For I had racked up quite a list of sins before then."

"A long and wicked life followed by five minutes of perfect grace gets you into Heaven. An equally long life of decent living and good works followed by one outburst of taking the name of the Lord in vain—then have a heart attack at that moment and be damned for eternity. Is that the system?"

I answered stiffly, "If you read the words of the Bible literally, that is the system. But the Lord moves in mysterious—"

"Not mysterious to Me, bud: I've known Him too long. It's His world, His rules, His doing. His rules are exact and anyone can follow them and reap the reward. But 'just' they are not. What do you think of what He has done to you and your Marga? Is that justice?"

I took a deep breath. "I've been trying to figure that out ever since Judgment Day . . . and Jack Daniel's isn't helping. No, I don't think it's what I signed up for."

"Ah, but you did!"

"How?"

"My Brother Yahweh, wearing His Jesus face, said: 'After this manner therefore pray ye:' Go ahead, say it."

"'Our Father, which art in heaven, Hallowed be thy name. Thy kingdom come. Thy will be done—'"

"Stop! Stop right there. 'Thy will be done—' No Muslim claiming to be a 'slave of God' ever gave a more sweeping consent than that. In that prayer you invite Him to do His worst. The perfect masochist. That's the test of Job, boy. Job was treated unjustly in every way day after day for years—I know, I know, I was there; I did it—and My dear Brother stood by and let Me do it. Let Me? He urged Me, He connived in it, accessory ahead of the fact.

"Now it's your turn. Your God did it to you. Will you curse Him? Or will you come wiggling back on your belly like a whipped dog?"

XXVIII

Ask, and it shall be given you; seek, and ye shall find;
knock, and it shall be opened unto you.
Matthew 7:7

I was saved from answering that impossible question by an interruption—and was I glad! I suppose every man has doubts at times about God's justice. I admit that I had been much troubled lately and had been forced to remind myself again and again that God's ways are not man's ways, and that I could not expect always to understand the purposes of the Lord.

But I could not speak my misgivings aloud, and least of all to the Lord's Ancient Adversary. It was especially upsetting that Satan chose at this moment to have the shape and the voice of my only friend.

Debating with the Devil is a mug's game at best.

The interruption was mundane: a telephone ringing. Accidental interruption? I don't think Satan tolerates "accidents." As may be, I did not have to answer the question that I could not answer.

Katie said, "Shall I get it, dear?"

"Please."

A telephone handset appeared in Katie's hand. "Lucifer's office, Rahab speaking. Repeat, please. I will inquire." She looked at Jerry.

"I'll take it." Jerry operated without a visible telephone instrument. "Speaking. No. I said, no. No, damn it! Refer that to Mr. Ashmedai. Let Me have the other call." He muttered something about the impossibility of getting competent help, then said, "Speaking. Yes, Sir!" Then He said nothing for quite a long time. At last He said, "At once, Sir. Thank you."

Jerry stood up. "Please excuse Me, Alec; I have work to do. I can't say when I will be back. Try to treat this waiting as a vacation . . . and My house is yours. Katie, take care of him. Sybil, keep him amused." Jerry vanished.

"Will I keep him amused!" Sybil got up and stood in front of me, rubbed her hands together. Her western clothes faded out, leaving Sybil. She grinned.

Katie said mildly, "Sybil, stop that. Grow more clothes at once or I'll send you home."

"Spoilsport." Sybil developed a skimpy bikini. "I plan to make Saint Alec forget that Danish baggage."

"What'll you bet, dear? I've been talking to Pat."

"So? What did Pat say?"

"Margrethe can cook."

Sybil looked disgusted. "A girl spends fifty years on her back, studying hard. Along comes some slottie who can make chicken and dumplings. It's not fair."

I decided to change the subject. "Sybil, those tricks you do with clothes are fascinating. Are you a graduate witch now?"

Instead of answering me at once, Sybil glanced at Katie, who said to her: "All over with, dear. Speak freely."

"Okay. Saint Alec, I'm no witch. Witchcraft is poppycock. You know that verse in the Bible about not suffering witches to live?"

"Exodus twenty-two, eighteen."

"That's the one. The Old Hebrew word translated there as 'witch' actually means 'poisoner.' Not letting a poisoner continue to breathe strikes me as a good idea. But I wonder how many friendless old women have been hanged or burned as a result of a sloppy translation?"

(Could this really be true? What about the "literal word of God" concept on which I had been reared? Of course the word "witch" is English, not the original

Hebrew . . . but the translators of the King James version were sustained by God—that's why that version of the Bible [and only that one] can be taken literally. But—*No!* Sybil must be mistaken. The Good Lord would not let hundreds, thousands, of innocent people be tortured to death over a mistranslation He could so easily have corrected.)

"So you did not attend a Sabbat that night. What did you do?"

"Not what you think; Israfel and I aren't quite that chummy. Chums, yes; buddies, no."

"'Israfel'? I thought he was in Heaven."

"That's his godfather. The trumpeter. This Israfel can't play a note. But he did ask me to tell you, if I ever got a chance, that he really isn't the pimple he pretended to be as 'Roderick Lyman Culverson, Third.'"

"I'm glad to hear that. As he certainly did a good job of portraying an unbearable young snot. I didn't see how a daughter of Katie and Jerry—or is it just of Katie?—could have such poor taste as to pick that boor as a pal. Not Israfel, of course, but the part he was playing."

"Oh. Better fix that, too. Katie, what relation are we?"

"I don't think even Dr. Darwin could find any genetic relationship, dear. But I am every bit as proud of you as I would be were you my own daughter."

"Thank you, Mom!"

"But we all are related," I objected, "through Mother Eve. Since Katie, wrinkles and all, was born while the Children of Israel were wandering in the wilderness, there are only about eighty begats from Eve to Katie. With your birthdate and simple arithmetic we could make a shrewd guess at how close your blood relationship is."

"Oh, oh! Here we go again. Saint Alec, Mama Kate is descended from Eve; I am not. Different species. I'm an imp. An afrit, if you want to get technical."

She again vanished her clothes and did a body transformation. "See?"

I said, "Say! Weren't you managing the desk at the Sans Souci Sheraton the evening I arrived in Hell?"

"I certainly was. And I'm flattered that you remember me, in my own shape." She resumed her human appearance, plus the tiny bikini. "I was there because I knew you by sight. Pop didn't want anything to go wrong."

Katie stood up. "Let's continue this outside; I'd like a dip before dinner."

"I'm busy seducing Saint Alec."

"Dreamer. Continue it outdoors."

Outside it was a lovely Texas late afternoon, with lengthening shadows. "Katie, a straight answer, please. Is this Hell? Or is this Texas?"

"Both."

"I withdraw the question."

I must have let my annoyance show in my voice, for she turned and put a hand on my chest. "Alec, I was not jesting. For many centuries Lucifer has maintained *pieds-à-terre* here and there on earth. In each He had an established personality, a front. After Armageddon, when His Brother set Himself up as king of earth for the Millennium, He quit visiting earth. But some of these places were home to Him, so He pinched them off and took them with Him. You see?"

"I suppose I do. About as well as a cow understands calculus."

"I don't understand the mechanism; it's on the God level. But those numerous changes you and Marga underwent during your persecution: How deep did each change go? Do you think the entire planet was involved each time?"

Reality tumbled in my mind in a fashion it had not since the last of those "changes." "Katie, I don't know! I was always too busy surviving. Wait a moment. Each change did cover the whole planet earth and about a century of its history. Because I always checked the history and memorized as much as I could. Cultural changes, too. The whole complex."

"Each change stopped not far beyond the end of your nose, Alec, and no one but you—you two—was aware of *any* change. You didn't check history; you checked *history books*. At least this is the way Lucifer would have handled it, had He been arranging the deception."

"Uh— Katie, do you realize how long it would take to revise, rewrite, and print an entire encyclopedia? That's what I usually consulted."

"But, Alec, you have already been told that *time* is never a problem on the God level. Or space. Whatever was needed to deceive you was provided. But no more than that. That is the conservative principle in art at the God level. While I can't do it, not being at that level, I have seen a lot of it done. A skillful Artist in shapes and appearances does no more than necessary to create His effect."

Rahab sat down on the edge of the pool, paddled her feet in the water. "Come sit beside me. Consider the edge of the 'big bang.' What is there out beyond that limit where the red shift has the magnitude that means that the expansion of the universe equals the speed of light— what is beyond?"

I answered rather stiffly, "Katie, your hypothetical question lacks meaning. I've kept up, more or less, with such silly notions as the 'big bang' and the 'expanding universe' because a preacher of the Gospel must keep track of such theories in order to be able to refute them. The two you mention imply an impossible length of time—impossible because the world was created about six thousand years ago. 'About' because the exact date of Creation is hard to calculate, and also because I am uncertain as to the present date. But around six thousand years—not the billion years or so the big-bangers need."

"Alec . . . your universe is about twenty-three billion years old."

I started to retort, closed my mouth. I will not flatly contradict my hostess.

She added, "And your universe was created in four thousand and four B.C."

I stared at the water long enough for Sybil to surface and splash us.

"Well, Alec?"

"You've left me with nothing to say."

"But notice carefully what I did say. I did *not* say that the world was created twenty-three billion years ago; I said that was its age. It was created old. Created with fossils in the ground and craters on the moon, all speaking of great age. Created that way by Yahweh, because it amused Him to do so. One of those scientists said, 'God does not roll dice with the universe.' Unfortunately not true. Yahweh rolls loaded dice with His universe . . . to deceive His creatures."

"Why would He do that?"

"Lucifer says that it is because He is a poor Artist, the sort who is always changing his mind and scraping the canvas. And a practical joker. But I'm really not entitled to an opinion; I'm not at that level. And Lucifer is prejudiced where His Brother is concerned; I think that is obvious. You haven't remarked on the greatest wonder."

"Maybe I missed it."

"No, I think you were being polite. How an old whore happened to have opinions about cosmogony and teleology and eschatology and other long words of Greek derivation; that's the greatest wonder. Not?"

"Why, Rahab honey, I was just so busy counting your wrinkles that I wasn't lis—"

This got me shoved into the water. I came up sputtering and spouting and found both women laughing at me. So I placed both hands on the edge of the pool with Katie captured inside the circle. She did not seem to mind being captive; she leaned against me like a cat. "You were about to say?" I asked.

"Alec, to be able to read and write is as wonderful as sex. Or almost. You may not fully appreciate what a blessing it is because you probably learned how as a baby and have been doing it casually ever since. But when I was a whore in Canaan almost four millennia ago, I did not know how to read and write. I learned by listening . . . to johns, to neighbors, to gossip in the market. But that's not a way to learn much, and even scribes and judges were ignorant then.

"I had been dead nearly three centuries before I learned to read and write, and when I did learn, I was taught by the ghost of a harlot from what later became the great Cretan civilization. Saint Alec, this may startle you but, in general throughout history, whores learned to read and write long before respectable women took up the dangerous practice. When I did learn, brother! For a while it crowded sex out of my life."

She grinned up at me. "Almost, anyhow. Presently I went back to a more healthy balance, reading and sex, in equal amounts."

"I don't have the strength for that ratio."

"Women are different. My best education started with the burning of the Library at Alexandria. Yahweh didn't want it, so Lucifer grabbed the ghosts of all those thousands of codices, took them to Hell, regenerated them carefully—and Rahab had a picnic! And let me add: Lucifer has His eye on the Vatican Library, since it will be up for salvage soon. Instead of having to regenerate ghosts, in the case of the Vatican Library, Lucifer plans to pinch it off intact just before Time Stop, and take it unhurt to Hell. Won't that be grand?"

"Sounds as if it would be. The only thing about which I've ever envied the papists is their library. But . . . 're-generated ghosts'?"

"Slap my back."

"Huh?"

"Slap it. No, harder than that; I'm not a fragile little butterfly. Harder. That's more like it. What you just slapped is a regenerated ghost."

"Felt solid."

"Should be, I paid list price for the job. It was before

Lucifer noticed me and made me a bird in a gilded cage, a pitiful sight to see. I understand that, if you are saved and go to Heaven, regeneration goes with salvation . . . but here you buy it on credit, then work your arse off to pay for it. That being exactly how I paid for it. Saint Alec, you didn't die, I know. A regenerated body is just like the one a person has before death, but better. No contagious diseases, no allergies, no old-age wrinkles—and 'wrinkles' my foot! I wasn't wrinkled the day I died . . . or at least not much. How did you get me talking about wrinkles? We were discussing relativity and the expanding universe, a really high-type intellectual conversation."

That night Sybil made a strong effort to get into my bed, an effort that Katie firmly thwarted—then went to bed with me herself. "Pat said that you were not to be allowed to sleep alone."

"Pat thinks I'm sick. I'm not."

"I won't argue it. And don't quiver your chin, dear; Mother Rahab will let you sleep."

Sometime in the night I woke up sobbing, and Katie was there. She comforted me. I'm sure Pat told her about my nightmares. With Katie there to quiet me down I got back to sleep rather quickly.

It was a sweet Arcadian interlude . . . save for the absence of Margrethe. But Katie had me convinced that I owed it to Jerry (and to her) to be patient and not brood over my loss. So I did not, or not much, in the daytime, and, while night could be bad, even lonely nights are not too lonely with Mother Rahab to soothe one after waking up emotionally defenseless. She was always there . . . except one night she had to be away. Sybil took that watch, carefully instructed by Katie, and carried it out the same way.

I discovered one amusing thing about Sybil. In sleep she slips back into her natural shape, imp or afrit, without knowing it. This makes her about six inches shorter and she has those cute little horns that were the first thing I had noticed about her, at the Sans Souci.

Daytimes we swam and sunbathed and rode horseback and picnicked out in the hills. In making this enclave Jerry had apparently pinched off many square miles; we appeared to be able to go as far as we liked in any direction.

Or perhaps I don't understand at all how such things are done.

Strike out "perhaps"—I know as much about operations on the God level as a frog knows about Friday.

Jerry had been gone about a week when Rahab showed up at the breakfast table with my memoir manuscript. "Saint Alec, Lucifer sent instructions that you are to bring this up to date and keep it up to date."

"All right. Will longhand do? Or, if there is a typewriter around, I guess I could hunt and peck."

"You do it longhand; I'll do a smooth draft. I've done lots of secretarial work for Prince Lucifer."

"Katie, sometimes you call Him Jerry, sometimes Lucifer, never Satan."

"Alec, He prefers 'Lucifer' but He answers to anything. 'Jerry' and 'Katie' were names invented for you and Marga—"

"And 'Sybil,'" Sybil amended.

"And 'Sybil.' Yes, Egret. Do you want your own name back now?"

"No, I think it's nice that Alec—and Marga—have names for us that no one else knows."

"Just a minute," I put in. "The day I met you, all three of you responded to those names as if you had worn them all your lives."

"Mom and I are pretty fast at extemporaneous drama," Sybil-Egret said. "They didn't know they were fire-worshipers until I slipped it into the conversation. And I didn't know I was a witch until Mom tipped me off. Israfel is pretty sharp, too. But he did have more time to think about his role."

"So we were snookered in all directions. A couple of country cousins."

"Alec," Katie said to me earnestly, "Lucifer always has reasons for what He does. He rarely explains. His intentions are malevolent only toward malicious people . . . which you are not."

We three were sunbathing by the pool when Jerry returned suddenly. He said abruptly to me, not even stopping first to speak to Katie: "Get your clothes on. We're leaving at once."

Katie bounced up, rushed in and got my clothes. The women had me dressed as fast as a fireman answering an alarm. Katie shoved my razor into my pocket, buttoned it. I announced, "I'm ready!"

"Where's his manuscript?"

Again Katie rushed in, out again fast. "Here!"

In that brief time Jerry had grown twelve feet tall—and changed. He was still Jerry, but I now knew why Lucifer was known as the most beautiful of all the angels. "So long!" he said. "Rahab, I'll call you if I can." He started to pick me up.

"Wait! Egret and I must kiss him good-bye!"

"Oh. Make it snappy!"

They did, ritual pecks only, given simultaneously. Jerry grabbed me, held me like a child, and we went straight up. I had a quick glimpse of Sans Souci, the Palace, and the Plaza, then smoke and flame from the Pit covered them. We went on out of this world.

How we traveled, how long we traveled, where we traveled I do not know. It was like that endless fall to Hell, but made much more agreeable by Jerry's arms. It reminded me of times when I was very young, two or three years old, when my father would sometimes pick me up after supper and hold me until I fell asleep.

I suppose I did sleep. After a long time I became alert by feeling Jerry sweeping in for a landing. He put me down, set me on my feet.

There was gravity here; I felt weight and "down" again had meaning. But I do not think we were on a planet. We seemed to be on a platform or a porch of some immensely large building. I could not see it because we were right up against it. Elsewhere there was nothing to see, just an amorphous twilight.

Jerry said, "Are you all right?"

"Yes. Yes, I think so."

"Good. Listen carefully. I am about to take you in to see—no, for you to be seen by—an Entity who is to me, and to my brother your god Yahweh, as Yahweh is to you. Understand me?"

"Uh . . . maybe. I'm not sure."

"A is to B as B is to C. To this Entity your lord god Jehovah is equivalent to a child building sand castles at a beach, then destroying them in childish tantrums. To Him I am a child, too. I look up to Him as you look up to your triple deity—father, son, and holy ghost. I don't worship this Entity as God; He does not demand, does not expect, and does not want, that sort of bootlicking. Yahweh may be the only god who ever thought up that curious vice—at least I do not know of another planet or place in any universe where god-worship is practiced. But I am young and not much traveled."

Jerry was watching me closely. He appeared to be troubled. "Alec, maybe this analogy will explain it. When you were growing up, did you ever have to take a pet to a veterinarian?"

"Yes. I didn't like it because they always hated it so."

"I don't like it, either. Very well, you know what it is to take a sick or damaged animal to the vet. Then you had to wait while the doctor decided whether or not your pet could be made well. Or whether the kind and gentle thing to do was to put the little creature out of its misery. Is this not true?"

"Yes. Jerry, you're telling me that things are dicey. Uncertain."

"Utterly uncertain. No precedent. A human being has

never been taken to this level before. I don't know what He will do."

"Okay. You told me before that there would be a risk."

"Yes. You are in great danger. And so am I, although I think your danger is much greater than mine. But, Alec, I can assure you of this: If It decides to extinguish you, you will never know it. It is not a sadistic God."

"'It'—is it 'It' or 'He'?"

"Uh . . . use 'he.' If It embodies, It will probably use a human appearance. If so, you can address Him as 'Mr. Chairman' or 'Mr. Koshchei.' Treat Him as you would a man much older than you are and one whom you respect highly. *Don't* bow down or offer worship. Just stand your ground and tell the truth. If you die, die with dignity."

The guard who stopped us at the door was not human—until I looked again and then he was human. And that characterizes the uncertainty of everything I saw at the place Jerry referred to as "The Branch Office."

The guard said to me, "Strip down, please. Leave your clothes with me; you can pick them up later. What is that metal object?"

I explained that it was just a safety razor.

"And what is it for?"

"It's a . . . a knife for cutting hair off the face."

"You grow hair on your face?"

I tried to explain shaving.

"If you don't want hair there, why do you grow it there? Is it a material of economic congress?"

"Jerry, I think I'm out of my depth."

"I'll handle it." I suppose he then talked to the guard but I didn't hear anything. Jerry said to me, "Leave your razor with your clothes. He thinks you are crazy but he thinks I am crazy, too. It doesn't matter."

Mr. Koshchei may be an "It" but to me He looked like a twin brother of Dr. Simmons, the vet back home in Kansas to whom I used to take cats and dogs, and once a turtle—the procession of small animals who shared my childhood. And the Chairman's office looked exactly like Dr. Simmons' office, even to the rolltop desk the doctor must have inherited from his grandfather. There was a well-remembered Seth Thomas eight-day clock on a little shelf over the doctor's desk.

I realized (being cold sober and rested) that this was *not* Dr. Simmons and that the semblance was intentional but not intended to deceive. The Chairman, whatever He or It or She may be, had reached into my mind with some sort of hypnosis to create an ambience in which I could relax. Dr. Simmons used to pet an animal and talk to it, before he got down to the uncomfortable, unfamiliar, and often painful things that he had to do to that animal.

It had worked. It worked with me, too. I knew that Mr. Koshchei was not the old veterinary surgeon of my childhood . . . but this simulacrum brought out in me the same feeling of trust.

Mr. Koshchei looked up as we came in. He nodded to Jerry, glanced at me. "Sit down."

We sat down. Mr. Koshchei turned back to His desk. My manuscript was on it. He picked it up, jogged the sheets straight, put them down. "How are things in your own bailiwick, Lucifer? Any problems?"

"No, Sir. Oh, the usual gripes about the air conditioning. Nothing I can't handle."

"Do you want to rule earth this millennium?"

"Hasn't my brother claimed it?"

"Yahweh has claimed it, yes—he has pronounced Time Stop and torn it down. But I am not bound to let him rebuild. Do you want it? Answer Me."

"Sir, I would much rather start with all-new materials."

"All your guild prefer to start fresh. With no thought of the expense, of course. I could assign you to the Glaroon for a few cycles. How say you?"

Jerry was slow in answering. "I must leave it to the Chairman's judgment."

368 | ROBERT A. HEINLEIN

"You are quite right; you must. So we will discuss it later. Why have you interested yourself in this creature of your brother's?"

I must have dropped off to sleep, for I saw puppies and kittens playing in a courtyard—and there was nothing of that sort there. I heard Jerry saying, "Mr. Chairman, almost everything about a human creature is ridiculous, except its ability to suffer bravely and die gallantly for whatever it loves and believes in. The validity of that belief, the appropriateness of that love, is irrelevant; it is the bravery and the gallantry that count. These are uniquely human qualities, independent of mankind's creator, who has none of them himself—as I know, since he is my brother . . . and I lack them, too.

"You ask, why *this* animal, and why me? This one I picked up beside a road, a stray—and, putting aside its own troubles—much too big for it!—it devoted itself to a valiant (and fruitless) attempt to save my 'soul' by the rules it had been taught. That its attempt was misguided and useless does not matter; it tried hard on my behalf when it believed me to be in extreme danger. Now that it is in trouble I owe it an equal effort."

Mr. Koshchei pushed his spectacles down His nose and looked over them. "You offer no reason why I should interfere with local authority."

"Sir, is there not a guild rule requiring artists to be kind in their treatment of their volitionals?"

"No."

Jerry looked daunted. "Sir, I must have misunderstood my training."

"Yes, I think you have. There is an artistic principle— not a rule—that volitionals should be treated consistently. But to insist on kindness would be to eliminate that degree of freedom for which volition in creatures was invented. Without the possibility of tragedy the volitionals might as well be golems."

"Sir, I think I understand that. But would the Chairman please amplify the artistic principle of consistent treatment?"

"Nothing complex about it, Lucifer. For a creature to act out its own minor art, the rules under which it acts must be either known to it or be such that the rules can become known through trial and error—with error not always fatal. In short the creature must be able to learn and to benefit by its experience."

"Sir, that is exactly my complaint about my brother. See that record before You. Yahweh baited a trap and thereby lured this creature into a contest that it could not win—then declared the game over and took the prize from it. And, although this is an extreme case, a destruction test, this nevertheless is typical of his treatment of all his volitionals. Games so rigged that his creatures cannot win. For six millennia I got his losers . . . and many of them arrived in Hell catatonic with fear—fear of me, fear of an eternity of torture. They can't believe they've been lied to. My therapists have to work hard to reorient the poor slobs. It's not funny."

Mr. Koshchei did not appear to listen. He leaned back in His old wooden swivel chair, making it creak—and, yes, I do know that the creak came out of my memories—and looked again at my memoir. He scratched the gray fringe around His bald pate and made an irritating noise, half whistle, half hum—also out of my buried memories of Doc Simmons, but utterly real.

"This female creature, the bait. A volitional?"

"In my opinion, yes, Mr. Chairman."

(Good heavens, Jerry! Don't you *know?*)

"Then I think we may assume that this one would not be satisfied with a simulacrum." He hummed and whistled through His teeth. "So let us look deeper."

Mr. Koshchei's office seemed small when we were admitted; now there were several others present: another angel who looked a lot like Jerry but older and with a pinched expression unlike Jerry's expansive joviality, another older character who wore a long coat, a big broad-brimmed hat, a patch over one eye, and had a crow sitting on his shoulder, and—why, confound his arrogance!—Sam Crumpacker, that Dallas shyster.

Back of Crumpacker three men were lined up, well-fed types, and all vaguely familiar. I knew I had seen them before.

Then I got it. I had won a hundred (or was it a thousand?) from each of them on a most foolhardy bet.

I looked back at Crumpacker, and was angrier than ever—the scoundrel was now wearing my face!

I turned to Jerry and started to whisper urgently. "See that man over there? The one—"

"Shut up."

"But—"

"Be quiet and listen."

Jerry's brother was speaking. "So who's complaining? You want I should put on my Jesus hat and prove it? The fact that some of them make it proves it ain't too hard— seven point one percent in this last batch, not counting golems. Not good enough? Who says?"

The old boy in the black hat said, "I count anything less than fifty percent a failure."

"So who's talking? Who lost ground to me every year for a millennium? How you handle your creatures; that's your business. What I do with mine; that's my business."

"That's why I'm here," the big hat replied. "You grossly interfered with one of mine."

"Not me!" Yahweh hooked a thumb at the man who managed to look like both me and Sam Crumpacker. "That one! My Shabbes goy. A little rough? So whose boy is he? Answer that!"

Mr. Koshchei tapped my memoir, spoke to the man with my face. "Loki, how many places do you figure in this story?"

"Depends on how You figure it, Chief. Eight or nine places, if You count the walk-ons. All through it, when

You consider that I spent four solid weeks softening up this foxy schoolteacher so that she would roll over and pant when Joe Nebbish came along."

Jerry had a big fist around my upper left arm. "Keep quiet!"

Loki went on: "And Yahweh didn't pay up."

"So why should I? Who won?"

"You cheated. I had your champion, your prize bigot, ready to crack when you pulled Judgment Day early. There he sits. Ask him. Ask him if he still swears by you. Or at you? Ask him. Then pay up. I have munition bills to meet."

Mr. Koshchei stated, "I declare this discussion out of order. This office is not a collection agency. Yahweh, the principal complaint against you seems to be that you are not consistent in your rules for your creatures."

"Should I kiss them? For omelets you break eggs."

"Speak to the case in point. You ran a destruction test. Whether it was artistically necessary is moot. But, at the end of the test, you took one to Heaven, left the other behind—and thereby punished both of them. Why?"

"One rule for all. She didn't make it."

"Aren't you the god that announced the rule concerning binding the mouths of the kine that tread the grain?"

The next thing I knew I was standing on Mr. Koshchei's desk, staring right into His enormous face. I suppose Jerry put me there. He was saying, "This is yours?"

I looked in the direction He indicated—and had to keep from fainting. Marga!

Margrethe cold and dead and encased in a coffin-shaped cake of ice. It occupied much of the desk top and was beginning to melt onto it.

I tried to throw myself onto it, found I could not move.

"I think that answers Me," Mr. Koshchei went on. "Odin, what is its destiny?"

"She died fighting, at Ragnarok. She has earned a cycle in Valhalla."

"Listen to him!" Loki sneered. "Ragnarok is not over. And this time I'm winning. This *pige* is mine! All Danish broads are willing . . . but this one is explosive!" He smirked and winked at me. "Isn't she?"

The Chairman said quietly, "Loki, you weary Me"— and suddenly Loki was missing. Even his chair was gone. "Odin, will you spare her for part of that cycle?"

"For how long? She has earned the right to Valhalla."

"An indeterminate time. This creature had stated its willingness to wash dishes 'forever' in order to take care of her. One may doubt that it realizes just how long a period 'forever' is . . . yet its story does show earnestness of purpose."

"Mr. Chairman, my warriors, male and female, dead in honorable combat, are my equals, not my slaves—I am proud to be first among such equals. I raise no objections . . . if *she* consents."

My heart soared. Then Jerry, from clear across the room, whispered into my ear, "Don't get your hopes up. To her it may be as long as a thousand years. Women do forget."

The Chairman was saying, "The web patterns are still intact, are they not?"

Yahweh answered, "So who destroys file copies?"

"Regenerate as necessary."

"And who is paying for this?"

"You are. A fine to teach you to pay attention to consistency."

"Oy! Every prophecy I fulfilled! And now He tells me consistent I am not! This is justice?"

"No. It is Art. Alexander. Look at Me."

I looked at that great face; Its eyes held me. They got bigger, and bigger, and bigger. I slumped forward and fell into them.

XXIX

*There is no remembrance of former things; neither shall
there be any remembrance of things that are to come
with those that shall come after.*
Ecclesiastes 1:11

This week Margrethe and I, with help from our daughter Gerda, are giving our house and our shop a real Scandahoovian cleaning, because the Farnsworths, our friends from Texas—our best friends anywhere—are coming to see us. To Marga and me, a visit from Jerry and Katie is Christmas and the Fourth of July rolled into one. And for our kids, too; Sybil Farnsworth is Inga's age; the girls are chums.

This time will be extra special; they are bringing Patricia Marymount with them. Pat is almost as old a friend as the Farnsworths and the sweetest person in the world—an old-maid schoolmarm but not a bit prissy.

The Farnsworths changed our luck. Marga and I were down in Mexico on our honeymoon when the earthquake that destroyed Mazatlán hit. We weren't hurt but we had a bad time getting out—passports, money, and travelers checks gone. Halfway home we met the Farnsworths and that changed everything—no more trouble. Oh, I got back to Kansas with no baggage but a razor (sentimental value, Marga gave it to me on our honeymoon; I've used it ever since).

When we reached my home state, we found just the mom-and-pop shop we wanted—a lunchroom in this little college town, Eden, Kansas, southeast of Wichita. The shop was owned by Mr. and Mrs. A. S. Modeus; they wanted to retire. We started as their employees; in less than a month we were their tenants. Then I went into hock to the bank up to my armpits and that made us owners-of-record of MARGA'S HOT FUDGE SUNDAE— soda fountain, hot dogs, hamburgers, and Marga's heavenly Danish open-face sandwiches.

Margrethe wanted to name it Marga-and-Alex's Hot Fudge Sundae—I vetoed that; it doesn't scan. Besides, she is the one who meets the public; she's our best advertising. I work back where I'm not seen—dishwasher, janitor, porter, you name it. Margrethe handles the front, with help from Astrid. And from me; all of us can cook or concoct anything on our menu, even the open-face sandwiches. However, with the latter we follow Marga's color photographs and lists of ingredients; in fairness to our customers only Margrethe is allowed to be creative.

Our namesake item, the hot fudge sundae, is ready at all times and I have kept the price at ten cents, although that allows only a one-and-a-half-cent gross profit. Any customer having a birthday gets one free, along with our singing *Happy Birthday!* with loud banging on a drum, and a kiss. College boys appreciate kissing Margrethe more than they do the free sundae. Understandable. But Pop Graham doesn't do too badly with the co-eds, either. (I don't force kisses on a "birthday girl.")

Our shop was a success from day one. The location is good—facing Elm Street gate and Old Main. Plentiful trade was guaranteed by low prices and Margrethe's magic touch with food . . . *and* her beauty and her sweet personality; we aren't selling calories, we're selling happiness. She piles a lavish serving of happiness on each plate; she has it to spare.

With me to watch the pennies, our team could not lose. And I do watch pennies; if the cost of ingredients ever kills that narrow margin on a hot fudge sundae, the price goes up. Mr. Belial, president of our bank, says that the country is in a long, steady period of gentle prosperity. I hope he is right; meanwhile I watch the gross profit.

The town is enjoying a real estate boom, caused by the Farnsworths plus the change in climate. It used to be that the typical wealthy Texan had a summer home in Colorado Springs, but now that we no longer fry eggs on our sidewalks, Texans are beginning to see the charms of Kansas. They say it's a change in the Jet Stream. (Or is it the Gulf Stream? I never was strong in science.) Whatever, our summers now are balmy and our winters are mild; many of Jerry's friends or associates are buying land in Eden and building summer homes. Mr. Ashmedai, manager of some of Jerry's interests, now lives here year round—and Dr. Adramelech, chancellor of Eden College, caused him to be elected to the board of trustees, along with an honorary doctorate—as a former money-raiser I can see why.

We welcome them all and not just for their money . . . but I would not want Eden to grow as crowded as Dallas.

Not that it could. This is a bucolic place; the college is our only "industry." One community church serves all sects, The Church of the Divine Orgasm—Sabbath school at 9:30 a.m., church services at 11, picnic and orgy immediately following.

We don't believe in shoving religion down a kid's throat but the truth is that young people like our community church—thanks to our pastor, the Reverend Dr. M. O. Loch. Malcolm is a Presbyterian, I think; he still has a Scottish burr in his speech. But there is nothing of the dour Scot about him and kids love him. He leads the revels and directs the rituals—our daughter Elise is a Novice Ecdysiast under him and she talks of having a vocation. (Piffle. She'll marry right out of high school; I could name the young man—though I can't see what she sees in him.)

Margrethe serves in the Altar Guild; I pass the plate on the Sabbath and serve on the finance board. I've never given up my membership in the Apocalypse Brethren but I must admit that we Brethren read it wrong; the end of the millennium came and went and the Shout was never heard.

A man who is happy at home doesn't lie awake nights worrying about the hereafter.

What is success? My classmates at Rolla Tech, back when, may think that I've settled for too little, owner-with-the-bank of a tiny restaurant in a nowhere town. But I have what I want. I would not want to be a saint in Heaven if Margrethe was not with me; I wouldn't fear going to Hell if she was there—not that I believe in Hell or ever stood a chance of being a saint in Heaven.

Samuel Clemens put it: "Where she was, there was Eden." Omar phrased it: "—thou beside me in the wilderness, ah wilderness were paradise enow." Browning termed it: "Summum Bonum." All were asserting the same great truth, which is for me:

Heaven is where Margrethe is.

ABOUT THE AUTHOR

Robert A. Heinlein, a graduate of Annapolis, served as a naval officer for five years.

He began writing science fiction in 1939 and is considered by many the most influential author in the field.

He has won the coveted Hugo award for the Best Science Fiction Novel of the Year on four separate occasions—an unequaled record. In 1975 he received the First Grand Master Nebula award from the Science Fiction Writers of America.

He lives in California with his wife, Virginia, in an extraordinary house of his own design.